OF HEAVEN

A GINNIE WEST ADVENTURE

Book Three

MONIQUE BUCHEGER

Leia,

Simply dreaming
your dreams isn't
good enough ... Live them!

Dream Big!

Monique Bucheger

Dedication

To my wonderful family who are usually very supportive while I write.

To my awesome husband who believes in me.

To Hillary Straga: Thanks for giving the Wests' their voices. ☺

To Gracie and Jessie: My "real-life" Ginnie and Tillie, thanks for loaning your beautiful faces to my book covers. ☺

To my fabulous friends and critique partners who give me great feedback.

And last but not least ... for Scott Livingston, who really came through for me with this book.

Thanks to everyone for their belief in my story, in the Wests, and most especially ... in me.

This was a great journey. ☺

WEST FAMILY TREE

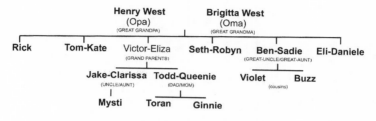

Henry West
(Opa)
(GREAT GRANDPA)

Brigitta West
(Oma)
(GREAT GRANDMA)

Rick **Tom-Kate** **Victor-Eliza** **Seth-Robyn** **Ben-Sadie** **Eli-Daniele**
(GRAND PARENTS) (GREAT-UNCLE/GREAT-AUNT)

Jake-Clarissa **Todd-Queenie** **Violet** **Buzz**
(UNCLE/AUNT) (DAD/MOM) (cousins)

Mysti **Toran** **Ginnie**

Bold denotes living family members

1

EVENTUALLY

Ginnie had waited long enough. It had been three weeks since her dad took her mother's journals away and said he would return them ..."eventually." If she had anything to say about it, "eventually" would be *TODAY*.

After all, Mama might not be here, but her journals still were. Hearing stories about the mom she lost when she was three-and-a-half-years old just wasn't good enough anymore, especially when Mama could tell Ginnie herself, in her own words.

Ginnie glanced around the chicken coop and let the cracked corn rain from the red scoop she held into the long slender feeding trough as hungry hens jockeyed for position to gobble their supper. The sound of the hard corn pelting the trough reminded her of a maraca.

Only today, the fun, clattering sound didn't amuse her like it usually did.

"Sorry, chick, no special seating." She moved her sneakered foot out from under one of the solid white hens. The hen squawked her displeasure.

Ginnie backed up and stumbled over two other hens. She tried to break her fall with her hands, but still landed on her rear with a thud.

Chicken feed flew from the scoop, skittering, and bouncing on the coop floor.

Hens mobbed the scattered corn.

"Fine! If you don't care about eating from the ground, why should I?" Ginnie wiped her stinging palms on her blue jeans, and slid her knees to her chest.

Rusty-brown feathered birds as well as black-and-white speckled hens blurred as they rushed to the fallen feed. They pecked greedily while Ginnie regrouped.

After scanning for some chicken poop-free space, she pushed herself into a standing position, and then begrudgingly showered another scoop of feed in the general direction of the trough, focusing more on her frustration than her chore.

Enough was enough.

She had more important things to think about ... like how to get Mama's journals back.

Sighing, she dropped the scoop into the plastic feed bin and pushed the lid down on the container until she heard the 'pop.' Ginnie searched her brain for the perfect argument to get Dad to change his mind. Nothing new appeared.

Water splashed her sneaker. The moat around the watering bucket overflowed. "Sugar Beets!" Ginnie hurried to the spigot and turned it off. "This day just keeps getting better and better. *Not!*" She pulled the hose out of the bucket and let the water drip into the moat.

A shadow fell across the coop. "Already having a bad day?"

Ginnie swiveled toward the doorway.

"The morning's just begun. Can I help?" Miss Amanda, the only woman Ginnie's dad had ever dated since her mom died eight-and-a half years ago, asked.

"Only if you can talk Daddy into giving me back Mama's journals," Ginnie retorted.

Miss Amanda frowned, then pushed her light auburn waves behind her ear.

Heat rose in Ginnie's cheeks. "Sorry. I didn't mean to be rude."

"I understand."

Ginnie sighed again. As much as she wanted those words to be true, she knew nobody *really* understood that when Dad took the journals, he ripped a gaping hole in her heart.

Not even her twin brother, Toran, got how horrible she felt.

"I'd like too," Miss Amanda offered with a warm smile.

Needing an ally, Ginnie decided to trust her. "Daddy told me Mama's secret didn't make her a bad person. If that's true, don't you think he should give me back the journals? Or at least give me a *good* reason why he took them away in the first place?"

"That's certainly a reasonable argument."

"Really?" Ginnie searched Miss Amanda's face for signs of teasing.

She couldn't find any.

"Of course." Miss Amanda entered the coop. "Just because he has a good reason for taking them, doesn't mean you have to be happy about it. And by the way, I've been impressed with how patient you've been with him through all of this. Thank you."

"You're welcome ... I guess." Ginnie's gaze dropped to her sneakers. "But—"

"But?" Miss Amanda lifted Ginnie's chin. "I thought you'd be happy he has a good reason."

"Well, yeah ... but if you say he has a good reason, then I have to wait longer." Ginnie felt like a whiny three-year-old but couldn't stop herself from adding. "I'm tired of waiting."

"I can imagine." This time, her understanding tone irritated Ginnie.

"Aren't *you* tired of him being a slow-poke about asking you to marry him? *Tillie* sure is."

"No." Miss Amanda shook her head and chuckled softly. "Tillie likes the idea of having a whole family again, and so do I. But there's no rush. Your dad and I want to enjoy the journey of getting to know each other better, at least for a while."

Ginnie squelched the urge to roll her eyes. "But you've known each other for years."

"True, but dating is different than being the parent of our daughter's best friend. Todd and I haven't even been going out for a month yet. You and Tillie wanted us to date, let us enjoy it a little."

"Well, that's true." Ginnie coiled the yellow hose and recalled how she and Tillie had plotted several outings to make their parents cross paths outside of their normal routines. Their scheming had been the push Ginnie's ostrich-like dad and shy Miss Amanda needed to start dating. "But you've been family forever." Ginnie blew out an impatient breath. "And just so you know, if he doesn't tell me *soon*, I'm gonna explode." Then she rolled her eyes. "Just saying."

"That's good to know. I'll see what I can do to nudge him along. However, I'm pretty sure exploding won't help." This time, Miss Amanda's tone *was* teasing. She rummaged in her black, leather handbag and fished out a thin paper bag. She handed it to Ginnie. "But maybe this will."

"Thank you." When Ginnie realized it was a book, she tried not to look disappointed. *She must have mixed me up with Toran.* Her twin could read any book at light speed.

Ginnie, well ... not so much.

Miss Amanda chuckled. "It's a diary, not a novel. I even bought gel pens to use in it."

Puzzled, Ginnie slid the book out of the sack. She was pleasantly surprised to find a picture of a chocolate brown thoroughbred with black mane and legs, much like her own mare, Calliope, on the cover. "It's beautiful! Thanks."

"You're welcome."

A package of brand new rainbow-colored gel pens slipped from the bag and fell into the straw. Ginnie picked them up. "Sorry."

"No worries. I know it must seem strange for me to give you a diary with all the recent drama over your mom's journals, but I've been trying to figure out a way to help both you and your dad through this. Then I saw the cover and thought maybe your mom was offering an idea or two."

"Seriously?" Ginnie locked her eyes on Miss Amanda's, surprised to hear her mention Mama. Even though Ginnie knew her mother and Miss Amanda had met a few times, it was still weird to think her mother and probable future step-mom had known each other.

Especially since Ginnie had so few memories of her mom.

"Of course. I told you we can still be just friends even though I'm dating your dad." Miss Amanda leaned toward Ginnie until their foreheads touched. "I'm still here for you ... and I *still* think you should get to know your mom."

Tell that to my dad. Ginnie bit back the retort.

"I thought you could use this journal to work through your feelings about everything, or write your mom—like she wrote you in that baby journal your dad let you keep." Miss Amanda tapped the cover. "This picture reminded me so much of Calliope that I decided you needed to have it. *You* decide what to do with it."

Ginnie adjusted her grip on the journal and pens, and let Miss Amanda envelop her in a hug, enjoying the smell of her perfume.

Until a few months ago, Ginnie hadn't even thought about Mama a whole lot. She was in her dreams every now and again, but not someone who existed in day-to-day life.

That all changed the day she found Mama's journals. Now she thought about her mom all the time. For the first time in eight years, Ginnie realized what she had truly lost ... a mother who not only cherished her, but actually understood her.

Ginnie didn't doubt Dad's love for her—he just didn't understand her—but Mama had.

As much as Ginnie wanted to be sisters with Tillie, it didn't change the fact that she also wanted to know her *real* mom.

Knowing Dad could give Mama back to her ... *at least a little* ... and he chose not to bugged her more each day. Until he gave her back the journals, Ginnie didn't see how she could be part of their new, big, happy family.

She had tried being understanding.

She had tried being patient.

She had tried being compassionate.

Now it was time to try something new.

2

NEW PLAN

*N*ew would be tricky. New would take some planning.

After Miss Amanda left, Ginnie finished with the chickens and then headed toward the farmhouse, clutching the bag with her journal and pens in one hand and the wire egg basket shaped like a chicken in the other.

She battled the good feelings that she had when Miss Amanda hugged her against her growing desire to know Mama better. She didn't want to hurt anyone's feelings, but she just *had* to get the journals back.

"Hey, Trouble," Dad's older brother, Uncle Jake, greeted as she came through the side porch door into their kitchen. Ginnie liked when he used his pet name for her.

"Hey, Uncle Jake." Ginnie smiled at her uncle and then her best friend. "Hey, Tillie." She put the eggs from her basket into the sink of warm, soapy water to soak.

"We're almost done," Tillie said, closing an egg carton. She and Uncle Jake were washing, candling, weighing, and sorting the 'farm fresh' eggs they sold to local families.

"I told your dad I'd take you guys out tonight so he can woo and pursue the lovely Amanda." Uncle Jake winked at Tillie, who grinned huge in return. "Where do you want to go?"

"Young's Jersey Dairy!" Ginnie replied.

"But that's an ice cream place," Tillie protested.

Uncle Jake shrugged. "What's the problem? You know—life's uncertain. Eat dessert first."

Tillie's mouth dropped open. "For real?"

Ginnie laughed at her friend. "Of course. That's the cool thing about Uncle Jake being in charge. Banana splits for dinner. Bananas, strawberries, and pineapple are fruit, ice cream is milk, and chocolate comes from cocoa beans. Three food groups right there."

Uncle Jake hitched a thumb at Ginnie and grinned. "You're my kind of girl."

"I just quoted you," Ginnie reminded him.

"Like I said ... *brilliant*." Uncle Jake winked at her and then finished washing the eggs in the sink and set them on the towel next to Tillie.

Tillie picked up an egg. "What does your dad think about dessert for dinner?"

Ginnie shrugged. "As long as Uncle Jake's buying, he doesn't usually care. Dad really likes breakfast for dinner when *he's* buying."

"He so needs to hurry and ask my mom to marry him. I want to be a part of your family ... *for real*." Tillie's cheeks flushed pink. When Tillie twirled her long brown hair around her finger, Ginnie realized her friend hadn't meant to blurt her thoughts.

She's starting to act like me. Maybe we really are turning into sisters. Ginnie wanted to laugh at that insight, but knew laughing would embarrass Tillie further.

Uncle Jake chuckled softly and pulled the plug on the sink. "It's all right, Turtle. He'll get around to proposing eventually. My brother's just enjoying the dating phase with Amanda. He rushed through it with Ginnie's mom."

"Why'd he rush through it?" Ginnie asked, curious at this new bit of information.

He turned on the water and sprayed the bubbles down the drain while thinking up a response.

Ginnie stared at him, hoping Uncle Jake would tell her the whole truth. Instead, he offered a bright smile and turned off the water.

"Your mom was a beauty queen, hence her nickname 'Queenie.' She had a fair amount of suitors. Once she gave your dad the time of day, he had to move fast." He shook his head and laughed. "It still floors me that she said 'yes,' but that's how she was ... impulsive. But hey ... they were happy and made cute kids."

When his gaze didn't quite meet hers *and* he wiggled his eyebrows while giving the compliment, Ginnie knew he was leaving something out ... something really important.

Before she could question him further, he wiped his hands on a dish towel and breezed past her. "Finish your chores. I need to change my shirt." He pointed to the wet spot on his navy work shirt and hurried to the dining room on his way to the staircase.

"Yeah, right." Ginnie muttered as he escaped through the door-frame. *Of course you do.*

By the time she decided to follow him, he had made it through the dining room, into the entryway, and dashed up the stairs. He was closing his door at the far end of the upstairs hallway as she rounded the banister. Clutching the new journal harder, Ginnie decided to put it in her room. She stopped at the second door on the left and cast a final look toward Uncle Jake's and Dad's room across the hall.

The door was still closed. "Sugar beets!"

She tossed the paper sack on her desk. It bumped the bright pink journal Mama had written in for Ginnie, chronicling her first year of life. She'd read it four times since Dad gave it to her out of the box of journals she had found in the barn loft.

She was ready to move on to the other journals, but Dad took them after giving her this one, promising to return them after he read them first. He didn't want any more surprises like Ginnie discovering that Mama had been pregnant when she died.

Ginnie and Toran had known about the pending birth of their baby brother, Cody, at the time, but had forgotten about him as they grew older. Dad said he wanted to tell them, but there never seemed to be a good reason to remind them of something so sad, so he did his ostrich act and hadn't mentioned their little brother.

Even though she understood why he didn't talk about Cody, Ginnie still wanted to know what the new secret was. The next morning he asked her to give him some time and space to deal with the new secret.

And Ginnie respected his request ... for the last three weeks.

Now she just wanted him to quit being an ostrich and tell her what new information he'd found but didn't know how to share. Frustrated all over again, she picked up the pink journal and let it fall open.

January 12

Dearest Gins,

You took your first step today! I love that you are so independent, but honestly, you are WAY too busy. Slow down, baby girl. You are only 8 ½ months. There's plenty of time to do lots of things. (And besides—if you start walking, your brother is going to think he needs to join you. I can barely keep up with you two as it is.)

Daddy laughed when I told him. "Well, what do you expect? She's just like you. Always trying to find something new and exciting. Slow down and maybe she will too."

He says I'M the smart aleck. 😊

SIGH He's the one who said he wanted our daughter to be just like me, but now that you are, I have a feeling he'll change his mind. He says he won't, but when you had a fit last night because he wanted you to stay in the playpen so we could enjoy a few minutes alone together, he gave in and scooped you up when you held out your tiny arms, crying "Dadadada." 😊

You're definitely a "Daddy's girl." When he comes home from work, you light up. He says it makes him feel like a rock star. I'll try not to be too jealous, since Toran's a "Mama's guy."

So much for a romantic dinner. There will be plenty of time for that later, I suppose ...

Maybe NOT plenty of time for a romantic dinner .... or anything else. Not even three more years as a family.

Ginnie closed the journal and sighed again ... feeling sad for Dad, for Toran, and most especially, for herself.

She glanced at the paper bag and then pulled the new journal out, trying to decide if she would toss it in a drawer or do what Miss Amanda asked. Ginnie didn't really want to write in it, but the gel pens were so bright and cheery that she opened them and sat in her white desk chair mulling over what she could write about.

The pens had a magnetic quality about them, especially the emerald green one, her favorite color. Ginnie picked it up, tapped the end on the desk, and opened the book to discover that the first page was filled with Miss Amanda's neat handwriting.

Dear Ginnie;

I'm giving you this diary in hopes that it will help you feel better until your dad gives you back Queenie's journals. I promise you, he does intend to give them back. Until then, the cover reminded me of Calliope and your mom. Her horse, Eternal Love, looked very much like Calliope as well. (Which isn't surprising since, of course, Eternal Love was Calliope's mom.) 😊

Anyway, I just want you to know that I was thinking about you and that you can talk to me about anything. If you don't want to right away, that's okay. Just know I'll always be here for you.

Sometimes when I am feeling lots of crazy, mixed-up emotions, I find that if I write down what I am feeling in MY journal, the craziness

*doesn't seem so crazy. And many times it helps me define what I am
REALLY thinking and feeling, not just what I THINK I'm feeling. Does
that make sense?* 😊 *Probably not—but please trust me and try it out
anyway. I love you, Ginnie West!*

Love, Amanda

*PS: Every night, even when I am too tired to write anything else in my
journal, I take at least 3 minutes and write 3 good things that happened
that day. Lately I find being with you, Toran, and your dad coming to
mind a lot. I challenge you to do the same.*

Try it, you might like it. 😊

Wow. A warm, cozy feeling enveloped Ginnie like a comfy robe. She
tapped the green pen on the journal and thought about what to
write. Her mind blanked. She tapped harder, concentrating on the
cover.

The horse did look like Calliope ... and Eternal Love. *Maybe
Mama did help Miss Amanda find the journal.*

Three things to be grateful for? Hmm.

*The first one is a no-brainer: Miss Amanda. She's turning out to be an
awesome sauce unofficial stepmom. Second? Mama's journals—if Dad
would give them back ... I bet I'd have even MORE to be grateful for.
Three: Calliope. If I didn't have her, I'd have gone nuts by now.*

Ginnie thought about all the horseback riding she'd done in the last
few weeks while giving Dad his 'space.'

Yeah, it's a good thing Uncle Ben talked Daddy into letting me have Calliope—even though Dad swore to never own another horse after Mama's accident.

While Ginnie couldn't blame her dad for feeling that way, she was extremely thankful for her great-uncle's influence.

Four: Uncle Ben. Not only did he raise Daddy since Grandpa and Grandma died when he was 11, Uncle Ben talked Daddy into letting me keep Calliope.

Since she came up with the three things to be grateful for so quickly, plus a bonus, Ginnie turned her attention to writing what she really wanted:

1) **Have Uncle Jake help me get the journals back (after all it's his fault Daddy took them.)**

2) **Figure out how to love Miss Amanda without feeling bad about wanting to know Mama.**

3) **Get Tillie to stop talking about "The Wedding"—because Daddy hasn't even asked Miss Amanda to marry him yet. Besides, he's a slowpoke about important things.** 😕

There. Hey, Miss Amanda's right. Things DO make more sense.

It may not be quite what her future step-mom intended, but Ginnie *did* feel better about having some kind of plan. Now, if she could just figure out a way to put it into action.

3

THE ARGUMENT

*O*nce Dad and Uncle Jake came home from work, everyone started on their afternoon chores.

Since Ginnie had promised her dad time and space about the journals, she calculated the odds of Uncle Jake unzipping *his* lips, hoping she could convince him to spill Dad's secret.

Giving a final glance around the hen house, Ginnie stopped thinking about the journals long enough to check off her chores:

Feed and water the chickens. Check.

Turn off the hose. Check.

Gather the few eggs they may or may not find ... Tillie found two. Check.

Put away the scoop. Check. Muck the worst of the chicken poop. Check.

Lay fresh straw. Check.

She turned to Tillie. "We're done?"

The statement came out more as a question.

Tillie nodded. "Looks done to me."

"Good. Let's go." Ginnie led the way out of the hen house. They corralled the few hens that lingered outside and shut the bottom half of the coop door. They lost a chicken to a fox last week, so now they made sure the hens were safely inside at night.

Ginnie debated again whether or not she would leave things alone or confront Uncle Jake. When they rounded the hen house and Ginnie spotted Uncle Jake heading to the hog barn, she got her answer, and made a beeline for him.

He offered a welcoming smile until she stood determinedly in front of him and put her hand up to block the late afternoon sun. His smile dimmed. "The journals?"

She nodded.

Uncle Jake adjusted the feed bucket in his gloved hand. "We've been through this, Trouble. Give it a rest. Your dad will come around when he's ready." He turned from her.

"But you promised." Ginnie stepped closer. "At least tell me *why* he took them."

"Trouble, *E-nuff.* Your dad'll let you know what you need to know, when *he* thinks you need to know it. Now drop it." He switched the bucket to his other hand and walked away.

Ginnie jutted out her chin and glared at his back. "I thought Wests don't lie?"

Uncle Jake turned around, set his bucket down and reached for Ginnie's basket. He handed it to Tillie. "Turtle, excuse us for a minute, will you?" It wasn't really a question.

Even though his voice was friendly, his aggravated eyes never left Ginnie's face.

Ginnie swallowed hard and glanced at her friend, who twirled her straight brown hair quickly around her finger. Tillie opened her mouth to speak.

"Thanks." Uncle Jake cut her off. "Ginnie'll be right in."

Sighing, Ginnie took another look at Uncle Jake and backed up a step.

Tillie threw her a sympathetic look.

While they waited for Tillie to get out of earshot, Ginnie scanned the pasture, wondering if she'd reached the limit of Uncle

Jake's patience or if she'd made a crack in his resolve to keep Dad's secret.

His growing frown didn't look too promising.

She swallowed hard.

"This is becoming a problem, Trouble."

"It wouldn't be if you'd just tell me *why*."

"Stop talking." A small smile lit his lips when Ginnie's mouth fell open and her eyes widened. He continued. "You know better than to interrupt an adult."

She crossed her arms and glared. "*You're* not supposed to be one of the adults. You're *supposed* to be on *my* side, *remember?*"

"I *am* on your side, but I promised your dad *before* I promised you. So cut me some slack, okay?"

Ginnie noticed Dad heading toward the main barn, which rested on a small hill up from them.

He won't be any help. He'll just bust me for aggravating Uncle Jake.

"I'm over here," Uncle Jake said.

Ginnie steeled her gaze on her uncle. "*Duh.*"

He pointed an angry finger at her. "You just turned twelve. We have a whole year before we need to deal with teenage attitude. Let's make this easy on both of us. *I* talk. *You* listen. Got it?"

After considering a few responses, she went with the one that would irritate him the most. "*Yes, sir.*"

His eyes narrowed.

She shrugged, knowing very well he hated it when she 'sir-ed' him. "What? You said you were an adult today. You know my dad expects me to 'yes, sir' and 'no, ma'am' adults."

"Just ... stop ... talking." He growled under his breath and leaned into her face. "*Now.*"

Tempted to 'yes, sir' him again, the words stopped in her throat as his look grew more menacing. 'Fun uncle' had hit the road. 'Angry uncle' was now in town.

She swallowed her snotty retort and tried not to blink.

After a long moment, Uncle Jake straightened and took a step back.

Ginnie blew out a light breath, wondering how long he would try to outstare her. He wagged a frustrated finger at her. "You seriously need to learn when to quit sassing."

Yeah, okay. Next? She clamped her mouth shut, and tried not to smile as she felt his anger grow. *He's the one who said to stop talking. What's he so mad about?*

He turned, muttered something she couldn't make out, and then faced her again. "Look, we're at an impasse here."

"What's that?"

"A wall. You're on one side and I'm on the other and the truth is, I'm really on your side, but I can't be because I promised your dad. Got it?"

"Huh?"

He tried again. "I know what you want and why you want it. Your dad does too. He'll come around. Just be patient, capiche?"

"I've been patient. For *three whole weeks*. He needs to give them back--or tell me why he took them." She glared at her uncle. "Or *you* should tell me why he took them."

"I can't. I promised." He wagged his finger again. After glancing at his finger, he rolled his eyes. "You've got me acting like *him*. *Stop it*. I don't like being mad at you."

While Ginnie struggled to remain quiet, her thoughts tumbled about like a whacked-out game of Hungry, Hungry Hippos. His look softened. "This isn't just about the journals anymore. Your impatience is causing trouble between you and me, as well as your dad and me. I'm working on him, but you have to let it rest, okay?" His eyes practically begged her for a 'yes.'

She nodded. "I hate being a kid."

"Being a grown-up isn't all apple pie and ice cream either. Are we good?"

She rolled her eyes. "Do I have a choice?"

"Let's go with no." He offered a gentle smile.

Try as she might, she couldn't keep from returning his smile.

He wrapped an arm around her shoulder and squeezed. "Drop this for now. I'm taking you guys out. Ice cream for dinner, remember? Let's have fun and not worry about the journals for a while longer, okay?"

"Not really."

"Please?"

Ginnie shrugged to irritate him, but offered a slight nod when he pulled his pathetic hound dog face.

He lifted his bucket. "Good. I've got this. Trust me."

"If you say so."

"I *do* say so." He headed for the hog barn as she turned toward the farmhouse.

4

EAVESDROPPING

illie and Ginnie let the screen door slam shut behind them as they walked out of the side porch. "What did Uncle Jake say, Ginnie? He seemed pretty angry."

"He was. He grounded me."

"For real?" Tillie's eyes widened.

Ginnie laughed. "No. He just wants me to leave him alone about the journals."

"What's the big deal?" Tillie grimaced. "Your mom wasn't a spy or something, was she?"

"Not that I know of."

They trudged up the hill to the main barn to stable Calliope for the night.

Usually Calliope would be in the pasture, but it was so hot and humid that Ginnie had rinsed Calliope off at the horse rack and stabled her after riding her so that Calliope could benefit from the huge fan circulating the air in the barn, rather than melting in the hot June afternoon sun. Since they were going out with Uncle Jake, Ginnie needed to tuck Calliope in for the night a little early.

Tillie followed Ginnie toward the back of the barn.

Ginnie stopped in her tracks when she heard her dad's scolding tone. "Back off, Jacob."

"No, I'm serious. What are you afraid of? The judge sided with *you*. You're giving Cabot too much power. *You* won," Uncle Jake replied.

After grabbing Tillie's hand, Ginnie pulled her friend into an empty stall and squatted. She put her finger to her lips as Tillie opened her mouth.

"You can't keep this from them forever, Todd. You're a good dad. Have some faith. Besides, Cabot ... " Uncle Jake must have turned, because his voice disappeared for a few seconds. "We have your back."

"I'm done discussing it." Dad sharpened his tone. "This is *my* problem and *I'll* solve it."

"Which is the wrong way to look at it."

"Jacob! Enough! If you can't handle Ginnie, *I'll* take care of her. But drop it already."

Goosebumps dotted Ginnie's arms. She exchanged anxious looks with Tillie.

"No thanks, you'll just ground her and then I'll be both a liar and a tattle-tale to her. I haven't been a tattle-tale since grade school. And no, wait. That was *you*. *I* never was a tattle-tale."

"*You* were a bully. That was worse."

"You need to check your stroll down memory lane," Uncle Jake mocked. "At any rate, I prefer being her knight in shining armor."

"Which is *my* job. *I'm* her dad."

"Give her back the journals and you will be. She just wants to get to know her mom. Queenie was amazing and so's your daughter. Cabot—"

They heard a rustling of boot steps and sliding sounds. "Hey!" Uncle Jake protested.

"I said I'm done discussing this with you." The finality of Dad's tone alarmed Ginnie.

She squeezed Tillie's arm and mouthed, "Sh!" Ginnie glanced around the stall, trying to figure out where they could hide better. No way did she want to get caught eavesdropping. Realizing they were trapped, they huddled closer as Dad continued to scold Uncle Jake.

"You've been bugging me for years to get on with my life. Now that I'm finally doing it, you're dragging up the past. I'll deal with it— my way—*in ... my ... own ... time*. Keep it up and I'll *make* you stop."

Uncle Jake snorted. "You and what army?"

"You don't get it, do you? I'm *done* losing. I lost my wife, my infant son, and almost my mind. I *won't* lose Ginnie and Toran. I'll deal with this, but trust me, if you keep bugging me, you *will* be sorry."

Ginnie swallowed hard. She wasn't sure what to think hearing Dad threaten Uncle Jake, but by the tone of his voice, she didn't doubt that Dad would win. She held Tillie tighter.

"That's what I'm saying!" Uncle Jake said. "Only don't fight me. Fight Cabot. *He* can't win. There are no grounds. Use that anger for him. He's earned it."

"Who's Cabot?" Ginnie and Tillie each mouthed to the other.

Both shrugged.

"Hey, has Ginnie stabled Calliope for the night?" Panic stained his words.

Ginnie heard footsteps crunching on straw and a stall door unlatch.

"Don't worry, she's probably in the kitchen telling Tillie I went psycho on her."

The footsteps hurried closer. Tillie and Ginnie scrunched together in the corner of the stall. *Don't let him see us. Don't let him see us. Don't let him see us.*

The handle of the milk pail squeaked as it was lifted.

"*Did* you go all psycho on her?" Dad's calmer voice asked.

"No, but I channeled you and Uncle Ben. She didn't stand a chance. She'll drop the journal thing for a while, but you need to get over being afraid. Cabot doesn't have any power. *You* do."

"I'm not afraid."

"Yes, you are."

"You need to stop talking." Dad's ire rose again.

"Make me," Uncle Jake taunted playfully.

Dad cleared his throat. "Do you really want to explain to Clarissa how you got a fat lip?"

"Only if you want to explain to Amanda about your black eye." Uncle Jake laughed as they walked by. "But even better will be watching you explain to Ginnie and Toran how your 'no hitting your sibling rule' only applies to them and *not* to you."

"That's the good thing about being the dad. I get to make the rules. They get to follow them."

Ginnie mimed sticking her fingers down her throat while rolling her eyes.

Tillie stifled a giggle.

Uncle Jake snorted. "I remember Uncle Ben having the same rule."

"What's he gonna do, ground me?" Dad joked.

"Probably not, but you know he'll come up with some way to make it look like a bad idea. Though honestly, why waste a good fight between the two of us? We have bigger fish to fry, namely your wife's ..."

Ginnie strained to hear the last words. The footsteps and voices faded.

All evidence of her dad and uncle disappeared.

She let out a relieved breath. "His wife's what?"

"I dunno." Tillie shrugged. "They're too far away."

"Let's get out of here. Daddy needs to see us coming into the barn or he'll know we heard." Ginnie led Tillie out the back barn door.

They raced from the back to the side of the barn, careful to skirt Dad's line of vision.

Dad and Uncle Jake hurried down the hill, carrying the milk jug between them.

Ginnie pointed to the woodshed. They rushed to it as quickly and quietly as they could. Once on the other side, Ginnie whispered, "Laugh loud."

They giggled and went around the woodshed into the open. "That's so funny, Tillie," Ginnie called loudly.

Her dad and Uncle Jake stopped, looking straight at them. Dad pointed to the main barn. "Have you put Calliope up for the night?"

"We're heading there now."

Relief swept Dad's face. "Good. Let me know when you're done."

"Yes, sir," both girls chorused.

Ginnie shot Uncle Jake a 'so there' smirk and dashed up the hill.

5

WANNA SHARE?

illie scooped the soiled straw in Calliope's stall into the wheelbarrow while Ginnie freshened her horse's water and took a square of hay from a bale. Ginnie concentrated on pulling the hay apart as she replayed Dad and Uncle Jake's conversation in her head.

Part of Ginnie wanted to confront her dad and demand some answers, but her sense of self-preservation opted for a 'wait-and-see' approach.' *Sugar beets! I won't be getting Mama's journals any time soon.*

"Who do you think Cabot is?" Tillie asked.

"I dunno."

"And how could he take you away from your dad? He doesn't hurt you like Jasper did me."

Ginnie always felt a little sad when Tillie called her birth father "Jasper" instead of "Dad." Tillie said it was because real dads didn't hurt their kids. "Why would anyone want to take you away from your family? They're the nicest people I know."

Ginnie shrugged. "I don't know."

"Well, whatever it is, your dad said he'll take care of it. So you don't need to worry."

Tillie sounded more worried than Ginnie felt.

"I hope not. But what does this Cabot guy have to do with Mama's journals? Daddy told me her secret didn't make her a bad person, but he almost got into a fight with Uncle Jake over it." Ginnie glanced around, making sure they were alone. "They tease a lot, but I've never heard Dad seriously threaten to hurt Uncle Jake. Something's going on."

"Yeah. But I don't think *we're* going to find out. Your dad won't even talk to Uncle Jake about it. And they usually tell each other everything, just like we do."

Ginnie smiled. "For best friends, they argue a lot, but that's probably because they're also brothers." She stroked Calliope's satiny neck and giggled. "I like it when Uncle Ben tells them to 'mind their manners' when they argue. Especially since Toran and I don't hardly argue at all. Daddy gets in more trouble for bickering than I do."

Tillie giggled. "That's fun for you. But it must be hard for your dad to be Uncle Ben's kid, your dad, and Uncle Jake's little brother all at the same time."

"I hadn't thought about it like that. And when he marries your mom, he'll be her husband too." Ginnie tapped her chin. "Do you think they'll start kissing each other more in front of us?"

"I like seeing him hug her and open doors for her. Jasper made her cry a lot, even when he didn't hit her. I'm okay with them kissing-- the more, the better."

The reality of Tillie seeing her father hit Miss Amanda always sickened Ginnie. Daddy always used a reverent or kind voice when he spoke of Mama. She couldn't imagine him hurting Mama, or Miss Amanda. Especially since he hardly ever spanked her or Toran when they were younger and he'd never slapped Ginnie in her entire life, even when she smarted off to him.

"Daddy would never hit your mom, *ever*. He doesn't even hit *me*, and I make him mad a lot."

"That's what I like about him. He doesn't yell much either. Jasper yelled a lot." Tillie set the shovel in the corner. She swiveled toward Ginnie and then away from her. Tillie tucked her hair behind each ear and then swallowed. "Ginnie?"

"Yeah?"

"If he adopts me, will you be okay with me calling him 'Dad' or 'Daddy' like you do?"

Ginnie stepped back. She leaned against Calliope and considered how to respond.

Most of her had no problem with sharing her dad with Tillie, but seeing the concern on her friend's face made her stop and really think about the question.

Tillie's cheeks changed from regular to pink to pale. She twirled her hair nervously around her finger.

After letting a few responses whirl through her mind, Ginnie smiled, wanting to relieve Tillie's discomfort. "I'm fine with that. You call everybody else in my family the same thing I do. Why not Daddy? I think he'd like it too."

A big smile lit Tillie's lips and then spread across her face.

The color returned to her cheeks.

She rushed across the stall and squeezed Ginnie into a big bear hug. "Thanks. You're the best sister ever."

6

THE DATES

Toran, Tillie, and Ginnie left the dining room together, walking into the entryway when they heard Uncle Jake coming downstairs. They had already planned their ice cream dinners.

Ginnie glanced their uncle's way, smiling as he did a jazzy box step in his descent. He wore a dark green button-down shirt with a skinny black tie, complete with black slacks.

Way overdressed for ice cream.

Buzz, Uncle Ben's son, followed behind Uncle Jake. Even though Buzz was Dad and Uncle Jake's cousin, they treated him more like a kid brother.

"What's up with the date clothes? I thought we were going to Young's," Ginnie said.

A guilty look quickly replaced Uncle Jake's playful grin. "Sorry. There's been a change of plans. Buzz is taking you guys out to ice cream and Clarissa's taking *me* out to dinner. Apparently she has something important to tell me that can't wait another minute."

Tillie giggled. "Oooohh, is she gonna propose?"

"I doubt it. We've only been dating a couple months." He picked a piece of lint off his shirt and made a big deal of rolling it into a ball before flicking it at Ginnie. "Besides, *I'll* be doing any proposing, if there's any proposing needing to be done."

"*Is* there any proposing needing to be done?" Tillie asked mischievously.

Uncle Jake shrugged. "Not tonight."

"That's not a 'no,'" Ginnie said.

"And it's not a 'yes,' either." Uncle Jake rolled his eyes. "Some people's kids."

"What about my kids?" Dad asked, descending down the staircase behind Uncle Jake dressed for his own date in black slacks and a royal blue shirt.

Uncle Jake hitched a thumb at Ginnie. "Miss Nosy thinks she's being clever."

"Hey! *Tillie* asked about proposing. I just mentioned you didn't disagree with her." Ginnie protested. "*You* said Clarissa wanted to ask you something important."

Dad cleared his throat. "That's *Miss* Clarissa to you. Mind your manners."

Ginnie squelched the urge to roll her eyes. "Yes, sir. But *Uncle Jake* started it."

"Todd ... didn't you and Queenie get married on your seven-week anniversary of meeting?" Buzz asked.

Dad nodded, looking a little uncomfortable. "What does that have to do with anything?"

"I was seven at the time, that info just stuck." Buzz pulled his keys out of his pocket. "I used to think all the kissing you and Queenie did was kinda gross, but now I know better."

Dad smirked at his cousin. "Kissing Queenie was a lot of things, but *gross* wasn't one of them." Dad winked at Ginnie and grinned.

"I said I know better, *now*." Buzz jangled his keys and motioned toward the door. "I'm just saying that Jake's been dating long enough to get serious about Clarissa—if it's possible for Jake to get serious about anybody--or anything, for that matter."

"You should talk." Uncle Jake hooked his thumb in a belt loop. "You and Faith have been going out for what? Four or five months already? And I remember you had a not-so-secret crush on Queenie, almost as big as Todd's."

"Gross. You had a crush on Mama?" Toran, Ginnie's twin brother, teased.

"Thanks a lot. I'd forgotten about that." Buzz grimaced at Uncle Jake and then winked at Toran. "I got over it quick. And remember, I was only seven. But *you* asked her to marry you."

"I did *not* ask my mom to marry me!" Toran shook his blond head. "Huh, Dad?"

When Dad coughed into his fist, Ginnie laughed out loud. "You mean it's true? *Finally*, an embarrassing little kid story *not* about me!"

"It's *not* true." Toran waved his hand, pointing from their dad to Ginnie. "Tell them, Dad."

Dad and Buzz exchanged shrugs and smiles. "Well, Tor. I would, but it *is* true."

Toran crossed his arms, frowning. "How old was I?"

"Three. Your mama thanked you kindly for the offer, but said she couldn't accept, because she was already married to me." Dad grinned and squeezed his shoulder. "You didn't talk to me for the rest of that day."

Ginnie and Tillie giggled.

Toran shook his head. "It's not funny."

"Oh, yes it is!" Ginnie laughed harder and pointed her thumb at her chest. "Now you know how *I* feel—they're always telling stories about me."

"Your mama thought it was sweet." Dad tugged one of Ginnie's blonde braids. "And being the kind and loving sister you are, you came up with a plan to help him out."

"What kind of plan?" Ginnie asked suspiciously.

His grin grew wider. "You asked *me* to marry *you*, so Toran could marry your mama."

"No way!" Ginnie objected.

Tillie and Uncle Jake roared with laughter.

"You couldn't let me have just one story where Toran looks bad and I don't?"

"Yes, way. And you don't need to feel bad, I was *very* honored, but like your mama, I had to decline." Dad winked, chuckling softly. "But thankfully, *you* were a bit more understanding than your brother and didn't hold a grudge. Your mom offered you a ride on Love, and all was well."

At the mention of Mama and her horse, Ginnie gave in and laughed along, picturing herself doing just about anything to ride horseback with Mama.

High heel shoes tapped across the front porch.

Dad opened the front door for Miss Amanda.

Ginnie didn't miss Dad's appraising glance at Miss Amanda's rose-colored blouse and black pencil skirt. Or how his smile grew bigger and his eyes brightened. Ginnie was still getting used to him falling for Tillie's mom, but it felt less weird and more 'right' every time they dated now.

Miss Amanda glanced around the group. "Hi, guys. Sorry I'm late. Traffic was crazy."

"You have impeccable timing. We're all headed out." Dad slipped his arm around Miss Amanda's waist and pulled her close. "Buzz, you're okay with doing the kids?"

"Sure. Faith is busy tonight." Buzz jangled the keys again. "You two go and have fun."

"We will." Dad wiggled his blond eyebrows at Miss Amanda and then kissed the top of Ginnie's head. "You three behave for Buzz. Bedtime at nine."

"You *do* realize it's summer break?" Ginnie protested.

"Not for Trixie and the chickens. They still need to be milked and fed on time. Tillie, if we're not home by then, would you be okay with spending the night?"

Now there's a dumb question. Ginnie caught herself before blurting her thoughts, knowing Tillie would have moved in years ago if she had her way.

A huge smile lit Tillie's face as she gushed, "Sure. You guys stay out as late as you want."

Dad hugged Tillie and then tousled Toran's hair.

Miss Amanda hugged Ginnie and then Tillie and Toran together. "I guess we're leaving. Be safe and have fun."

Ginnie, Toran, and Tillie replied, "You too."

They laughed at their unintentional chorus. Dad smiled and offered Miss Amanda his arm.

Trying to imagine Mama on Dad's arm, and not being able to, tugged at Ginnie a little. She sighed, torn between wanting Dad and Miss Amanda to get together and wishing Mama could be here as well.

7

YOUNG'S JERSEY DAIRY

*a*t Young's, Buzz ordered two extra-large plates of chili cheese fries to go along with their banana splits. Although more laid back than Dad, Buzz wasn't quite as into 'dessert for dinner' as Uncle Jake. But he *was* approachable ... and Dad wasn't here.

After stabbing her spoon into her treat several times, Ginnie decided to quit slicing her bananas to pieces and ask what was on her mind. "Buzz, do you know Dad's secret?"

He shrugged. "I'm not sure what you're talking about."

Ginnie rolled her eyes. *How could he not know?*

"Mama's journals? Daddy promised I could read them," she hinted impatiently. "Do you know why he took them?"

Buzz shook his head. "I don't remember any secrets, but I had just turned twelve a few days before Queenie died. However, I do remember that your mom made me feel better about losing *my* mom the year before. Then Queenie died. That was a rough year."

Ginnie sliced the banana chunks with her spoon as she mulled over her cousin's words.

A lump caught in her throat. Swallowing didn't help.

"It was a pretty awful time." Buzz picked up the salt shaker and jiggled it, before setting it back down. "Jake had to stay in the Army for a few more weeks before he could come home for good. I was really glad when he moved back in. Both of our dads were grieving, and Jake made everyone laugh again."

"That's so sad, Buzz," Tillie said, her eyes shining with tears. "It must have been hard on you to lose your mom and then Ginnie's mom. I don't remember either of them."

Uncle Jake and Tillie's birth dad were friends as teenagers, but Ginnie and Tillie only remembered meeting in kindergarten.

Ginnie fondly recalled the day they met. A little boy had the nerve make fun of Tillie and called her a crybaby when she started crying. He laughed at her. Ginnie had taken matters into her own hands and poured a carton of milk over his head, asking him if he thought *that* was funny.

He ended up bawling and Ginnie had to take a time out.

But she and Tillie had been best friends ever since.

"Join the club, Tillie." Toran pointed a spoonful of pineapple topping at her. "I only remember Mama a little as well. She called me her 'little man' and let me feed Eternal Love apples and carrots with her." He laughed. "One time Love snatched a bite of my watermelon, which pretty much took the whole thing. Mama helped me feed her the rest of it and got me another slice."

Buzz laughed. "That horse loved fruits and vegetables. I even lost a piece of Oma's strawberry *bread* to her once. She snatched it right off my plate."

Ginnie laughed along, but her mind drifted back to the journals. She figured Buzz knew more than he was telling. After all, Dad and Buzz were pretty good friends and more alike than Dad and Uncle Jake. "He hasn't said anything to you, *at all*?"

Buzz shrugged. "Todd *is* thirteen years older than me. He's also pretty involved with Amanda right now and I haven't been around much with my college and work schedules. Not to mention hanging out with Faith. Sorry, Gin. *If* there is a secret, he didn't tell it to me."

Ginnie had a hard time believing Buzz knew nothing, but it *was* true that he hadn't been home much the last few weeks. She studied his face, but couldn't find any trace of intentional deception.

Nuts.

Now she needed a different plan.

8

TWITTERPATED

O n the drive home, Ginnie stared unseeing out the backseat window of Buzz's truck. Trees flew by unnoticed on the country roads that led to their nine-generation old farm, "Heart of the Wests."

She stared past the knee-high cornstalks on her left and the neck-high alfalfa lining the right side of their lane, quickly creating and discarding several arguments to convince Dad to give the journals back.

While Toran and Tillie plotted to retrieve a treasured amulet in Toran's new computer game, Ginnie realized that simply *talking* to Dad wasn't going to get her what she wanted after all.

She needed *action*, so she formed a new plan.

It didn't take long to work out the details. Normally at least two of the five family vehicles were parked side-by-side in front of the two-story red-brick farmhouse they called home. Today only Miss Amanda's silver-blue car and several pairs of dried, muddy ruts greeted them.

That never happened.

Her plan could succeed.

Usually the adults outnumbered the kids around the farm, but tonight, the odds were in Ginnie's favor. She was determined to make good use of this rare opportunity.

Once Tillie and Toran settled in the family room with Toran's computer, Ginnie slipped out to the side porch and opened the dryer door. A load of men's jeans. *Perfect.*

She scanned the back waistbands and found two marked with the letter 'T' for Todd, her dad, three pairs with the letter 'J' for Uncle Jake, and two pairs with a 'B' for Buzz. *Jackpot.*

Now she had the perfect excuse to be in Dad's room without permission. She folded the jeans into a neat pile and plucked it up.

Dad had asked her to not bother him about the journals for a while.

But if she *found* them and read them without his knowledge, she'd really be doing *him* a favor. Because then she could figure out whatever it was that had hurt him, and he wouldn't have to actually *tell* her.

Hadn't he called her a kind and loving sister? Sparing him hurt feelings would make her a kind and loving daughter as well. And since he really was a pretty good dad—when he wasn't being *too* lame —she *owed* it to him to be a good daughter.

Feeling pretty good about her justifications, Ginnie ventured from the porch to the kitchen. She adjusted the pile of jeans and smiled, happy that her mission was no longer sneaky, but noble.

She made her way up the stairs and turned. One, two, three, four, five closed doors. Clear sailing. Her heart beat wildly, thinking how close she was to getting the journals back.

She kept going straight, pausing to glance out the window facing their lane. No sign of Dad, Uncle Ben, Vi, or Uncle Jake. She let out a relieved breath, and approached the room Dad and Uncle Jake had shared off-and-on since they were orphaned at age eleven and thirteen.

No need to knock. She shifted the jeans and reached for the door knob.

A quick glance around the room confirmed the absence of its occupants.

Whew! The pounding in her chest eased.

After setting Buzz and Dad's jeans on Dad's perfectly made bed, she dropped Uncle Jake's on his hastily made one before opening the closet door.

She glanced at the shelf above the hangers full of shirts and pants. Her dad's clothes were all sorted by type, size, and color of slacks, jeans, and short-and-long-sleeve shirts. Uncle Jake's shirts were grouped by themselves, his jeans and slacks mingled, and his hangers hung at odd angles.

No boxes.

Slippers, running shoes, cowboy boots, work boots and a couple of shoe boxes. Swiveling, her eyes swept the room. Still no box of journals. She pushed the hanging clothes with her arm. Nothing behind them.

She closed the closet door, knelt in front of her dad's bed, and lifted the navy blue comforter. His bed was too short for the original box to slide under, but maybe he'd put them in a couple of smaller boxes. Then a strange thought occurred to her.

He's hidden them! How could he? Doesn't he trust me?

Aggravated, she looked and felt under the bed. She pulled two plastic totes toward her. One held papers and the other regular books, but not journals.

Why would he hide Mama's journals? I told him I'd leave him alone about them. He has no right to hide them!

Ginnie shoved the totes back where she found them and crawled over to Uncle Jake's bed. Under his was a disorganized mess covered with dust bunnies.

Leaning back on her heels, she scanned the room again.

No sign of the original box.

Maybe the journals are in his drawers?

A quick open-and-closing of each drawer revealed piles of neatly folded socks, underwear, T-shirts, ties, and belts wound into spirals.

The bottom drawer held neat piles of papers and last year's school pictures, but no journals.

Boots thudded softly up the stairs. The floor creaked as someone neared the hallway window. "Ginnie? Where are you?" Buzz called from the hallway.

A tremor jolted through Ginnie as she scrambled to her feet. She snatched Buzz's jeans from her dad's bed and tiptoed to the door.

Ginnie took a breath and turned the doorknob.

Buzz jerked toward her, surprise coloring his face. "What are you doing in Todd's room?"

Shrugging, she held out Buzz's jeans. "Just putting his and Uncle Jake's laundry away. These are yours."

He reached for the pile. "Why was the door closed?"

Umm. She opened the door wider and glanced at Dad's nightstand. On it stood a picture of Mama and Daddy holding hands together at a rodeo competition when they first met. "I-I was just looking at the picture of Mama." Her cheeks heated. "They look so happy together. I was just imagining what they must have been thinking."

It wasn't a real lie. She *had* wondered that over the last couple weeks since Dad first showed her and Toran the picture he had previously kept hidden in the nightstand drawer.

"You should probably ask your dad," Buzz said, studying her face. "But I don't know why you'd need to close his door."

His suspicion turned her awkwardness at being caught to defensive anger. "You remember *your* mom. I just wanted to spend a little time with *mine.*" She whirled away from him, sliding her hand on the banister as she inched past his six-foot-one frame, intent on getting away from him as fast as she could. "It's no big deal."

"Hey! Stop a minute." He moved to intercept her.

Ginnie backed up a step, keeping an arm's length between them.

"I get it." His understanding tone kept her feet planted where she stood. "I may remember my mom better, but I know how you *feel.* I understand latching on to her photo."

Relief at his kindness mixed with growing guilt at her unintended deception.

I WOULD have studied the picture more if I'd had time.

Dad looked so mesmerized by Mama in the photo that Uncle Jake teased him about being 'twitterpated.' When Ginnie asked Dad what 'twitterpated' meant, he had replied 'crazy in love' and worn the word proudly. Ginnie thought it was cool that Dad loved Mama so much that she refused to let Uncle Jake's teasing turn the fun new word into a bad thing.

'Twitterpated' seemed like a good way to be with someone you were married to.

"Ginnie?"

She shook her head, trying to clear her mind of the photo, not wanting Buzz making trouble for her with her dad. "Yes?"

"Are you okay?"

"Do you think Dad loves Miss Amanda as much as he loved Mama?"

Where did THAT come from? I wasn't even thinking about Miss Amanda.

Ginnie swallowed hard, turning so Buzz didn't see the pink rising in her cheeks.

"I don't know."

Good going, Gin. You need to ditch Buzz, not make him worry so he tells Dad.

"I don't think you can quantify something like that. And even if you could, I don't think it matters. Queenie and Amanda are two different people and these are two very different situations. Love isn't a measurable commodity."

Leave it to Buzz to sound like a science teacher. But what did she expect? He and Toran spent a lot of time together discussing scientific experiments. They analyzed everything ... to death.

"But I know *this*, if Queenie were still alive, Todd wouldn't even consider looking at another woman."

Ginnie glued her eyes to Buzz's, liking this revelation.

"They had something special ... like they belonged to an exclusive country club. I can't explain it, but whenever they looked at each other, you could tell they only saw the other one, at least until you and Toran came along."

Buzz winked at her. "They let the two of *you* into their private club, and even though they loved the extended family a whole lot, they loved their own little family a tad bit more."

His words wrapped around her like her favorite comforter: gentle, warm, and cozy.

He shifted from one foot to the other and chuckled. "I know he loves Amanda. But I don't think it matters whether he loves her more or less than your mother. Or rather it shouldn't. It's a different love. Does Todd loving your brother take away from him loving you?"

"Of course not." She grimaced at his question. "I know people can love more than one person. But if he loved Mama so much and they were happy, can he love Miss Amanda enough to make *her* happy too?"

Buzz leaned against the banister next to her and crossed one brown work boot in front of the other. "I guess that would be a question for Amanda to answer. But I think the real question you're asking is: Can *you* be happy if your dad marries Amanda?"

Ginnie shook her head. "Nuh-uh."

"Well, Todd and Amanda seemed pretty enamored with the idea of going out tonight, so I don't think *their* happiness is in question here."

Ginnie's hands flew indignantly to her hips. "I want them to be happy. I'm okay with them getting married. I just want ..." She swiveled away from him, not really sure how to put the elusive feelings into words.

"You want to know your mom won't be forgotten?" Buzz quietly finished for her.

"I *already* forgot her." She shook her head and turned further away. "What kind of person does that?"

He put his hand gently on hers.

Ginnie forced herself to glance at her cousin.

The horrified look on his face told her everything she needed to know.

Horrible people forget their dead moms.
That's who.

39

9

ZZZT ZZZZZT

*G*innie snatched her hand out from underneath Buzz's and rounded the banister, intent on putting as much distance between them as possible.

"Hey. Come back. Why're you leaving?" Buzz asked, grabbing Ginnie's elbow as she headed down the stairs. "What's wrong?"

"You know what's wrong!" She tugged her arm out of his grip. She pushed through the screen door, scurried out onto the front porch, and down the concrete steps.

He reached his arm around her and pulled her close.

The screen door slammed shut.

She ducked out of his hold and fell on the gravel and dirt, scraping her hand. The sting pulsed while she rubbed her palm on her blue jeans.

When Buzz offered her a hand up, she shook her head, and leaned on her elbows, away from his hand. She scooted back a few steps, then hugged her legs to her chest, blinking back hot tears.

"We were having a nice conversation until you freaked out." His concerned tone turned to frustration. "Why did you run?"

Ginnie hid her face with her knees. *Like you don't know.*

Fuzzy white noise buzzed in her ears.

Then a long zzzzt zzzzzzzzzzzzzzzzzt zzt sounded.

She jerked her head toward the woodshed.

The bug zapper hanging off the eaves glowed purple as it barbequed a mosquito.

Buzz squatted next to her. "Are you afraid your dad won't have time for you?"

Ginnie shook her head. "What are you talking about?" Then she realized what he meant. "I told you I'm okay with him marrying Miss Amanda. I just shouldn't have forgotten Mama."

"You were three. It's allowed." Buzz picked a piece of grass and stood. "I don't remember things that happened to me when I was three."

"But you remember your mother."

"Because she died when I was *ten*."

"But that shouldn't matter."

"You're not making any sense. I had my mom seven years longer than you had Queenie. Of course I remember her better." Buzz's face scrunched in a mixture of concern and amusement. "Don't beat yourself up. Your dad was eleven and Jake thirteen when their folks died. They still ask my dad about Aunt Eliza ... and Uncle Vic too."

At the mention of her grandparents' names, Ginnie calmed some. *That's true.*

Daddy had asked Uncle Ben just the other day about Grandpa and some camping trip they had gone on.

But still, forgetting your very own mom couldn't be a good thing.

10

TUMBLE, ANYONE?

a loud rumbling and thudding made Tillie jerk her head from the laptop and scan the family room. "What's that noise?"

"Sounds like someone falling down the stairs," Toran answered, closing his laptop. He set it on the couch and bolted toward the kitchen.

Tillie followed behind as they raced to the hallway.

No one was in a heap at the bottom of the staircase.

"Outside." Toran held the screen door open for her.

Tillie rushed through and froze.

Ginnie sat sprawled on the grass, her arms behind her and legs in front. She looked worried. Buzz reached an arm to her. Ginnie fell on her elbows, further from him and backed up.

Did he hit her? Swallowing an old fear, Tillie willed her legs to move.

"Are you okay, Gin?" She dashed down the steps.

Buzz glanced at Tillie as she approached, then backed up a step.

Tillie searched Ginnie's face. *No handprints.* Relief bubbled inside. *Buzz wouldn't hurt her. Nobody in Ginnie's family hits. They hardly even yell. Why does Buzz look so weirded out?*

Ginnie cast a quick look to Buzz and rose to her feet. "I'm fine. I just slipped."

Tillie didn't see any red spots on her friend's arms. *Did Buzz push her?*

"Down the stairs?" Toran pointed toward the house. "How did you get out here?"

A puzzled look crossed Ginnie's face. "I slipped on the grass."

Again, her eyes met Buzz's.

They exchanged looks detailing a conversation that Tillie got the feeling wouldn't be shared with her. Buzz gave a quick shrug and offered a welcoming smile.

Buzz isn't a hitter. He's too much like Uncle Ben.

Tillie almost missed the slight shake of Ginnie's head at her cousin.

Great. Another secret.

Ginnie was full of secrets lately.

Tillie wanted her best friend back, the one who told her everything.

They were so close to finally being sisters for real ... and Ginnie didn't seem as happy about their parents dating as she should be ... and she wouldn't say why.

"Oh." Ginnie laughed at Toran. "No, Buzz and I ran outside. I slipped on the grass. Buzz was just helping me up." She turned. "I need to take care of Calliope. Finish your game. I'll play the winner."

So that's how she wants to deal with this? Like nothing's wrong? Fine. Two can at play that game. Tillie offered Ginnie a friendly smile. "I'll help you. I love how Calliope's lips tickle my palm when I feed her an apple."

"Next time, walk down the stairs, Gin. I thought someone fell," Toran scolded and turned to Buzz. "Wanna play Jewel Quest?"

Buzz nodded. "In a minute. Gin, are you sure you're okay?" He held out his hand for Ginnie's and looked it over. "You should wash this right away. Need some help?"

"No thanks. I'll clean it after I take care of Calliope." She whirled toward the main barn.

Tillie ran behind her friend. "Wait up, Gin."

Ginnie slowed, looking surprised that Tillie had followed. "I got this. Finish your game."

"Toran just clobbered me. I'd rather see Calliope."

Instead of a welcoming smile, Ginnie gave a quick nod. "I'm just making sure Calliope is stabled for the night. No big deal."

"Then it'll be twice as fast with two of us." Tillie joined in step with Ginnie. "Unless you don't want me to come."

Ginnie rolled her eyes. "Of course you can come. I just didn't want you to be bored."

Somehow her words didn't match the anxiety on her face.

Ginnie's eyes darted around, like she was looking for someone ... or rather, like she didn't want someone to see her.

"I'm not bored. I love Calliope." Tillie kept what she hoped was a pleasant smile glued on her lips. "Maybe I can even get my own horse and we'll race them. Mom said she might buy me a horse after our folks get married."

"Good luck with that," Ginnie muttered as she slid the barn door open.

Tillie's heart stopped. "You don't think they'll get married?"

"What?" Ginnie stared at her like she'd grown a third arm.

"Why'd you say 'good luck with that?' You don't want them to get married?"

"Don't be silly. Of course they'll get married."

"Then what did you mean?"

Ginnie let out a quick breath. "Just don't count on getting a horse. I tried to talk Daddy into giving you one for your birthday and he said 'no.' I doubt he'll change his mind."

"Why? *You* have one. Mom thinks it's a good idea."

"Because my mom *died* when her horse threw her." Ginnie turned and walked away.

Tillie followed silently, not trying to catch her.

When they reached Calliope's stall, Ginnie swiveled toward her and softened her tone. "Maybe your mom can talk him into it. I just don't want you to get your feelings hurt if Daddy tells you no."

"I bet he won't tell me no."

Ginnie sighed impatiently. "I know you think he's perfect, Tillie, *but he's not.*"

"What's that supposed to mean?"

"You'll find out." She opened Calliope's stall and entered, not looking back to see if Tillie followed.

11

WHAT TO DO ABOUT TILLIE?

*G*innie tried to figure out how to ditch Tillie without hurting her feelings.

Getting a sister was becoming too complicated.

As much as she loved her best friend, having Tillie around all the time was getting harder to take. Ginnie needed room to think ... and thinking was a lot easier when she didn't have Tillie around making a big deal out of nothing. *Just like Buzz had.*

Dad and Miss Amanda were pretty much a done deal.

That was a no-brainer. But just because Dad was falling in love with Tillie's mom, didn't mean Ginnie didn't have a right to find out about hers.

After tearing a square of alfalfa from the hay bale, Ginnie separated it into strands. She offered a little to Calliope and put the rest in her mare's feeding trough.

Out of the corner of her eye, Ginnie watched as Tillie stood outside the stall, twirling her straight brown hair around her finger. She always did that when she was nervous or uncomfortable.

Great! Now I have to fix Tillie AND try to find Mama's journals. Why couldn't she go back inside with Toran and finish their game? Ginnie forced a smile to her lips.

She looked up toward the loft where she had found Mama's journals three weeks ago.

It had occurred to her about the same time Tillie and Toran came outside that Dad might have put the journals up in the loft again, given how he was a bit OCD about things being put back where they belonged.

But even obsessive-compulsive Dad couldn't believe Mama's journals actually belonged hidden away in the loft any more.

Grieving, 'ostrich dad' probably had, but 'moving-on-with-his-life dad' wasn't that sad person any more. Somehow she doubted he had returned the journals to their hiding place, but with Tillie standing between her and the loft, she probably wouldn't find out tonight.

Sure, Tillie might play along and be a good sport, but more likely, if Tillie knew how badly Ginnie wanted Mama's journals, she'd freak.

Tillie *acted* like it was okay for Ginnie to want Mama, but secretly, Ginnie was pretty sure Tillie wasn't as okay with it as she said.

As far as Ginnie knew, Tillie had a picture of her ideal family in her mind and that image probably didn't include Dad's first wife.

12

DT

D T will TOO let me get a horse. I know he will.

Tillie watched as Ginnie fed Calliope alfalfa hay. *He will. He has to.* Tillie fought back tears. *Quit bawling. DT didn't say no. GINNIE SAID that he said no. I know Ginnie's mom died in a bad accident, but DT let Ginnie get Calliope and Ginnie's his own kid. Surely he won't tell ME I can't have a horse.*

Squaring her shoulders, Tillie blinked, determined not to worry about this until she had to.

DT probably said no because horses are expensive. Of course he's not going to spend a few hundred dollars on a horse for me ... yet. But Mom will. Mom wants a horse, too.

Tillie didn't feel as comforted as she usually did when she used her own private nickname for Ginnie's dad: DT... AKA ... Daddy Todd.

Even Ginnie didn't know about her secret name for him.

Tillie had christened him that one day about four years ago when she was feeling sorry for herself that Jasper had called drunk and made Mom cry. Tillie had fallen and scraped her knee. DT had dried her tears, cleaned the wound, and assured her she'd be fine.

Tillie realized that day she didn't need her birth father to ever come back. He wasn't a nice dad like Ginnie's, anyway. If Jasper stayed away, she could pretend that DT was her dad.

And Jasper *had* stayed away, for six whole years.

Last month, she and Ginnie had set up Mom and DT to start dating ... and they went for it.

If DT would hurry up and ask Mom to marry him, I won't have to pretend much longer.

DT will be my dad ... FOR REAL.

When her finger started pulsing, Tillie realized that she had wound her hair tightly around it again. She unraveled the hair. *I hate how Jasper makes me nervous. He isn't even here and he worries me. When DT adopts me, I won't have to be afraid anymore.*

She sighed. *But DT has to marry Mom first.*

Tillie took another look at Ginnie, wishing she could be as brave as her best friend. "Hey, Ginnie ..."

"Yeah?"

Tillie opened the stall door, waiting until Ginnie glanced at her before continuing. "Do you still want to be sisters?"

"Of course not." Ginnie rolled her eyes and then grinned like Uncle Jake did when he teased. "Stop being silly. They'll get married. Daddy's just slow about making important decisions. It's annoying, but that's how he is. He took forever to change his mind about Calliope, and to give me a raise in my allowance, and to date your mom. And he still hasn't given me back Mama's journals." Ginnie turned away quickly, her cheeks pinking.

Why's she blushing over the journals? In some ways Tillie wished that DT would just give them back. Then Ginnie could move on to more important things, like being sisters.

But what if the journals made Ginnie want her real mom so much that she doesn't want MY mom? Shuddering, Tillie turned away. She couldn't bear it if Ginnie didn't want Mom to be her stepmom. DT had told Ginnie once that he wouldn't date Mom if she didn't want him to.

Quit being silly, Matilda! He's already fallen in love with Mom. Even if Ginnie changed her mind about them getting married, DT wouldn't change his ... or would he?

13

PLAN B

Ginnie spent the rest of the night avoiding any subject that might lead back to her dad as she didn't want to listen to Tillie defend him. Ginnie couldn't believe he had the nerve to hide the journals. Hadn't she agreed to give him space?

Hadn't she dropped the subject ... for *three whole weeks? At least to HIM?*

Now that she'd figured a way to help *him* out, as well as herself, she realized he didn't even trust her.

How is that even possible? I'm not the one keeping secrets.

Her angry thoughts churned so much that she couldn't concentrate on the movie she was watching with Toran, Tillie, and Buzz in the family room.

After mumbling about getting something from upstairs, Ginnie walked to the kitchen and then rushed to the front staircase. She hurried up them, stopping only when she got to her cousin Vi's room at the top. Vi was Uncle Ben's daughter and Buzz's older sister.

Ginnie tiptoed to the hallway window. *Still just Miss Amanda's car and Buzz's truck.*

Relieved, she tiptoed back to Vi's door, turned the porcelain handle, and slipped inside. She crossed Vi's room to the second door that opened to their food storage room and turned the knob. Of course it had to squeak *loudly*, making her heart nearly jump out of her chest. *Get a grip, Gin!*

She entered the food room and scanned rows and rows of canned goods, glass jars of jellies, and veggies from their garden, paper products, and boxes of cereal and pasta.

Yum. Cocoa Crunchies. Focus Gin, you don't have much time.

"It's the food room, I'm allowed in here," Ginnie argued with herself, before adding, "just not through Vi's room."

She walked over to the row of shelves where she had hidden the box of journals after finding them in the loft. If only she hadn't handed them over when Dad found out she was reading Mama's pregnancy journal. Ginnie looked over the shelves again. *Nothing.*

Where did Dad put them? Her gaze searched every place she'd already looked, then twice more. No sign of the box. She shook her head and went back to Vi's room.

Boots pounded on the stairs. Her knees buckled.

Judging by the sound of the footfalls, it had to be Buzz.

Great! I can't let him catch me in Vi's room. He'll tell Dad for sure.

Glancing around, Ginnie spotted the food room door. She tiptoed to the door, opened it an inch at a time, and slipped through, reversing her movements until the knob clicked shut.

Vi's main door squeaked open. "Ginnie?"

Grateful Buzz couldn't see her, Ginnie snatched the box of Cocoa Crunchies off the shelf and hurried down the back stairs, tearing open the box of cereal while entering the kitchen as quietly as she could. She poured herself a bowl of cereal and splashed it with some milk.

Footsteps pounded down the front staircase.

Ginnie put the milk away and grabbed a spoon on her way to the family room. Just as she sat with the bowl of cereal, Buzz rounded the corner. "Toran? Do you know where—?" He stared straight at Ginnie. "How'd you get here?"

Ginnie showed him the bowl. "I just wanted something chocolate. Anybody else want some?"

Buzz opened his mouth. "But ..."

Ginnie smiled and locked her gaze on Buzz's. She ate a spoonful of cereal. "Mmm."

Buzz shook his head again and dropped into Uncle Ben's moss green armchair.

When everyone turned back to the TV, Ginnie took another spoonful and forced herself to chew and swallow each bite, even though it now felt like eating sand.

14

JASPER TAYLOR

*W*hen nine o'clock came and went, Tillie happily got ready for bed at the farm. She loved spending the night with Ginnie. The sounds of chirping crickets and the occasional barking of Uncle Jake's two watchful hunting dogs, Bandit and Reckless, made her feel safe.

The only thing not right was how quiet Ginnie was. She hadn't said much all night. Tillie changed into her pajamas. For some reason her birth dad, Jasper Taylor, came to mind.

The last time she saw him, he was yelling at Mom in their bedroom.

Mom was in tears.

Tillie had stood in the hallway, out of his line of vision.

"Jasper, calm down. I've got a job. We'll manage."

Jasper shook his fist. "It's not supposed to be like this."

The anger in his voice made Tillie's belly tremble. She put her hands over her ears to muffle the words, but couldn't take her eyes off Mom. *Please don't hurt her.* .

Mom had reached a comforting hand to Jasper, but he raised his own and pushed hers away. The tremble in Tillie's belly radiated over her whole body.

"Jasper, let me help," Mom had begged.

He turned back to her, hand raised.

Tillie ran forward. "Don't hurt Mommy!"

"I'm ..." Jasper stopped and glared.

She grabbed Mom's leg and buried her face in her mother's jeans. She'd done it now. He would hurt *both* of them. Jasper jerked her away from Mom. "Tilda, look at me."

Tillie scrunched her eyes closed and tried to move her shoulder to protect her face.

"Tillie, I didn't hurt her. *Look* at me."

But she couldn't look at him. She just couldn't.

"Daddy wasn't going to hurt me." Mom's quiet voice said. "He promised to stop. It's okay."

Tillie shook her head and scrunched her eyes shut harder.

He'd promised to stop hurting Mom many times, but he never kept that promise.

"My own kid doesn't ..." Jasper grabbed Tillie's arms. He squeezed her arms and shook her once.

"Jasper, don't!"

He let go.

Tillie stumbled backward.

"Jasper, she didn't mean ..."

Tillie opened her eyes in time to see Jasper pick up a vase and throw it against the wall behind Mom. Tillie screamed as it crashed into a zillion pieces.

He pointed a finger at Tillie and then opened his mouth.

No words came out.

He grabbed his jacket off the bed and shook his head. "I'm done."

Tillie latched onto Mom's leg as he rushed past them. Mom tried to follow him. Tillie grabbed harder and burst into tears. "Tils, it's okay. Jasper! Come back."

The front door slammed so hard it bounced open.

Tillie shivered, glanced around Ginnie's room, and rubbed her arms to smooth the goose bumps dotting them.

"Are you cold?" Ginnie asked. "We can close the window."

"No. I'm fine." Tillie lifted the emerald green satin comforter and slid between the sheets.

Ginnie turned on the bedside lamp. "You look a little freaked out."

Tillie forced a smile. "I'm fine."

"You sure?"

Tillie nodded and plumped her pillow. "Yeah, I'm sure."

You have your secrets. I have mine.

15

THE NIGHTMARE

*a*fter Tillie got into bed, Ginnie couldn't sleep. She couldn't get comfortable and she couldn't turn off her hurt and anger about Dad not trusting her after she had tried so hard to not bug him about the journals.

Then she remembered the diary Miss Amanda had given her.

Ginnie wasn't feeling very grateful, but she did recall how good she felt reading Miss Amanda's words to her. *Almost as good as Mama's entries.* Once Tillie's breathing evened into sleep, Ginnie slipped out of bed and padded on the soft royal purple carpet to her desk.

Ginnie re-read the passage Miss Amanda wrote to her. And then read her own thoughts.

Uncle Jake must have kept his promise to try again with Daddy— because they fought about whatever was keeping Dad from giving me the journals. Cabot somebody.

She added to the list:

4. Figure out who Cabot is.
5. Find out why Dad is afraid of him.

Then she thought about three things to be grateful for. She tapped the pen. *Got it.*

1. Buzz—he was really understanding and didn't pry when he could have.
2. Miss Amanda: she promised to work on Dad. They're on a date. Maybe she'll have better luck than Uncle Jake. After all, she can hug and kiss him. 🙂
3. Vi: She's been a great substitute mom. But I'm gonna miss her when she marries Preston and moves out after her wedding.

There, three things. Now if Miss Amanda asks, I can tell her the truth. I did what she asked.

Ginnie closed the diary and put it in the top drawer with the pink journal, crept back to bed, and thought about Mama and Miss Amanda working together to help her with Dad.

Her anger and hurt subsided. She willed her favorite dream to come to her, riding with Mama when she was three. Ginnie leaned back into Mama's arms, breathing in the smell of her floral perfume. Mama's long, blonde curls tickled her cheeks. Ginnie giggled.

"What's so funny, Princess?" Mama had asked.

"Your hair's tickling me." Ginnie leaned forward in the saddle, trying to move in front of Mama's hair. Mama snuggled Ginnie tighter in her arms and laughed.

Their bodies moved in rhythm to Eternal Love's strides.

They cantered around the frosted dirt of last summer's corn field.

A peaceful feeling enveloped Ginnie. The crisp morning breeze kissed only her cheeks. The rest of her body felt warm, nestled securely in Mama's arms.

They continued to ride, past the gray paint-weathered hay barn and up the gravel path behind the main barn. As they approached their woods, Ginnie giggled again and pointed. "Look, Mama! Doggies!"

Before Mama could respond, a pack of wild dogs headed straight toward them, jaws snapping.

Each dog was a different breed.

Black ones ... brown ones ... white ones.

Medium and large-sized dogs. A white one with a brown patch over its eye bared its teeth as it jumped in front of them, gnashing its teeth and growling, moving back and forth in a menacing pattern.

Eternal Love lurched and jumped over it.

Ginnie sat straight up in bed, heart pounding.

"Are you okay?" Tillie's sleepy voice asked.

Shuddering, Ginnie blinked, trying to figure out where she was.

The moonlight drifted in her window. She made out the familiar lumps and bulges of her bedroom at night. Tillie lay beside her in her full-sized bed. "I'm fine. Bad dream. Go back to sleep."

"'Kay. Night."

Ginnie barely heard Tillie's muffled voice as she adjusted into her pillows.

Turning over, Ginnie pulled up her comforter and tried to recall her dream, before the dogs. She often replayed this dream in her mind, riding with Mama. She never remembered it clearly during the day, except when she rode Calliope.

Willing herself back to sleep, she imagined herself nestled in Mama's arms again. Soon she and Mama moved as one on Love. They rode for what seemed like a long time before panic surged through Ginnie, waking her again.

Ginnie stumbled into the hallway, thinking a drink of water from the bathroom would help. Instead of the bathroom, she found herself in front of her dad's bedroom. She jerked her hand to her side just before her knuckles rapped on his door.

"What do you mean, what're you going to do?" Dad's voice scolded. "If she's your daughter, you get involved with her life."

Ginnie shook her head like an Etch-A-Sketch and let her eyes adjust to the soft glow of the night light directly in front of her, under the window that faced out toward their lane.

This is the hallway. That's Daddy and Uncle Jake's bedroom door. Why am I here?

"It's not that easy," Uncle Jake protested. "Clarissa lied to me, *for years*. What kind of woman doesn't tell a guy she gave birth to his kid?"

"Apparently the kind of woman *you* made a baby with. You knew better than that. What were *you* thinking?"

Uncle Jake doesn't have a baby, does he? Ginnie pressed herself against the wall. Nightmare or not, this wasn't the time to interrupt. She knew she should leave, but couldn't make herself go.

"*Don't* judge me! I was still reeling from Aunt Sadie and Queenie's deaths and trying to move heaven and earth to get back here to help you with Ginnie and Toran. I was overwhelmed ... and Clarissa ... well, she was a good listener. And apparently pretty good at keeping secrets."

"Ya think?"

Uncle Jake must not have appreciated Dad's snarky reply because he snapped. "Knock it off! This is serious."

"Well, it could be worse."

"How so?"

"You could be in high school. At least you have a job and insurance and if you had to, you could buy a house and support your family."

"Stop smiling. It's not funny."

Dad cleared his throat. "Actually, it kinda is. And it's *not* the end of the world. You like Clarissa, you wanted a kid, and now you have both. Win. Win. It's time to grow up, Peter Pan."

"Only I don't want Clarissa anymore. How can I forgive her? My child is *seven-and-a-half years old*. She's over halfway to being a teen and I haven't even met her."

Ginnie heard someone drop onto a bed. The springs creaked.

"You better figure it out. Your daughter needs you. Contrary to popular belief, dads are important. Suck it up and make nice with Clarissa. You have rights. *Exercise them.*" Dad's voice softened. "What's my niece's name?"

"Mysti. Mysti Rose Lawson. And it's spelled weird: M-Y-S-T-I. What's up with that? And another thing, if she's my kid, why doesn't she have *my* name? And why did she have to be a girl? I don't know anything about girls. Wests make *boys*. Maybe she's not mine after all."

Ginnie clamped her hand over her mouth, wanting to protest.

Dad spoke up. "So what's Ginnie? Chopped liver? And Vi? Uncle Ben and I figured out how to make girls, the first time out. That excuse doesn't wash. *Next*."

Go, Daddy!

"It's not an excuse. Ginnie likes dirt and toads and snakes. I get *her*. Mysti's a girly-girl. Check this out."

Ginnie leaned into the half-inch crack to see better.

Uncle Jake stood and fished his wallet out of his back pocket. He handed Dad two pictures. "Pink, frills, ruffles. What am I supposed to do with her? She's a princess."

"Even princesses need their dads." Dad cocked his head to the side. "And she looks like Mama. Queenie used to dress Ginnie up like this. Remember all those pageant dresses? They were even frillier than this. I loved it when Ginnie was my pink, frilly princess. I was the guest of honor at a lot of high class tea parties."

He handed the picture back. "You'll like it too."

Uncle Jake moaned. "You think she's mine, don't you?"

"What's more important is if *you* think she's yours." Dad handed back the photos. "But yeah, she does look like you and Mama. You said the dates matched up."

"Clarissa says she's easy-going most of the time but she has a bit of a temper. After all I put Uncle Ben and Aunt Sadie through, it serves me right to get a spitfire for a kid. But I'm not sure I can handle one."

"You'll do fine. You're great with my kids."

"*Your* kids are easy. And when they're not, I just have to threaten to get you involved. You're good at being the heavy." He moaned again. "I stink at it. You said so yourself, I'm Peter Pan."

"Then, grow up. You've got a supportive family. Isn't that what you just said to me? We're here for you." Dad slapped him lightly on the back, still smiling. "Besides, it's one thing to tell Uncle Ben you have a child out of wedlock, it's quite another to tell him you're not going to do right by her. If that's the case, you'd best pack up and get outta Dodge, 'cause Uncle Ben'll blow through you like a tornado in a trailer park." Dad shook his head and chuckled. "Not a pretty sight."

Imagining quiet Uncle Ben as a tornado made Ginnie smile.

She'd never seen him actually blow his top, but imagined that Uncle Jake had a time or six, having heard quite a few stories of Uncle Jake's prank-pulling teen days.

"Will you help me?" Uncle Jake asked Dad.

"Help you what?"

"Tell Uncle Ben about Mysti ... and help me parent her. You're the best dad I know."

"Thanks for the vote of confidence, but this is *your* news to tell. And I don't want to parent your kid. I want to be the fun uncle—the one who encourages Mysti to do naughty things and then talks you out of punishing her for it!" Dad teased. "Just like *you* do with *my* daughter!"

Ginnie laughed out loud, clamped her hand over her mouth, and whirled toward her door. She slinked across the hallway—but not fast enough.

Dad's door opened.

Ginnie's heart dropped to her toes.

16

BUSTED

"*V*irginia Maie Stratton West, *the second.*"

Dad's quiet, but menacing voice caused a shudder to course through her. "*Freeze.*"

Ginnie froze.

"Come here."

Swiveling slowly, Ginnie blew out a breath.

After darting his eyes around the empty hallway, Dad motioned her inside his room.

She swallowed hard and skirted by him, only to bump into Uncle Jake, whose pale face looked as horrible as she felt.

Dad pointed to his perfectly made bed. "Sit."

Ginnie sat. A shiver ran through her in spite of the hot, humid June night.

She wanted to apologize, but no words formed in her mind.

"What did you hear?" Dad's words were more of an accusation than a question.

She shrugged.

Uncle Jake slapped his thigh. "You know about Mysti, don't you?"

Ginnie jerked her head toward him.

Dad frowned. "If she didn't before, she does now."

Uncle Jake threw Dad a 'no, duh' look. "How can she not know? Look at her. Men on death row look more innocent than that."

She struggled to form a complete sentence in her mind.

"What are we going to do?" Uncle Jake asked.

"*We* aren't doing anything." Dad chuckled. "*You're* a dad now, *you* figure it out."

"But Ginnie's *your* kid. Make her keep my secret."

Ginnie clamped her jaw shut to keep from laughing at the horrified look on Uncle Jake's face.

"*You* make her. Mysti's *your* secret." Dad shot Ginnie a 'behave' look, but turned away when he couldn't keep his own face straight.

"Stop laughing. This is *not* funny." Uncle Jake threw each a disgusted look, but Dad didn't catch his. Instead, Dad's body shook with silent laughter.

Uncle Jake glared at him, then took out his wallet and fished out two twenties. "Here. I'm not above bribing you. Keep my secret, okay?"

Dad turned back in time to swipe the cash out of Uncle Jake's hand and shook it at him. "No way. Give this money to *your* daughter."

"You want me to handle it, so I'm handling it." Uncle Jake grabbed it back and thrust it at Ginnie.

Ginnie reached for the money. "Thanks."

"Virginia Maie, *don't you dare.*" Dad snatched the money from her and handed it to Uncle Jake. "You're not bribing her. And she's not accepting it."

"Geez, Todd. Make up your mind. In or out. I'm okay with bribing her. It's all good."

"No, it's not. *Reason* with her. I have faith in her good judgment."

Uncle Jake rolled his eyes. "Ginnie, this is easy, right? I pay you. You keep your mouth shut."

When Dad's eyes narrowed, Ginnie shrugged. She wanted to say "*Sure!*" but the warning expression on her male parental unit's face kept her mouth glued shut.

Dad gave Uncle Jake's chest a slight push to back him up. He knelt in front of Ginnie, eyeball-to-eyeball. "You can see that you knowing about Uncle Jake's surprise daughter has him a little wigged out, right?" When Ginnie nodded, Dad sighed. "This is *his* news to tell. Please don't say anything to anyone until he does, okay?"

"Even Toran and Tillie?" Ginnie asked.

Uncle Jake groaned. "*Especially* Toran and Tillie."

"I tell them everything."

Uncle Jake pushed Dad aside and took his place. "I need to tell Uncle Ben first. Your dad was the good son and I was the screw-up. I was finally getting to a point where I thought I couldn't possibly do anything more to embarrass the old man and here we are. I know this is huge news, but please don't spill the beans until I do. As a favor to me, your favorite uncle and buddy."

Remembering how aggravated he was when she asked him to unzip his lips earlier in the pasture, Ginnie felt tugged between sympathy and slightly amused at his discomfort.

"Please, Trouble? *For me?*"

A glance at Dad unglued her lips. "Okay. I won't tell."

"Thank you." Uncle Jake hugged her. "I owe you. Catch me when the warden isn't around."

Dad cleared his throat. "I heard that."

"It's okay. Daddy's right. Just don't take too long telling Uncle Ben." Ginnie didn't think it was possible, but he actually looked sicker.

"A couple, three days, tops. I have to meet her first. If she's not mine there's no reason to stir that hornet's nest." Uncle Jake glanced at Dad and grimaced. "But since she probably is, I'll figure out how and when to tell him. Preferably without causing him to have a stroke."

"Uncle Ben's pretty understanding. He'll still love you," Ginnie offered.

"I know. And Mysti truly is a blessing--just a very unexpected one. I have to get my head around this before I can tell him. Just keep my secret for a while, okay?"

"Okay." Ginnie smiled at him. "Can I leave now?"

Dad nodded. "But wait a minute. Why were you here?"

"I had a nightmare."

"I'm sorry. Are you okay?" Dad reached an arm around her shoulders. "What was it about?"

"I don't remember. I woke up outside your door. I didn't mean to listen, but I couldn't leave." Ginnie let him envelop her in a hug, liking how safe he made her feel.

"I'm sorry. I didn't realize. I'll tuck you in, okay?"

Ginnie nodded and then offered Uncle Jake a hug. He squeezed her a little too tight, but his arms felt good to her as well. "Uncle Jake?"

"Yes?"

"Mysti's lucky to have you for a dad. Besides, we need more girls around here."

"We do?" Dad asked, chuckling.

"Duh. There's too much testosterone in our family." She rolled her eyes.

Uncle Jake roared with relieved laughter.

"Stop rolling your eyes." Dad pointed a warning finger, no longer smiling. "And where did you hear *that*?"

"Vi, of course. Why do you think she wants to get married so much? Five guys in our family and two girls. You need to hurry up and marry Miss Amanda so we can even things up."

Dad smirked. "I'll get right on that."

Cool. Tillie will be happy. Ginnie grinned. "Really?"

"No. Yes. I *mean*, say good-night to your uncle." Dad play-glared at Uncle Jake when he laughed louder. "And *you* ... just wait. See how much fun having a daughter is?"

"Yeah." Uncle Jake rolled his eyes. "Lookin' forward to it."

Dad walked Ginnie to her room, tucked her in, and adjusted her comforter. "I know it's asking a lot, but please keep Uncle Jake's secret." Dad nodded at Tillie. "Please?"

"Sure,"

He kissed her goodnight and wished her pleasant dreams, and

then walked around the bed to adjust Tillie's covers and kiss the top of her head as well.

Ginnie snuggled into her covers and thought about Mysti.

She realized her new cousin was the biggest secret she had ever been entrusted with.

Thankfully, since Toran and Tillie were asleep, she would be able to keep Uncle Jake's secret tonight ... at least.

17

ZIPPED LIPS ARE NO FUN

*T*he next morning, Ginnie did her best to think about anything besides her new cousin. She wanted to tell Tillie so badly about Mysti, that she thought she might explode.

Not telling Toran was easier. His chores were different than hers.

When she and Tillie were on her way to the chicken coop, Dad gave her a quick hug and whispered. "I know you can keep Uncle Jake's secret. Thanks."

Ginnie nodded and then bristled. *Of course I can. I'm a West, aren't I?* Then she thought about Mama's journals and sadness swept over her. She bit back a plea for them and sighed.

That's what we do now, isn't it? Keep secrets? And hide things from each other?

Dad squeezed Tillie into their hug and headed to the main barn.

I wonder if keeping Uncle Jake's secret will make him want to share Dad's? Or maybe if I threaten to tell, he will unzip his lips? Hmmm.

Shame warmed Ginnie's cheeks as she pictured Uncle Jake's face last night.

Remembering his misery heated her cheeks even more.

You promised Uncle Jake--just like he promised Dad.

An ugly pit burrowed in her belly when she recalled him saying

"I *am* on your side. But I promised your dad before I promised you. So cut me some slack, okay?"

She still didn't want to cut him any slack, but she understood his position better.

Tillie's grin grew as she watched Dad leave.

Shame battled guilt as Dad's faith-filled "thanks" glued her lips shut. She blinked away her traitorous thoughts and gripped the egg basket tighter.

Ginnie would have liked to bask in the faith Dad showed in her ability to keep her word, but she felt undeserving. She headed for the hen house, with Tillie following like an eager puppy.

Ginnie searched her brain for a safe topic, but everything she thought of led back to the journals, Mama, Dad and Miss Amanda's wedding, or Mysti, all of which she either wasn't allowed to talk about or she didn't want to talk about ... with her very own best friend.

They entered the hen house.

The chickens dashed around and squawked their impatience.

"What's wrong?" Tillie picked up two eggs and put them in her chicken-shaped basket. "Why are you so quiet?"

Because Uncle Jake has a daughter and I can't tell you.

Ginnie shrugged, put the yellow hose in the waterer, then walked over to the wall to turn the spigot. "I just don't have anything to say." *At least, nothing I CAN say ... to YOU.*

"Your dad seemed to be in a good mood this morning." Tillie chatted happily. "I hope that means he and Mom had a fun time."

"Probably. He always seems to." Ginnie turned away, not certain how much thinking time Dad had to devote to Miss Amanda since becoming an uncle last night.

"Uncle Jake didn't look so happy. I wonder what Miss Clarissa wanted to ask him?"

"Um." Ginnie swallowed hard, trying not to blurt the news. Then an interesting idea occurred to her. She tried not to grin. "I didn't ask him. Maybe *you* should."

"Okay." Tillie picked up an egg and pointed it at Ginnie. "If it wasn't a proposal, maybe she won a trip somewhere? And wants to take him? Wouldn't that be cool?"

"Sure, or maybe she won a free dinner." Ginnie turned the water off and giggled softly. *Or he won a free kid.*

"That would be fun too." Tillie moved over to the other side of the coop for eggs while Ginnie scooped chicken feed into the feeding troughs.

The hens gobbled greedily.

I wonder how Uncle Jake would answer if Tillie asked him straight out? Wests aren't supposed to lie.

She turned from Tillie, scooped more feed, recalled the events of the last twenty-four hours, and sighed again. *But we certainly know how to keep a secret.*

18

"YES, SIR."

A shadow crossed the door of the hen house. Ginnie glanced up. Uncle Jake stood in the doorframe looking a little concerned. *I didn't tell her!*

Uncle Jake winked at Ginnie and then flashed a bright smile to Tillie. "Hey, Turtle. Do me a favor and fill the cat and dog feeders, will ya please?"

Tillie looked from Ginnie to Uncle Jake and back.

When Ginnie nodded, Tillie shrugged, and smiled. "Sure, Uncle Jake."

"Thanks." He opened the bottom half of the hen house door and waited for her to leave. He entered, closed the door again, and squatted next to Ginnie.

"I didn't tell her." Ginnie plucked up three eggs and put them in her basket.

"You said you wouldn't." Uncle Jake's quiet words calmed her racing heart. "I trust you."

"Then why are you here?"

"Because I'm embarrassed."

Ginnie locked her eyes on his.

He wiped his forehead with his arm and turned from her. "I'm not ashamed of Mysti. I told you last night that she's a blessing." He swiveled back. "I still believe that."

Several seconds passed like molasses through a strainer.

"I know you know how these things happen." He paused and then cleared his throat. "I'm not embarrassed that you know I most likely have a daughter. I'm just not wild about you knowing I have a daughter and that I'm *not* married to her mother."

"It's okay, Uncle Jake."

"No, Ginnie, it's not." He sighed and glanced around the chicken coop. "We both know I'm not always the best example for following the rules, but in this case, I don't want you thinking it's okay to do what I did. It's not." Uncle Jake's gaze bore through her. "You do a lot of things I do, *that I probably shouldn't.*"

"Okay, I won't." She snapped the lid down on the feed bucket.

"Look at me, please."

Ginnie pushed the chicken feed container against the wall and hesitantly met his gaze.

"I mean it. I want you to do things the right way. And 'yes sir' would be appropriate here."

Her mouth dropped open.

Over the years, he'd scolded her many times for 'sir-ing' him, but she couldn't recall one single time when he'd *insisted* she 'sir' him. "Okay. I-I mean. Yes, sir."

"You're catching flies." He chucked her gently under the chin. "I still don't like being 'sir-ed', but I want you to know I'm serious."

"Yes, sir."

He smiled. "You can stop now."

Ginnie grinned. "Yes, sir."

"I mean it. *Stop.*" He stood, strode toward the door, and turned. "Oh, and Gin?"

"Yeah?"

"This is one of the few things that are off limits for us to joke about. Please respect that."

" I understand." Her gaze dropped to his work boots. "I'm sorry I eavesdropped. I didn't mean to."

"Yeah, me too. But since you overheard quite a bit, I didn't have to look you in the eye and tell you. If Mysti *is* my daughter, I'll have to have this chat with Toran and Tillie as well." Uncle Jake locked his gaze on hers. "You and I have always been close. I don't want that to change."

"It won't. I like that you're my buddy."

"Good, I just wanted to make sure that we are on the same page. But if you follow my example in this way, buddy or not, I *will* tan your hide."

Ginnie swallowed hard enough for her ears to pop. "No, sir, I won't."

"Good. You believe me." He pointed his finger. "Your folks did it the right way. I expect you to follow *their* example, not mine." He took two steps back to her. "Now please give me a hug, I need to get back to work."

"Got it. Get married first, *then* have babies." Ginnie let him hug her tight, relieved he was smiling again.

"I'm glad you were paying attention. Hurry up in here." He took a step back from her. "We need to eat breakfast and get started on the hay truck."

"Uncle Jake?"

"Yeah?"

"Miss Clarissa always sounds very nice when I take messages for you. I'm sure Mysti is nice too. Will I get to meet them? Or are you still mad at her?"

"I am *very* angry with her. Clarissa betrayed me and that will take a while for me to look past. I'll call her and work this out *with her...* *later*. I'm too angry to be civil, so throwing hay bales will probably be good for me today. Just don't say anything until you hear from me, okay?"

Ginnie knew only one answer would do. "Yes, sir."

19

MISS CLARISSA

Whenever Ginnie was tempted to tell Tillie about Mysti, she heard Uncle Jake's quiet voice say "I trust you." She just couldn't break her promise to him.

After breakfast, Vi asked Ginnie and Tillie to wash the dishes while she changed for work. Toran helped Dad and Uncle Jake unload bales of alfalfa from the hay wagon into the hay barn. Their other best friend, Austin, came over to help. Austin was the fourth member of 'The Four Musketeers' as Uncle Jake dubbed Toran, Tillie, Austin, and Ginnie.

"What's wrong?" Tillie pulled a plate out of the drying rack and wiped it with a purple towel.

Ginnie shook her head and rinsed the next plate. "Nothing."

"Wests aren't supposed to lie."

Ginnie caught the teasing tone to her friend's words, but she didn't find them funny.

Maybe not, but they're supposed to know how to keep a promise .... and a secret.

"Tell me what's wrong."

"Nothing's wrong." Ginnie added a plate to the dish rack. "I just want to help in the hay barn."

"That's hot, scratchy work." Tillie put away a plate. "How long do we have to do it?"

"Until it's done. Uncle Ben and Buzz are in the field baling and loading the other hay wagon. After we unload this one, Dad will take the rest of us to the field to help."

"Though not you," Vi said, entering the kitchen.

Ginnie jerked toward her cousin. "Why not? I want to go."

"Because I have to work. You need to be at the house to answer the phone and take care of the egg and milk customers. Mrs. MacGregor and Mrs. Adams will be by after I leave for the diner."

"Ugh!" Ginnie complained. "Couldn't *you* take care of Mrs. McGregor? She's so annoying!"

"Be nice." Vi lightly pinched Ginnie's cheek. "She's just lonely since her husband died."

Ginnie rolled her eyes. "You do realize that if Mrs. McGregor gets her way, she'll marry Uncle Ben, and *you'll* have one not-so-lovely stepmother to entertain?"

Vi offered a mischievous smile. "That won't be a problem for *me* ... I'm getting married and moving out. *You two* would have to entertain her."

"That's not funny," Ginnie protested. "Uncle Ben wouldn't dare marry *her!*"

Vi and Tillie giggled. "Probably not," Vi agreed. "Aren't you glad your dad's dating Amanda instead of someone like Mrs. McGregor? Pretty soon, we'll each get a new sister."

"If Daddy dated someone like Mrs. McGregor, I would go all kinds of prank happy on her ... and *him* too ... for doing such a thing."

Tillie's happy smile grew. "Yeah, and I'd help you. I wouldn't wish Mrs. McGregor on anyone."

Vi wagged a scolding finger at each of them. "You two better be nice to her. She's one of our best customers and Ginnie Maie ... Mrs. McGregor had an interesting tale to tell about you and Calliope jumping over the hood of her car last month. One I *didn't* share with your dad ... *but I could.*"

Ginnie didn't miss the warning in her cousin's words.

It was true. She and Calliope had sailed over the hood of Mrs. McGregor's car, but only after Mrs. McGregor nearly squished her and Calliope into horseburgers.

Even so, Dad wouldn't be very happy about the knowledge since he'd forbidden her to do tricks on Calliope and had threatened to sell her horse if Ginnie ever disobeyed him. He'd probably make an exception for that time, since jumping the car had saved them from a bad accident, but no sense taking chances.

Ginnie swallowed hard. "Yes ma'am, we'll be nice to her."

"Yes'm." Tillie echoed, raising her eyebrows in question. "What else do you want us to do?"

"Good. We're on the same page." Vi offered a sympathetic smile. "I'm setting the oven timer. When it beeps, please add this jar of barbecue sauce to the pulled pork I have in the crock-pot. I made snickerdoodles last night. Set up lunch when the guys come in from the field. Also, please catch up the laundry and do the eggs. All easy."

"I love doing the eggs. Can I candle them?" Tillie asked.

"Sure." Ginnie put a plate in the rack. "Then what?"

"Nothing. Just do the dishes and clean up after lunch." Vi stirred the pork. "Tillie, your mom and I are going wedding shopping tonight. Want to come?"

Tillie grinned. "I'd love it. Ginnie, you come too."

"What are we shopping for?" Ginnie rinsed a glass.

"Flowers. The craft store has flowers on sale—I need to snap up as many violets as I can for corsages and boutonnieres."

"Sounds like fun ... *not*." Ginnie whispered the 'not' under her breath after she turned the water on higher. She'd try to figure a way out of the shopping trip later.

However, Vi and Miss Amanda were good about stopping for ice cream when they took her and Tillie shopping, so maybe she'd just be a good sport and go along.

Miss Amanda was even nicer to her these days than she used to be, since she most likely would be her new stepmom. Ginnie loved spending time with her.

On the other hand, with Vi's wedding coming up, the only mom she had ever known would soon be moving to a new home.

Then Miss Amanda might or might not take her place. Ginnie scrubbed some silverware and tried not to think about any of her 'moms': Vi, Mama, or Miss Amanda.

She really wanted to see Austin and help the guys with the hay wagon. Austin would understand about the journals and maybe even help her figure out a way to get them back.

Vi offered to finish the dishes so Ginnie and Tillie could help stock the hay barn for a while.

It was easy to forget about Uncle Jake's secret daughter while lining bales and pushing them into place after the men got them in the general area.

Toran and Austin joked about the swimming hole and Dad promised to take all of them later in the week.

Vi called Ginnie and Tillie away about the time the wagon was unloaded, but before Ginnie had time to ask Austin to help her brainstorm. She swallowed her frustration, knowing better than to argue with Vi when her dad was around. He would just tell her to do what Vi asked.

Dad winked at her as she walked by him.

Ginnie forced a smile and followed Tillie and Vi back to the house.

After Vi ran through the to-do list again, she left.

Mrs. Adams showed up for eggs. Tillie took care of her while Ginnie ran for the phone.

"Hello, West residence, Ginnie speaking."

"Ginnie!" The voice on the other end sounded relieved. "Hi honey. This is Clarissa, is your Uncle Jake there, please?"

"I don't think so." Ginnie walked out on the porch. Dad had already driven the tractor pulling the empty hay wagon down the lane. "He's in the field. Can I take a message?"

"Don't take this wrong, but is he really in the field or did he just tell you to tell me that?"

Ginnie bristled. "He would *never* ask me to lie for him. He's in the field."

"I'm sorry. Of course he is. I just need to talk to him."

I'll bet you do. Something about Miss Clarissa's voice hovering between anxious and sad made Ginnie feel sorry for her. Given Uncle Jake's fury last night with Dad, she could imagine that Uncle Jake's last words to Miss Clarissa weren't the most comforting.

"He said he'd call you later," Ginnie offered, feeling a little guilty for repeating Uncle Jake's words to the lady he considered an enemy at the moment.

But she couldn't help herself. She hated it when Uncle Jake was mad at her.

She could imagine how awful Miss Clarissa felt. Dad was right. Uncle Jake would have to get over being mad at Miss Clarissa for Mysti's sake.

Maybe Ginnie could help. "It'll be a few hours. They have to load both hay wagons."

"No, that's fine. Thank you." Hope seemed to replace the sadness in her voice. "He has my cell phone number. If he said he'll call, I'm sure he will. Thank you."

"You're welcome. Bye now."

"Bye, honey."

Ginnie smiled as she hung up the phone.

Then her stomach flipped.

Now that Miss Clarissa sounded happy, Ginnie wasn't so sure she'd done the right thing by Uncle Jake. She forced herself to take a few breaths to calm the uneasiness in her belly.

She felt downright sick, but couldn't figure out why and worse ... she couldn't talk to Tillie about it.

This secret was becoming a huge burden.

Uncle Jake better figure out whether Mysti's his kid or not ... and soon. I can't take much more of this.

Ginnie made herself a glass of ice water, sat at the kitchen bar, and gulped away the queasiness.

When she spotted the cookie jar, she grabbed a few snicker doodles to share with Tillie.

"Mrs. Adams gave us a tip." Tillie said, as she came through the kitchen archway holding up a ten dollar bill. "Cool, huh?"

"Very cool. Want some cookies?" Ginnie handed her friend two.

"Mmm." Tillie bit into a cookie and then put the money into a purple crockery jar printed with raised black lettering that said: 'Egg Money.'

Most things around the farmhouse were purple and green, Aunt Sadie's favorite colors. Since Aunt Sadie had a thing for goats and violets, their kitchen and family room still sported drapes, plates, pillows, canisters, knickknacks decorated in one or both themes.

On the one hand, it made Ginnie think that Aunt Sadie was watching over their family and that always made her feel warm and cozy. On the other, she wished they were surrounded with things that had been important to Mama as well.

But they weren't.

The farmhouse hadn't been Mama's home, just Dad's home ... and Toran's ... and Ginnie's.

Vi's full name was Violet Elizabeth West, so Ginnie understood the violets, but her only experience with goats was Uncle Ben's nanny goat, Gertrude, a spiteful excuse for an animal.

Ginnie was sure Gertrude held a grudge against her personally for some unknown reason and if Ginnie had her way, Gertrude would disappear.

Tillie slid onto the bar stool next to Ginnie and took another bite of her cookie.

"I hope the guys are done in the field in time for Uncle Ben to milk Gertrude," Ginnie said, pointing a cookie at Tillie. "Otherwise you get to milk *her* and I'll milk Trixie."

Tillie laughed. "Gertrude's not so bad."

"She's evil. And she makes bad things happen."

"Like what?"

The doorbell rang.

A voice called out in a thick Scottish accent. "Yoo-hoo! It's Mrs. McGregor comin' to buy a fresh quart of goat's milk."

Ginnie smirked. "Exhibit 'A.' Mrs. McGregor."

Tillie giggled and stood.

Ginnie groaned, dropped her head onto her arm, and wished she could melt into the countertop.

20

NOT AGAIN

*T*he guys came home late for lunch, done with haying for the day. After they ate, Dad showered and got ready for work. Ginnie folded the last load of jeans and took them upstairs. As she approached her dad's room, she heard him and Uncle Jake arguing.

Great ... not again.

"Please, Todd? Seb's only expecting one of us. Let me take Ginnie. She'll keep me calm."

Take me where?

"Amanda wants to take the girls shopping. She wants to spend time with Ginnie, especially. And I think it would be good for her. Maybe if she can spend more time with Amanda, she won't miss Queenie so much."

I doubt it. Ginnie felt instantly ashamed at her response. *I do love Miss Amanda, but she can't replace my mom.*

"I'm working nights tomorrow. I need to know if Mysti's mine or not—*for sure.* Let me bring Ginnie. If I get crazy, she can keep Mysti occupied. I need her. Please?"

"Jake, she's twelve. This is an adult situation. I don't really want her involved. I already told Amanda that Ginnie could go with her."

"She's *already* involved. Besides, if I take her with me, it'll be easier for her to keep my secret. Like you said, she's twelve. This is huge news and Tillie's always with her. It's got to be eating her up. I don't know if I could have kept such a big secret at her age."

Wow, he does understand.

Ginnie backed up and headed toward the stairs. She wanted to go with Uncle Jake, but even more, didn't want to get busted for eavesdropping.

Stomping up the last three steps, she called out loudly, "Daddy? Uncle Jake?'

Dad opened his door as she rounded the banister. "Think you're making enough noise?"

She shrugged. *I wouldn't want to interrupt anything.*

"I wasn't sure if you were still in the shower. Here are your jeans. Laundry's caught up."

"Thanks, honey."

Uncle Jake came up behind Dad and nudged him.

Dad glanced around the second floor hallway and motioned Ginnie into his room. Trying not to grin, she widened her eyes innocently. "Am I in trouble?"

Uncle Jake pushed his way in front of Dad. "No, I need a favor."

Dad elbowed him back. "She can choose."

"Fine." Uncle Jake rolled his eyes and said in the most inviting circus ringmaster voice: "Trouble, do you want to spend the night with Clarissa, Mysti, me, *and* a pocketful of tokens and *all* the pizza you can eat at Quincy's Pizza Palace and Game Emporium o-r-r-r do you want to go shopping with Vi and Amanda?" He said 'shopping' like he might suggest drinking a large glass of warm vinegar.

"Hmmm, both things sound like so much fun," Ginnie teased.

She glanced at each of them, trying not to laugh. She wanted to go, but wasn't against making Uncle Jake sweat a little. After all, he'd do the same to her. "Well, Miss Amanda usually buys us ice cream ..."

"Fine, I'll buy ice cream. Just come, okay?" The sharpness of his answer took the fun out of teasing him.

Dad shook his head at her, but didn't quite manage to hide his smile. He offered a conspiratorial wink.

"Sure, Uncle Jake. But you know ..." Ginnie tapped her chin and grinned. "Now that you're a dad—you're a lot crankier than when you were just my buddy. You might want to chill out some before meeting Mysti. Like Uncle Ben's always saying: You only get one chance to make a good first impression. You wouldn't want Mysti to think you were weaned on a sour pickle."

Dad burst out laughing when Ginnie quoted one of Uncle Jake's favorite sayings.

"Sure, encourage her to kick me when I'm down." Uncle Jake backhanded Dad softly. He shook his head and smirked. "That's why I need you to come with me. You know how to work me. Just go easy on the teasing. I'm not my normal jolly self."

"No kidding." Ginnie rolled her eyes.

Dad narrowed his. "Stop that."

"Hah!" Uncle Jake high-fived her. "Let's ditch the stiff."

Dad frowned. "It's only one-thirty. I've got to get to work, but isn't Clarissa already *at* work? And you can't leave until after chores."

"Probably, but Ginnie and I can meet her right after."

"I'm sure she'll want to. She was anxious to talk to you," Ginnie said.

Uncle Jake leveled her with a stare. "When did *you* talk to her?"

Ginnie took a step toward Dad. "She called earlier. I told her you'd call later because she sounded so miserable."

"And when did I say I'd call her?" His words were more accusing than questioning.

She swallowed hard and hitched her thumb toward the window. "In the hen house."

Uncle Jake slapped his thigh. "UN--*BE-liev-able*. Whose side are you on? *She betrayed me*. Geez, Trouble."

Dad reached a gentle hand to Ginnie's shoulder. "Jake, back off. You don't need to kill the messenger. You have your own kid to terrorize now, leave mine alone."

Dad's voice was both protective and teasing, and caused several emotions to skirt across Uncle Jake's face.

Ginnie stepped into Dad's hug.

Uncle Jake grimaced. "See? If you don't come I might end up scarring Mysti for life and wouldn't that be a fine how-do-you-do?"

"Not so much." Ginnie agreed and rolled her eyes at him, knowing Dad couldn't see. Then she turned to her dad. "What are you going to tell Miss Amanda? I don't want to hurt her feelings."

"The truth. Jake's insane and needs you to keep him out of trouble." Dad twirled one of Ginnie's braids around his finger. "Though on second thought, maybe that's just asking for gasoline to fan the flame."

"Very funny, Daddy."

Dad grinned and opened his door. "*I* thought so. I need to get to work. Behave, okay?"

"Sure." Ginnie wrinkled her nose. "Whatever you say."

21

GOLF

*G*innie thought about what she would say to Tillie when she and Uncle Jake ditched her tonight while making her way to the back of the house. She nearly ran into Uncle Jake as he tried to move into the dining room at the same time she tried to enter the kitchen.

"Beep, beep. Careful, Trouble."

"Sorry." Ginnie mumbled, keeping her head down, suddenly irritated with her uncle.

He was the cause of all her frustration today.

It was Uncle Jake's fault that she didn't have Mama's journals, it was *his* kid Ginnie was trying to keep secret, and it was because of *him* she needed to come up with a non-lie to tell Tillie, to keep from hurting her best friend's feelings.

"Trouble, what's the matter?"

She glared at him, made a beeline to the cupboard, and took out a glass.

"Did I do something wrong?"

Ginnie rolled her eyes, opened the freezer door, and grabbed a handful of ice. "Nope."

Except for ruining my whole entire life, not a thing.

The puzzled look on his face didn't escape her, even though she turned quickly. He stepped in front of her, eyebrows raised in question. "Is there something we need to talk about?"

"Nope." She looked pointedly at his shoulder, then at the glass behind him. "I just need a glass of water."

He stepped aside and let her pass.

After dropping the ice cubes into her glass, she wiped her cold palm on her blue jeans, filled the glass with water, and then turned her back to him, willing him to leave.

He didn't.

She gulped the water, turning just enough to see him standing with a slight smile on his lips, waiting for her to tell him why she was mad.

He can wait until chickens lay duck eggs for all I care.

Ginnie swiveled toward the family room and drained her glass. The rush of ice cold water gave her brain freeze. She sucked a breath through her teeth and tried not to grimace.

Uncle Jake cleared his throat and stepped into the middle of the kitchen where she would have to either go through him or around him.

Great. Now what do I do?

Pretty certain he wasn't planning to move until she spoke, she set her glass on the counter, glanced at him, and noticed a slightly bigger smile. *Fine.*

Ginnie did an about-face, marched into the family room, snapped on the TV, dropped onto the couch, and refused to make eye contact, gluing her gaze on the television screen.

Golf? Seriously? She groaned. *DOUBLE GREAT!*

Out of the corner of her eye, she noticed an even bigger smile on his lips.

Her anger boiled.

She concentrated on the TV. Still golf.

Now what?

Uncle Jake crossed into her line of vision. "Are you sure there isn't something you wanted to say to me?"

"Nothing you want to hear."

Sugar beets! Quiet, Gin. Just ignore him.

"Fair enough. But maybe there's something I *need* to hear?" His amused look fled, quickly being replaced with concern.

"Nope." *Of course there is. You're so smart. Figure it out.*

"Wow. One word, lotsa attitude." His eyebrows knit together. "Is this about what you heard last night?"

"Nope."

"Want to give me a hint?"

"Nope. If you knew me at all, you'd know what the problem is."

"*Really?*" He made a half-whistle, half-laugh noise and smirked. "You're twelve. I didn't expect to hear that line to come out of your mouth until you started dating at least. Is there something we should discuss with your dad?"

His playful tone only fueled her fury.

She jumped off the couch, dashed around his outstretched arm, bolted through the kitchen, and out the side porch door.

He followed quickly, catching up to her as she flew out of the second porch door.

Before she could tell her feet whether to flee toward the barn, the pasture, or the front of the house, Uncle Jake stood in front of her, worry coloring his face. "Don't make me jump any hoops. Just tell me what's wrong. And don't say 'nope' or 'nothing.' Wests don't lie."

"But they sure know how to keep secrets, *don't they?*" Ginnie let the words drip with spite. She crossed her arms. "Too bad Wests don't keep their promises."

"Didn't we just have this conversation?"

She toggled her head. "I *told* you that you didn't want to hear what I had to say. Too bad you didn't listen, *huh?*"

"Wow, even *more* attitude." His eyes narrowed. Then worry crept into his voice. "Is this how you're gonna act tonight? Because I *thought* you had my back."

"I have your back as much as you have mine." She took a sideways step.

He matched her move. "I *do* have your back. *You* need to have some patience."

"No, sir." Ginnie shook her head so hard her blonde braids flipped from one shoulder to the other. "What I *NEED is* a dad who isn't afraid of his past, an uncle who keeps his promises, a best friend who doesn't have to talk about weddings all the time, and a brother who isn't perfect."

Uncle Jake hung his thumb on his jean pocket and asked quietly. "Anything else?"

"As long as you're asking, a mom who *isn't* dead would be nice." She blinked quickly and jutted her chin. "But since pigs don't fly, I got *nothing.*"

She brushed the bangs out of her eyes and glared just past his shoulder. "*Leave. Me. Alone.*"

22

LOOSE LIPS SINK SHIPS

*W*ow." Uncle Jake took a step back and then locked his gaze on hers. "How much of that is spite and how much is really bugging you?"

Ginnie rolled her eyes.

He winked. "I know how annoying it is to have a perfect brother, but I don't think Toran's that big a problem." His expression grew serious when she refused to respond to his playfulness. He reached a hand to her shoulder. "Seriously, Todd's finally moving on with his life, so if you must keep being mad about the journals, please keep directing it at me ... at least until he gives them back."

You got it. No problem there.

"That last bit about wanting a mom who isn't dead ... I think Amanda's pretty awesome. *And* she's very much alive. So if you really want a mom, she's available."

Ginnie shrugged, determined not to speak.

"You know, you *can* have both. Amanda has always been good to you and Todd's not against you getting to know Queenie. If there's something you need or want to know, just ask."

"If I had the journals I wouldn't *have* to ask." She yelled and then blinked back hot tears. "I'd just know."

"Maybe." He lowered his voice. "But maybe not. What do you think the journals will tell you?"

Good question. Ginnie shrugged, not sure how to respond. "Stuff."

Stuff? Lame answer.

"Like?"

Ginnie shrugged again. "I dunno. Her favorite color? Her favorite song? Just stuff I'd know if she were still here."

"I can help you out a little there. Her favorite color was emerald green, like yours. You'd have to ask your dad about her favorite song." He rubbed his chin, thinking a minute before he continued. "She could listen to the same song fifty times in a row if she was in the mood. For some reason, she always managed to burn toast, but she also made this delicious chicken dish that I forgot the name of."

Although interesting, Ginnie wanted more. "That's not the same as reading words *she* wrote."

"I know, but it's *something*." He blew out a long, slow breath, reminding Ginnie of a punctured bike tire. "Look. I'd still like your help with Mysti tonight, but *only* if I know you're not gonna flip out on me."

A vulnerable look replaced his normally confident one.

She turned away.

"This is probably—hands down—the most important night of my life." He squeezed her shoulder, his voice catching.

Ginnie reluctantly met his gaze.

"If Mysti *is* my kid … that makes me a dad … forever and always. I'm a little freaked about it. I can't have *you* freaking out too. So let me know if you're in or out, just don't make this harder or weirder than it already is."

She let his words run through her mind a couple of times before responding. Each time they repeated, his anxiety increased and her anger diminished.

Ginnie took a step into his outstretched arms and let him envelop her in a bear hug.

The rest of her anger melted.

After a minute, she stepped back and smiled. "Don't worry so much. You're an awesome uncle. You're gonna be an awesome dad."

"The two aren't exactly the same thing." He weaved her braid through his fingers and sighed. "But I hope I can be a good dad. My dad was pretty awesome and so's yours and Uncle Ben. I'd hate to mess up *that* family tradition."

The porch door slammed, causing each of them to turn.

Ginnie's eyes widened as a light green hue washed over Uncle Jake's face.

Oh man! Of all the people to hear!

23

THE CAT'S OUTTA THE BAG

*illie pulled several handfuls of grass, angry that she couldn't put into words what she was thinking and feeling ... and growing even angrier that she couldn't figure out what was on Ginnie's mind. Her best friend hadn't said much at all last night and even less this morning.

After Uncle Jake asked Tillie to feed the cats and dogs so he could talk with Ginnie alone, Ginnie didn't even hint at what they talked about. *Normally she would have told me everything.*

Tillie snatched at several more lumps of grass.

Great. Another new secret. Ginnie's full of them lately: the journals, how she really feels about Mom and DT getting married, whatever Uncle Jake wanted to talk about, and that Cabot guy.

Rascal trotted up to her, panting in her face. She stroked his neck, then pushed him gently away.

Come to think about it, DT has a lot of secrets too. Why was there a judge? Who IS that Cabot guy? And why can he take Ginnie and Toran away from their dad?

She froze, horrified at her next thoughts. *Will that Cabot guy make DT not marry Mom? Does Uncle Ben know? Can Uncle Ben fix it?*

The familiar worry Tillie struggled to keep away, crept inside her, making it hard to breathe.

She threw a handful of grass into the brook, willing her bad vibes to float away with the current.

Chill, Tillie. There's nothing so bad that Uncle Ben can't fix it. That's what he does ... he fixes bad things and bad people.

The uneasiness lifted when she reminded herself that Uncle Ben had made Jasper go away. Jasper was *really* bad. *Uncle Ben will make this Cabot guy go away too.*

Happy to have a plan, Tillie brushed off the rest of the grass and went to find Ginnie and reassure her as well. Tillie made her way to the kitchen, but didn't see any sign of her friend.

Continuing on to the family room, she was surprised to find golf playing on the television. *Who's watching this?*

Tillie switched off the TV and retraced her steps to the kitchen.

"If I had the journals I wouldn't *have* to ask."

That's Ginnie. She sounds mad. Maybe she's cornered Uncle Jake.

Tillie walked to the side porch. *Maybe he'll tell her about Cabot.*

Uncle Jake stood facing mostly away from the house with a thumb hanging off his front pocket. Tillie saw enough of his face to realize he was trying to stay calm. "I know, but it's *something*." He blew out a long slow breath. "Look. I'd still like your help with Mysti tonight, but *only* if I know you're not gonna flip out on me."

Who's Mysti? And why does he need Ginnie's help with her? She can't go anyway. We're going shopping with Mom tonight.

Tillie opened the screen door and took a step through.

"If Mysti *is* my kid ... that makes me a dad ... forever and always. I'm a little freaked about it. I can't have *you* freaking out too. So let me know if you're in or out, just don't make this harder or weirder than it already is."

Uncle Jake has a baby? Wow! But why'd he tell Ginnie and not the rest of us?

Uncle Jake hugged Ginnie when she laughed. "Don't worry so much. You're an awesome uncle. You're gonna be an awesome dad."

"The two aren't exactly the same thing." He weaved her braid through his fingers. "But I hope I can be a good dad. My dad was pretty awesome and so's yours and Uncle Ben. I'd hate to mess up that family tradition."

The screen door slipped through Tillie's sweaty fingers and slammed shut.

The shocked looks on Ginnie and Uncle Jake's faces rushed the awful lead balloon feeling Tillie tried to avoid at all costs, straight to her belly. Her knees buckled as she tried to breathe through fuzzy white noise pounding in her ears. "S-s-orry. It slipped."

Uncle Jake slapped his thigh and groaned. "Not again."

Ginnie took a step toward Tillie. "Hey, Til, what's up?"

"Um, not much, how about you guys?"

"Cut the small talk, I can't stand it." Uncle Jake scanned the area. "Is anyone *else* listening?"

"Toran's at Austin's and everyone else is at work. It's just us three," Ginnie pointed out.

"And you couldn't have reminded me of that five minutes ago?" he asked, shaking his head.

"Sorry, Uncle Jake. I was just trying to ..." Tillie stopped, not sure how to finish the sentence.

His eyes narrowed. "Just trying to what?"

"Umm. Find Ginnie?"

"You found her all right." He grimaced. "Thanks, Trouble."

"This isn't *my* fault. I told you I didn't want to talk to you." Ginnie planted her hands on her hips. "*You* followed *me* outside. I was trying to get away from you."

"Note to self: next time Trouble has a meltdown, just ignore it." The sarcasm in his voice made Tillie want to giggle, but the look on his face squashed that impulse.

He pointed a finger at Ginnie. "Knock it off, it's not funny."

Good, Ginnie thought it was funny too.

Tillie clamped her jaw shut to corral a smile.

"On the bright side, Tillie can go with us tonight," Ginnie said.

"Go where?" Tillie shook her head, trying to figure out what Ginnie was talking about. "Mom and Vi are taking us wedding shopping."

Ginnie turned to Uncle Jake. "It'll be easier for her to keep your secret if she comes with us."

"Maybe, but I don't need a ... hey!" He leaned toward Ginnie, frustration crossing his face. "Did you eavesdrop on your dad and me earlier?"

"Not on purpose. You left your door open. Remember Daddy saying I made a lot of noise? I was trying not to listen," she answered.

Uncle Jake lifted his hand.

"Don't hit her!" The words escaped before Tillie even thought them. "Please!"

Ginnie's mouth opened. No words came out.

"I wasn't going to hit her." Uncle Jake lowered his hand. "For the record, Turtle, I never have." He pointed a finger between them and took a step closer to Tillie. "But I might consider grounding you guys if you two keep listening to conversations that aren't meant for your ears."

Tillie swallowed hard.

"Though probably not." Uncle Jake squeezed her shoulder. "Now what do I do with you?"

"Take us both. We'll play with Mysti if you need to talk to Miss Clarissa," Ginnie suggested.

"I don't *want* to talk to Clarissa. I don't even want to talk to the *two of you* about this, but it looks like I don't have much of a choice."

"Sorry, Uncle Jake. I didn't realize the conversation was private." Tillie looked to Ginnie for help. "Is Miss Clarissa Mysti's mom?" Ginnie nodded. "I thought Miss Clarissa just moved to town a couple of months ago." Tillie pushed her hair out of her eyes. "How old's Mysti? A newborn?"

"Not hardly. She's *seven years old*." The way Uncle Jake said 'seven' made goosebumps rise on Tillie's arms.

"Seven?"

"Yeah, *seven* ... and a half." He motioned them toward the porch, held open the screen door, and grimaced. "Let's go inside. I need a drink and since I don't drink alcohol, root beer's gonna have to do."

24

MAKE IT GOOD

*U*ncle Jake handed Tillie and Ginnie each a can of cold root beer and looked at the clock on the microwave. "You have ten minutes to ask me whatever questions you want. Make them good, but not *too* good."

Ginnie tried not to giggle when he grimaced.

"Then I want you to drop all questions until I figure out whether or not Mysti is my child, capiche?"

"Capiche," both answered in unison.

Tillie swiveled her chair toward him. "How long have you known Miss Clarissa?"

"About ten years. We dated for a little over a year and I decided to propose to her." Uncle Jake lifted his can of soda, jiggled it, and then set it back down.

"You were married to her?" Ginnie asked, puzzled.

Uncle Jake shook his head. "I got a call from Uncle Seth saying Aunt Sadie had died about an hour before I was to take Clarissa out and propose. He said Uncle Ben wanted me to come home as soon as I could. So of course, I spent the night making travel arrangements instead of proposing. It kind of took the joy out of the moment."

"No kidding." A sick feeling swept over Ginnie. "Sorry, Uncle Jake."

"Yeah." He tapped the soda and sighed. "It took a few months to move past that. Aunt Sadie had been my mom slightly longer than Grandma had been my mom." Uncle Jake glanced at each girl, and then took a sip of root beer. "I came back here for Christmas the next year. Uncle Ben insisted that if I still loved Clarissa, I should go ahead and ask her to marry me."

"Did you?" Ginnie asked.

He shook his head. "I had planned to. Since your dad and I didn't have any sisters, and I'm older, Aunt Sadie kept my mom's engagement ring for me to give to my future bride. I flew home at Christmas to pick it up and brainstormed with Queenie on how to make a magical night for Clarissa. Queenie insisted New Year's Eve would be a fun night to propose. And it might have been if ..."

His gaze dropped to the counter.

"If Mama hadn't died on December twenty-eighth," Ginnie finished for him.

"Yeah," he agreed.

"Wow. That's a lot of sad nights," Tillie whispered.

Uncle Jake cleared his throat. "Clarissa put up with a lot that year and a half. I should have just married her then, but I didn't. And I got it into my head that with both Aunt Sadie and Queenie dying, maybe Clarissa wasn't the one for me."

Ginnie leaned forward. "Then how did you get Mysti?"

She clamped her hand over her lips, realizing too late that her thoughts had fallen out of her mouth. Her cheeks burned. "Sorry."

Tillie threw Ginnie a look that clearly said: "You seriously didn't just ask him *that*, did you?"

He planted his elbow on the counter and dropped his face into his hands for a few seconds before looking up and shaking his head. "Because I was impulsive and didn't think about the consequences. See what happens? Your whole life can change in an instant."

Uncle Jake took a long drink of soda, glanced at the microwave, and blew out a breath. "After Queenie's funeral, I put in my papers for terminal leave."

"What's that?" Tillie asked.

"Permission to get out of the Army as soon as I could. Everything here was turned upside down. Clarissa didn't want to leave *her* family, who all live in Texas, and I had to get home to mine. The night before I left Texas for good, let's just say we lingered our goodbye a little longer than we should have. Fast forward to today and here we are."

He glanced at the microwave and stood. "Time's up."

25

TWILIGHT ZONE

*U*ncle Jake didn't take a chance on anyone else hearing about Mysti. After giving them a quick history of his courtship with Miss Clarissa, he insisted Ginnie and Tillie start the afternoon chores a little early.

Once Toran showed up on Calliope to do the hogs and finish his chores, Uncle Jake gave him permission to go back to Austin's for the rest of the night.

Ginnie and Tillie hurried through their chores.

Just as Ginnie snapped the lid on the chicken feed bucket, Uncle Jake entered the hen house. "Are you two about done?'

Tillie nodded.

"We just finished."

"Good. Get cleaned up. Jeans and a nice shirt, okay? It may be the pizza place, but we're probably meeting my daughter. I want to make a good impression, capiche?"

"Got it. Don't worry, we'll make you look good," Ginnie insisted. They hurried to Ginnie's room to change into clean clothes and brush out their hair.

"You should leave your hair down. You've got such pretty blonde curls," Tillie suggested.

Ginnie cast an appraising glance at the mirror. "Nah. I like my braids."

'You're insane. I'd die for hair like yours." Tillie pulled her own straight medium brown hair taut. "Mine's not even a pretty color."

"Yes it is. And straight hair doesn't get knotted as easy as curls. You're lucky." Ginnie divided one side of her hair into three parts and braided the lengths together. She remembered the pictures of her mom she'd seen with long pretty curls and stopped braiding.

Mama was beautiful. Everyone said that Ginnie looked just like her mom. But Ginnie didn't consider herself beautiful.

She thought about wearing her hair down, then decided not to and finished the braid. *Maybe another time.* She wrapped a ponytail holder around the end.

Tillie rummaged through Ginnie's jewelry box. "Let's wear our friendship bracelets, only you wear mine and I'll wear yours so they match each other's shirts."

Tillie held up two bracelets, one purple, one green.

"Sure." Ginnie reached for the purple one. Tillie handed Ginnie a pair of purple heart earrings as well.

Ginnie shook her head. "I don't wear jewelry."

"We're going into the seventh grade. You need to start," Tillie scolded. "Besides, Uncle Jake wants us to dress up."

Groaning, Ginnie put the earrings in her ears.

Tillie nodded her approval. "How about me?"

"Beautiful." Ginnie glanced at the two of them in the mirror. She leaned toward Tillie and smiled. Even though Tillie was a brunette and Ginnie was a platinum blonde, they were starting to look more and more like sisters. *Weird ... and way cool.*

They raced down the stairs, only slowing when Uncle Ben and Uncle Jake walked into the entryway from the study. Uncle Jake motioned them to the door. "We'll be back about nine. I'm looking forward to taking Turtle and Trouble out. I never get a surprise night off. We're gonna have fun, huh, girls?"

Ginnie grinned. "Of course. Pizza and token wrist bands to play all of the games we want. What more could we ask for?"

"Just time with your favorite uncle," Uncle Jake teased.

Uncle Ben raised an eyebrow and smiled.

Tillie hugged him. "You're our favorite *great*-uncle."

"The greatest." Ginnie gave Uncle Ben a hug.

Uncle Ben laughed and looked each of them in the eye. "If I didn't know any better, I'd say you three have something up your sleeves." His gaze rested on Uncle Jake. "And if I were a betting man ... which I'm *not*, but if I *were* ... Jacob Douglas West, I'd bet a dollar to a donut it's not just your arms."

"Uncle Ben, Uncle Ben, Uncle Ben. You sure are getting suspicious in what should be your carefree years," Uncle Jake chided softly, hamming an innocent grin. "Want some pizza? We'll bring you back a slice or two."

"No thanks." Uncle Ben's eyes narrowed, but his smile grew. "And I'm not suspicious. I just happen to know you *very* well, Jacob. Girls, keep him out of trouble."

"Yes, sir," Ginnie and Tillie chorused.

It's a little late for that. Ginnie pushed the screen door, fighting an urge to both laugh and confess; only she wasn't sure what *she* needed to confess too.

Tillie and Uncle Jake followed quickly and hurried to Uncle Jake's tricked out black truck.

They climbed the silver running boards and scrambled into their seatbelts.

Uncle Jake backed the truck and honked his horn, which blasted the Army Calvary charge, before leaving the farmhouse in a cloud of dust. He glanced backward and shook his head at Ginnie. "Welcome to the Twilight Zone. We just went back in time to my teens. Did you enjoy the ride?"

Tillie scrunched her eyebrows and leaned forward. "I'm not sure what you mean."

"Uncle Ben knows something is up." Uncle Jake slapped his palm on the steering wheel. "He's got like super-sonic 'dad radar.' *Geez.* I spent most of my teens in trouble because I was too stupid to figure that out. The man is impossible to fool for very long."

"That's how my dad is too," Ginnie said, looking pointedly at Tillie. "Just saying. But on the plus side, when Uncle Ben finds out about Mysti, he probably won't ground you."

"That won't make telling him any easier." Uncle Jake flipped on his turn signal and groaned. "Do yourselves a favor and learn from my mistakes. Not that Mysti is a mistake, just how she got here."

Ginnie nodded, trying to imagine telling her own dad the same kind of news. Her queasiness rushed back.

Recalling how Dad always teased about not letting her even date until she turned thirty-seven seemed more of a warning than it usually did.

She glanced at Uncle Jake, who seemed to be carrying on a conversation with an invisible Uncle Ben.

Ginnie swore he was turning green. *There's a conversation I never want to have with Daddy.* She glanced at Tillie, who nodded, like she had just read Ginnie's mind.

Weird.

26

QUINCY'S

*A*s they approached Quincy's Pizza Palace, an excited feeling rushed through Ginnie. She hadn't been here in forever.

Uncle Jake reached a hand to each of their shoulders, stopping them just before they entered. "I don't want Mysti to even think I could be her dad. I'm just Clarissa's boyfriend tonight, okay?"

His face twisted with displeasure.

"You're not going to be a very good boyfriend if you can't say Miss Clarissa's name without looking like you've been weaned on a sour pickle," Ginnie teased.

"Don't worry about me. I'll do what I need to do."

"You asked us to help you look good," Tillie pointed out. "Sour pickle faces don't look so good."

Uncle Jake gently chucked each of them under their chins. "You two spend too much time together." He smirked at Ginnie. "Your smart aleck mouth is rubbing off on her."

Ginnie winked at her friend. "That's okay. We're gonna be sisters. We should act alike."

"Then act like Turtle. She *used* to know how to behave."

"Where's the fun in that?" Ginnie rolled her eyes back at him.

"You didn't like having a perfect little brother. I don't need a perfect brother *and* a perfect sister. Give me a break."

"I'm starting to see Todd's point about you rolling your eyes. It's kind of annoying. Stop it."

"You started it," Ginnie replied.

He rubbed his palms down his jeans. "Just stop."

Tillie hugged him. "It's okay. Mysti's gonna love you, either way. And even if you're not her real dad, you can still be a family. Mysti probably needs a dad."

Uncle Jake's angry look melted into a kinder, more loving expression.

He held the door for them.

Once inside, it was like being at their local swimming pool. Little bodies bobbing around, chasing peers, running from caregivers, and squealing. Young kids ran, tugging at their parent's hands, calling out, "Let's play *this* game, Daddy!"

Ginnie searched for little girls that looked like Uncle Jake. She wasn't much help with finding either Mysti or Miss Clarissa as she'd only met Miss Clarissa once. "Maybe they aren't here yet?"

"They're here. I saw Clarissa's car." He turned and pointed toward the kiddie rides. "There's Clarissa. The little girl on the purple pony must be Mysti."

Miss Clarissa was talking to a little girl in red shorts with bright red strawberries across the front of her shirt. Ginnie focused on the girl's face. Her dark blue eyes danced. A deep dimple appeared in her left cheek, just like Uncle Jake's. Her dark honey blonde waves were held in place by a red headband with a large strawberry on the side.

"She's really cute," Tillie whispered.

"She *is* really cute, isn't she?" A huge grin spread across Uncle Jake's face. His eyes seemed to zoom in on Mysti. "Do you think she *looks* like me? Yeah, she's cute, but so's her mom."

Ginnie nodded. "She has your dimple. And almost your hair color. I'd go with 'yes.'"

"Okay, but remember, today I'm *just* Clarissa's boyfriend, *not*

Mysti's dad. I want to get to know her a little before spilling that kettle of beans."

"Yes, sir," Ginnie teased.

"Knock it off." He walked toward Clarissa and Mysti.

"Stop teasing him," Tillie scolded. "He's nervous enough."

"That's how we roll. He does it to me all the time."

Tillie shook her head. "How would *you* like not having a dad? Maybe Mysti really wants a dad who will be nice to her. Uncle Jake would be so cool to have as a dad. *Don't. Bug. Him.*"

Ginnie got the feeling her friend was no longer talking about Mysti.

Not knowing how to respond, she kept step with Tillie until they caught up to Uncle Jake.

27

BACON... REALLY?

*U*ncle Jake stopped next to Miss Clarissa, startling her. She recovered quickly. "Hi, Jake. Hi, Ginnie. Hi, Tillie." Miss Clarissa held out her hand. "It's so good to see you again."

Ginnie reached for it, feeling a slight tremble before Miss Clarissa gripped her hand a little too tight.

Miss Clarissa darted her gaze toward Uncle Jake, then Mysti, then back to Ginnie and Tillie before she replied, "Thanks for coming."

"You're welcome." Ginnie brightened her smile when Mysti looked up. "This is a fun place."

"It's *very* fun." Mysti slid off the pony. "Wanna play Whack-A-Frog? I'm really good at it."

"In a minute, Mysti." Miss Clarissa caught Mysti's hand as she tried to dash by. "I want you to meet my friend, Jake. He's been looking forward to meeting you."

Mysti paused impatiently and peeked at Uncle Jake. She tilted her head to the side when he smiled at her. "Do you know how to play 'Whack-A-Frog? 'Cause her last boyfriend stunk at it."

Miss Clarissa's cheeks pinked. "Mysti Rose. Be nice."

"Well, he did. I beat him all the time." Mysti turned to Ginnie, shook her head, and whispered loudly. "And he smelled funny too."

Uncle Jake didn't seem to know if he wanted to laugh or say something mean to Miss Clarissa. He must have settled on a compromise. He smiled at Mysti while shaking his head. "Well, I *am* pretty good at Whack-A-Frog, so we can play after I order some pizza for everybody. What kind would you like, Mysti Rose?"

Mysti frowned. "Cheese only. *Of course.* And I'm Mysti. *Only Papa* calls me Mysti Rose."

"Oka-a-a-y." Uncle Jake acted like he was counting to ten in his head. "Mysti it is. To be fair though, your mom just called you Mysti Rose."

"That's 'cause she's mad at me, but I don't know why. I *just* told the truth." Mysti threw an irritated look at her mom and then smiled at Ginnie and Tillie. "Let's go play."

Ginnie glanced at Uncle Jake.

Disappointment flashed across his face. "In a sec, Mysti. Gin, Tillie, what do you want on your pizza?"

"Sausage and bacon?" Ginnie suggested.

He smiled. "You got it."

Mysti wrinkled her nose. "Yuck, I hate bacon."

Ginnie stifled a giggle, knowing Uncle Jake could live on bacon if he had to. And he wouldn't be unhappy about it.

He threw Miss Clarissa an 'Are-you-sure-she's-*my*-kid?' look.

Then he narrowed his eyes at Ginnie, who struggled harder to be serious.

"Uncle Jake, are you gonna buy us lots of tokens?" Mysti asked.

"Sure. Only you can call me just Jake. Do you like to ride the rides or play the games the most?"

"I call *all* of Mommy's boyfriends 'uncle,' huh, Mommy?" She rolled her eyes with a 'Duh, get-with-the-program' look and then shook her head, spilling her dark honey waves across her cheeks. "I like both. But you can only get tickets for playing games. I like to win toys *and* candy."

"I like to win prizes too." His smile widened for Mysti as his eyebrows arched at Miss Clarissa. "How many other boyfriends?"

"I dunno." Mysti shrugged. "Uncle PJ, Uncle Sean, Uncle Robert,

Uncle Derek, Uncle Teddy, Uncle Sam, Uncle William, Uncle Eric, Uncle Jesse, Uncle Xavier, Uncle Scott, Uncle James, Uncle Frank, he's the one who smelled funny."

Uncle Jake sucked in a sharp breath, clamping his jaw shut tighter as the list of names grew.

Miss Clarissa looked like she couldn't decide between wanting to crawl in a hole or stuffing a sock in Mysti's mouth.

Ginnie tried to keep from laughing. She felt Uncle Jake's anger grow, but had a hard time not laughing at Mysti's obliviousness to everyone's reactions.

"*Just* Jake is fine. I'll order the pizza." Uncle Jake turned on his heel and left.

This is gonna be an interesting night.

Mysti grabbed one of Ginnie's hands and one of Tillie's. "Come on. Play with me."

Miss Clarissa handed Ginnie and Tillie each a wrist band. "They are already loaded with tokens, just tap the game and they should work. Have fun."

Ginnie offered her an encouraging smile. "We will."

Miss Clarissa seemed grateful and a little relieved, until each of them glanced at Uncle Jake. He stood in the ordering line, fisting and unfisting his hand.

Ginnie could swear she heard a sucking air sound, like a can of soda pop opening.

Only instead of feeling the excitement of a cool drink, all the amusement sucked right out of her.

Like having a new cell phone fall out of a pocket and bounce into the path of an oncoming car.

For Uncle Jake's sake, she hoped this night would improve ... and soon.

Ginnie did her best to be a good sport as she played Whack-A-Frog with Mysti.

Tillie seemed to have more patience.

Mysti wasn't very good at taking turns, but she was pretty good at playing the game itself. She beat each of them a couple of times.

Uncle Jake walked up. "Can I have a turn?"

"Sure, Uncle Jake. Mysti's really good at this game," Tillie said.

He pointed at Ginnie's play band. "Supposedly those just got loaded with more credits to play more games. Play until the pizza's ready, okay?"

Ginnie nodded, happy he'd found his good humor again.

Mysti looked up, eying him suspiciously. "Are you *sure* you know how to play?"

"I'll watch you and *make sure.*"

Mysti grinned at his answer. "Okay." She pounded the poor frogs with the cushioned mallet as quickly as their heads popped out of the holes, making her best score yet.

"Nicely done, Mysti." Uncle Jake bowed graciously and waited for her to hand him the mallet. He tapped the band against the start button of the game, so he could play with Mysti and took his turn, smacking frog heads as soon as they dared to show themselves. Although he moved quickly, he didn't quite beat her score.

"You're not *too* bad," Mysti admitted.

"Thank you. Want a rematch?"

Grinning, she nodded. "Sure, Uncle Jake."

Uncle Jake cringed, but didn't say anything. Instead, he tapped the start button twice and did a funny imitation of a frog voice complaining that all of the pounding was giving him a headache.

Mysti giggled and decided she should voice the two girl frogs while Uncle Jake voiced the three boys. The two of them took turns saying things like: "Oh my! I can see stars!" and "Stop! I'll eat my green vegetables!"

They talked in high-pitched cartoon voices.

Tillie smiled and nodded toward the big kid area.

Ginnie followed her to a Skeeball alley. "What do you think about Mysti?"

"She's interesting."

"You say that like it's a bad thing." Ginnie grinned and tapped her band against the game. "Dad's gonna have a lot of fun with her."

"Why do you say that?"

Ginnie repeated the conversation she overheard last night, laughing harder when she told Tillie how she got caught eavesdropping by giggling when Dad mentioned he wanted to be the "fun" uncle and help Mysti get into mischief instead of having to be the rule-following dad.

"That's too funny," Tillie agreed. "But your dad *is* fun."

"Not as fun as Uncle Jake."

"He's nice, and that's the most important thing."

"If you say so." Ginnie pushed the "start" button.

There was no point in arguing with Tillie.

Sure, it was great that Dad was nice, and that Ginnie didn't need to be afraid of him, but she wished he wasn't so afraid of Cabot or whoever was keeping him from returning the journals.

Tillie really shone at Skeeball. Her balls seemed to go wherever she wanted them to.

Her third ball went into the bonus hole just as Ginnie's went into the gutter.

Uncle Jake and Mysti came over, hand-in-hand.

"Wow, Tillie! That's a lot of tickets!" Mysti squealed, pointing to the row of tickets the game had spit out. "Can I try?" She didn't wait for an answer and plucked up a ball.

"Whoa there, little lady." Uncle Jake did his best imitation of John Wayne and put his hand over Mysti's. "Please wait for Tillie to say yes or no."

Mysti looked at him like his head had grown three sizes.

Ginnie imagined that people didn't often tell Mysti "no" and if they did, she didn't consider it a legitimate response.

Of course, Tillie nodded. "Sure, Mysti. Go ahead."

After smirking at Uncle Jake, Mysti snatched her hand from his and threw the ball hard.

It hit the plexiglass instead of the ramp so that it bounced straight back at her.

Uncle Jake pulled Mysti out of the line of fire and caught the ball just before it could smash into her chest. "Whoa. Okay, maybe you need a quick course on how Skeeball works." He glanced at Tillie. "Turtle, why don't you show her?"

"Why did you call Tillie 'Turtle'?" Mysti asked.

"Because I think she's brave," Uncle Jake replied.

"Turtles aren't brave," Mysti protested.

Uncle Jake winked at Tillie. "Sure they are. When they need to, they get all curled up inside their shells to protect themselves from danger. But eventually, they have to come back out and live their lives. And besides, I think it's kinda cool to have a built-in camper shell. It doesn't matter how far they travel, a turtle is always home."

"Thanks, Uncle Jake." Tillie handed Mysti a new ball. "Watch what I do and then you do it."

Tillie rolled the ball along the alleyway. It went straight until it hit the bump and continued into the scoring area. It landed in the 500-point hole. Four tickets spit out.

Mysti took a turn. Her ball landed in the 200-point hole.

"Good job." Uncle Jake offered her a high five. "The pizza's ready. Turtle and Trouble, you two finish and meet us at the table. Mysti, let's help your mom serve the pizza, okay?"

"Okay, Uncle Jake." Mysti put her hand in his.

He seemed to force a smile before they left.

"Why do you think it bugs him to have Mysti call him 'Uncle Jake'?" Tillie asked. "He doesn't act like it's a problem when *I* do it."

Ginnie shrugged. "I dunno, but I get the feeling that if he decides Mysti *is* his kid, he'll be biting his tongue a lot. She's quite a handful."

"I'll say. She has lots of opinions."

"I wonder if she'll like Uncle Jake being her dad? At least she wants to hang out with him."

Tillie giggled. "And he doesn't smell funny."

"Yeah, because that would definitely be a deal breaker." Ginnie rolled her eyes as each of them dissolved into a fit of laughter.

28

MISS IMPATIENCE

*J*t didn't take long for Tillie and Ginnie to use up the rest of their balls and head back to the table. Mysti was happy to see them. "Mommy, Tillie is super awesome at Skeeball. She got like a zillion tickets."

"A zillion, huh?" Miss Clarissa smiled at Tillie. "That's very impressive."

"It wasn't really a zillion. More like fifty," Tillie corrected.

"Well, I won too, Mommy, but Uncle Jake *almost* did. He's almost as good as me."

"Almost, huh? I'm impressed, Jake."

"She's had more practice." Uncle Jake motioned Mysti to slide down the bench. "I guess we'll just have to come back here so I can get as good as she is."

Mysti giggled. "Yay."

Ginnie and Tillie followed Mysti, leaving Uncle Jake to sit next to Miss Clarissa.

Mysti ate half a slice of pizza before bouncing on the seat. "Let's go play some more."

"At least eat one whole slice. The games will still be there in a minute," Miss Clarissa said.

Mysti frowned. "But I'm done, *now*."

Ginnie glanced at her uncle to see what he would do about Mysti's whining. He gave a slight shake of his head ... to Ginnie ... not Mysti. Ginnie widened her eyes.

Whining wasn't allowed at home.

Even Uncle Jake would frown at her when she disagreed with her own dad *too* much.

"Be patient please, everyone else just started." Miss Clarissa implored.

Mysti pushed her lips into a pout as she tried to stand. "Please?"

Ginnie arched her eyebrows at Uncle Jake. *Are you gonna be her dad or what?*

Uncle Jake narrowed his eyes at Ginnie, then cleared his throat.

Miss Clarissa let out an exasperated breath. "Mysti, please cooperate."

"Mysti, please sit down and do as your mother says. One piece of pizza and then I'll play with you. *After* I eat my pizza, okay?" Uncle Jake bargained.

Finally. "Come on Mysti, I'll race you." Ginnie took a big bite of pizza.

Mysti nodded and bit into her pizza.

Miss Clarissa mouthed, "Thank you."

Ginnie smiled, then took another bite.

Mysti finished her pizza.

Uncle Jake gobbled his second piece and followed Mysti to the games.

Ginnie ate more slowly after they left.

Miss Clarissa cleared her throat. "Thanks for being patient with her."

"I like little kids," Tillie said.

"Yeah," Ginnie added.

Miss Clarissa glanced toward Uncle Jake and sighed. "I wasn't sure what to think when Jake said he was bringing you girls, but I'm glad he did. It made tonight easier. I really messed up with him." She let out a soft sigh. "I don't blame him for being angry with me. I'm just happy he decided to come."

An uncomfortable silence hovered over them.

Ginnie thought about Dad saying he didn't want her involved in adult business.

I guess this conversation is why.

Eager to put Miss Clarissa at ease, Ginnie said, "Me too. It'll be okay. Uncle Jake doesn't hold grudges for very long. He's just mad because he's missed so much of her life. Why didn't you tell him about her?"

About the same time a hurt look crossed Miss Clarissa's face, Ginnie realized she had said too much. She took a huge bite of pizza, wishing she hadn't said anything at all.

Tillie threw her a look that clearly said: *Seriously?*

"Because I thought I was helping him. Making his life easier by not having to choose between Mysti and me, or you and your family." She looked away and lowered her voice. "I realize now that I was wrong. But at the time, I really thought I was doing the right thing."

Miss Clarissa's misery made Ginnie think back to a time when she was about Mysti's age and had played with a cigarette lighter and caught a bale of hay on fire.

At first, she could only think to push the bale away from the other bales and hide the evidence, but she couldn't move it very far and the fire spread quickly, until she had no choice but to tell her dad so that the fire wouldn't burn the barn down as well.

Dad had hefted the burning bale, dropping it outside where he put the fire out safely.

Ginnie remembered feeling helpless, afraid, and ashamed--as well as wanting to avoid the punishment she knew she had earned, but didn't want to receive.

After he put the fire out, Dad had scolded her, until she burst into scared and sorry tears.

Then he held her as she apologized over and over.

When she couldn't stop crying, he stood her in front of him, wiping her tears. "Ginnie, it's okay. The fire is out. You did the right thing coming to tell me. You were very brave."

Her crying slowed as his soothing words repeated through her mind. "You're not mad at me?"

"I was, but I'm not anymore." He offered her an encouraging smile. "You realized you couldn't put the fire out without my help. Seeing how upset you are, I'm sure you thought I would be really mad and punish you--*but you asked for my help anyway.* That was very brave ... *and* the right thing to do. If you had waited any longer, the fire would have been a lot worse."

Blinking, she searched his face for signs of anger.

She only found kindness and concern.

He reached his hands to her face, enveloping her cheeks in his palms, his thumbs swiping gently at her tears. "The most important thing is that *you* didn't get hurt. You saw how fast the fire traveled. I'm very grateful that you didn't get burned or worse. I couldn't stand it if I'd lost you."

She had thrown grateful arms around his neck while fresh tears streamed down her face.

He had assured her over and over that her mistake was forgivable.

Surely Miss Clarissa's mistake is also forgivable.

Ginnie felt a light kick on her shin.

She caught Tillie's frown as her friend mouthed, "Say something."

Glancing at Miss Clarissa, Ginnie tried to put her thoughts into words. "Miss Clarissa?"

"Yes?"

Uncle Jake's laughter and Mysti's giggles lighted in Ginnie's ear as she reached an awkward hand to Miss Clarissa's and squeezed. "It'll be okay. Uncle Jake seems to care about Mysti already. He's mad tonight, but he doesn't hold grudges for long. Eventually, he will be more grateful that he has Mysti in his life than mad at you for not telling him right away."

The relief and hope that swept Miss Clarissa's face made Ginnie both happy and uncomfortable.

At least I HOPE he won't hold this grudge for long.

After all, Mysti might be seven years old now--but she still had a whole lifetime ahead of her that Uncle Jake could be a part of.

Things would work out all right--just like telling her dad about the burning hay bale had.

Now that Uncle Jake had Mysti in his life, Ginnie was pretty sure he would do whatever he had to ... to *stay* part of her life.

He might be a little freaked out about being fast tracked to father-hood, but knowing Uncle Jake, he'd make it work.

And eventually ... he'd figure out how to make it a fun adventure.

When Ginnie and Tillie finished their pizza, Tillie wanted to play Skeeball again and Ginnie decided to play a pirate-themed pinball game while Miss Clarissa joined Uncle Jake and Mysti.

Ginnie was doing well until her ball went down the middle into No-Man's Land. "Sugar beets!"

Uncle Jake chuckled. "So, I take it you're not winning?"

"I'd do better if the ball would cooperate." Ginnie smacked the pinball game with her palm. "But that's the third time it's done that. Neither flipper can touch it."

"Do you want to play me? Clarissa took Mysti to the restroom."

"Sure. Mysti seems to like you." Ginnie studied his face. "Are you feeling better about this?"

"It's working out. Let's just play." He tapped his band against the game twice, then pushed the start button twice and motioned for her to go first.

Ginnie started the ball and watched it zing back and forth between two silver gates. Hoping the ball would drop to the side, Ginnie groaned when it dropped straight down the middle, guttering immediately.

Uncle Jake took his turn. His ball behaved impressively--going where he wanted it to go: pinging and bouncing around, setting off bells and whistles, tripping lights and a bonus ball. "How did you get it to do that?" Ginnie asked.

He shrugged. "What were you and Clarissa talking about?" He juggled two balls skillfully, landing one in a treasure trunk, while playing the other. It took a while, but finally each of his balls landed in No-Man's Land.

Ginnie shrugged. "Just stuff."

They switched places.

Her ball was released straight at the flipper. She smacked it into the gates area again.

"Stuff like...?" Uncle Jake prompted.

Ginnie concentrated on the ball, pushing the paddle quickly, but missing it until it ponged across the way to Dead Man's Gulley and released another ball.

At the same time, she measured her words, wanting Uncle Jake to stay happy. "Like Miss Clarissa really likes you and she's happy that you and Mysti are getting along. She told me thanks for being nice to Mysti."

"I'd rather you not talk to her about me, okay?"

"If you say so."

"I do say so."

Ginnie glanced at his face.

His gaze didn't move from hers. He grimaced. "Stick to talking about pizza or games or anything but me."

Frowning, she tried to figure out why Miss Clarissa liking him would offend him. "She didn't say anything mean."

"That's nice. Don't talk to her about me."

His tone left no room for argument.

Ginnie tore her glance away just in time to see her balls go into No Man's Land.

He blew out a frustrated breath. "Sorry. You can take my turn."

Shaking her head, Ginnie took a step back. "Go ahead. I've been playing for a while."

Uncle Jake gave a quick nod and started the next ball into play.

Following the ball with her eyes, Ginnie tried to figure out why he was still so mad.

Asking him wouldn't help since he pretty much shut her down.

Not wanting to risk making him angrier, she watched his ball bounce along the top arch of the game twice before pinging back and forth between several gates and doors, setting off lights and bells.

The longer she tried to figure out how to help him be his regular jolly self, the more irritated she became.

Mysti seems to like him. He seems to like her. Why is he putting so much effort into being mad at Miss Clarissa?

This moodier Uncle Jake was getting on her nerves.

Uncle Jake's ball flew around the inside of the game, setting off bells and lights until it got trapped in a treasure trunk and an extra ball was released. Then he pinged and popped two balls around until first one ball, and then the other, went down the middle of the game.

"Can I play, Uncle Jake?" Mysti squealed as she ran toward them.

"Can you call me just Jake?" he teased.

Mysti frowned. "Ginnie calls you Uncle Jake."

"Because I'm her uncle. I'm not *your* uncle, so I'd rather you just call me Jake."

Mysti rolled her eyes and the same annoyed look that flashed across Dad's face when Ginnie rolled her eyes at her dad, flashed across Uncle Jake's face.

Ginnie stifled a giggle.

Uncle Jake smirked. "Your turn, Virginia."

Mysti laughed. "Virginia's a dumb name. I like 'Ginnie' better."

Ginnie rolled her eyes at Uncle Jake and swiveled toward Mysti. "Me too."

"Mysti! That's not nice. Say you're sorry," Miss Clarissa scolded. "Virginia's a pretty name."

Uncle Jake cleared his throat and lowered himself to Mysti's eye level. "Ginnie was named after a very special lady, her mother. And her mom was a very good friend of mine. I was just teasing Ginnie, but it's not nice to make fun of people's names. Please remember that, okay?"

"Was she your girlfriend?" Mysti asked, wide-eyed.

"No, she was my sister-in-law. Ginnie's dad is my little brother. That's why I'm her uncle." He stood and smiled. "Just call me 'Jake' and we can keep playing, okay?"

"Okay." Mysti started her ball. It didn't take long to gutter. "Will you help me, Uncle Jake?"

"Yes, if you'll call me just Jake," he repeated, less pleasantly.

"Ginnie calls you Uncle Jake," Mysti repeated.

"We just went over this Mysti. I'm *her* uncle, not *yours*, so please just call me Jake, okay?"

"*No!* I want to call you *Uncle* Jake ... just like Ginnie," Mysti declared.

Ginnie giggled.

Uncle Jake threw her an ugly look.

"Sorry, Uncle Jake."

"You act like Ginnie's dad." Mysti crossed her arms. "You're bossy to her."

"I'm not trying to sound bossy. I just want *you* to call me Jake."

"Tillie calls you Uncle Jake," Mysti pointed out.

"Because Ginnie does," Uncle Jake answered, then shook his head in defeat.

Mysti stomped her foot. "Then why can't *I* call you Uncle Jake?"

"Because I'm not your uncle, I'm your *dad*." Uncle Jake snapped, then did a quick face plant into his palm.

So much for not telling Mysti. Ginnie glanced at Uncle Jake and then looked around for Tillie. *She's going to be mad she missed the big reveal.*

Mysti's mouth dropped open.

Miss Clarissa threw him a look that clearly said: "Are-you-out-of-your-everlovin'-mind?"

Uncle Jake knelt in front of Mysti. "That's not how I wanted you to find out. Sorry, honey."

Miss Clarissa enveloped Mysti in her arms. "Honey, Jake's not just Mommy's boyfriend. He's your daddy ... the real one you've been asking about."

"You're really my daddy?" Mysti glanced at her mom for confirmation, then steeled her gaze on Uncle Jake. "If you're my daddy, why haven't I seen you before?" Her lip trembled. "Didn't you love me?"

Frustration colored Uncle Jake's face.

He clamped his jaw shut, and turned away.

The squished cell phone feeling swept over Ginnie again.

29

FAMILY PICTURES

*G*innie could swear she heard a game show countdown clock chime its way to the dreaded buzzer as silence enveloped them.

Miss Clarissa's hand shook as she tucked her hair behind her ear. "Sweetie, that was my fault. Don't blame Jake. It's complicated, but when I found out you were in my tummy, I wanted to keep you all to myself. If I had told Jake about you, he would have been a good daddy to you. I'm sorry. You have every right to be angry, but only with me, not *him*, okay?"

Miss Clarissa's explanation must have softened Uncle Jake's heart. "Honey, she told me about you last night, so I wanted to meet you today. I think you're the best surprise I've ever had." He hugged her tight. "We'll be seeing a lot of each other."

"Can I come stay with you, since you're my dad? I don't like my babysitter. I want to play with Ginnie, I like her," Mysti said excitedly. "And Tillie. They're nice."

Uncle Jake tilted his head at Miss Clarissa.

"Sweetie, we can talk about it. Jake has a job too, like Mommy. You still need to go to the sitter's. But we'll visit Jake, Tillie, and Ginnie. I promise."

Mysti's face scrunched in confusion. "So Ginnie's my sister?"

"No honey, she's your cousin." Miss Clarissa let go of her. "Her mommy is your Aunt Queenie, like my sister, Aunt Mellissa."

Mysti grinned. "My aunt is a *queen*? How cool is that? Does she live in a castle?" Mysti grabbed Uncle Jake's hand. "Can I visit her?"

"Sorry, honey." Uncle Jake shook his head sadly at Mysti. "Aunt Queenie lives in heaven. So, no, you can't visit her for a very long time."

"Oh. Can I see pictures of her?" Mysti persisted. "I've never had a queen aunt before."

Ginnie smiled at her cousin.

Picturing Mama as 'queen who lived in a castle' and then as a 'queen ant' amused her.

Not that Ginnie herself had any regular aunts, just great-aunts.

They were all married to Uncle Ben's brothers.

Uncle Jake was the only regular uncle she had.

Unless he decides to marry Miss Clarissa. Hmmm. She glanced at Mysti's mom. *If Uncle Jake gets past being mad at her, Miss Clarissa might be fun to have around.*

Uncle Jake started to shake his head, then stopped. He pulled his wallet out of his pocket. "Wait. I do have a picture of her."

"Really?" Excitement surged through Ginnie as she stepped in front of Mysti.

"It's the last family picture you guys took." He nodded and held the picture so each of them could see it. "This is my brother, *your* Uncle Todd, and Ginnie, and her twin brother, Toran. They were three years old here, and this beautiful lady is your Aunt Queenie."

Mysti's eyes grew huge. "She's very pretty." Mysti glanced at Ginnie. "You look like her. You're pretty too."

"Thanks, but I'm not pretty. I'm just me." Ginnie tried to memorize this newest picture of her mom.

She had seen it years ago, but had forgotten about it.

"Yes, Ginnie's *very* pretty," Uncle Jake agreed. "*And* she's very smart and funny and kind—just like her mom. Her mom was a rodeo queen as well as a beauty queen, which is how she got the nickname

'Queenie.' Do you want to see a picture of your other grandpa and grandma?"

Mysti nodded. "Sure."

Uncle Jake led her to a table and pulled out all the pictures in his wallet.

While he was trying to explain why he was raised by Uncle Ben and Aunt Sadie, instead of Grandpa and Grandma West, Ginnie decided to go find Tillie and catch her up.

30

NOW WHAT?

*H*e told her? How did she react? Was she super-happy?" Tillie grabbed Ginnie's hands and happy-danced with her. "I can't believe I missed that! Mysti must be ecstatic!"

Ginnie happy-danced along, acting more amused at Tillie's reaction than Mysti's good fortune.

But Tillie didn't care.

If Mysti could get Uncle Jake for her dad, then maybe it wouldn't be too long before DT would become Tillie's. She peppered Ginnie with questions, wanting to know every little reaction Mysti had.

"Um, why don't we just go over to the table and you can see for yourself?" Ginnie suggested.

"But it's their private moment. How cool is it that Mysti has no idea who her dad is and then, bazinga! It's Uncle Jake? That's totally awesome sauce!"

"Tillie, it's Quincy's." Ginnie made a wide sweep of her arm, taking in the many arcade and video game booths and play areas. "Nothing's private."

Even though Ginnie had no idea how important this night probably was to Mysti, Tillie sure did. "Okay, let's go." She followed her friend to the table, joy bubbling inside.

Mysti sat on Uncle Jake's lap, questioning him about six wallet-sized pictures on the table in front of her. "Look, Tillie. It's Uncle Jake when he was in the Army! Hey, wait." Mysti locked her eyes on Uncle Jake's. "If you're really my dad, then I'm calling you 'Daddy,' okay?"

The question came out more as a demand.

He hammed an "is-that-so?" look. Then his eyes went wide, almost like he was scared.

True to Uncle Jake's personality, he recovered quickly from his shock and nodded. "Well then, Little Lady, I guess I'm *'Daddy'*, now." Uncle Jake hugged her tight. "Which is fine by me."

Tillie scanned his face to make sure it really was fine with him. His panicked look disappeared as a warm smile lighted his lips and a sincere peace seemed to envelop both he and Mysti.

Joy-filled tears burned Tillie's eyes.

If Uncle Jake could embrace a daughter he didn't even know he had, surely DT could love the daughter of the woman he was dating and had known since she was a baby.

Either way, Tillie was so happy she could burst.

Uncle Jake hugged Mysti again and then tickled her until she giggled loudly before setting her on her feet. He stood and pulled a bunch of tickets out of his pocket. "Turtle, why don't you take her to the prize line and let her pick whatever prizes she wants, okay?"

"Sure, Uncle Jake."

Ginnie glanced at Uncle Jake and Miss Clarissa, hoping the private conversation he had just orchestrated would smooth his mood. He nodded for Ginnie to join the other girls. She offered a hopeful smile to Miss Clarissa and arched an eyebrow at him, mouthing, "Be nice to her. You wouldn't want her to think you were weaned on a sour pickle."

He offered a sarcastic smile, shook his head, and narrowed his eyes at Ginnie, hitching a thumb toward Tillie and Mysti.

They locked eyes. *He wants to be the adult in charge.*

She smirked at him, saying "Yes sir, understood." in the friendliest tone she could muster.

He rolled his eyes at her and raised his pointer finger. Ginnie giggled as she realized he'd grown a "dad" finger. He took a second look at his finger and grimaced. "Good bye, Virginia Maie."

Not wanting to make him testy for Miss Clarissa, she winked at him and replied pleasantly. "Bye Uncle Jake. Bye Miss Clarissa."

He raised a second finger and mouthed, "I'll get you, my pretty."

Hoping she hadn't made him angry for Miss Clarissa's sake, she smiled at them both, turned toward the prize counter, and hurried to catch up to Tillie and Mysti, where Mysti tried to make up her mind between a larger toy prize and a handful of candy.

A few minutes later, Uncle Jake and Miss Clarissa came and told them it was time to leave ... about the same time Mysti finally decided on a blow-up ball, nine Tootsie rolls, and two lollipops. "Anything else we need to do before we go?" Uncle Jake asked.

"I need a new backpack for the sitter's. My strap broke today, huh, Mommy?"

Her mom nodded. "We'll get that on the way home."

"Or we can go now." Uncle Jake took Mysti's hand. "What kind of backpack do you want?"

"Can it be a princess one?"

Uncle Jake kissed the top of her head. "It can be any kind you want, Princess."

"Yay!" Mysti squealed.

The uneasy expression on Miss Clarissa's face turned into a full-fledged smile.

A tingling sensation coursed through Tillie as Uncle Jake's grin grew even bigger.

Tillie fist-bumped with Ginnie and whispered: "Awesome sauce!"

Ginnie grinned. "Totally."

31

SHOPPING

*O*nce they arrived at the store, Uncle Jake bought Mysti pretty much whatever she wanted. And she wanted everything in pink, purple, and princess. They found puzzles, pink Lego bricks, a couple of play outfits, a princess nightgown, a princess toothbrush, younger kid games, coloring books, and crayons. Uncle Jake offered to buy her a doll and Mysti made a beeline to a princess ballerina complete with a change of clothes and a balancing beam.

"Jake, that doll's pretty expensive," Miss Clarissa protested.

The look he sent Miss Clarissa made Tillie cringe.

Ignoring Miss Clarissa, he handed the box to Mysti with an exaggerated smile. "A princess for my princess."

Mysti giggled. "Thank you, Daddy."

"You're very welcome." Uncle Jake picked up a dark chocolate-colored stuffed horse with black legs and mane. He put it in the cart. "Hey Gin, look. It's Calliope!"

"You don't have to buy that for me," Ginnie said.

He shrugged. "We're celebrating. It's not every day you get a new cousin. Turtle, what do you want?"

Glad he included her, Tillie peeked at the art supplies on the other side of the aisle. "A drawing tablet?"

"Sure and some pencils?" He put the ones she pointed to in the cart. "Let's get Toran a new model and some paint." He took Mysti's hand and headed for the model airplanes.

Ginnie smiled. "At least he's happier now."

Miss Clarissa nodded. "True, but he's going overboard and she's spoiled enough."

"I don't think I'd tell *him* that." Tillie wanted this night to be perfect for Mysti, just like it would be for her when DT finally got around to asking Mom to marry him.

"I guess it could be worse. He could have just run when I told him." Miss Clarissa pushed the cart slower and smiled conspiratorially. "I shouldn't complain."

"Probably not." Tillie agreed.

They followed along as Uncle Jake picked out three new model airplanes and assorted paint brushes. Buzz and DT enjoyed building model cars and airplanes as much as Toran.

Mysti insisted Uncle Jake buy pink and purple paint as well, because she was very sure her new uncle would love a pink airplane as much as she did.

Tillie smiled, thinking DT probably wouldn't, but decided it would be fun to watch *him* explain that to Mysti.

"Games, clothes, toothbrush ... we got the basics covered, anything else, Princess?"

Mysti laughed. "A new backpack?"

Uncle Jake chuckled. "I guess that was the reason we came in here. Let's go."

They hurried over to the backpacks and found a princess one Mysti adored. It didn't take long for Mysti to suggest a pair of cowboy boots like Ginnie's and for Uncle Jake to agree that to be a proper cowgirl princess, Mysti would need a matching cowgirl hat for the pink boots they found.

Her mom agreed that both completed Mysti's ensemble nicely, but narrowed her eyes at the two bags of candy Mysti added to the cart.

Tillie felt for Miss Clarissa when Uncle Jake pretended not to notice her frustration.

"He's just being spiteful," Ginnie whispered to Tillie.

"At least Mysti thinks her dad is awesome," Tillie whispered back.

"Just wait until he tells her 'no', then we'll see what happens."

Tillie tried not to giggle at Mysti's future probable meltdown.

Mysti hugged Uncle Jake's legs. "You're the best daddy ever."

He hugged her back. "You're a great princess."

Mysti smiled sweetly.

Tillie's excitement bubbled, like *she* was the one who was getting everything she wanted.

Uncle Jake lifted Mysti into his arms, grinning even wider when Mysti rested her head happily on his shoulder. He picked up the biggest bag and nodded for Ginnie and Tillie to take the other three.

"When will I see you again, Daddy? Tomorrow?"

"Yep, bright and early. You'll spend the day with me, until I have to go to work. We'll have lots of fun, okay?"

Mysti nodded. "I can bring my stuff over?"

Uncle Jake set her down when they reached Miss Clarissa's car and opened the princess ballerina doll. He pulled out his pocket knife to cut the plastic ties. "I'm going to take everything to my house for you to have when you visit me, except for the doll and backpack." He hugged the doll and knelt, laying her in Mysti's arms. "You keep her with you so when you need a hug from me, she'll give you one until I can see you again, okay?"

Mysti's lower lip trembled. "I'm gonna miss you."

Tillie wanted to cry for them both, but especially for Mysti.

"I'll miss you too. But it's almost bedtime and you'll wake up and come see me. You can help Ginnie and Tillie gather eggs and maybe go riding on Calliope. That'll be fun, won't it?"

Her eyes widened. "You have *real* chickens?"

Uncle Jake grinned. "And baby hogs, kittens, dogs, cows, and an ornery ol' goat. We even have ducks that you can play with in the brook. Put a swimsuit in your new backpack and we'll go wading in the creek. I'll introduce you to the rest of the family, chickens included."

"Did you hear that Mommy? Ducks and chickens and everything!" Mysti squeezed Uncle Jake's neck. "I like this daddy." She kissed his cheek.

Uncle Jake gave her a final hug, and buckled her into a pink carseat in Miss Clarissa's car before closing the door and waving. He gathered the bags of toys and clothes, and tossed them onto the backseat of his truck.

Ginnie and Tillie climbed in.

His grin seemed to grow even bigger. "That went better than I thought it would." He winked at Tillie and backed out of his parking space.

Tillie laughed. "That was fun. But now I'm wondering who's gonna bring more gifts at Christmas, you or Santa?"

"We'll just have to wait and see, now won't we?" Uncle Jake started whistling.

She sat back, enjoying his good mood.

Uncle Jake turned on the radio and drummed his fingers on the steering wheel to the beat of the song. When they were a couple minutes from home, Uncle Jake stopped whistling. His eyes darted around the cab. He muttered something Tillie didn't catch before parking his truck and gathering the bags. "Thanks for going with me. I just need you guys to keep my secret a little longer, okay?"

Ginnie nodded. "You're not going to tell Uncle Ben?"

"Yeah, I'm gonna tell him. I'm just working up my nerve." He opened the door and slid out.

After shutting her door, Ginnie met him in front of the truck. "What's the worst thing he'll do to you? It's not like he'll ground you or anything."

He shrugged. "Worse. He'll give me his 'I-can't-believe-you-did-that' look. I always hated that more than anything. I'd rather he beat me. The hurt and disappointment of those looks still cut me deep. I tease him a lot, but I love the old man. And I really hate it when I disappoint him."

Ginnie thought back to the day she had to tell her dad about the burning hay bale--since he'd been *very* clear about her not playing with matches or cigarette lighters--a similar look had crossed his face before he put the fire out. That disappointed/betrayed look was seared forever in her mind. She shivered. "I understand."

Tillie and Ginnie each took a smaller bag and followed him up the sidewalk to the side porch door. He led the way through the kitchen to the family room, where all of the family were gathered together watching a movie.

Uncle Ben sat in his armchair.

Mom sat next to DT on the love seat with his arm around her shoulder.

Toran sat on the floor with his computer on his lap.

Vi and her fiancé, Preston, sat on the couch, with Buzz at the other end. Vi Sat upright.

Uncle Jake set the bags on the floor and glanced around the room.

DT picked up the remote and paused the show, arching a questioning brow at them.

Uncle Ben glanced at Ginnie. "That's a lot of pink. I thought your favorite color was green?"

"It is green. *Emerald* green. That's not my stuff." Ginnie pulled out the stuffed horse. "Except this. Looks just like Calliope, huh?"

"Very nice." Uncle Ben said. "Whose stuff is it then?"

Uncle Jake sucked in a deep breath. "I know I owe you a classier way to tell you this, Uncle Ben, but everybody's here and I just want to get it over with."

DT's eyes widened as he shook his head.

"The night before I left Texas to come home and help Todd with the kids, Clarissa and I got a little cozier than we should have and well ... um ... we have a seven year-old daughter. Clarissa told me about her last night. Tillie, Ginnie, and I met her tonight. Her name's Mysti and she's coming to visit with us tomorrow. I hope that's okay, because I wouldn't know how to tell her it's not."

Uncle Ben's mouth popped open, then shut as he closed the footrest of his armchair.

Vi squeezed Preston's hand and jumped to her feet, making her way quickly to Uncle Jake. "Well, I had planned to ream you for taking the girls and ditching Amanda and me, but I guess you have a pretty good excuse. Do you think Mysti would want to be my flower girl? Ginnie and Tillie keep complaining that they're too old."

Uncle Jake swept her into his arms and grinned, relief flooding his face. "Let's ask her."

"Congrats on your daughter! That's wonderful!" Preston clapped him on the back and teased. "I thought West men didn't know how to make girls."

"No one's ever accused me of being a rule follower." Uncle Jake took a step back and chuckled. "Which is probably why I find myself in these situations."

DT stood, shaking his head. "Ya think?" He pointed between Ginnie, Vi , and Uncle Ben. "And some of us figured it out." He met Uncle Jake's gaze, then grinned. "Welcome to the 'Dad-of-a-West-girl' club. We meet every third Wednesday in the study. The newest member always brings the pie."

"Thanks. As long as it doesn't have to be a humble pie." Uncle Jake rolled his eyes, then widened his smile. "Mysti's a cutie. That's probably more her mom's doing than mine, but she does look like a West."

Uncle Jake looked to Ginnie for confirmation.

She nodded. "Mysti definitely looks more like the rest of you than Daddy, Toran, and I." Ginnie's gaze swept the room. "Her hair's a little lighter brown like Uncle Jake's and wavy like Vi's. She has Uncle Jake's deep blue eyes and his dimple."

"That's okay. Todd's been the white sheep of the family forever with his platinum blond hair--as was our dad. It shows up every now and again." Uncle Jake hugged his group of well-wishers and winked at Ginnie. "Of course, with him being married to your mom, you and Toran couldn't help but be towheads."

Alarm coursed through Tillie as she realized once again that she and Mom didn't look much like DT, Ginnie, and Toran.

DT leaned over and kissed Mom's cheek. "Jake's right, you look more like my family than I do. And you fit right in, just fine." He reached a hand to Tillie's shoulder and gave her a gentle squeeze. "You too."

Gratitude swept through Tillie like a tidal wave. "Mysti's adorable. You'll love her."

"Clarissa's going to drop her off in the morning. I'll take her back to her mom on my way to work, unless you guys are okay with her staying here until Clarissa gets off work. I told her we'd play that by ear."

"Mysti'll probably want to stay. We got along fine." Ginnie turned to Toran. "She wants to meet the chickens."

Toran didn't say anything right away.

Tillie took a closer look at his face. *What's he mad about?*

He shook Uncle Jake's hand, saying stiffly, "Congrats."

"How cool is that? Mysti is kinda like getting a little sister. I've always wanted one of those," Tillie gushed, before glancing shyly at DT. "If you guys get married."

He winked at her. "Cousin, sister, friend. There's lots of names for family, huh, Uncle Ben?"

DT's question seemed to jumpstart Uncle Ben into "good dad" mode, complete with a welcoming smile. "Of course. Children are always a blessing. Congratulations on your little girl, Jacob."

Tillie winced at Uncle Ben's use of Uncle Jake's proper name.

Uncle Jake let go of Toran and made his way to Uncle Ben. "I'm sorry you found out like this, but I'm not sorry I have her." He stopped in front of his uncle, who stood. "But you'll love her, I know you will. She looks a little like Mama and she's got an ornery streak like me. I'm sure you'll get lots of opportunities to enjoy some payback for my teen years."

For once, Uncle Jake didn't sound self-confident.

"I'm sure she'll make a nice addition to the family." Uncle Ben reached a hand to Uncle Jake's back and lowered his voice. "How are you feeling about her mother?"

After glancing around the room, Uncle Jake lowered his voice as well. "Let's go for a walk."

"Let's do that." Uncle Ben motioned him to go ahead.

Buzz grinned. "Busted."

DT laughed and moved out of Uncle Jake's way.

"We're good, right Uncle Ben?" Uncle Jake hammed a pathetic look.

Everyone laughed.

"I guess that would depend on what you have to say," Uncle Ben replied, arching an eyebrow.

For a split second, Uncle Jake looked genuinely concerned. Then he shrugged and replaced the worried look with an irreverent one. "Think of it this way. I keep your blood pumping. You're always saying we should give service. I'm just doing my part to keep you going."

"That you do, Jacob. That. You. Do." Uncle Ben followed Uncle Jake through the parting crowd of family.

Uncle Jake elbowed DT. "If we're not back in an hour, come looking for me, okay?"

"Nope." DT shook his head. You deserve whatever you get, Peter Pan."

"Some brother you are." Uncle Jake turned to Preston. "*You've* got my back, right?"

"I did until my future father-in-law just shook his head." Preston nodded at Uncle Ben. "Sorry, Jake, it's been nice knowing you. I'll remember you fondly."

The anxiety Tillie tried to keep squashed in a dark corner of her mind tried to get unsquashed.

"Cry." Vi squeezed Uncle Jake's arm, smiling. "He's a sucker for tears. Works every time."

"I'll get right on that ... *not*." Uncle Jake grimaced and escaped out the side porch door.

Uncle Ben followed as everyone laughed.

"Glad I'm not Jake," Buzz teased.

The anxiety reached out and squeezed Tillie's chest. "Why? What'll Uncle Ben do to him?"

"Besides, kill him with kindness? Not a whole lot," DT told her, still laughing. "Uncle Ben's got a gift for being so understanding, you want to punish yourself."

"Very efficient parenting," Buzz mused.

"And annoying." Vi rolled her eyes and headed for the kitchen. "Let's have some cake. I brought a double fudge devil's food from work. What's Mysti like?"

Ginnie and Tillie took turns describing their new cousin.

When Ginnie got to the part where Mysti asked why Uncle Jake didn't love her enough to get to know her, a disturbing quiet fell across the room.

"Clarissa had better have a very good reason for that," Vi insisted. "I've got a good mind to tell her off—and I won't be nice about it like my dad would!"

When Mom, Preston, Buzz, and DT nodded their agreement, Tillie swallowed hard, wondering if this was what being in front of a firing squad might feel like.

32

NEANDERTHAL CLUB

*M*ysti seemed really happy when she found out Uncle Jake was her dad. She lit up like a Christmas tree," Tillie offered, wanting DT to like Miss Clarissa.

After all, Mysti's pretty lucky to score a great dad like Uncle Jake. The only one luckier will be me, if you'd ever get around to asking Mom to marry you.

"We should probably meet Clarissa again before we tar and feather her." DT took the cake Vi offered him. "Having Mysti is a shock, but she may be just what Jake needs to settle down and become the family man he's always wanted to be."

Preston nodded. "I have to say, your uncle handled that better than I imagined he would."

"Don't get any ideas." DT winked at Preston and turned on his "lecture" voice. "My cousin may have an engagement ring, but until she's wearing a *wedding band*, just remember she has two older brothers and a younger one duty bound to protect her honor—even if one of them didn't use his best judgment in a similar situation."

Vi slapped DT's chest lightly. "Knock it off. You said so yourself, Jake has *no* room to talk."

Tillie clamped her mouth shut before she could protest Vi's treatment of DT. She liked it when DT was protective of the women in his family, even if Ginnie and Vi hated it.

Jasper was awful, he shoulda been like DT.

"Jake knows he was wrong." DT glanced between Toran, Tillie, and Ginnie. Tillie stood straighter, wanting him to know she was paying attention. "But he'll *also* do right by Mysti and Clarissa." He smiled at Vi. "And that'll make him all the more protective of *you.*"

Ginnie rolled her eyes when DT turned.

Tillie frowned at her and mouthed, "Don't."

"I'm not afraid of Jake," Vi scoffed.

"*You're* not the one who needs to worry." DT turned to Preston. "A word to the wise, Jake *hates* being wrong. Don't give him a reason to make *you* his scapegoat. Been there, hate that."

Vi shook her head, glared at DT, and wrapped her arm defiantly around Preston's waist. "Ignore him. Todd's a Neanderthal. Amanda, I take back all the nice things I said about my *brother.*" She spat the word like a piece of spoiled meat. "*Run.* Before it's too late."

Mom shook her head. "No way. He may be a Neanderthal, but he's *my* Neanderthal." The possessiveness in her voice radiated sweet warmth over Tillie, like heated syrup over fresh pancakes. *Yay, Mom!*

"Hah!" DT pulled Mom close and kissed her.

She returned the kiss and then went right on kissing him.

The longer they kissed, the tinglier Tillie felt.

Strobe lights at the skating rink had nothing on the light inside Tillie.

"Hey!" Vi slid her fingers between their lips. "What happened to personal space, buddy? Back up. We'll be dusting Amanda for fingerprints and your mitts better *not* show up on her."

Panic swept through Tillie's middle. "It's okay Vi, they're dating. He can kiss her."

Laughing, DT winked at Tillie. "That's my girl."

The strobe light feeling shone brighter.

Vi grimaced. "You say that *now*, Matilda Grace, but trust me. Todd won't be returning the sentiment. When your first boyfriend comes a-calling, don't plan on actually being allowed within six feet of him. I know from experience. He and Dad ruined many of my dates."

Ginnie giggled at the warning in Vi's voice.

Tillie glared at her friend.

"Now honey ... that's okay." Preston pulled Vi close. "They just kept you safe for me."

Buzz and DT laughed louder and exchanged a fist bump.

Mom shook her head at DT, but didn't say anything.

She must like his protectiveness as well.

"*Don't* encourage him!" Vi whirled on Preston, tossing her auburn waves angrily. "They made my life miserable."

"Nope. Just did our job," DT said.

Preston leaned in to kiss Vi. She shook her head and waited a few seconds before allowing him to kiss her. After about three seconds though, DT cleared his throat.

Preston's hazel eyes widened before a grin formed on his lips. "I got the memo, Todd. The lovely Violet West deserves only the best." His grin widened as he hugged her closer. "And if you recall correctly, her daddy deemed *me* the best. That earns me a pass on the inquisition as well as full admission into the Neanderthal Club, right brother?"

"Absolutely." DT nodded along with Preston. "Right after the wedding. Full-fledged membership. But until then, keep your hands and lips where I can see them."

Tillie giggled.

Ginnie grimaced. "Dad, that's a little hypocritical, don't you think? *You* were smooching on Miss Amanda."

"But I know what *my* intentions are. So it's all good."

Tillie locked her eyes on his. *What are your intentions? Tell me ... now!*

"Todd--I believe I declared my intentions the night I asked your uncle for permission to marry my incredibly amazing fiancee." Preston pointed out. "I think admission to the Neanderthal Club should be a done deal."

"You are definitely well on your way to full membership," DT agreed, still nodding. "Once the 'I-do's' are official--so is your full-fledged membership."

"You're certifiable, Todd Benjamin. And you, Preston? Really? You *want* to join their little club?" Vi pushed him away. "My own fiancé is acting like my family. *Pathetic*."

"Honey, don't be mad," Preston offered Vi a friendly wink. "Now that Jake has a little girl, I'm feeling much better at the prospect of *us* having a daughter. Since West girls are rarer than hen's teeth, I'll do my best to make sure her suitors are properly screened." Preston hitched a thumb at DT. "They used to irritate me, but I know your dad and brothers have your best interests at heart. And now that I've made it through the worst of it, I'm really looking forward to being on the *other* side of the magnifying glass."

Ginnie and Tillie exchanged "Oh, brother!" looks and burst out laughing.

"Amanda, you're supposed to be on *my* side," Vi complained. "Todd can kiss *you*, but Preston *can't* kiss me? What's wrong with that picture?"

"Sorry. But I kind of like him, Neanderthal and all."

DT smiled bigger and held Mom closer.

Good. Maybe he'll hurry up and propose.

"It's okay." Buzz reached his arm around Vi's shoulder. "If it makes you feel any better, the three of us will be watching Jake and Clarissa a little closer, being's how *her* brothers are out of state. Todd has a proven track record of using his self-control. Jake? Well ... not so much."

Vi backhanded him lightly in the chest.

"Stop talking. You guys make me sick. Just for irritating *me*, you two can wash the dishes." She picked up two dish towels and threw a purple one at DT and a green one at Preston.

They exchanged nods and smiled. "Yes ma'am."

"See, Vi? They aren't complete cavemen, they do dishes." Miss Amanda laid her head on DT's shoulder.

He laughed and then kissed her.

"Enough." Vi grimaced and pointed to the sink.

DT winked at Ginnie and Tillie. "We won the war. We'll give her the battle." *Whatever that means.*

"Have fun." Mom kissed him again. "I'll take a few minutes to catch up with Ginnie."

Feeling pretty good about the way things were turning out, Tillie glanced at her friend.

Why does Mom want to talk to her? The anxiety Tillie liked to avoid rushed back when Ginnie blinked away a surprised look.

Uh-oh, she doesn't want to talk to Mom. Why not?

The anxiety ratcheted up a notch.

Ginnie better not mess things up.

33

MISS AMANDA

K nowing she couldn't decline, Ginnie glanced at Dad. He gave a quick nod, confirming he expected her to obey Miss Amanda's request. She followed Miss Amanda through the dining room and into the front entryway.

"Tillie wants to know if she can stay the night, since it's so late. Are you okay with that?"

Ginnie nodded. "That's fine."

"Is it?" Miss Amanda searched Ginnie's face. "I know she loves being here all the time, but I was wondering if *you* are okay with it."

Now that Miss Amanda mentioned it, Ginnie had to admit that sometimes she wasn't as happy about having Tillie around all the time as she thought she'd be.

But she's my friend, I'll deal with it. Ginnie shrugged. "We have fun together."

"That's good. I just want you to know that I care what *you* think as well as what Tillie thinks."

"I know you do. I even wrote three things I was grateful for--the day you gave me the diary--and last night." Ginnie turned slightly away. "You're one of them. I'm glad you're dating Daddy. He's happier than he's been in a long time."

"You didn't have to do that. That's very sweet of you."

"Of course I did. You're helping me." Ginnie smiled at her. "Did you talk to him about giving me back the journals?"

"Some. He isn't quite ready."

"But he will? Soon?"

"Hopefully." Miss Amanda touched her forehead to Ginnie's. "I mentioned that you were doing your best to not bug him, but if he didn't hurry up, you'd probably pop like a shaken soda can, and he would only have himself to blame."

"Did that help?" Ginnie imagined the mess that would make and giggled.

"He smiled and said he knew. You know how he is about messes."

Ginnie grimaced. "Yeah, he never lets me go anywhere if my room isn't clean."

"This time it worked in your favor."

"I hope he also gets around to proposing soon." Ginnie pointed her thumb toward the kitchen. "Tillie's gonna do some exploding of her own if he doesn't."

"You two just need to have some patience." Miss Amanda scolded. "For one thing, we haven't even dated for a whole month yet and two ..." Her cheeks pinked before she looked just past Ginnie's shoulder. "He's fun to date."

Someone's been eating too much granola. Dad's the lamest guy in the whole world.

Miss Amanda glanced toward the kitchen and then turned her back to it. "I know you see him as your dad and as overly protective and responsible, *and he is*, but he also has a very creative, fun side. Let's just say Prince Charming has nothing on him."

My dad? Ginnie rolled her eyes. "Miss Amanda, I think you might need to sit down. You must've spent too much time in the sun or ate something weird, or ..."

She laughed again. "Neither. Your dad is a great guy."

"Oka-a-y." Ginnie pointed to the stairs. "You *definitely* need to sit."

"Virginia Maie Stratton West *the second*, your dad *is* a great guy."

Miss Amanda shook her head. "After all, he raised two terrific kids. He couldn't do that if he wasn't a good person."

"I didn't say he wasn't a good person, and yeah ... Toran and I are pretty cool, but still ... *My dad?* Prince Charming?" Ginnie wrinkled her nose. "Come on."

"Yes. *Prince Charming,*" Miss Amanda said firmly.

Ginnie swallowed, not sure if Miss Amanda was angry with her or not. "Yes'm."

"You don't have to believe me, but it's the truth. And even though Vi protests about him being a Neanderthal, she also knows he just wants her to find a man who will cherish her. Trust me, that's much better than being married to an angry man who can't see past his own hurt."

Oh. She must be talking about Mr. Taylor. Daddy's definitely better than HIM.

Miss Amanda sighed and then smiled again. "Let's change the subject. I want to reschedule our night out, okay?"

"Yes ma'am."

"Stop 'ma'aming' me." Miss Amanda rolled her eyes and giggled. "Maybe we'll do dinner and have a sleepover at my place. With Tillie over here all the time, the apartment is very lonely." She wagged a warning finger. "But no ditching, got it?"

"Yes ma'am." Ginnie grinned and put her hands up in mock-fear when Miss Amanda narrowed her eyes and wagged her finger harder. "I got it, *no* ditching. Somehow I doubt Uncle Jake has any more surprise kids, so I don't think that'll be a problem."

"Shhh." Miss Amanda put a finger to her lips and glanced out the screen door. "I think Uncle Ben and Jake are down the lane. Todd's working nights tomorrow, so that'll be a good time to go out. Pencil me in, okay?"

"Yes ma'am."

"Virginia *Maie,*" Miss Amanda scolded playfully.

Ginnie burst out laughing. Normally it irritated her when people used her formal name, but tonight it felt kind of nice to be scolded by Miss Amanda.

Somehow, Ginnie was pretty sure her own mom would have responded to her teasing in the very same way.

34

GIGGLES

*a*fter Tillie fell asleep, Ginnie couldn't stop thinking about Miss Amanda calling Daddy 'Prince Charming.'

While pretending to gag at the thought, Ginnie turned on her side-table lamp shaped like a Thoroughbred, got out of bed, and padded over to the drawer where she kept the pink journal. She brought it back to her bed and let the journal fall open.

April 12

Dearest Giggles;

That's your newest nickname. I think we are up to 26 for each of you. ☺ *You have the cutest giggle and Toran has the biggest smile, so now we are calling you Giggles and Grins. It's a bit 'twinny.' but still cute, yes? Sometimes we mix it up and call you Gins and Grins as well.*

Speaking of nicknames, today I've decided to call your dad 'Mr.-Too-Good-to-Be-True.' He actually turned down an all-expense paid party/business trip this weekend because we couldn't go with him. When I asked him why, he said: "I'd miss you guys too much. Why would I want to hang out with a bunch of guys from work, when I can hang out with the most wonderful woman in the world and the two greatest kids?"

How am I supposed to argue WITH THAT?!!!

Ginnie laughed and then groaned. *Not you too, Mama. I want you to be mad at Daddy also.*

Because of course, he is absolutely right. 🙂 *Why WOULD he want to leave us ... even for a weekend? We ARE wonderful.*

One of the last things my mama told me before she passed was: When you think you've found the man for you, watch how he treats his family before you decide for sure. If he treats HIS mama and sisters well, he'll probably treat you right, but if he doesn't ... RUN like your life depended on it, because it just might.

I listened to my mama and I'm passing her advice on to you. Though your daddy didn't have any sisters and his own mama passed a long time ago, your daddy is a good son to Aunt Sadie and Uncle Ben and a good brother to Vi and Buzz—when he's not being an overprotective Neanderthal.

Between you and me, I feel sorry for whoever marries Vi. She went on her first date last week and I doubt the young man will be back. Uncle Ben and your dad were unbelievable—polite, but U-N-B-E-L-I-E-V-A-B-L-E: talking about shot guns, and dusting Vi for fingerprints and warning the young man that they had best not find any of his prints ANYWHERE on her.

The poor guy didn't even dare hold her hand. 😦

Don't laugh—your daddy says YOU'RE not dating until you're 27. And as much as I love him and his family, the menfolk are a bunch of Neanderthals when they get together and discuss Vi and you dating.

Ginnie giggled, all too familiar with such rantings. Only now her dating age was supposedly thirty-seven. Since Dad was only thirty-four, she wasn't too worried he'd hold to thirty-seven, if she could actually find a boy she might want to date sooner than that.

Then a brand new and *totally awesome sauce* thought occurred to her. Even though she had read this entry before, she just now realized that although Vi had always called Dad and Uncle Jake Neanderthals, it was probably because *Mama* started it.

Realizing that Mama was still part of her life, even though she was no longer here, warmed Ginnie like the hot fudge Vi drizzled on her cream cheese brownies.

Remember how I told you that Vi and you are the 1st and 2nd West girls born in 5 and 6 generations? Well, let's just say it's a good thing you have ME in your corner. If your daddy has his way, (which I will make sure he won't), you won't be getting your first kiss until you're 35 AND been married for 8 years. NO ONE is going to be good enough for his little girl.)

And while that's true: no one will ever be good enough for you, my perfect baby girl, I'll try not to make you crazy, but I'm not sure even I can rein in your daddy ... so my apologies in advance.

Ginnie laughed until she realized that Mama wouldn't be around to help her out after all.

I wonder what Miss Amanda would say if Daddy acts like a Neanderthal to one of my dates?

Usually, Ginnie thought of Mama and Miss Amanda as polar opposites.

Somehow, I think Miss Amanda could stand up for me if I need her to. She divorced Mr. Taylor to keep Tillie safe.

Sorry, Gins. I started off writing how much I love your daddy, and then I go off on a rant. The truth is, WITH ME, he's a kind, gentle man who is utterly devoted to our little family and I find his devotion endearing and sweet.

On the other hand, he just wants to make sure that Vi is treated well.

His desire for her to find the perfect man comes off as both endearing AND annoying.

Maybe by the time you're old enough to date, he'll tone it down. Don't hold your breath, Giggles, but we can hope.

Not hardly. Ginnie rolled her eyes, recalling tonight's little feud with Vi, one of many she'd heard over the years.

Mama and Miss Amanda seemed to love Daddy in spite of that though ... and maybe quite possibly because *of it.*

Another new thought.

Ginnie shook her head, trying to sort out her own feelings about her dad. Right now, she seemed to be the only one in the whole wide world having an issue with him.

Tillie loves how protective Daddy is ... but that's because her father was a jerk. Miss Amanda is a ga-ga over him because she thinks he's Prince Charming, Toran thinks the Neanderthal jokes are a badge of honor, just like the rest of the men in our family.

But if Daddy really wants to be a rock star TO ME, he needs to give me back the journals and .... soon.

Ginnie closed the pink journal and sighed, wondering for the zillionth time what other things she'd learn from the unread journals.

35

MEETING MYSTI

The next morning, Ginnie sat perched on the front porch steps with Tillie watching as Miss Clarissa pulled her red Jeep into the parking space next to her dad's hunter green sedan. Mysti bolted out of her mom's car as soon as Miss Clarissa stopped. She ran to Uncle Jake squealing. "Dadd-E-E-E!"

"Mysti-E-E!" Uncle Jake imitated her pitch and snatched her up in a bear hug.

The rest of the family poured out of the house to meet her.

Even Miss Amanda had come by early to greet them.

Miss Clarissa joined them in the hastily formed circle of family, looking a little nervous.

Ginnie offered a welcoming smile.

Uncle Jake held Mysti tight and made the introductions, as the family circled closer, starting with Uncle Ben. "You're like my daddy's daddy, right?" Mysti asked.

"Just like that." Uncle Ben shook her hand.

Uncle Jake took a step to Uncle Ben's side. "And you know Ginnie."

"I like Ginnie!"

Ginnie hugged her. "Good to see you again."

Uncle Jake pointed to Dad. "This is Ginnie's daddy, *your* Uncle Todd."

"It's nice to meet you, Mysti. Welcome to the family."

Mysti reached for Dad and gave him a quick hug.

"Uncle Todd's look-alike here is Ginnie's twin brother, Toran." Toran smiled and waved.

"And you met our sweet Tillie last night." Tillie beamed and hugged Mysti.

"This lovely lady is her mom, Miss Amanda." Uncle Jake leaned toward Mysti and whispered loudly, "And if Uncle Todd had a lick of sense, he'll get around to asking her to marry him sooner than later so she can be your auntie." He rolled his eyes heavenward feigning an innocent look. "Just saying."

"Hey," Dad complained good-naturedly. "The best things are worth waiting for."

Miss Amanda chuckled. "It's nice to meet you, Mysti."

"Are you a queen, too?" Mysti asked.

"No, just a regular mom," Miss Amanda said.

"Don't believe her, she's an *awesome* mom." Uncle Jake replied and turned. "This is Vi. She's really my cousin, but she's more like my little sister."

"Hi, Mysti." Vi gently squeezed Mysti's hand.

"And this strapping young man who towers over her is Vi's baby brother, Buzz."

"Buzz is a funny name," Mysti said.

"That's my fault, but only because he was a funny kid." Uncle Jake winked at Buzz. "He used to fly a plane around all the time, buzzing it through the air when he was younger than you. I started out calling him 'Buzzer Boy', then it got shortened to 'Buzz' and stuck."

Mysti giggled. "That's a funny story."

"And it's true." Buzz tossed Uncle Jake a not-so-appreciative look. "Your dad is good at giving funny nicknames. Just ask Turtle and Trouble here." Then he pointed to Toran. "And The Professor. I'll show you my plane collection sometime—though a few of them are flying around Toran's room."

"For real?"

"Well, on fishing line from my ceiling," Toran agreed.

"Daddy says you have kittens." Mysti wiggled out of Uncle Jake's arms and ran over to Toran. "Can I play with them ... right now?"

"Sure. Is that okay, Uncle Jake?" Toran asked.

"Knock yourselves out."

Just as Mysti ran off, Miss Clarissa called her name, adding, "Can I at least have a good-bye hug?"

Mysti dashed back, gave an impatient hug, called loudly, "Bye Mommy, love you!" and ran back to Toran.

Tillie followed them.

Ginnie knew she would want to 'big sister' Mysti.

Tillie loved little kids.

Ginnie stayed, wanting to see if Uncle Jake was still holding a grudge.

Miss Clarissa bit her lip and seemed to force a smile. "I guess I don't need to worry about her. You've got kittens, a horse, and chickens. What more could she ask for?"

"Just her dad," Uncle Jake insisted, his tone a bit spiteful.

Uncle Ben cleared his throat.

"I meant that in a good way." Uncle Jake took a step closer to Miss Clarissa. "Thanks for bringing her. I'm looking forward to getting to know her better."

Miss Clarissa nodded, smiling a little more confidently.

"Don't worry." Miss Amanda gave her a hug just as Ginnie thought about doing so. "Tillie's been coming here since she was tiny and has always been well cared for. If my daughter had her way, she'd never come home. Mysti'll be fine."

"Thanks." Miss Clarissa sighed. "Until we moved here, I've only left her with family."

"And she's *still* with family." Uncle Jake insisted, an angry edge to his voice.

Ginnie wanted to shout: *Be nice! Can't you see she feels bad?*

Uncle Ben shook his head at Uncle Jake.

Good, he's busted.

Uncle Jake seemed to realize his tone wasn't the nicest. "Sorry. We'll take good care of her."

"I know you will." Miss Clarissa eyed Uncle Ben warily. "I handled this badly and I'm sorry. I just wanted to uncomplicate Jake's life, instead I made a huge mess."

"You did what you thought was best. That's your job as her mom." Uncle Ben offered a friendly wink. "We're just glad you're sharing her with us. She's one of us now and *so are you.* You might regret that, but you can't change it," he teased, his gray-blue eyes twinkling.

Miss Clarissa allowed Uncle Ben to hug her. "You're just as nice as Jake said you were."

"He's okay; just don't go around blowing up his outhouse." Uncle Jake rolled his eyes. "That makes him a little bit cranky."

"Since *you* did the last one in, I think she's safe there," Dad joked.

"It was *your* idea," Uncle Jake protested.

Ginnie snapped her eyes to Dad's face and laughed when he shook his head, looking both guilty and incredulous. "In what reality, Jake? *You're* the one who said the dynamite was a dud."

"*You* suggested using the outhouse as target practice."

When Ginnie laughed, Dad grimaced. "Don't be getting any ideas. It's funny *now*, but we earned quite a few chores for our brilliance."

"It was still better than using the real house," Uncle Jake insisted.

Buzz looked at Uncle Ben. "When did we have an outhouse?"

"When you were a baby ... at least until Jake and Todd blew it up." Uncle Ben shook his head. "My brothers and I were talking about modernizing when these two took matters into their own hands." He glanced at Miss Clarissa. "My folks still lived here then. Opa, my dad, wasn't real happy about the damage, but Oma, my mother, thought it was high time we had more indoor plumbing."

Miss Amanda laughed. "Why Todd West! I can believe that about Jake ... but you?"

Dad winked at Ginnie. "What can I say? I told you my brother was a bad influence on me."

"It's all good. Oma was happy. She had wanted to build a second bathroom inside and to fill the outhouse in once and for all." Uncle Jake teased. "It *was* kinda convenient for emergencies, but Aunt Sadie didn't shed one tear. Though I did have to hide from Uncle Ben until he cooled off."

Ginnie's eyes widened. "Seriously?"

"Yeah. Uncle Seth had our back, though." Uncle Jake snapped his fingers. "But now that I think of it, it was *his* idea. He gave us the dynamite. Honest, Uncle Ben, he did."

Uncle Ben smiled. "I know. He told us. But since you two hid, we thought we'd make you sweat a little. You guys owned up to your future shenanigans quicker after that."

Ginnie and Miss Clarissa burst out laughing.

Miss Amanda wagged a scolding finger at Dad. "Naughty, naughty, naughty. *Never* mess with Uncle Ben."

"*I* learned that lesson eventually." Dad grinned and hitched a thumb at Uncle Jake. "But I'm not sure my brother *ever* did."

"Enough of this stroll down memory lane. I'm sure Clarissa is anxious to get to work." Uncle Jake slipped his arm around Miss Clarissa's waist and swept her toward her car. "I want to spend some time with my daughter."

"I think it's been a good stroll." Ginnie laughed, picturing her dad and Uncle Jake as teens in trouble.

The image was *very* satisfying.

Dad followed suit with Miss Amanda, although he added a couple of kisses, which Miss Amanda didn't seem to mind, not even one little bit.

Ginnie followed a few steps behind.

"Ginnie, please tell Tillie goodbye for me. I do need to run." Miss Amanda hugged her and then turned to Miss Clarissa. "Let's do lunch sometime."

"I'd love to." Miss Clarissa waved to Uncle Ben, Vi, and Buzz, and then smiled at Miss Amanda, Ginnie, Dad, and Uncle Jake. "Bye. Thanks for watching Mysti. Jake, call me if you need me."

He nodded.

Ginnie waved back. "Bye!"

Dad whispered something in her ear and then kissed Miss Amanda yet again.

This time Ginnie wondered what Dad said to make her eyes light up.

"Todd?" Uncle Jake asked after both women backed up their cars and drove down the lane.

"Yeah?" Dad reached his arm around Ginnie's shoulder and pulled her close.

"I don't think them becoming friends is a good idea."

"Why not?"

"Because we're brothers. I'm more interested in being a dad than a husband. With all this talk of you proposing to Amanda, I don't want Clarissa getting any ideas."

"You mean all *your* talk about proposing?" Dad stopped walking, making Ginnie stumble. "Which you need to stop. The joy is in the journey *as well as* the destination."

Whatever that means. "So, when are you gonna ask Miss Amanda to marry you, Daddy?"

"When the time is right." Dad pointed up the hill toward the barn. "Go find your brother, sister, and cousin."

Ginnie grinned. "Sister, huh?"

"Eventually ..." He shook his head. "Could you two just leave my love life *to me*, please?"

Uncle Jake laughed. "That's all I'm saying, bro."

Dad whirled toward him. "Two days ago you were all set to propose to Clarissa, for the *third* time. And now that you have a ready-made family, one *you* made, I might add, you're being a flake. *Grow up.*"

"He has a point, Jacob." Uncle Ben folded his arms and gave Uncle Jake 'the look.'

"I get it. I messed up." Uncle Jake shook his head and glared. "I'm fixing it, but I'm doing it *my* way and I'm gonna start with Mysti."

Vi grimaced. "Jake, you're certifiable. Clarissa seems lovely.

Forgive her and move on. She may have come to the wrong conclusion, but her heart was in the right place."

"Maybe, but she can't give me back the last seven years of my daughter's life. Until I can get past *that*, there's *no* future for us." Uncle Jake clamped his jaw shut and stormed off, leaving them all standing open-mouthed.

36

HORSIE

*L*ook, Toran! A horsie!" Mysti yelled and ran straight at Austin and Traxx, his black gelding as they rode up next to the woodshed.

Toran ran after her, intercepting his new cousin before she could spook Traxx. "Whoa, Mysti. You might get hurt. Walk up *next* to a horse, don't run straight at them."

Swinging down from the saddle, Austin nodded at Mysti as Tillie caught up to them, asking, "Who's this?"

"My cousin." Toran turned to Austin. "Mysti, this is my friend, Austin, and his horse, Traxx."

"Cousin, huh?" Austin scrunched his face in confusion. "All of your cousins are *boys*. Did somebody adopt a girl?"

"My name's Mysti Rose Lawson. I'm *not* adopted. I'm for real ... and so is my daddy." She stomped her foot and glanced around. "See? *That's* my daddy." She pointed to Uncle Jake, who carried a baby hog down the side porch sidewalk toward them.

Austin's eyes got big.

"Shhh!" Toran hissed. "I'll explain later."

Mysti ran over to Uncle Jake. "Can I ride this horsie Daddy? She's beautiful."

Uncle Jake adjusted the baby hog in one arm, took Mysti's hand in his hand, glanced at Austin, and quickly hid an embarrassed grimace by smiling at Mysti. "Well, that horse *is* a beauty, but *she's* a *he*. Traxx is a boy. Check out our runt hog. His name is Hamilton."

He knelt down so Mysti could pet him.

Hamilton squealed.

Mysti matched the pitch of Hamilton's squeal.

She giggled before reaching a hesitant finger to stroke him.

Austin arched an eyebrow at Toran.

"Where's his mommy, Daddy?" Mysti asked.

"With his brothers and sisters. She's kinda big. I didn't want her to scare you."

"I'm not scared of pigs!" Mysti stomped her foot at him. "But why is he black and white? Pigs are *supposed* to be pink."

"Hamilton is a British saddleback. They're black and white. His mama is too."

"Can I see her?"

"If you want to." Uncle Jake stood, tossed Toran a 'I-trust-you-to-have-my-back' look, took Mysti's hand, and led her to the hog barn.

Austin jabbed a finger at Toran. "When did Uncle Jake get a kid? And who's her mom?"

"His girlfriend, Miss Clarissa," Tillie answered.

"Oh! I get it now." Austin laughed. "For a second there, I thought you were serious. Mysti is his girlfriend's kid. She's just calling him 'Daddy.'"

Toran shook his head. "Wrong. Mysti's his real kid."

"Get out of town!" Austin looked at Tillie for confirmation.

She nodded.

"Whoa. This is one story I gotta hear."

"Yeah. Add Mysti to the growing list of secrets around here." Toran glanced at Tillie, only feeling a little bad when her mouth dropped open at his snarky tone. "You might want to ask one of my *sisters though*, since I always seem to be the last one to find these things out."

37

BOWLING BALLS

illie licked her lips and tried to steady her wobbly legs. She and Toran had many experiences over the years, but him being mad at *her* wasn't one of them.

Austin shrugged when Tillie stared at him wide-eyed.

She glanced at Toran.

He turned away.

The all-too-familiar anxiety weighed her belly down like a ten-pound bowling ball. "I'm sorry I couldn't fill you in about Mysti, but Uncle Jake asked Ginnie and me not to tell."

Toran turned back to her. "You could have hinted."

"How do you hint about a kid?" Tillie put her hands on her hips. "And what other secrets have we kept from you?" *I mean, besides the Cabot guy who wants to take you away from your dad?*

"My mom's journals." Frustration colored Toran's face. "Ginnie told *you* before she told me. If she hadn't blabbed to Uncle Jake, I might not even know about them *now*."

"If it makes you feel any better, she wishes she *hadn't* told him." Tillie swallowed hard, wanting to fix things between them. "And it wasn't her idea to tell him. He forced her."

The only downside to Mom and DT getting married that Tillie

could see was that she and Toran couldn't date when they got older because Toran would be her brother.

In second grade, when she and Debbie Ross played a jump rope game where Debbie insisted Tillie name the boy she was going to marry when she grew up. Tillie had blurted Toran's name because his name came first to her mind.

Then, the idea of marrying him for real grew on her.

In the four years since, not only hadn't she found anyone she liked better, she realized he was the only boy who didn't gross her out.

He didn't eat bugs, say mean things, pick his nose, or burp as loud as he could.

In fact, Toran was the exact opposite of most of her boy classmates: kind, polite, thoughtful, smart, and shared with Tillie all kinds of scientific theories. Treating her like she was smart and her opinions actually mattered. If Toran chose to stay mad at her, Tillie wasn't sure what she would do.

"Ginnie was going to tell you about the journals after she read them. She just wanted to have your mom to herself for a little while. You can understand that."

He looked at her like the top of her head had sprouted a water fountain. "I can, but I wouldn't do that *to her*. I can't believe she did it *to me*."

"I don't think she meant to do anything *to* you." Tillie protested. "She just misses your mom."

"And I don't?" Toran swiveled toward Austin. "Let's put Traxx in the pasture."

"Okay, but what are you so mad about?" Austin shook his head. "You told me you were only a little mad about your dad taking the journals. Why are you acting like Tillie's the enemy? That's not like you."

Grateful that Austin was taking her side, Tillie searched Toran's face while waiting for him to answer. The ten-pound bowling ball was replaced with a five-pound one.

Toran opened his mouth to respond, only to be drowned out by a loud wail. The three of them turned as Uncle Jake scurried up the side porch sidewalk with Mysti in his arms.

Austin reached for Traxx's reins.

Toran and Tillie ran to see what happened.

Uncle Jake waved them off with a quickly mustered smile. "She just got a little muddy. Carry on with what you were doing. No need to worry."

Tillie glanced at Toran, very much *not* wanting him to carry on being angry with her.

38

WASHING DISHES

*I*nstead of following Uncle Jake to the barn to find the other kids, Ginnie went into the farmhouse, tired of his mood swings. Even though she knew Uncle Jake had every right to be mad at Miss Clarissa, Ginnie didn't have to spend time with him when he was being so ridiculous.

She gave an extra hard squeeze to the bottle of green dish soap and sprayed water into a growing ball of iridescent bubbles. She washed the breakfast glasses and then dropped some silverware into the hot water.

Dad came in the kitchen and took a pitcher of milk out of the fridge. "I appreciate you doing the dishes, but why aren't you with the other kids?"

"Uncle Jake's getting on my nerves." She dropped a handful of rinsed silverware in the drying rack. "I like Miss Clarissa. He *used* to like her and she *still* likes him. Mysti likes them both. *He's being dumb.*"

Ginnie looked him straight in the eye, daring him to argue.

Dad backed up against the counter and smiled. "I can't say I disagree with your logic. But he'll come around." He poured a glass of milk.

"And *you* like Miss Amanda. So how come you haven't asked her to marry you yet?'

"That's different." He opened the fridge door and put the milk away.

"How? You know she'll say 'yes.' It's kind of a no-brainer."

"That's not the point."

She rolled her eyes. "*You're* not making sense either."

"Stop that." He turned and stacked some dirty plates. "I want to do things differently this time around. We rushed things, your mom and I, and I don't want to do that again."

Ohhh?

"Why'd you rush things?" Ginnie rinsed a plate and set it in the rack.

"Just because."

"Because she was pregnant?"

"No! Of course not." He lowered his voice, growling. "Thanks, Jake."

"Well?" Ginnie turned and leaned against the sink. "Toran and I *were* born nine months after you got married."

"Because you guys came *three* weeks early! If there had been just one baby, you'd have come almost ten months after our wedding."

Ginnie rinsed a plate. "So what was the big hurry?"

Dad drank most of the milk before setting the glass on the counter. He wiped his mouth with a napkin. "I guess you're going to figure it out soon enough."

He's actually gonna tell me his secret?

She shut off the water and glued her eyes on his. *Miss Amanda is amazing!*

"It was your mom's idea to have a quick engagement. She wanted—hey, what's that?"

A loud scream pierced the air and grew closer. "It's okay Mysti, it's okay."

Dad opened the side porch door to find Uncle Jake carrying a bawling, mud-covered Mysti.

"Owie, owie, ow-i-E-E-E!"

"Let's wash off the mud and check out the damage, okay Princess?" Uncle Jake adjusted Mysti in his arms as he came through the door. "I'm sure it looks worse than it is."

Dad motioned Ginnie away from the sink and took her spot. He cleared it of clean dishes and held out his hand to Mysti. "Let me help you rinse off. What happened?"

"She was checking out the baby hogs and the mama oinked loudly and scared her. She backed up and fell in the mud. I don't think she's hurt, just muddy." Uncle Jake kissed Mysti's forehead. "It's a good thing we bought you some extra clothes, huh Princess?"

Her tears dried instantly. "Can I wear my purple outfit with the gold crowns?"

Uncle Jake shrugged. "If you want."

Dad rinsed her arm and looked at Ginnie. "Please start her a bath. You'll need to help her wash her hair, Vi just left for work."

"But Uncle Jake's her dad," Ginnie protested.

Dad shook his head. "That wouldn't be appropriate."

"Why not?" Ginnie glanced at each of them.

An uncomfortable look crossed Uncle Jake's face.

He nodded at Mysti.

"Oh ... fine." Ginnie walked over to the bathroom behind the kitchen bar and started the bath. She called to Mysti. "Do you want strawberry or lavender bubbles?"

"Strawberry."

Uncle Jake toweled off more mud. "Let Ginnie help you. When you're cleaned up, we'll play one of the games I bought you, okay?"

"Okay." Mysti pointed to his shirt. "You're muddy too."

He rolled up the towel. "I'll change while you get a bath. Check out the tub." He wiggled his eyebrows at her. "I bet you haven't seen one like that before. It has lion-shaped feet. It's a hundred years old."

"It's as old as you?"

Ginnie laughed. "Not quite."

"Very funny." Uncle Jake smirked at Ginnie and then smiled at Mysti. "It's older than Uncle Ben's daddy, Opa. And he's eighty-six."

"Opa's a funny name." Mysti walked over to Ginnie. "You have a lot of funny names around here."

"Opa is German for grandpa," Dad explained. "Opa is Uncle Ben's dad, your dad's grandpa, and your *great*-grandpa. He married Oma, who was born in Germany."

"Oh. I just call Mommy's parents Nana and Papa. Do you know them, Daddy?"

"Yes, but I haven't seen them since I left Texas. I went hunting with your grandpa a couple of times." Uncle Jake grinned at Ginnie. "I made the mistake of out-shooting him. He said he wanted a challenge, but he really didn't. I'm a little surprised he hasn't come looking for me."

Before Ginnie could respond, Dad motioned him toward the dining room. "Let's not get into that. You get changed and I'll check on Toran and Tillie. Where are they?"

"Side yard. Mysti wanted to see the hogs, so I took her."

Ginnie helped Mysti into the tub and remembered too late that Dad was going to tell her his secret.

She dumped a cup of water over Mysti's head and groaned.

Sugar beets!

39

FRENCH BRAIDS

*A*fter her bath, Mysti changed into her new purple short set and asked Ginnie to French braid her hair.

Ginnie patted the blue leather bar stool. "I can try, but I'm not very good at French braids, just regular braids."

Dad and Uncle Jake came into the kitchen from the family room. Dad smiled and held out his hand for the comb Ginnie was holding. "I can help you out, Mysti."

"You're a boy." Mysti shook her head. "Boys don't do hair."

"Oh, yeah?" Dad winked at Ginnie. "They do when they have daughters who don't like getting their long hair full of knots. Want me to show you?"

Mysti tapped her cheek suspiciously with a finger. "If I don't like it, I'm gonna take it out."

Ginnie glanced at Dad to see how he would deal with Mysti's rudeness.

Instead of scolding her, he offered a confident smile. "It's a deal."

Hey! Ginnie opened her mouth to protest, but Dad shook his head.

She moved so he could stand behind Mysti's chair.

Glancing at Uncle Jake to see what he thought, Ginnie was a little aggravated when he just shrugged. *He just wants Mysti to like him, but if that had been me, I'd be hearing about it.*

They each knew Dad was very capable of French-braiding Mysti's hair.

For once though, Ginnie wasn't the model and had a bird's eye view as she watched Dad weave the strands in a tight, even fashion. She was actually impressed with how skillfully he managed the braiding. In no time, he fastened ponytail holders onto each of the braids.

Dad turned the barstool toward the bathroom. "Check out your hair in the mirror. If you don't like it, you can take it out."

Mysti reached a hand to her hair and patted it softly.

Her face squished into a puzzled expression while she continued to feel the braids. She bolted to the bathroom and peeked in the mirror. "Hey! It looks even better than when Mommy does it."

"I'm glad you like it." Dad grinned at Uncle Jake.

"Show off." Uncle Jake smirked at Dad and then grimaced at Ginnie. "See what I am meant about perfect little brothers?"

"Duh. Toran's *my* brother, remember?" Ginnie teased back.

"It's got nothing to do with being a brother." Dad buffed his nails against his shirt. "You belong to the 'Dad-of-a-Daughter' Club now. Doing hair is a requirement to stay in good standing. I can teach you how if you want to learn. It's not that hard."

"Maybe it's necessary for someone married to a beauty queen." Uncle Jake hitched a thumb at Mysti, who was still admiring her hair in the mirror. "But the rest of us can muddle along without such skills."

"Suit yourself." Dad counted out three fingers, one at a time, mouthing. "One. Two. Three."

As if on cue, Mysti came back and hugged Uncle Jake. "Can you do my hair too?"

Dad laughed. "Tell *her* you don't want to learn."

Ginnie high-fived her dad, impressed with how well he knew Mysti. "How did you do that?"

He shrugged. "Daddy magic. It comes with the job."

She searched his face, wanting to believe there was such a power.

The twinkle in his eye suggested he might be teasing, but even so, Ginnie decided to give him the benefit of the doubt. "Daddy Magic" had come to her rescue a few times over the years.

Who knows? His "daddy magic" might kick in so he realizes I need Mama's journals sooner than later.

"I'm still going with you being a show off," Uncle Jake said. He plucked Mysti up and hugged her. "Let's play hide-n-seek with the other kids. Mysti and I'll be 'It' first."

40

HIDE-N-SEEK

*T*here you are!" Ginnie called, coming through the pasture gate to join Tillie, Toran, and Austin. "Uncle Jake says he'll be 'It' if we want to play hide-n-seek."

"Cool," Austin said.

Toran didn't really want to spend time with either Ginnie or Tillie, but with Austin on board, Toran nodded to keep from having to come up with a reason to ditch them.

Dad, Uncle Jake, and Mysti joined them before moving to the front part of the farm, where trees, the woodshed, and assorted family vehicles made hiding easier. Only Dad's hunter green sedan, Uncle Jake's tricked-out black truck, and Buzz's royal blue low-rider truck were parked there today.

Uncle Ben and Buzz had just left in his great-uncle's old white-and-rust workhorse truck to deliver a load of alfalfa bales to the Heider's farm in the next county.

The gigantic maple trees offered shade and relief from the humidity while they hid.

Uncle Jake helped Mysti a little too much by swooping her up and out of the way when anybody tried to tag her.

"That's cheating!" Toran protested.

"No, it's not." Uncle Jake moved out of his reach. "It's called 'leveling the playing field.' You're twice her size."

"And you're twice ours," Ginnie complained.

"Deal with it." Uncle Jake deposited Mysti into the bed of his black truck, which was too tall for any of them to reach her easily. "I know you can hold your own." He danced around Toran, mocking his attempts to tag him.

Toran lunged toward Uncle Jake as he rounded the end of the truck bed and felt his sneakers slide on the gravel. Toran smashed into the truck bumper, then hit the ground, unable to cushion the inevitable meeting with the gravel and dried mud.

It took a second to realize the horrendous sound he heard came from his own body, the vibration and pain in his throat the only clues to ownership of the horrific scream.

A burning sensation flooded his side.

"Toran!" several voices yelled as one.

Uncle Jake arrived just as Ginnie did, his face drained of color. He motioned Ginnie back and dropped to his knees. "Where does it hurt, Tor?"

His uncle's words unscrambled into a coherent sentence about the same time Toran unscrunched his eyelids. Toran pushed Uncle Jake's hands away, pressing his own palms to his sides in an effort to quell the growing pain. He clamped his jaw tight.

"Daddy! He's bleeding!" Mysti screamed from above.

"Move over," Dad said, appearing out of nowhere.

Toran barely registered the panic in Dad's voice before Uncle Jake disappeared. Dad knelt beside him, gingerly lifting his yellow T-shirt. Scarlet drops of bloodied shirt disappeared into Dad's fisted hand.

Dad let out a quick breath. "It's not so bad."

"It hurts like it's bad," Toran protested, pain battling his efforts to breathe.

"I believe it. But the important thing is you'll live."

Toran didn't find the prognosis quite the no-brainer Dad did.

Blood filled the eight-inch gash now carved from his side to chest.

Dad guided him into a sitting position, slipped the T-shirt over his head, and pressed it onto the scrape. "Help me lift him, Jake." Dad held the shirt against the wound while lifting Toran's arm.

Uncle Jake reached for Toran's right arm and helped him to his feet.

"Can you walk?" Dad asked.

Toran nodded and then stumbled.

"Sure you can," Uncle Jake teased.

Toran felt Uncle Jake lurch to the side and wrap his free arm around his new cousin, and guide her down his body to the ground. "Mysti, he'll be fine, don't cry."

"Mysti, let's go see the kittens," Tillie suggested, taking the little girl's hand.

"Ginnie, please wrap some ice in a dish towel and come back as quick as you can," Dad ordered, steadying Toran.

"Yes, sir." Ginnie bolted toward the house.

"I've got him." Dad scooped Toran up and climbed the front porch stairs. "Door please."

Uncle Jake reached for the red wooden door.

"Dad, I can walk." Toran pushed on the shirt again, increasing the pain before making it ebb.

"No problem, I've got you." Dad adjusted his hold as he walked through the front door, turned left, and sidestepped through the living room doorway. "What happened?"

"I slid on the gravel and scraped my side on the bumper edge on the way down." Toran reached for the back of the burgundy couch as Dad eased him onto the cushion. "Ow."

"Sorry." Dad lifted the shirt again. Blood filled the scrape, but slower than before. "It's starting to bruise."

"Here's the ice." Ginnie appeared through the other living room door. "Yikes, Toran. That looks awful. Are you okay?" She handed Dad the towel.

"Yeah." Seeing her worried expression made him almost forget he was mad at her.

"Thanks." Dad placed the ice lightly on the scrape. Toran sucked in a painful breath. "Gin, get the spray antibiotic/pain reliever. Green can." Dad's face scrunched in sympathy. "Please."

"Yes, sir." Ginnie whirled around and left.

"I'm okay, Dad."

"I know." He lifted the towel. "That's going to leave quite a mark. How bad is the pain?"

Toran tried to smile. "It only hurts when I breathe in."

"It's starting to swell." Dad glanced at his watch. "I wonder if we should have this x-rayed. You might have a cracked rib. With a little luck, I can get you seen before I have to leave for work. Jake, what do you think?"

"If it's bruised or cracked, they won't be able to do much," Uncle Jake said.

Dad lifted the towel and gently touched the outer edge of the wound. A white-hot pain shot through Toran, making him gasp for breath. "Owwwww!"

"Yeah, we're having this x-rayed," Dad insisted.

"Here." Ginnie arrived and handed over the green can.

"Sorry in advance, but this should help." Dad moved the towel and sprayed the scrape. A cool, soothing mist took the immediate sting out of the wound, but not the worry from Dad's face. "Jake, enjoy Mysti. Either we'll be back in time for work or we won't. Tor, do you want to walk or have me carry you?"

"I'll walk. But Uncle Jake said they can't help."

"I want this x-rayed." Dad offered his arm to help him off the couch. "Just to know exactly what's wrong."

Toran gritted his teeth and sucked in a quick breath, trying not to moan as he stood. He caught a sympathetic look from Uncle Jake. "Sorry, bud. This is my fault."

"It was just an accident," Toran mumbled automatically and then glanced at his sister.

And if anyone's to blame, it's her. She's the one who made me so mad I didn't pay attention.

41

GO FISH

*A*fter Dad and Toran left, Uncle Jake offered the rest of them Popsicles and suggested a game of Go Fish. Mysti happily agreed. It didn't take long to figure out she was good at remembering who asked for which card and knew who to ask for their matches when it was her turn.

Uncle Jake didn't seem to mind losing to her, in fact he seemed quite happy and proud that she beat him fair and square. Ginnie giggled, remembering the look on her uncle's face last night when Mysti announced that she hated bacon.

After Mysti won the second game of Go Fish—without help— Uncle Jake beamed his approval.

Joking with the rest of them took Ginnie's mind off Toran's injury. She wasn't one to worry, but seeing her twin's gash surrounded by swelling purple flesh concerned and sickened her.

She knew Tillie and Austin were just as worried, though Austin kept one-upping jokes with Uncle Jake. Just as Tillie dealt the third game, Austin's mom called him home for a forgotten dental appointment.

Austin grimaced. "That's lame. Toran gets hurt and I have to go to the dentist?"

"Totally lame sauce," Ginnie agreed.

Uncle Jake pulled a mocking face. "Them's the breaks, Mr. Comedian."

Ginnie and Tillie accompanied Austin to the pasture to retrieve Traxx. While watching her friend mount his gelding, Ginnie had an overwhelming urge to ride Calliope.

That would take her mind off Toran's injury.

"See ya, Austin," Tillie said.

Ginnie closed the pasture gate, waved to Austin, and tried to figure out how to ditch Tillie, preferably without hurting her feelings. Ginnie needed to ride and she needed to ride ... *alone*.

She walked Tillie back to the farmhouse.

After entering the porch, Ginnie heard Mysti ask Uncle Jake about the decorations above the kitchen sink.

Several wooden butter molds hung by their handles. Each had a different 'stamp' with a simply carved shape.

The stamps sported strawberries, sheaves of wheat, a daisy, and a heart. Hanging also was a two-piece wooden butter mold of a sheep as well as one of a cow.

Uncle Jake explained to Mysti how they sometimes made home-made butter by shaking heavy cream in a canning jar until it formed lumps of butter.

"I want to try that," Mysti said.

"We could make some butter, couldn't we, Uncle Jake?" Tillie asked.

"Sure. Vi made banana bread last night. Nothing tastes better on it than fresh butter."

When Uncle Jake and Tillie started gathering supplies for butter making, Ginnie found her excuse to ride alone.

42

THIS IS IT!

"W hoa girl, slow down," Ginnie called, stroking her
mare's neck. She eased Calliope into a slow canter.

An expensive-looking silver car turned into their gravel lane from
the main road. Ginnie tugged Calliope's reins gently to the right and
urged her horse onto the grass lining the lane.

The car slowed.

Ginnie smiled pleasantly, waved at the driver, and wheeled
Calliope completely around. With a gentle kick of Ginnie's heel,
Calliope picked up speed and galloped down the lane toward their
two-story red-brick farmhouse. Ginnie motioned for the driver to
follow, all the while puzzling about who she might be.

The car was too fancy to belong to any of their regular egg-and-
goat-milk customers.

Ginnie urged Calliope up the lane near the house, to their
hundred-and-sixty-year-old iron horse-head hitching post and slid
off her mare's back.

She tied the reins through the iron loop of the hitching-post-
horse's mouth and waited for the driver to park the car.

Long, platinum-blonde, curly hair fluffed around the woman's
face when she exited the car.

Large dark-tinted sunglasses hid most of her face.

And yet, there was something familiar about the woman, even though Ginnie was pretty certain she'd never seen her before. Forgetting that it wasn't polite to stare, Ginnie concentrated on the woman's face, walking closer, almost in a hypnotic daze.

She knew this woman, but had no idea why.

The woman smiled pleasantly. "Ginnie?"

"Yeah?"

"You don't remember me?" Her soft southern accent beckoned recognition, only Ginnie couldn't place her.

"Should I?"

"I had hoped you would, but it's been a while." The lady sighed, reached a hand to her sunglasses and slid them to the top of her head. Her curls adjusted around the stems. "It's so good to see you again, sweetheart."

Shaking her head, Ginnie sucked in a quick breath and took a step back. She *did too* know who this woman was. Ginnie's heart hammered in her chest.

Her voice was barely able to speak the name that jumped to her lips. "Mama?"

43

PHOTOS

*M*ama?" Ginnie repeated, shaking her head like an Etch-A-Sketch, trying to make sense of what she was seeing.

The woman's hand flew to her mouth. "Oh, honey, no! I'm so sorry."

She reached a hand to Ginnie's shoulder.

Ginnie stiffened, certain the hand would go straight through her like sunlight. *You can't feel ghosts, right?*

Instead, the hand pulled her closer. The woman's other arm slipped around her shoulders and squeezed Ginnie into a bear hug. She started to resist, then recognized the floral scent of her mother's perfume.

The arms released her.

"Sweetheart, I'm *so* sorry! I didn't think about that ... I mean ... I'm sorry. I'm *not* your mama."

Feeling like she'd just stepped off the Tilt-A-Whirl at the fair, Ginnie lurched to the side.

The woman wiped her eyes.

Ginnie tried to make sense of her words.

"I'm your *aunt* ... Aunt Roni." She waited for Ginnie to recognize the name. When Ginnie just stared blankly, the woman tried again. "Roni *Stratton*? Your mom's sister? We're identical twins, your mama and I."

Ginnie took a step back and continued staring.

"Wow! You look so much like your mother! You could be our triplet!" "Aunt" Roni babbled on in a soft Southern accent before Ginnie could form an answer. "Even *mah* little girls don't look as much like us as *you* look like us. Of course my husband is the tall, dark, and handsome type. Ginnie, well, I suppose *you* know her as '*Queenie*', preferred blonds, like your dad." The lady sighed again. "You can't pick who you fall in love with. If you could, our lives would've been very different, now wouldn't they? How's Toran?"

Confusion turned to indignation.

"My mama didn't have a sister, and certainly not a *twin* sister. *I'm* a twin." Ginnie shook her head. "My dad would've told me if Mama was a twin as well. Who are you ... *really*?"

"Who I said. I *am* your mother's twin sister. Your daddy didn't tell you about me?" "Aunt" Roni's voice hovered between disbelief and hurt. "I knew Todd was angry, but it's *been* eight-and-a-half ye-ahs."

Ginnie crossed her arms. "Prove it."

"Prove what?"

"That you're my mom's twin sister."

"I look like her, don't I?" Her Southern accent caught Ginnie off guard. Then she remembered Vi teasing Daddy about Mama's accent and how she called him Honey Pie and Sugar Pie, only the 'pie' sounded funny. "You are most certainly your mother's daughter. *Suspicious*." Roni smiled, then shook her head, causing her curls to sway. "How do I prove it? I look like her. *You* look exactly like *us* when we were twelve. Oh, wait a minute. I *can* prove it."

She strode over to her car, her two-inch heels clicking on the gravel. Roni plucked her purse out of the front seat and came back. "Can we sit on the steps at least. Or on the swing? Please?"

Ginnie nodded.

Roni dug in her purse. "Do you still go by Ginnie or did your daddy rename you after your mama passed?"

"I'm Ginnie."

Roni continued digging in her purse. "I know your mama wasn't happy with Todd for naming you after her at first, but it was probably a comfort for him after what happened."

Not sure how to answer, Ginnie just stared at this babbling, impeccably dressed woman who looked too much like her dead mother. Roni sat on the top porch step and patted the space next to her. "You know, I knew your mama as 'Ginnie' or 'Widget' her whole life and then your daddy comes along and renames her. But I think it's sweet how he called her 'queen of his heart.' I'll say this for your dad, he loved my sister. And *she* most definitely loved *him*."

Ginnie had a hard time keeping up with her southern-accented, breathless chattering.

Roni handed Ginnie a small photo album. "Go on, open it. You'll be glad you did."

The first page showed two look-alike blonde girls with curls, hamming for the camera. "That was our fourth birthday. Turn the page."

Ginnie obeyed.

A little girl dressed in an emerald green dress sat on a brown miniature horse with a white star-shaped birthmark on its head and on the opposite page an identical little girl in a bright pink dress sat on a brown miniature horse with a white circular birthmark.

Each girl wore a tiara with jewels matching the color of her dress.

"Can you guess who is who?" Aunt Roni asked.

Ginnie didn't need to guess. "Mama is in green."

"You're right. When we were born, our mama always dressed me in purple and Widget in pink, to tell us apart. Then sometime around the time we turned two, *your* mama decided her favorite color was green. Her wardrobe turned into various shades of green. Her engagement ring had an emerald in it. Did Todd keep it for you?"

Ginnie tried to picture the ring and shook her head. "I don't think I've ever seen it."

"Oh." Roni's hopeful look fell.

The next page showed the girls playing in a tree. "That was our castle and we had to stay in it to be safe from the goblins. Your mama loved to make up stories about kings and princesses and knights in shining armor. She called Todd her 'knight in denim armor.' but you probably don't remember that, do you?"

"No." Ginnie turned the page.

The same two little girls were dressed in pageant dresses, one purple, one green, each standing next to trophies taller than they were and wearing tiaras on two differently styled blonde hairdos.

"My sister won Ultimate Queen Supreme that day, and I won Queen Supreme. She would almost always place just higher than me. We were identical, but some of the judges thought she had more 'dazzle.' Then she got more into rodeo stuff and barrel racing. I wasn't quite as daring as her at first. When we'd barrel race against each other, I held my own in those competitions, but then she kicked it up six notches by becoming a trick rider. Sugar, turn the page."

Ginnie did and found a picture of two little girls on a beautiful chocolate Thoroughbred. The girl in purple knelt on the horse's back with her arms stretched out straight while the girl in green stood behind her, with her arms in a "V" shape.

"How old were you?" Ginnie asked.

"Nine. That horse was my daddy's favorite stud. His name was Romeo. He sired two of your mama's favorite horses, Eternal Love and Gypsy Queen. He sired my favorite horse as well. Her name is Sweet Dreams."

"My horse is named Calliope." Ginnie pointed at her mare. "Her mom was Eternal Love."

"Really?" Roni glanced at Calliope. "Your mama loved that horse. Love was born on our twelfth birthday. Ginnie claimed her. I wanted her too, but Daddy always gave in to Widget." She sighed. "It's just as well. Sweet Dreams was born a day later." She met Ginnie's gaze. "I don't suppose you remember seeing your mama compete on Love?"

"No, I only remember us riding together."

She gave an understanding nod. "I swear they read each other's minds. They were magic together. I wanted to buy Love after the funeral, but Todd wouldn't sell her to me."

179

Her chattering stopped when her voice caught.

"He sold her to Mr. Davis after Mama died," Ginnie explained, lowering her voice. "He said it hurt too much to see her without Mama and that Love missed Mama."

"I know, but he should have let *me* buy her. I could have helped Love ..." Tears welled in the woman's blue eyes. She took a tissue from her purse. "It would've helped with losing my sister ... she was everything to me."

"That doesn't sound like him." Ginnie couldn't figure out why Dad would deny Roni the horse *he* didn't want any more. "Daddy's strict, but he's not mean."

"Todd was very angry with my father." She wiped her eyes. "I can't say I blamed him. But I had hoped he would change his mind about Eternal Love. He just nevah did."

The sadness in her voice moved Ginnie to justify Dad's actions. "Mr. Davis wanted Love before Mama died, so Daddy sold her to him and Mr. Davis bred her. She had Calliope." Ginnie pointed at her horse again. "Mr. Davis gave Calliope to me because he was dying of cancer and thought Queenie's daughter and Eternal Love's daughter belonged together." It was Ginnie's turn to sigh. "He was right. Daddy told him no at first, for a long time. Eventually he said 'yes,' thank goodness. I love Calliope almost more than anything."

"Of course you do." Aunt Roni wiped her eyes. "Then it's probably good Todd sold her to *him*. Otherwise you might never have gotten a horse." She patted Ginnie's knee. "So you trick ride like your mama?"

Ginnie shook her head. "I'm not allowed. My dad said he'll sell Calliope if I do. But that's okay. I'd rather have Calliope just to ride than not at all. She's my friend."

"That's fine too. Sometimes when you're competing all the time, you forget to just enjoy your horse." Aunt Roni stared straight ahead.

Ginnie was sure she wasn't seeing the growing alfalfa and corn fields that lined their gravel lane.

"We practiced for hours every day as kids. Our daddy wanted us to be champions, like his horses. Widget sometimes stole away on Love or Gypsy Queen. It made Daddy furious. Widget warned him that he was pushing too hard, but he didn't listen. Once, she filled a backpack with provisions and disappeared for a couple of days."

"What did he do?" Ginnie asked, awestruck at her mother's nerve.

"What *could* he do? She stayed away long enough for him to cool down from missing the competition and for him to fear she might be hurt or worse. She called him in the middle of an important meeting and gave him her terms." Aunt Roni's smile brightened. "My sister had pretty incredible timing."

"Wow, my dad would never put up with that. I'd be grounded until I was eighty-seven."

Aunt Roni laughed. "Nobody ever stands up to Cabot Alexander Stratton, *except* your mother. Even *my* mother didn't openly defy him."

Ginnie sucked in a breath. "Did you say, *Cabot*?"

"Yes. Is something wrong?"

"I don't think I can talk to you anymore." Ginnie jumped off the porch, her heart pounding so hard she thought it might pop out of her chest.

44

CABOT

Ginnie rushed over to Calliope and unfastened her reins. Aunt Roni followed. "What's the matter?"

"I can't talk to you." Ginnie waved her away. .

"Why not? I *am* your aunt."

"Cabot tried to take me away from my dad." Suddenly, the overheard conversation made sense. "If you're related to *him*, I don't think my dad wants me to talk to you."

"He told you about *that*, but not about *me*?"

"He didn't *tell* me about anything." Ginnie put her boot in the stirrup, and swung into the saddle. "But I found out. Why does Cabot want me and Toran?"

"He doesn't." Aunt Roni held Calliope's bridle and stroked her neck. "I mean, he does, but not like that ... at least not anymore."

"Not like what?"

"Back up a minute. If Todd didn't tell you anything, how do you know about your grandfather and not about *me*? I had nothing to do with that lawsuit. I begged Daddy to drop it."

"What lawsuit? What grandfather?" Ginnie stilled her heel before she could tap Calliope. "I don't have any grandfathers. They're all dead, except Opa."

"It may not be for long, but for the moment at least, Cabot Alexander Stratton is very much alive." Aunt Roni locked her eyes on Ginnie's. "He's your mother's father, which makes him *your* grandfather."

Ginnie shook her head. "No way. Her dad can't be alive. Mama never mentioned him." Then another thought occurred to Ginnie. "And for that matter, she never mentioned *you* either. You *can't* be her sister. She would have said so, even if Dad didn't."

"As much as I'd like you to remember *me*, I understand why you don't." She thrust the photo album at Ginnie. "Look—it's your mom, and *me*, her twin sister. You asked for proof and I gave it to you. Who *else* would look so much like her?"

"Besides *me*?" Ginnie blinked and turned away.

None of this made any sense. Daddy never mentioned an Aunt Roni, at least not that she could recall.

Uncle Jake didn't mention Mama having a twin.

Or Vi.

Or Buzz.

Or Uncle Ben.

Or Mama. Most especially not Mama.

Why would Mama never mention her twin sister, if she actually had one?

"If you're my aunt, why wouldn't my mom tell me?"

Aunt Roni's face scrunched in confusion. "Because you were just a baby when she passed. How could you possibly remember everyone she ever knew? You haven't seen me since just after her funeral." Exasperation painted Aunt Roni's words. "As much as I'd like you to remember *me*, I understand why you don't."

"I was three-and-a-half." Ginnie jutted out her chin. "And that's not what I meant. She didn't mention you in the journal she wrote for me. If you are her sister *now*, you woulda been her sister, *then*. Who are you, *really*?"

Aunt Roni flipped through the album. "Look." She held it open. The left page showed a picture of what had to be Mama and this woman, together, each holding a baby.

Ginnie recognized the babies as herself and Toran.

On the right page, the women were holding the opposite baby from the left page. Ginnie couldn't tell the difference between the women, except one wore a blue blouse and one wore green. One of the women was definitely Mama. The other had to be this woman claiming to be her twin sister.

"I don't get it," Ginnie whispered. "Why wouldn't she write about you in my journal?"

"Because." Aunt Roni's lip quivered. She swallowed and then straightened, her voice firming. "Because we had a falling out. Our father disowned her when she married Todd. My dad made me choose between Widget and him. I thought by choosing *him*, I could make him see reason and fix things." Aunt Roni stared past Ginnie for a few seconds. "Eventually they each behaved more reasonably. But before they could fix things completely, she died."

"Oh." Ginnie's anger deflated like a popped balloon.

"My sister had a lot of great qualities, but she could hold a grudge. She was also used to getting whatever she wanted. Our dad gave her an ultimatum: come home *without that farm boy* or he'd cut her off. Queenie wanted your dad ... and she got him. But she lost pretty much everything else she'd ever had or known. For once, she couldn't have it all."

Anger and confusion welled in Ginnie. She couldn't believe what she was hearing. "Why would Cabot tell her that? Daddy loves Mama. Everyone says so. Even *you* said so."

Ginnie tapped Calliope's side, needing to get away and think this new information through.

"I'm sorry. I was prepared to not be welcomed with open arms, but it never occurred to me that you would know *nothing* about your mother's family." Aunt Roni held the bridle, keeping Calliope from leaving. "Please dismount and talk to me. You and Toran are all I have left of my sister. I miss her so much."

Ginnie blinked back tears, hearing true sorrow in her aunt's voice.

She knew a little something about missing Mama. "Will you tell me about her?"

"Of course." Aunt Roni held out her hand.

Ginnie dismounted and let her aunt envelop her in a hug.

Just as she nestled against Aunt Roni's shoulder, a waft of Mama's favorite perfume drifted by.

Ginnie could swear she felt another pair of arms embrace her.

It didn't make any sense, and she didn't even care that it made no sense.

As sure as she stood in her favorite riding boots, Ginnie knew Mama was here ... with her ... and with this woman who looked too much like her mother.

45

AUNT QUEENIE

*M*ysti looked up from the jar she was shaking. Daddy smiled and shook his jar faster. A yellow-white blob bobbed in the sloshing liquid. Mysti peeked at her own jar. No blob.

"Wanna trade for a little while?" Daddy asked.

She nodded, exchanged jars, and then shook the new jar.

The butter bobbed up and down quicker.

"Uncle Jake, can we color the butter? I bet Mysti would like to see orange butter," Tillie suggested.

"Or maybe green, huh, Princess?"

"Ick. Green butter?" Mysti shook her head. "I like yellow butter, but this isn't super yellow, like at the store."

"We don't add coloring like the stores do," Daddy said. "Unless we add it for fun. The carotene from the grass the cows eat turns it yellow. Sometimes we like to play with it and turn it other colors."

"Oh." Mysti caught movement through the doorway. "Hey! It's my kitty, Sushi. Be right back." She slid off the bar stool and rushed into the dining room.

The kitten ran into the entryway.

Mysti followed.

She plucked her up and held her tight. "Naughty kitty. Daddy says you have to stay outside." She glanced out the front door.

A pretty lady with the same color hair as Ginnie stood next to Calliope, hugging her cousin.

Mysti went back to the kitchen. "Daddy?"

"Yeah, honey?"

"If Aunt Queenie is supposed to be in heaven, how did she get in the front yard to hug Ginnie?"

46

NIGHTMARES IN DAYLIGHT

hat?" Tillie dropped the jar she was shaking. It slid down her dark-blue-jeaned legs before she could stop it from rolling onto the multi-shaded blue throw rug, thankfully unbroken.

She jumped off her bar stool. "What are you talking about, Mysti?"

"Aunt Queenie's on the front porch."

Tillie scooped up the jar and set it on the counter.

She glanced at Uncle Jake.

He sucked in a breath. "No way." He set his jar next to Tillie's. "Mysti, stay with Tillie."

"What's wrong, Uncle Jake?" Tillie asked.

He glanced at Tillie. She knew he didn't see her. "She can't be here. Todd's gonna flip his lid."

Anxiety replaced all the fun and carefree feelings Tillie had been enjoying. "Why? Who's here?"

"Nobody." Uncle Jake pointed to the bar stool she just vacated. "Stay here. Keep Mysti with you. *Please*." He turned and hurried through the doorway.

Mysti shook her head at Tillie. "I'm not staying."

"Me either." Tillie followed Mysti through the dining room to the entryway.

Uncle Jake stopped so suddenly that Mysti and Tillie piled into him. He wagged his finger at each of them. "I told you to stay in the kitchen."

"I came to get Mysti." Tillie peeked through the screen door, gasping when she saw Ginnie's mom. "She's not dead?" Tillie grabbed Uncle Jake's arm, fear and disbelief coursing through her. "Why isn't Ginnie's mom dead?"

"What?" Uncle Jake looked straight through Tillie like an x-ray machine. "Of course Queenie's dead."

"Then who's that?" Tillie demanded, pointing to the woman that looked like an older version of her best friend.

"*That* isn't Queenie." Uncle Jake lifted an impatient Mysti into his arms. After shushing Mysti, he locked his eyes on Tillie's. "*That* is my brother's second-worst nightmare, up close and personal."

47

OLD FRIENDS

*T*he front porch screen door creaked.

Ginnie whirled to see who opened it.

Uncle Jake held Mysti, his mouth half-open. He closed and opened it again, but no words spilled out.

Behind her uncle, Tillie stood frozen like she'd been hit with an immobility spell, except for her lips, which trembled.

With fear or illness, Ginnie couldn't tell, but she knew her friend's warning signs for crisis.

Tillie's wide eyes and horrified look only intensified in her statue-like state.

"Oh, dear," Aunt Roni whispered.

"Hi, Aunt Queenie!" Mysti kicked her way out of Uncle Jake's arms and ran to Aunt Roni. "Daddy said you were in heaven. I didn't know that God lets the angels come back and visit. Did you bring my bunny, Abraham?"

"Why, hello there." Aunt Roni hugged Mysti and then smiled at Uncle Jake. "What's your name, sweetie?"

Uncle Jake closed the distance quickly. "She's not your Aunt Queenie, Mysti. She's..."

"Aunt Roni," Ginnie finished.

"Yes." Uncle Jake glanced around their little circle and rested his gaze on Tillie. "And she's *not* Ginnie's mom. *Or* an angel. She's Queenie's identical twin sister." He narrowed his eyes at Aunt Roni. "She's also someone who's *not* supposed to show up here uninvited."

"Like *you're* a good example of a rule-follower." Aunt Roni teased, offering an apologetic smile. "It's been over eight ye-ahs. It's high time for a truce."

"Whether I may be inclined to agree with you is *not* the issue," Uncle Jake insisted. By his tone, Ginnie got the impression that he *did* agree with Aunt Roni. "The judge made it very clear that Todd gets to choose who sees his kids and who doesn't. The last time I checked, *you* weren't on the 'get-to-see' list."

"Which is totally unfair. Ginnie and Toran are as much my niece and nephew as they are yours. Why should *you* get to see them and I can't? *I* didn't do anything wrong."

"Sorry, Roni. I didn't make the rules."

"What rules? Why can't she see us?" Ginnie glared. "And why didn't *you* tell me about her? Don't you think I had a right to know about Mama's very own twin sister?"

"As a matter of fact, I did." He nodded. "But convincing your *dad* to share the information with you, when he felt you were better off *not knowing*, complicated things a bit."

Ginnie rolled her eyes. "That's *crazy*."

"No, it's not. He has some good reasons for not shaking every branch of your family tree." Uncle Jake opened the screen door and motioned them inside. "As long as you're here though, Roni, come in and get out of the heat. The girls can offer you lemonade while I figure out how to let Todd know you're here and make this family reunion work."

Mysti tugged Aunt Roni's hand toward the door.

Ginnie felt an overwhelming urge to unclasp their hands.

Aunt Roni stopped in front of Uncle Jake and smiled, relief showering her face. "Thank you. I was hoping I could count on your sense of chivalry. I just want to see Ginnie and Toran, not cause trouble."

"Good luck with that. Trouble seems to follow you Strattons

around." Then he glanced at Mysti and rolled his eyes. "But I guess it comes more honestly to some of us than others. Come in—before I change my mind."

48

GUMMY WORMS AND FAMILY TREES

illie led the way to the kitchen. She forced a smile and motioned Ginnie's aunt to the family room. Mysti skipped along, holding the lady's hand and chattering nonstop.

When Ginnie followed without even looking at Tillie, a pit burrowed deep in Tillie's insides. She wanted to be happy for her friend.

But seeing a woman who looked so much like Ginnie's dead mom had Tillie's head spinning. *What if DT likes her? Wait, Uncle Jake said DT doesn't want her around. He couldn't like her like that then. Why is she here?*

Ginnie's aunt sat next to Mysti on the plum leather sofa and patted the spot next to her for Ginnie, who smiled and sat, her eyes never leaving the woman's face.

A tremor rumbled through Tillie's belly.

Uncle Jake stood in the doorway between the kitchen and family room, turning one way, then the other, like he couldn't decide what to do or where to go.

"Want to see my butter, Aunt Roni?" Mysti asked.

Wait, is Aunt Roni Mysti's aunt? My mom'll be Mysti's aunt when they get married, right?

Tillie handed Mysti two jars of the homemade butter, while puzzling out Mysti's family tree and how it related to this look-alike woman and DT's first wife.

Tillie groaned. Trying to figure out how everyone was related was like trying to sort out a bag of multi-colored gummy worms without touching them.

"Check it out, Aunt Roni! Real butter!" Mysti squealed.

"Aunt Roni" smiled like she was being shown a national treasure.

Ginnie frowned and sat back on the couch a few inches, acting as if Mysti was an annoying intruder.

Swallowing hard, Tillie realized that she herself found this woman's very presence to be a terrible intrusion and threat to her plan of happiness.

I'm not being a good friend at all. I just want Ginnie's aunt to go away.

Uncle Jake took two steps into the family room. "Mysti, she's not *your* Aunt Roni. She's *Ginnie's* aunt. Ginnie's *mom* would be your aunt."

Tillie moved to the spot Uncle Jake just vacated.

"But she *looks* like Aunt Queenie." Mysti spoke as if that fact changed the reality of the situation. Her stubbornness amused Tillie.

"You can call me 'Aunt Roni' if it's okay with your dad. I love being an auntie." Her welcoming smile upped the "dazzle charts" by ten. If Ginnie's mom smiled so beautifully, Tillie could see why DT loved her so much.

"My husband has a brother with two sons. Ginnie is my only niece. Don't tell my nephews, but I am partial to little girls. You look about the same age as my oldest daughter. Mysti, how old are you?"

"Seven ... *and-a-half*."

Husband? Oldest daughter? She's married ... and has a family?

Tillie instantly liked "Aunt Roni" a whole lot better.

"I thought so. So is my little girl."

"I'm gonna call you 'Aunt Roni' then." Mysti informed the woman. "And Tillie can call you Aunt Roni *too*, because she's gonna be Ginnie's sister."

"She is?" Aunt Roni seemed confused, and then smiled again,

sending a questioning look toward Uncle Jake. "Todd's getting remarried?"

"He's considering it," Uncle Jake confirmed.

Hey, you should be saying, "Yes, he absolutely is!" Bumblebees invaded Tillie's middle.

"Good for him." Aunt Roni patted Ginnie's knee. "Are you happy about getting a sister?"

Ginnie nodded. "Tillie's my best friend. We're already like sisters."

Soft fluttering butterfly wings replaced the frantic bumblebees.

"That's wonderful. Sisters *should* be best friends. I miss my sister terribly. We were so close growing up." Aunt Roni's eyes searched Ginnie's face, then Tillie's, and then Uncle Jake's.

For sympathy, Tillie was certain.

Although Tillie's mind screamed that she needed to be wary of this beautiful stranger dressed in perfectly fitting designer clothes who looked just like DT's first wife, Tillie's heart felt a kinship with the woman who honestly just seemed to want to be a part of Ginnie's life.

Tillie knew *that* feeling *very* well.

Ginnie smiled at her aunt. "You'll love Miss Amanda, Tillie's mom. She's very nice. She told me she doesn't want to take Mama's place, that she and I can just be friends. She knew Mama a little. Did you ever meet her?"

"Amanda?" Aunt Roni glanced at Uncle Jake. "Was she at the funeral?"

He nodded. "She was married at the time to Jasper Taylor, my friend from high school."

The bumblebees returned.

Uncle Jake slipped his arm around Tillie's shoulders. "Turtle's eleven days younger than Ginnie, so they've always been roughly the same size. She was at the funeral as well."

Aunt Roni studied Tillie and then smiled. "I *do* remember you, *and* your mama at the memorial luncheon. You were wearing a purple dress. You, Ginnie, Toran, and a few other kids had a little picnic. A lady named Lauren, I believe, helped your mom keep you children busy while the adults tended to the condolences and such. Your mom has light brown wavy hair, yes?"

Tillie nodded, liking this woman more and more. "Yes."

"Lauren is probably Austin's mom. She and Mama were best friends," Ginnie said.

Aunt Roni nodded. "Yes. Austin's mom. Queenie thought the two of you made a cute couple." Her eyes twinkled. "Do you still see Austin?"

"Most every day. He's Toran's best friend. And he's my buddy, so *no way* could he be my boyfriend." Ginnie rolled her eyes and waved away the suggestion.

Tillie giggled, trying to picture Austin and Ginnie as a "couple." The image didn't work for her.

"Hey! Where is everybody?" DT's voice called out.

Tillie backed up a little and peeked through the doorway leading to the dining room.

DT and Toran walked toward them.

"Hi, Till!" DT grinned at her and then lowered his voice. "Who's visiting? Nice car."

Uncle Jake crossed in front of Tillie. "How's Toran?" He stopped walking when he reached DT and asked quietly, "How come you didn't answer your phone?"

"I was driving and almost here." DT leaned to look past Uncle Jake. "I tried calling before we left the hospital, but the phone just rang. I thought maybe you took the girls out for ice cream or something, to get their minds off Toran's injury. His ribs are bruised, but he'll be fine."

"That's good to hear." Uncle Jake sent an appraising look Toran's way. "Brace yourself. In about thirty seconds, I guarantee Toran's injury is gonna feel like old news."

When alarm lit DT's face, the all-too-familiar anxiety pummeled Tillie's belly, pushing her onto the bar stool behind her.

49

TORAN'S TURN

oran glanced at Uncle Jake, who stood in front of Tillie, biting his lower lip. *This can't be good.* Uncle Jake was usually self-confident to the point of being obnoxious. Toran couldn't tell what Dad was thinking from where he stood, but he noticed the color draining from Tillie's face.

Her lip trembled, making Toran realize the light wasn't playing tricks on him. She was definitely concerned about something ... or someone.

She turned toward the family room.

Whoever drove the silver Mercedes parked in front of the farmhouse is a problem, but for who? Dad? ... Tillie? ... Me?

Toran moved around Dad and entered the kitchen, brushing off Uncle Jake's hand as he hurried past. *I'm done with all the secrets. Who's here?*

It didn't take long to figure out why Uncle Jake tried to stop him.

Once Toran reached the family room doorway, an invisible force immobilized his entire body as surely as if he'd walked into a wall.

There, on the couch, sat his twin sister and a woman who looked very much like her.

That can't possibly be our mother. Mama is dead ... isn't she?

Before Toran could form the question his brain wouldn't let him believe, Dad gripped his shoulders lightly, moved him forward a step, and rushed past him before stopping in front of the couch.

The woman rose. She offered a nervous smile.

Ginnie stood next to her. "Hi, Daddy."

Toran half-expected Dad to sweep the lady into his arms and hug her happily.

He didn't.

Instead, an expression composed of a multitude of emotions crossed Dad's face so quickly it was like watching a fast-forwarding movie.

Anger, fear, relief, sadness, frustration, sorrow, and then anger again.

Lots of anger.

That's not like Dad.

Before Toran could finish his thought, Dad shook his finger at the woman. "What are *you* doing here? You can't just drop by any old time you feel like it. How *dare* you."

Ginnie's eyes grew huge, like the size of duck eggs.

"How dare *me*?" The woman's smile disappeared. "I came to see if you'd call a truce and let me reconnect with my niece and nephew only to find out *my sister's kids have no knowledge of her family.*" The woman hugged Ginnie to her and then pointed her own finger. "How *dare YOU!*"

Her sister's family?

Mama's sister?

Mama has a sister?

Toran's brain searched the puzzle pieces dropped in front of him, trying to put together a clear picture of the facts. One his mind could comprehend. "Mama has an identical twin sister?"

Toran knew the question came from him, but didn't recognize his own voice, strangled with incredulous disbelief.

Of course! If this woman who looked like Mama was actually her, Dad would be happy to see her ... and Dad was NOT happy to see her.

An identical twin sister explained things ... and opened up a whole boatload of new questions ... *like why does Ginnie know about a twin sister and I don't? First she hides Mama's journals from me and now Mama's sister? Maybe we aren't as close as we used to be, but when did she decide not to share anything important with me?*

"Yes, she does." Dad hung his thumb on his front jean pocket. "I'm sorry, Toran. This is your aunt, Veronica Stratton." He turned to Ginnie. "She's the biggest reason I didn't give you back your mother's journals ... well part of it. I haven't seen her in years ..." He glared at Aunt Roni. "... and I don't really want to see her *today*."

Ginnie's mouth dropped open, frustration crossing her face.

Then understanding.

She practically whispered, "Is Cabot the other part?"

Who's Cabot? An uncle? Even more secrets?

Aggravation colored Dad's face and lit Toran's own fuse.

He crossed the room quickly, wanting very much to call Ginnie out on her newest pile of betrayals.

Some kind of twin YOU are! Traitor!

Before he could speak, he caught the glare Dad directed at Veronica Stratton. "Thanks a lot. You could have called first, so I had time to prepare my kids."

"By *my* count, you've had eight-and-a-half *ye-ahs* to prepare them. I've been praying you were the decent man I used to know and that you hadn't poisoned Ginnie and Toran against us, but it *nevah* occurred to me that you'd erase us completely out of their lives."

Wait a minute. Erase us? Erase ... who?

Ginnie blinked, looking very vulnerable, stopping the ugly accusation in Toran's throat. *What am I missing?*

Fragments of thoughts and possible conclusions swam wildly around his head as incongruent as an octopus in freshwater or frogs in saltwater.

Mama's twin released Ginnie and squared herself to Dad, looking him straight in the eye. "Here I comforted myself with the thought that at least my niece and nephew had a good dad, even if their mama and I couldn't be around them. How could you erase *me*? I know my *daddy* hurt you, but *I've* never been a problem for you. Didn't my sister mean *anything* to you?"

"Don't. You. *Dare!*" Dad roared. He reached for Ginnie's upper arm and tugged her behind him. "Queenie meant *everything* to me, but her *family? Not. So. Much.*"

Dad spit each word with such force Toran had to look twice to make sure the man before him was indeed his dad. The hurt and anger this man spewed was palpable and extremely un-Dad-like.

A tremor pulsed through Toran.

Mysti burst into tears.

The woman's mouth dropped open.

Tillie shuddered as her eyes went wide. Her hands flew to her mouth.

Ginnie jerked her arm, but couldn't free it from Dad's grasp.

Fear crossed her face as her lip trembled.

Dad didn't seem to notice any of their reactions as he steeled his gaze on this mystery aunt. "*Your* family made a horrific time *excruciating. Get out!*" Dad demanded, pointing toward the doorway Uncle Jake was coming quickly through. "I don't have to let you see *my* kids."

Toran slid in front of Uncle Jake, reaching Dad first.

"Daddy! You don't mean that." Ginnie snatched her arm from his hold and stood next to their aunt. "Stop being hateful. *You* don't have to talk to me about Mama anymore if you don't want to. Aunt Roni can tell me what I need to know." Tears rolled down Ginnie's cheeks. "*Don't send her away. I ... need ... her.*"

Hearing the rawness of his sister's plea, Toran realized she didn't know any more than he did.

He heard his voice speak before he recognized that the words coming out of his mouth had just whirled through his mind. "Dad, calm down and tell us what's going on. You promised to tell us why you took the journals. *Now* would be good."

Uncle Jake scooped up Mysti and reached a comforting hand to Ginnie. "Toran's right, Todd. It's way past time."

50

THUNDERSTORMS

*D*ad clamped his jaw shut and jerked his fingers through his blond waves. He opened his mouth, then closed it again.

Ginnie had seen him angry on occasion, but this was more than anger. She blinked away her tears and tried to care about the hurt and confusion crossing his face.

But she *couldn't* care.

No way could she let him send Aunt Roni away.

When Dad didn't respond to Uncle Jake, Ginnie tried appealing to his sense of fairness.

She mustered all the calm she could, then willed her voice to stay even. "You always say there's each person's side and then there's the whole truth. I want to hear Aunt Roni's side, Daddy, even if you can't or won't tell us yours."

Dad found his voice, still hard and bitter. "Not until I find out *why* she's here." He motioned to the big couch and waited for Aunt Roni to sit.

"Tillie, c'mere." Ginnie sat next to her aunt and patted the seat next to her for her friend.

Tillie darted her gaze between Daddy and Aunt Roni.

Dad must have noticed her panicked expression, because he

mouthed, "Sorry," as he took in a breath and let it out, frustration and dismay battling one another as he slowly shook his head.

"My, you've grown." Aunt Roni said, reaching for Toran's hand as he approached the couch. "You're very handsome. The spitting image of your dad."

Dad grimaced. "Flattery will get you *nowhere*, Veronica."

Uncle Jake set Mysti on her feet and then guided Dad to the matching loveseat.

"It's the truth. He does look just like you." She sighed softly. "I'm not your enemy, Todd. I just want to see my sister's kids. I've missed them."

Giving a wide sweep of his hand, Dad locked his eyes on Aunt Roni's. "You've seen them. And since I have a court order saying that you *don't* have that right, please explain to me why I shouldn't have you arrested, right here and now."

"Dad!" Toran and Ginnie chided as one.

"*Don't judge me.*" He glared at each of them in turn. "You don't know what she and her father put me through."

"We would if you had *told* us," Ginnie retorted, no longer feeling the least bit sympathetic.

"Whoa, Todd. Count to ten." Uncle Jake grabbed Dad's arm as he jerked forward. "Ginnie, this would be a good time to practice some self-control and keep quiet."

"Why should she?" Toran moved to his feet and waved the advice away, shocking Ginnie. He never defied their dad. "Ginnie's right. Dad's had plenty of time to tell us about Mama's family. *Especially* if they're the reason he took the journals. I think we have a right to know *everything.*"

"That may be so, but I'd appreciate it if you'd speak more respectfully. He's still your dad." All eyes turned toward the doorway, where Uncle Ben stood frowning at Toran. "You know better."

Buzz stood next to him, eyes wide.

Their great-uncle's scolding tone turned more pleasant. "Buzz, I see you don't remember her, but this is Roni Stratton, Queenie's twin sister. You met her at the funeral. Roni, my son ... Buzz. I'll presume the rest of you made the proper introductions."

Uncle Ben's casual remembering of Mama's long-lost sister reminded Ginnie that he had kept this information from her for weeks, waiting for Dad to get a grip. She made an effort to push away her anger, hoping her great-uncle would keep Dad from blowing his top again ... if need be.

Buzz nodded his head. "Hi, Roni. I remember you now."

"A pleasure to see you both again." Aunt Roni's soft Southern accent soothed Ginnie like hot cocoa on a stormy day. "You were Toran's age when I saw you last."

Buzz smacked his forehead, having an "ah-ha" moment. "Gin, I'm sorry. She's the secret you were asking about?"

"Apparently." Ginnie nodded. "I didn't have a clue either."

Uncle Ben strode over to his moss green recliner, offered Aunt Roni a welcoming smile, and sat. "It's nice to see *you* again."

Good. Uncle Ben likes her. Then she can't be a bad person. Ginnie snuggled closer to her new-found aunt, feeling better that her great-uncle had given his approval.

He raised a finger and pointed it at Aunt Roni. "Provided you really are here just to get to know Ginnie and Toran. If you pull any of the nonsense Cabot did after the funeral, this will be the *last* time you will be welcome in our home. You have my word on that." He popped the footrest opened and leaned back. "Don't make me keep it."

Ginnie sucked in a shocked breath and still heard Tillie gasp in surprise. Ginnie caught a slight but satisfied smile cross Dad's lips as she turned to see how Aunt Roni would respond.

Instead of cowering like Ginnie had imagined, Aunt Roni straightened and faced Uncle Ben, wearing a pleasant expression. "I wouldn't dream of it. May I still call you Uncle Ben?"

"If you're here as family."

"Yes, sir. I came with Daddy's blessing. He isn't long for this world and wants to make amends before he meets his Maker." She paused. When Uncle Ben's look softened, she spoke again, her words apologetic. "His biggest regret is cutting off my sister and trying to take her kids, when he couldn't have what he wanted."

"Take us where?" Toran asked.

"Away from your dad." Tillie glared at Aunt Roni and folded her arms angrily across her chest. "What was *that* about? I want Ginnie's dad to marry my mom so I can have a *good* dad. Why would *your* dad do something so hateful?" Tillie's cheeks flamed bright red.

She stared straight ahead until Dad caught her eye. "Thanks, Tillie. If this doesn't go well, I'm glad to know *you're* on my side at least." Dad leaned forward and sent Ginnie a questioning glance.

Ginnie refused to acknowledge it, not willing to commit to him before she got to know Aunt Roni better. She peeked at her friend. Tillie winked back at him, her cheeks becoming a lighter pink as her grin grew.

That figures. Tillie thinks Dad is perfect.

Aunt Roni reached across Ginnie to give Tillie's knee a gentle squeeze. "That's a very good question. The truth is simple. He got caught up in pride. He realizes now the pain he caused Todd and he wants to make things right." Aunt Roni locked her eyes on Dad's. "If you'll let him, he'd like to apologize to you personally."

Dad's slight smile turned into a frown.

Ginnie could tell he wanted to believe Aunt Roni's words, but he wasn't ready to let bygones be bygones.

I guess Daddy does have a good reason to hold a grudge.

The seconds passed like hours.

Uncle Ben cleared his throat and tapped his watch. "I'm not sure what you want to do about this information, but it's twenty-five till two. At least two of you need to be heading to work in the next ten minutes, or calling in to make other arrangements."

His gaze volleyed between Uncle Jake and Dad.

Dad slid his palms down his jeans and stood.

Uncle Jake spoke first. "Uncle Ben, are you okay with me leaving Mysti? With Toran getting hurt and Roni showing up, I completely forgot to call Clarissa and make arrangements to meet her."

"What happened to Toran?" Uncle Ben and Aunt Roni asked in unison.

Uncle Ben lowered his footrest.

"I had a disagreement with Uncle Jake's truck bumper," Toran joked. "I bruised two ribs, but the good news is I can breathe now."

Aunt Roni hugged him.

Toran gasped.

"Sorry." Her face crinkled.

He smiled through a grimace. "No worries."

His light-hearted response didn't make Ginnie feel any better about forgetting he'd been hurt in the first place. "You'll be okay?"

"Yeah. But I won't be able to help hay tomorrow."

"Great, I forgot about that," Dad said.

"Sorry," Toran apologized.

"That's not what I meant. You're fine." Dad shook his head. "I can't take tonight off because we have to hay tomorrow and I'm already taking tomorrow night off. Sorry Roni, I have to go and I'm not okay with you being here without me." He put his hand up in a 'stop' motion for Ginnie's benefit. "I'm glad Cabot wants to make amends, but after eight years of angry silence, I'm not feeling inclined to leave my children in your care. How long are you going to be in town?"

Before Aunt Roni could reply, Ginnie ignored his motion, rushed to her dad, and grabbed his wrist. "Please let Aunt Roni stay. Please, Daddy? Don't send her away."

"No." He pulled his wrist out of her grasp. "Roni should have called before she came. Say your good-byes." He glanced at his watch and then Ginnie. "You have five minutes while I change."

"Daddy!"

He clamped his jaw shut and shot Ginnie a warning look.

"Todd," Uncle Jake said quietly.

"DON'T!" Dad swiveled toward him, jabbing a finger at his chest. "*I'm their dad and I said 'no.'* Now leave it alone."

Fuzzy white noise buzzed in Ginnie's head.

Uncle Jake and Dad stared each other down.

Ginnie wanted to continue her protest, but something about her dad's stance, both threatening and vulnerable, stopped the words, like an invisible hand pressing against her mouth.

Uncle Ben cleared his throat.

Uncle Jake looked away first, sinking Ginnie's hopes.

A feeling she could only describe as 'desperate' percolated inside her.

Tears burned her eyes.

She blinked and then glanced at her great-uncle.

He raised a finger to his lips and gave a quick shake of his head.

She turned to Uncle Jake, hoping he would help.

He pinched his lips together and shrugged.

Ginnie knew he wouldn't press the issue, at least while there were witnesses.

The fuzzy white noise grew louder.

Her thoughts swirled like ugly black storm clouds.

The desperate feeling grew, surrounding her, stealing the oxygen from the air.

Making it hard to breathe.

She searched each face in the room, looking for a glimmer of hope.

Hope for what?

Ginnie couldn't be sure.

Her heart raced.

Her throat hurt.

Her eyes burned.

The white noise pounded.

Then the storm clouds burst.

And Ginnie knew—without a doubt—she would drown in the misery engulfing every fiber of her being.

51

BOOMING SILENCE

Tillie shuddered.

The warning look on DT's face reminded her of Jasper.

Fear froze Tillie where she sat.

Toran swiveled, glancing between his dad and sister.

Uncle Jake ducked his head and took Mysti's hand.

Everyone moved in slow motion.

Ginnie blinked. Her mouth opened, but no words escaped. Her eyes darted around the room, desperate for something.

Helpless.

Vulnerable.

Hurt.

Tears burned Tillie's eyes with sympathy for her friend.

No one said anything.

The quiet boomed.

Anxiety pulsed through Tillie.

She glanced at Ginnie again.

Her friend's mouth opened wider, her lips trembling.

Tears shone in Ginnie's anguished eyes.

Tillie blinked away her own tears and found herself standing in front of DT, pleading. "Please? Ginnie needs her aunt. Please don't send her away."

I can't believe I said that.

Apparently DT couldn't either. He looked at Tillie, but she knew he didn't see her.

He glanced at Ginnie.

A tear streamed down her cheek, her eyes pleading for his approval. "Please, Daddy?"

His head moved in a shaking motion and then stopped.

Tillie followed his gaze to Uncle Ben, who gave a quick nod and said in a firm, quiet voice. "I'll be here."

DT turned from Uncle Ben and studied Ginnie's face.

She blinked, wiping her cheeks with her lime green T-shirt sleeve. "Please?" Ginnie's sad voice cracked as she repeated her desperate plea. "Daddy, *I ... need ... her.*"

Tillie held her breath.

The silence grew louder.

The anguished look on Ginnie's face jumped to DT's.

He gave a quick nod and escaped from the room.

WINNING? NOT SO MUCH

G innie didn't know what to say, think, or feel.

Dad's nod meant that Aunt Roni could stay.

Ginnie had won. Then why did she feel so terrible?

Uncle Jake kissed the top of Mysti's head, set her on Uncle Ben's lap, and followed Dad out of the room.

Ginnie barely felt Tillie's arms embrace her. She froze instead of joining her friend in a happy dance. She'd gotten what she wanted, but "winning" didn't feel good at all.

Dad's final look before he left haunted her.

She couldn't define it completely, but betrayed seemed close.

Hurt, sad, and bewildered also hovered nearby.

"Maybe I should go. Todd's right. I should have called first." Aunt Roni swept Ginnie into a hug and then gently touched Toran's cheek. "I've hurt Todd again. That's the last thing I wanted to do. My family's done that enough. I'd hoped enough time had passed, but I guess not." She let go of Ginnie and wiped her eyes with a tissue. "I'm sorry, Uncle Ben. Please assure him I meant him no harm."

Aunt Roni picked up her purse and rifled through it.

Ginnie froze, unable to make sense of what was happening.

She'd just won Dad's permission, but Aunt Roni was still leaving.

What's wrong with this picture?

Uncle Ben scooted Mysti off his lap and stood. "Now, Roni ... we can work this out."

She handed him a business card with a horse on it. "This has my cell phone number. I'll be in town another day or two. Todd can call me if he wants to make arrangements."

Panic blazed through Ginnie. "Don't go!"

"I'm sorry, honey. Todd doesn't want me to stay. He *is* your daddy. As much as I want to see you, this isn't right. You can understand that, can't you?" Aunt Roni lifted Ginnie's chin. "Your mama loved him *so* much. Out of respect for her ... as well as him, I need to go."

"But he doesn't talk about her." Ginnie tried to blink the burning in her eyes away. "I need to know about my mom." She held Aunt Roni's hand to her chin. "Mama would be okay with us getting to know you. I know she would."

"Not like this." Aunt Roni sighed. "I love you so much. You know about me now. Todd and I'll talk. I'll make it work. I promise."

Her reassuring words didn't feel the least bit reassuring.

Ginnie glanced at Toran, hoping her brother could fix this. He looked as torn as she felt.

"Why are you crying? Uncle Todd *did this*." Mysti nodded her head emphatically at Aunt Roni. "You can stay. My daddy will make him feel better."

Her confidence amazed Ginnie. "How do you know? You've only known Uncle Jake since last night."

Aunt Roni did a double take. "Last night?"

Mysti jutted out her chin and folded her arms across her chest. "So? He made *me* feel better. He'll make Uncle Todd feel better too. That's what daddies *do*."

Then Ginnie realized what else she'd seen in her dad's face—a willingness to sacrifice his happiness and comfort for hers. He had set aside his anger and fear to help Ginnie find what she needed ... her mom.

Even if it was in the form of a woman whose family had caused him unbearable pain.

"Please stay." She gripped Aunt Roni's wrist tighter. "I'll make it better with my dad."

Before Aunt Roni could protest, Ginnie rushed from the room, calling behind her, "Toran, Uncle Ben, make her stay. I'll be right back."

53

NOW WHAT?

*G*innie stopped when she reached the top step. She forced a smile and followed the cherry wood banister the length of the hallway, feeling better with every footstep.

When she reached her dad's bedroom door, she lifted her hand. Before she could knock, it opened.

"Eavesdropping *again*? I'm losing my patience with that, young lady," Dad scolded.

"I ... I ... I ..."

"You what?" His angry tone cleared her mind as quickly as a whiteboard eraser. He motioned to the staircase. "Why aren't you downstairs?"

"I ... I ..."

"Well?" He glanced at his watch. "I don't have time for this. Enjoy visiting with your aunt." He hurried quickly down the hallway, without looking back.

Anger and hurt seized Ginnie's throat.

She no longer wanted to make him feel better.

Instead, she wanted to throw something at him. She glanced at Uncle Jake.

He arched an eyebrow and asked in a quiet, defeated voice. "Did you need something?"

Ginnie shrugged at him, swallowed her frustration, and turned toward her dad, who had stopped on the second step.

He was now looking straight at her.

"*Did* you need something?" Dad's kinder tone made her swallow an ugly retort and remember why she had come upstairs.

"I wanted to say 'thank you' for letting Aunt Roni stay."

"Oh." He backed up a step and ducked his head. "I'm sorry. This has been a crazy day. First Mysti came, and then Toran got hurt. Now Roni showing up. I'm not handling that very well. Sorry I took it out on you. Please forgive me."

"I'm sorry too." Ginnie swallowed hard. "Aunt Roni's *not* staying. She's leaving."

"Why?" Dad asked, alarm filling his voice.

"She doesn't want to hurt you anymore." Tears filled Ginnie's eyes. She blinked. Instead of stopping the tears, they overflowed. "I want her to stay, but not if you really don't want her to be here. She says Mama would want her to leave. Is that true?"

"I wish she were here to ask." Dad walked over to Ginnie and wiped her cheek with his thumb. "Do you think Roni is serious about leaving?"

Ginnie nodded. "She gave Uncle Ben a business card with her cell phone number so you can call her. I told her to wait till I talked to you, but I don't know if she did."

"What a mess. I didn't even want her here, but if Roni's feeling bad enough to leave, then I don't mind her staying so much." He slipped Ginnie's hand in his. "Let's fix this quick. I have to get to work. You coming, Jake?'

"I wouldn't miss it." He winked at Ginnie as he dashed by. "I have my own little girl to say good-bye to now." They followed Uncle Jake downstairs.

Dad sighed. "We've had quite the family reunion, haven't we?"

"Yeah, but if you don't want us to meet Cabot, that's okay with me."

Dad grimaced. "As much as I'd love to never lay eyes on that man again, I won't hold my breath. Knowing my luck, he'll outlive me out of spite, the ornery old coot."

"Don't say that." Ginnie shuddered. "I don't want anything to happen to you. But if it did, would he get us?"

"*Never.*" He squeezed her hand and let out a breath. "I've made sure of that."

The quiet strength of his reply calmed her rising panic.

Getting to know Mama is one thing, but getting to know her family isn't feeling so good.

54

SURPRISES

*W*hen Ginnie, Dad, and Uncle Jake reached the family room, Mysti sat on the floor facing Aunt Roni, Tillie, Buzz, and Toran, who all sat on the large plum couch listening as Mysti explained how she had come to be part of the family.

Ginnie took note of their amused smiles.

"Mommy said I was such a great present that she didn't want to share me. But then she realized she was being very selfish." Mysti plastered a stern look on her face. "It's not nice to be selfish, so she told Daddy about me so that they could share me."

"He's lucky to get you." Tillie leaned forward and brushed a stray hair near Mysti's eye.

Mysti pointed her thumb at her chest. "Daddy said I was the best surprise ever."

Uncle Ben chuckled from his recliner. "You were that."

Mysti smiled even bigger when she spotted Uncle Jake. "Huh, Daddy?"

"Abso-posilutely," Uncle Jake agreed.

"Of course, Mysti. Who wouldn't want a sweet little girl for a surprise?" Aunt Roni's words seemed sincere, but Ginnie didn't miss the teasing look she sent Uncle Jake.

Uncle Jake swept Mysti into his arms, making her laugh. When Mysti wasn't looking, Ginnie noticed Uncle Jake exchanging odd looks and funny faces with Aunt Roni.

Like they were old friends. *Hmmm.*

"Are you feeling okay, Tor?" Dad asked, eyeballing Toran's side. "You can have more pain reliever at four-thirty. Ginnie, Tillie, please help him with his chores, he's not supposed to lift anything heavy for a while." Dad motioned to Tillie, who came to him. He pulled Tillie and Ginnie into a quick hug and lowered his voice. "Please help with Mysti."

"Yes, sir." Tillie and Ginnie chorused.

When's he gonna talk to Aunt Roni?

Dad hugged them harder. "I love you. Listen to Uncle Ben." He smiled and let go of them. "Toran, take it easy. Mysti, please keep the big girls out of trouble." He gave Toran's shoulder a quick squeeze, Mysti a hug, and then turned toward the couch. "Roni, will you please walk to Jake's truck with me?"

"Certainly." She joined him near the doorway.

He motioned for her to go ahead and then followed her through the kitchen.

"What do you think he'll say to her?" Tillie asked.

Ginnie shrugged. "I don't know, but at least he's happier about her being here."

"Maybe I'll go find out." Uncle Jake winked and gave Mysti one last hug. "Tell your mom about all the fun we had today so she'll bring you back tomorrow, okay?"

"Sure, Daddy. I like being here." She looked around. "Am I gonna meet anybody else?

"Everyone's here except Vi and Miss Amanda. They'll be back later." Uncle Jake stood. "Aunt Roni is a *bonus* aunt."

"Just wait until everybody shows up for Vi's wedding. Mysti's only the third West girl in six generations." Buzz picked up a stuffed goat and made it leap toward Mysti. She giggled and ran from the goat. "That'll make her a pretty popular cowgirl."

"Just like a rockstar." Ginnie chuckled as she thought of her well-meaning—but seriously over attentive—great-aunts and great-uncles descending on Mysti like a bunch of locusts.

Better her than me.

Having Mysti around might prove more useful than Ginnie first thought.

55

TORAN ATWATER

*A*unt Roni joined everybody in the family room after her walk with Dad—visibly happier than when she left.

"What did he say?" Ginnie caught a shake of Buzz's head, but pretended she hadn't. "Well?"

"We came to an understanding of sorts. There are a couple things he'd like to tell you." She lifted Ginnie's chin, smiling as she seemed to read Ginnie's mind. "And I intend to honor my word to him so that he allows me to keep seeing you. So, any questions after they eloped need to go through your dad."

"They eloped?" Toran, Ginnie, and Tillie asked as one.

"Oh, dear." Aunt Roni cast a pleading look at Uncle Ben. "Didn't he tell them *anything*?"

Uncle Ben stiffened. "I don't think Todd considers his wedding an elopement."

"Whatever it was—it was not the wedding my sister had planned since we were little girls."

"Why not?" Ginnie asked.

Aunt Roni's cheeks pinked. "I don't mean to sound bitter, but given my dad's ultimatum, there was no way I could attend their wedding without making things worse."

"What ultimatum?" Toran questioned.

Uncle Ben cleared his throat.

Aunt Roni sighed. "Let's talk about something else." She looked around the room before lingering her gaze on Toran. "Ginnie said my sister wrote each of you a journal. Did she mention how you got your nickname?"

After Toran nodded, her countenance brightened considerably. "Wonderful. Toran Atwater was a good friend of ours. A hero, really. He deserves a namesake."

Ginnie glanced at her brother, fairly certain neither of them had ever heard about a "Toran Atwater" or any other Toran for that matter. As far as she knew, it was a name her mom made up for her brother, at least that was what their dad had said.

"We made a pact, Ginnie and I. I *mean—Queenie* and I." Aunt Roni turned to Ginnie and offered a flustered smile. "Sorry, your mom is still 'Ginnie' to me—or Widget."

Ginnie nodded, barely hearing Aunt Roni's nervous chatter after catching a puzzled look on her brother's face.

"We made a pact, Widget and I, that whoever had a boy first would name him after Toran."

Toran's smile turned to a slight frown.

His blue eyes narrowed, reminding Ginnie of their dad just a few minutes before, suspicious of Aunt Roni.

She continued her story. "The other day, I was looking through an old jewelry box of your mom's and guess what I found?"

Aunt Roni's excited tone made Ginnie forget about Toran's growing grimace. "What?"

"A 'to-do' list. Among other things, she'd written down that she wanted to have boy-girl twins and a couple of alpaca." Aunt Roni's eyes twinkled as she glanced around. "She wrote it in sixth grade, but still ... that's pretty amazing that she actually got what she wanted. Though on second thought, it shouldn't surprise me."

"Really? She wished for us?" A happy squeal escaped Ginnie. She glanced at her brother. "How cool is that?"

Toran's frown only deepened. "Who is Toran Atwater?"

Aunt Roni's smile disappeared. "A friend from school. Our first crush." Her eyebrows knit together. "You said your mom told you about your name."

"Dad said my name came from each of my grandfathers' names. Vic*tor* from Grandpa West and Alex*an*der from Grandpa Stratton." His eyes narrowed. "Mama said she named me after her friend--but she didn't mention that he was an old *boyfriend*."

He spat the word with such disgust, Ginnie locked her gaze on his.

The loud quiet from earlier exploded, showering each of them in uncomfortable silence.

56

BUCKET LIST

*T*oran glared at his so-called aunt. All along something had been bothering him about Aunt Roni, but her story about Mama naming him after an old boyfriend ratcheted his suspicions up ten-fold.

No way would Mama do that, at least not the Mama who wrote in his journal how much she loved Dad and their little family. *That* Mama wouldn't deceive Dad.

Ginnie seemed to be falling for Aunt Roni's soft, southern-accented explanations, but Toran wasn't so gullible. He folded his arms across his chest and silently dared her to explain this obvious slur on his mother's character.

"Don't look at me like that. *I* said he was our first crush, which he was. *You* said he was her boyfriend, which he *wasn't*. I *also* said Toran was a hero." She pointed between Ginnie and himself. "If it wasn't for Toran Atwater, you two might not even exist."

Toran scowled. "How do you figure?"

Buzz looked intrigued with the tale from his perch on the loveseat.

Tillie's mouth dropped open next to him.

On the other side of her, Ginnie's eyes opened wider.

Mysti couldn't care less. She sat by the hearth coloring.

Uncle Ben had on his 'tolerant' face.

Toran figured Aunt Roni had maybe twenty seconds to explain herself before his great-uncle would change the direction of this conversation.

"I declare, Toran, you are so suspicious," Aunt Roni drawled, pinching his cheek in a playful way. "Toran Atwater was just about the nicest, bravest individual to ever walk the earth. You should be honored to bear his name."

"Why should I? I don't know anything about him." The anger and frustration he'd been holding in check, boiled over. "Why would my mom marry my dad if she had feelings for another man? And then name their son—ME— after him?" Toran stood straighter, fisting his hands. "You make her sound like an awful person."

"Oh honey, no. I certainly didn't mean to imply *that*." Aunt Roni's hands flew to her face. "We met Toran when we were nine and had just started barrel racing. He lost his left leg below the knee to cancer when he was three. He stayed in remission for years until he lost a valiant fight to that horrible disease just after his sixteenth birthday."

"Oh." His anger deflated. "How old were you?"

"Almost fifteen. Toran promised he'd stay long enough to celebrate our birthday with us. He managed to linger another three weeks. He was older than us by a ye-ah and five days."

"That's so sad ... and brave," Tillie said.

"I agree, Tillie. Toran was inspiring. He loved soccer and could work a ball better with his prosthetic leg than most kids with both original legs. He had such a cheery outlook on life, in spite of how much pain he was in at the end." Aunt Roni cupped Toran's chin in her hands. "He truly was a hero. I know you were named for your grandfathers, but also for your mama's dear friend."

Toran searched his aunt's eyes for a sign of deceit. He couldn't find any. "That Toran sounds like a nice person."

"He certainly was. And wise beyond his years." Aunt Roni brushed his cheek with her thumb before letting go of his chin. "You remind me of him. Your dad does as well."

Toran bristled. "Are you saying my mom married my dad because she couldn't have the other Toran?"

"*Of course not.* Your mom married your dad because he was her soulmate. They completed each other. They had something very special." She turned away and took a breath before continuing. "But if Toran Atwater hadn't died, I don't know that Widget would have had the courage to defy *our* daddy to actually go through with her marriage to Todd."

"I don't get it. What does that other Toran have to do with Mama and Daddy?" Ginnie asked.

Aunt Roni's curls swayed as she sat on the couch again. "Widget made what you would now call a 'bucket list.' Things she wanted to do before she died as well as attitudes she wanted to embrace as she lived her life. After Toran died, Widget focused on racing, trick riding, and trying new things ... sometimes crazy things like skydiving and stock car racing, and other, less crazy things like she quit counting calories and she chose to enjoy all things chocolate."

"Do you really have to give up chocolate to be a beauty queen?" Tillie asked. "I don't think it'd be worth it."

Aunt Roni laughed, looking relieved to lighten the subject. "Chocolate is a serious sin in some circles. We found that when we quit worrying so much about every calorie and finding the perfect dress, we relaxed and enjoyed our competitions more." She reached across Ginnie to pat Tillie's leg emphatically. "Which actually led to more wins. It was freeing, and a great life lesson. One Widget took to heart, to our daddy's dismay."

Ginnie frowned. "What was *his* problem?"

"That's a little complicated. Our father groomed your mother to take over his businesses. She was very much like him: goal-oriented, charismatic, driven. Then Toran died. She decided to start living her own dreams as well as our daddy's." She paused a moment, taking in a breath. She glanced at each twin, before continuing. "Unfortunately, our mama died a year later, further impressing on each of us that life could be way too short."

"No kidding." Toran shrugged, feeling for his mom.

He often thought it was sad that their family had lost Aunt Sadie and then Mama within fifteen months of each other, but he didn't remember much about them.

It would be far worse to lose a friend *and* your mother at his age now. *Mama must have been devastated.* "But you'd think he'd be sympathetic and not want to push Mama away."

Aunt Roni patted the spot next to her on the couch for Toran.

He sat.

"He never intended to push your mother away. He just didn't expect Todd and Queenie to connect so thoroughly *and* so quickly." Aunt Roni squeezed Ginnie's knee. "Todd was different from the other boys we knew. He was totally into my sister, not just her achievements, or her beauty. He could even tell *us* apart--*most* of the time--which not many people could do."

She glanced at Uncle Ben, who nodded his agreement, then looked between Ginnie and Toran again. "Your mama and daddy connected on a level that she had never experienced before. She used to say that Todd was a calming anchor in her stormy life. And when they were together, the crazy in her life didn't seem so crazy."

Ginnie nodded. "She wrote that in my journal."

"She wrote in mine that Dad was the shade tree to her sunny day." Toran shook his head, a little embarrassed to be repeating such a sappy thought. "And other girly stuff."

Everyone chuckled.

Ginnie turned toward their aunt. "So why didn't Cabot like our dad? Couldn't he tell how much they loved each other?"

Aunt Roni blew out a breath and seemed to want to choose her words carefully.

"Once my sister decided she couldn't live without Todd, she told our daddy that she was certain she had found the man for her, fully expecting Daddy to share her vision." She glanced at Uncle Ben, then dropped her gaze to the living room carpet. "Not only did Cabot Stratton *not* want to give Todd the time of day, he informed Widget that he had already picked out the perfect husband for her." She rolled her eyes as she shook her head. "As you can imagine, that didn't go over very well."

Buzz whistled. "I'm thinking a train wreck would be a good analogy."

"Or a lead balloon," Toran quipped, further disgusted with the grandfather he didn't want to meet. *No wonder Mama married Dad in spite of her father--Cabot Stratton sounds like a nutcase.*

Aunt Roni gave a quick nod. "It was downright ugly. Widget brought all of her ammunition: tears, threats, pleadings, drama, promises, blackmail, contracts. She even came up with a presentation to convince our daddy to give Todd a chance."

Ginnie rolled her eyes. "Did Cabot ever quit being so dumb?"

"I doubt it." Toran said, smirking. "We didn't know we had a grandfather until half an hour ago."

"And you'd be right. Daddy would have none of it, and usually he gave in to her when she dug in." Aunt Roni sighed. "Instead *he* dug in even harder. But again, he didn't realize that Todd and Widget had a real connection. I realized--but our daddy refused to see it. He thought she was just being stubborn and if he stood his ground, she'd cave." Aunt Roni wiped at her eyes. "Many of her good qualities come from our father, but so does her stubbornness."

"What good qualities? He sounds like a total loser!" Ginnie jumped to her feet. "I'd elope too if my dad wouldn't even *meet* my boyfriend."

Buzz laughed. "Which is a problem *you'll never* have."

Toran smiled, knowing Buzz was right.

He could see their dad offering Ginnie a short list of candidates that he approved of, but even Dad wouldn't go so far as to pick out her future husband.

And Dad would certainly never make Ginnie choose between her family and anybody else.

"So, did he eventually meet our dad?" Toran asked.

"Yes, but by then, so many ugly words had passed between my sister and our father that it didn't do much good. The short story is that Todd professed his love for her and he even offered to put things on hold, asking for a do-over of sorts, so Daddy and he could get to know each other better. Then Daddy said something snide and Widget was done listening. She told Todd that they were leaving and made him choose between Daddy and her." She looked to Uncle Ben for approval.

He gave a quick nod.

"Of course Todd chose Widget. My sister decided our dad would eventually come around. She convinced Todd that they should get married and hoped for the best."

"How could they if her dad said no?" Tillie asked.

"She was nineteen. Legally, Cabot couldn't stop them from getting married," Buzz interjected.

"True, but that didn't stop him from trying." Aunt Roni grimaced. "After they married, our dad tried to get it annulled. Then Widget found out he couldn't annul the marriage if she and Todd had a baby. So she decided to start a family, figuring that once she presented our daddy with a grandchild, he'd forgive and forget and everything would go back to the way it used to be."

"But that didn't happen," Toran surmised.

"No ... it didn't." Aunt Roni squeezed his knee. "And when she found out you were a boy--she thought that would win him over for sure. But for once, her defiance made him more angry than proud."

"Why would he be proud of her being defiant? My dad gets really mad when I don't do what he wants," Ginnie interjected, *"Especially* when I refuse to change my mind."

Aunt Roni glanced at Uncle Ben again, who gave a slight nod.

She continued, "... because, quite often when she stood her ground against him--he would bend, impressed with her tenacity. But for whatever reason, giving him a grandson didn't give her the edge she thought it would." Aunt Roni sighed and patted Ginnie's knee. "That's not saying anything against you--but like Wests tend to have boys, Strattons tend to have girls. Your mama was the son he always wanted and never had. She was the child he pinned all of his dreams on--until she chose your dad over him." She brushed some blonde waves behind her ear. "He was always good to me, but *she* was his favorite. When she chose your dad over him, and wouldn't back down, it broke something in him. He dug in every bit as hard as she did."

The many wrongs of the situation coursed an anger through Toran unlike anything he had ever experienced. He felt a need to protect his mom ... his sister ... his dad ... and even this new aunt ... from this pigheaded, unknown grandfather.

Before he could express his raging thoughts, Aunt Roni pulled a tissue out of her designer jean pocket. "I don't want you to hate him."

It's a little late for that.

Ginnie rolled her eyes, but didn't say anything--*for once*--but Toran totally understood her disgust.

"He *is* your grandfather and before your dad, Cabot Stratton was the most important man in your mother's life."

A resigned sadness clouded Aunt Roni's face. "By answering your questions honestly from that time, I haven't painted a very good picture of my father. He's no longer that person and wants to make amends. Do you think you could let him?" She glanced at Ginnie first, and then locked her eyes on Toran's. "It would mean the world to both of us. He can't apologize to my sister, but he would love the opportunity to apologize to her children."

Toran found his voice first. "I'll have to think about it. But I wouldn't get your hopes up. And even if I agree--I don't think Dad is going to be very open to Cabot, *ever.* Dad doesn't even want *you* here." He pointed at his sister. "He only let *you* stay because he loves Ginnie more than he must dislike your dad--and that's saying something-- I've never seen my dad blow up like he did when he first saw you. I didn't think it was possible for him to be that outraged."

"That was scary." Ginnie nodded her agreement. "I've never seen my dad that furious."

Toran stood. "Somehow, I don't see him welcoming the man who was too pigheaded to attend his own daughter's wedding, after blowing our dad off without even trying to get to know him."

57

WESTERN PLEASURE

*O*nce Toran said his piece, Uncle Ben reminded them all that they had chores to do. Aunt Roni seemed relieved at the distraction, acting almost as excited as Mysti to gather the chicken eggs. Uncle Ben and Tillie offered to help Toran with his chores while Aunt Roni shadowed Ginnie doing hers.

When the chores were done, Mysti wanted to play with the kittens, so Tillie followed her to help her look for them. Princess had a bad habit of moving them, probably to keep them away from Uncle Jake's hunting dogs, Rascal and Bandit.

Aunt Roni ran her hand down the side of Calliope's chocolate neck, before leading the horse out of the pasture. "She's lovely, Gin.

"Thanks." Ginnie closed the gate and beamed.

Her aunt slid a finger under the nose band and then the throat latch. She measured the nose band again by putting two fingers between the band and the under part of Calliope's chin. "This is only supposed to be one finger wide. Up here, under her throat can be three fingers wide."

"Oh." Ginnie stepped closer, disappointed that her aunt found something to fix. "I thought I was doing it right."

Aunt Roni gave her shoulder a reassuring squeeze. "They slip. I'll tighten it and it'll be right as rain."

Aunt Roni continued adjusting the rest of the tack, checking the reins, harness, and saddle. She pulled the saddle pad higher under the saddle. "Calliope's wither is a little high, so she would do better with a pad that has a higher gullet for better air flow. The more comfortable she is, the better your ride."

Ginnie nodded. "I have another pad, but it's the same as this one."

"No problem. I can help you out." Aunt Roni lifted the fender of the saddle and checked the cinch and stirrups. "You do know to keep the stirrups up until just before you ride, so the flapping doesn't bother Calliope, yes?"

"She doesn't act bothered."

"Trust me, sugar, it bothers her. Horses don't like the unnecessary bumping when they walk." Aunt Roni slid the stirrup up the cinch where it lay flat against the pad. "Do you and Toran share her?"

"Kinda. Calliope's *my* horse, but Toran rides her sometimes."

"I see. Does Toran like to ride?"

"I guess. But I think he likes his computer more. Austin has a horse, so we take turns. Sometimes we borrow Traxx so Tillie and I can ride together, and sometimes, Toran rides Calliope so he and Austin can ride together."

Aunt Roni traced her finger around an intricate pattern of hearts stamped on the saddle fender and skirt. "Did you know this saddle was a gift from your grandfather to Widget on her fourteenth birthday?"

"Really?" A surprised, but happy feeling swept through Ginnie. She knew the saddle was Mama's, but knowing she was almost the same age as Ginnie when she got it, made Mama seem more real somehow.

"Widget saddle broke Love with it. Daddy had it custom-made for her. He thought the hearts went well with Eternal Love's name." Aunt Roni sighed, seeming both happy and sad. "Mine had roses on it."

"It sounds like your dad cared about my mom ..... at least a little,"

Ginnie added, trying to reconcile her image of a crotchety old grandpa with her own father, who almost always greeted Toran, Tillie, and herself with a smile.

"He cared about her *very* much." Aunt Roni patted Calliope's neck. "He was heartbroken when she left."

"But that was his own fault." Ginnie steeled her eyes on Aunt Roni's back, having no sympathy for Cabot Stratton. "My dad's only crime was falling in love with my mom. *And Mama loved him back.* She wrote that in my journal over and over. Cabot shouldn't have punished her for that."

"I agree." She nodded. "Your granddaddy's pride cost him more than you'll ever know."

Ginnie stiffened, not wanting to claim in any way the man who had caused her parents so much pain.

"So, did you take lessons when you got Calliope, or did you just start riding?" Aunt Roni asked, reminding Ginnie of Toran when he changed the subject to keep the peace.

"My dad showed me. He's picky about us wearing riding helmets and not doing tricks on Calliope, but otherwise, he's okay with us having Calliope. He doesn't ride much, but he knows about horses." When Aunt Roni blinked at her defensive tone, Ginnie felt her cheeks heat. "Sorry."

Aunt Roni brushed Ginnie's bangs out of her eyes. "Well, he certainly couldn't be married to my sister and not know a few things about horses, sugar, now could he?"

Her gentle tone made Ginnie realize that Aunt Roni hadn't meant to criticize Dad. "No ma'am." Then a thought occurred to her. "Did *you* like my dad when you met him?"

"I did. Believe it or not, I still do."

Hmmm. "Did you help my mom try to change Cabot's mind about him?" Ginnie persisted, folding her arms across her chest. "Or did you tell my mom to give up my dad when *your* dad was being so hateful?"

Each of them seemed to know that how Aunt Roni answered could greatly affect their budding relationship. "It was complicated. I liked Todd when I met him, which for the record wasn't until the fourth time your mom did."

"Really?"

"Really. They met at your state rodeo. I was competing in a race that weekend several hours away. Widget told me about this cute blond guy, but she didn't go into a lot of detail, figuring she'd never see him again."

"Why not?" That didn't seem right. *Mama adored Daddy. She said so herself, in my baby journal--over and over.*

"Because ... and don't take this wrong, your mama was a pretty popular cowgirl." Aunt Roni ducked her head as pink colored her cheeks. "She literally had lines of interested cowboys at all of her competitions. At first, she figured Todd was just another of her many admirers."

"But he wasn't like that! Dad told me he fell in love with her the first time he ever saw her!" Ginnie shook her head before remembering that Dad himself had said Mama had blown him off the first time they met. Ginnie took a calming breath. "When did Mama realize he loved her?"

"The third time they met. He drove six hours to see her compete and she hadn't even told him where she'd be. I still don't know how he found out." Aunt Roni gave Ginnie's cheek a playful squeeze. "But somehow she knew he'd be there. And when he was, everything changed for her. She fell in love with him and the rest is history."

"*Unread* history ... for me at least." Ginnie thought about the hidden journals and rubbed her other cheek on Calliope's satiny neck, debating on whether to press Aunt Roni's loyalty to Mama. She couldn't stop herself from speaking. "So, *did* you help my mom?"

"I tried. But as you know, it didn't do any good. My father and sister could be as immovable as mountains." Aunt Roni reached for the bridle and clicked. "Your mama knew my sister was stubborn, eh Calliope?" Aunt Roni sighed, then brightened measurably. "Have you ever thought about breeding Calliope?"

"I talked to my dad about it."

"Was he open to the idea?"

"Yeah, but he said it was expensive."

"Given Calliope's pedigree, it would definitely be worth the money to get a good stud."

"That's what Daddy said."

"I'm glad he agrees. Eternal Love was an incredible horse. Maybe Calliope could produce a filly like her grandmama." Aunt Roni ran her hand down the length of Calliope's back and side. "She's in good shape, the right age to breed. She would make a great mama."

"I think Calliope would like that, wouldn't you, girl?" Ginnie stroked her mare's neck and grinned at Aunt Roni. "Do you know any good studs?"

"I just *might*." Aunt Roni pointed to the stirrup. "Why don't you mount her and I'll watch you ride. You seemed to be enjoying yourself when I drove up. You startled me, actually. For a second I thought you were my sister."

"People say that to me all the time. At least the ones who knew my mom." Ginnie studied her aunt's face and felt a kinship. "But you hear that too, don't you?"

She nodded. "Yes, but not much anymore. When we were kids, it bugged me to always be compared to Ginnie. Now ... I just wish she were here."

Ginnie didn't know how to respond, but she knew that sentiment very well.

58

COUSINS

*G*lancing at the sadness coloring Aunt Roni's face, Ginnie had to do something. She put her left foot in the stirrup and then mounted Calliope in one smooth movement.

"Nicely done. Have you ever been to a horse show?" Aunt Roni patted Ginnie's shin, her voice brightening measurably.

"I've been to rodeos."

"Those are fun, but not what I meant." Aunt Roni walked along as Ginnie urged Calliope forward along the side of the house. "I'm talking about a western pleasure show, where you control Calliope's movements with leg pressure and quiet hands. Using signals that the judges either don't notice or barely note as you have her walk, jog, trot, back up, and stop."

An-all-too-familiar frustration surged through Ginnie. "I know what they are, but my dad won't let me compete." Hearing her own anger, she softened her tone. "He doesn't want me to end up like my mom."

"Well, I can certainly sympathize with him, but western pleasure isn't the least bit dangerous. You were riding down the lane faster than you would in a competition. My daughters compete in English pleasure. Which is similar to western, but a different discipline."

"I know about western and English. Like this is a western saddle. Why do your girls do English instead of western--and what are their names?" Ginnie asked quickly and then looked away, embarrassed about not asking about her cousins sooner.

"Genna-Maie is seven, a few months younger than Mysti, and Niqi is five. They ride English because I used to compete in English competitions. Queenie competed in western. We had to compete against each other in pageants because as twins, we were always the same age. We didn't want to do it on our horses. Oh, and their dad— your Uncle Sterling—is British."

"Genna-Maie--like Mama?"

"Yes. Maie was *my* mama's middle name--Serafina Maie. I thought about naming Genna after your mama, but held out hope that Todd would eventually let me reconnect with you and I didn't want that to be awkward." Aunt Roni gave a soft chuckle. "Having two Virginia Maies running around. So I compromised to Genna-Maie--sometimes your mama went by Ginnie Maie."

"Daddy calls me Ginnie Maie sometimes, but it's usually when I'm *almost* in trouble--he calls me Virginia Maie when he's mad at me--or when he's teasing."

"My sister heard her full name quite often when she tried *our* daddy's patience." Aunt Roni offered a conspiratorial wink. "But I think that is a mama and daddy thing--I tend to use my girls' full name when I want them to behave, though I use my younger daughter's full name more than Genna-Maie's."

"Genna-Maie has another name?"

"Yes, We're from the south, so double first names are common. Her full name is Genna-Maie Lucille Stratton Brooks. The 'Lucille' is my mother-in-law's name, so we honored both Sterling and my mamas as well as my sister. My younger daughter is Veronique Joie"

"Veronique? That's different, " Ginnie mused.

"Veronique is french for Veronica. My husband decided to take a page from *your* daddy's book and name her after me--with a french twist." Aunt Roni rolled her eyes and smiled. "My full name is Veronica Joie--spelled J-O-I-E to match the unique spelling of Maie.

We call her Niqi, spelled N-I-Q-I for short. My husband likes 'Q's', and so do I."

"Veronique is pretty *and* unique." Ginnie stroked Calliope's neck. "You know, all my life I have only had boy cousins, twenty-eight of them actually, and all of a sudden--in the last two days I have three girl cousins ... thanks to you and Uncle Jake."

"Jake's had quite the couple of days, hasn't he?" She teased. "I'm glad Jake was here. We dated a couple times, you know."

"No way!" Ginnie tried to imagine Mama's sister and Daddy's brother as a couple. Aunt Roni seemed relaxed in her designer clothes and perfectly applied make-up, but picturing her with prankster Uncle Jake, wasn't working. "And how would I know? You were a huge secret until a couple hours ago."

A hurt look passed over Aunt Roni. "I'm still getting used to that myself."

"If it makes you feel better, we didn't even see pictures of our *mom* until a few weeks ago."

Aunt Roni's hand flew to her mouth. "Really?"

"Yeah. After Mama died, Toran would stand in front of her pictures and cry until he threw up or fell asleep. Daddy said he took her pictures down to help him deal with her death." When Aunt Roni's eyes widened, Ginnie hurried to add. "He meant to put them back up, but he just never did."

"Oh, poor Toran!" Aunt Roni shook her head in sympathy. "He had a hard time dealing with me at her funeral as well. He knew I wasn't her, but he wanted me to be. For his sake, I wished I could have been."

A strange sensation rushed through Ginnie as she recalled briefly being held in a tight hug by a sobbing Aunt Roni. "How did *I* react to you?"

"You knew she was gone. Probably because you were ..." She turned as Vi's purple convertible VW bug slid to a crunchy stop in her parking spot.

Vi got out of the car in a hurry.

The look on Vi's face was indescribable.

Fury and disbelief collided with hurt.

Or perhaps just incredible fury.

Ginnie wasn't exactly sure what emotions she saw, but her belly clenched as Vi stormed toward them, her face a kaleidoscope of unpleasant expressions.

59

MAMA BEAR

By the time Vi reached them at the front of the house, her "Mama Bear" face was set firmly in place. Aunt Roni's friendly smile dimmed. "Hi, Vi."

"Veronica Stratton ... it *is* you." Vi planted her hands on her hips and eyed Aunt Roni suspiciously.

"Yes, it's me. I've missed you." Aunt Roni moved to hug Vi.

Vi stiffened. "Before we act like nothing's happened, *why* are you here?" She gave Ginnie and Calliope a good once-over before folding her arms over her chest.

The front door opened.

Tillie stepped out onto the porch and then jogged down the steps.

"I just came to get reacquainted with my niece and nephew." Aunt Roni nodded at Tillie as she came to a stop in front of Calliope. "And a new niece ... I hope. I miss my sister terribly and being a part of her kids' life. Before you blow up, Todd and I called a truce."

Vi took a step closer to Ginnie. "And how are you?"

"Just fine, Vi." Ginnie tried to keep from laughing at her cousin's serious attitude. "As Uncle Jake would say, you can stand down. She hasn't tried to kidnap us or anything."

Vi crooked her finger and waited for Ginnie to lean forward

before whispering. "I used to love Roni, but your loyalty needs to be to your dad first. Understood?"

"Yes'm." Ginnie swallowed hard, realizing Vi was serious. "But she's not gonna hurt us."

"I hope not." Vi turned her gaze to Tillie. "And you?"

Aunt Roni backed up a step, seeming a bit surprised at Vi's prickliness.

She's not the only one. Geez, Vi.

"She's been really nice to me. I like her," Tillie said.

"Hmmm." Vi turned her magnifying glass on Aunt Roni. "Well, this is the deal. Half of me wants to hug you and go back to being friends. The other half, *the half that's helped raise Ginnie and Toran since Queenie passed*, needs to know that if I let you back in; Todd and the kids won't regret it. We can't go through that again, Roni *We. just. can't.*"

Aunt Roni nodded. "I want a chance to be a part of Ginnie and Toran's lives." She slipped her arm around Tillie's shoulders. "And Tillie's ... and Todd and Amanda's ... if they'll let me. I can't very well embrace Ginnie and Toran and not acknowledge the people they care about most, now can I? Ginnie says she is thrilled to have her best friend become her sister. I know a little about how important that is--*that's* why I'm here. I miss my best friend and sister *so much*. Seeing Ginnie and Toran again for even this short time has healed some hurt immeasurably. I wouldn't dream of becoming a problem for any of them--I can't lose them again."

"I would hope not--because I'm pretty sure you won't be getting a third chance if you cross Todd--or his kids." Vi pointed a determined finger at Aunt Roni. "My family will see to that."

"I remember how well Uncle Ben and his brothers 'circled the wagons' around Todd and the kids after the funeral--so to speak." Aunt Roni gave a resolute nod and then shuddered. "I wouldn't dare invite *that* ire back." She softened her tone. "My daddy isn't long for this world--he would like to mend a few fences before he passes."

The head of steam that Vi was amassing fizzled some as Aunt Roni shared her thoughts.

"My uncles and aunts are *very* protective of Todd and his kids. They *would* make you regret it," Vi assured Aunt Roni, her voice determined--then softening a little before taking on a defensive tone again. "And Queenie's sister or not--I *would* join forces with them--as would *all* of my cousins. As much as I love them--and get frustrated with their Neanderthal ways--*we Wests do look out for our own*--make NO *mistake about that*. Queenie died a West--and honoring Todd's will concerning her and her memory is more than enough motivation to unleash their ire--as you put it. They would definitely be a force you *don't want* to reckon with."

Vi took a step back and searched Aunt Roni's face--for what, Ginnie wasn't sure. But whatever she needed to find, must have been there, because Vi calmed a little. "Well, I know you aren't Queenie, but seeing you here makes me miss her so much." Vi took a step toward her and then stopped.

Ginnie sucked in a concerned breath.

She studied Aunt Roni again, shook her head, and then after a very long minute, gave a sharp nod.

They held each other so tight, Ginnie thought one of them might break or pass out.

When they finally let go of each other, each had tears streaming down her cheeks. "I mean it, Roni. I want to trust you, but if you hurt these kids, you won't get another chance. I'll see to that." She wiped at her tears. "Queenie was the best big sister I could ever ask for."

"You've done a great job with her kids. I know Widget would be pleased." Aunt Roni hugged her again. "And, although she was only older by twenty-three minutes, I agree, she was a very good big sister."

Ginnie blinked back tears for the hundredth time that day.

She glanced at Tillie.

Her best friend's eyes shone as well.

At least they aren't sad tears.

They each giggled at their silliness.

Vi patted Ginnie's shin and Calliope's neck before sweeping Tillie into their hug. "Queenie knew the coolest hairstyles and always did my makeup for dates. It was our tradition." Vi blinked and let out a slow breath. "Now I'm getting married and neither she—nor my mom—will be here for my biggest day ever."

Ginnie felt the sorrow in Vi's voice. She knew Vi and Mama were friends, but hadn't really thought about how Mama being gone would affect her cousin.

"Well, I'm not my sister, but I know a thing or two about hair and makeup. I'd love to help, if you'd be okay with that," Aunt Roni offered.

"It's a nice thought, but I don't expect you to make a second trip so soon." Vi wiped her cheeks. "Though you're welcome to come if you'd like."

"I would love to."

Vi smiled. "Are you sure?"

"Definitely." Aunt Roni gave a determined nod. "I'll be there."

"Aunt Roni, will you help me with my hair too?" Ginnie asked, surprising herself as the words left her mouth.

"You never want to do your hair," Tillie protested.

Ginnie shrugged. "I think I'm tired of braids. Like you said, we're going into seventh grade. I should try some new hairstyles."

Vi eyed her suspiciously.

Like Tillie, Vi had tried many times to talk Ginnie out of her braids.

Ginnie locked her eyes on Vi's. *Please don't make a big deal out of this.*

Vi seemed to understand her silent plea. "Clarissa and Amanda will be here soon. Girls, why don't you start the chores and Roni and I'll catch up while we start dinner."

Ginnie wanted to keep visiting with her aunt, but swallowed her protest when Vi shot her a warning look. "Yes ma'am. Can Tillie and I go for a quick ride first?"

Vi glanced at her watch and nodded.

Ginnie patted the saddle. "Tillie, want to ride with me?"

"Sure." Tillie followed them to one of the wrought iron chairs next to the side porch to help her mount.

Ginnie offered her hand to Tillie and helped her up behind the saddle. Tillie slid her arms around Ginnie's waist. "Oh, Aunt Roni? Uncle Ben wanted me to let you know you got a phone call. He didn't answer it because it was in your purse, but he thought you'd want to know."

"Thank you, Tillie. I'll check it in a minute. Ride safe you two." Aunt Roni gave a soft pat to Ginnie and Tillie's legs and then turned to Vi. "Shall we start dinner now?"

Vi waved goodbye to Ginnie and Tillie. "Go get a riding helmet for Tillie."

"Yes ma'am," they chorused, with Ginnie adding an eye roll.

Aunt Roni opened the side porch door and waited for Vi to walk through.

Tillie giggled. "They act like old friends."

"I think they were." A pang of jealousy struck Ginnie. "But you couldn't tell a couple minutes ago. I thought Vi was going to take Aunt Roni's head off."

"That's not good."

"No kidding. But guess what?"

"What?"

"Aunt Roni might be able to get us a good deal on a stud fee. Wouldn't it be cool to train a colt or filly from birth? Like Mama did with Eternal Love?"

"But you don't know anything about training horses."

"So? Aunt Roni does. She'll help me. You heard her. She just wants to be a part of our lives." Ginnie tapped Calliope's side and steered her up the hill toward the barn to get the helmet. "I may not have my mom, but I have Aunt Roni. How cool is that?"

Ginnie felt Tillie's arms tighten around her waist. "Yeah, how cool."

60

LAME IS IN THE EYE OF THE BEHOLDER

*I*t's *NOT cool! It's not cool AT ALL!* Tillie wanted to scream. *Aunt Roni is going to ruin everything! You'll want her more than my mom, and then we won't be a real family.*

Tears burned Tillie's eyes. *Why did DT's secret have to be Ginnie's mom's identical twin sister?*

Cringing, Tillie recalled pleading with DT to let Aunt Roni stay for Ginnie's sake.

She shivered, hating how she now regretted helping her best friend.

I'm horrible. Ginnie's finally happy and I'm miserable. I'm a lousy sister.

"I hope Calliope has a filly. Wouldn't it be cool if my future daughter could ride Calliope's future daughter? And carry on that tradition? That would be totally awesome sauce!" Ginnie practically sang the words.

"Sure." Tillie forced the word to sound enthusiastic.

"And Aunt Roni was telling me about a horse competition my dad can't object to. No way could I get hurt. And the best thing is, my mom used to do it! And I bet she rocked at it. I'm sure I can't ask him right away, but maybe after he gets over being mad that Aunt Roni came, he'll be open to the idea. What do you think?"

I think it's not fair that you get a horse and I don't.

Tillie shrugged. "He's already told you 'no.' Maybe you shouldn't bug him about it."

Or ... maybe you should and he'll change his mind and send Aunt Roni away because she's a bad influence.

"Tillie, quit being lame."

"Fine. Ask him. And while you're at it, see if he'll let me get a horse too. My mom said she'd buy me one if we could afford to care for it. When they get married, your dad would let me stable a horse in the barn, right?"

"Duh. Hmmm. Well, he did say he didn't want to give you a horse for your birthday, because he didn't always like having Calliope. But on the other hand, he also said he'd consider breeding her, so maybe he'll change his mind. After all, you're right." Ginnie swiveled to grin at Tillie. "We're gonna be 'for real' sisters. You should have a horse if I have one."

"True." *No argument there.*

The gloomy feeling that had begun to tangle itself into Tillie's belly loosened. "And Christmas is coming. Do you think they might be married by then?"

"Your mom says she doesn't want to rush things."

"No, she didn't!" Panic lashed through Tillie.

"Yes, she did." Ginnie moved to face her friend. "She told me she liked dating my dad because he was fun and romantic ... like Prince Charming." Ginnie rolled her eyes. "I told her she was nuts, but she acted serious. She also said she wasn't in any hurry to get married."

The tangle-y feeling twisted into a knot. "She wouldn't say that. She *wants* to marry him."

"Oh, she wants to marry him all right. But she wants to date him for a while first." Ginnie laughed, making the tangle-y knot tighten.

Tillie clenched her fists. "It's not funny."

"Yes, it is. And as opposite as our moms are, they both seem to love him ... *a lot*, for whatever reason." Ginnie's voice lost its teasing tone. "I just can't figure out *why*."

"There's nothing to figure. Your dad's *nice*."

Ginnie faced forward and stopped Calliope at the end of the lane. "Well, he's something. Now that we know his secret, maybe he'll quit being so lame."

She wheeled Calliope around and headed back toward the farmhouse.

"He's *not* lame," Tillie shouted.

And for the first time ever, she smacked her very best friend.

61

HARD TRUTHS

*H*ey!" Ginnie turned to find Tillie's jaw hanging open like the back flap of a pair of old-fashioned long-johns. Her friend's look confirmed what she thought she'd felt ... Tillie did too slap her back. "What gives?"

"He's *not* lame," Tillie growled.

Ginnie didn't know how to respond.

She stopped Calliope and swiveled to face her friend.

Tillie's cheeks flamed red. "Your dad is awesome and you don't even realize it."

"You hit me because of my dad? He's okay, but ..."

"He's *more* than okay." Tillie steeled her eyes on Ginnie's. "Why do you think I want our folks to get married? *I hate Jasper*. He hurt me. Your dad treats me better than Jasper ever did." Her voice vaulted to a higher pitch. "I *hate* it when you call him lame. He's *not* lame. He loves you so much and you're too *pigheaded* to realize."

Indignation burned.

Ginnie's eyes narrowed.

She jabbed her finger at Tillie. "I *do* know he loves me. I *also* know he's not perfect ... which *you* think he is. He's *not*. He shouldn't have kept Aunt Roni from me."

Tillie clamped her jaw shut and looked away.

A fury ignited in Ginnie. "If he had let her see me, I wouldn't have felt so ... I don't know ... like something important was always missing."

"Well, maybe it's better to not have a mom than to have a dad who hates you." Tillie toggled her head and grimaced. "The last time I saw Jasper, Mom had to stop him from hurting me and then he threw a vase at her. It hit the wall instead and crashed into a million pieces."

Horror replaced Ginnie's fury.

Tears burned Ginnie's eyes as she pictured Tillie's bruised face on a long ago night in kindergarten when Miss Amanda had arrived at the farm, begging for help.

Ginnie hated how helpless she had felt that night.

Tillie had cried, shaking uncontrollably when Ginnie had hugged her.

No matter what she or the other people in her family tried to do to comfort Tillie, her friend shook, her eyes haunted by a memory they couldn't erase.

"I'm sorry I don't sound like a good friend, but I'm *NOT* sorry you had *two* parents that loved you when I only have *one*." Tillie's sarcasm kicked the rest of Ginnie's anger to the curb.

Frustration percolated as she considered Tillie's words, but completely fizzled out when her friend's hands flew to her face and she broke into sobs.

Ginnie wanted to stay mad, but couldn't.

Her self-appointed role as Tillie's protector kicked in.

She didn't know how to fix this, but she wanted Tillie to feel better.

"Sorry," Ginnie mumbled. "Sometimes I feel like you're only my friend because you want my dad."

"That's not true. But I want him to love me." Tillie's voice dropped to a whisper. "Jasper doesn't. Do you know how it feels to be hated by someone who's *supposed* to love you?"

"Jasper loves you. Uncle Jake told you he left so he wouldn't hurt you anymore. And that he used to brag about you. It's not as cool as doing stuff with you, but it still means he loves you."

"You don't get it."

"Get what?"

Tillie swallowed hard and folded her arms across her chest. "If your dad adopts me, that means he chooses me. If he *chooses* me, then I'm lovable. If someone as nice as him can't love me, then nobody *else* will ever love me either."

It was Ginnie's turn to drop her jaw like a long-john flap.

She turned away.

The pain in her friend's eyes was just too hard to see.

62

TILLIE'S DUNGEON

The hot June breeze swept Ginnie's face, surprising her when her cheeks felt cool. Her efforts to not cry must have been in vain—too stunned by Tillie's words to feel the tears streaming down her cheeks. Pressure pounded behind her eyes as she shook her head to erase the pain of Tillie's words.

But the pain didn't stop.

It scratched and slithered into places Ginnie didn't want to see, dripping with hurt and venom, staining each comforting word she tried to utter with an ugly black truth she didn't want to acknowledge.

Of course Tillie is loveable.

I love her.

Dad loves her.

Our whole family loves her.

How can Tillie believe what she just said?

Another glance at her friend confirmed Ginnie's suspicion, sickening her.

Tillie DID believe what she said.

As wrong as she was, Tillie believed her words to be true.

Ginnie knew it didn't matter whether Dad adopted Tillie or not, he would always love her.

After all, he still loved Mama.

But Tillie wouldn't hear those words.

Her friend was imprisoned in a false picture of herself that only Tillie could see and feel.

Numb, Ginnie forced her gaze back to Tillie's face.

She could no longer see the horrors behind her friend's eyes.

Tillie's hands covered them.

Her friend cried harder, her body wracked with sorrow, shaking uncontrollably as her misery deepened.

And still, Ginnie couldn't move, paralyzed by Tillie's agony.

Ginnie's back ached, protesting the uncomfortable position she'd placed it, contorting out of her physical comfort zone. She resisted moving to ease the discomfort.

She couldn't worry about her own physical pain when she couldn't fix Tillie's emotional pain. She reached to hug her friend and had to stop.

Her body couldn't twist that far. She slid back in the saddle and arched her leg over Calliope's neck. Ginnie had to grip both ends of the saddle to keep from sliding off her mare.

Her movements jarred Tillie, who lowered her hands.

The misery that emanated from Tillie's eyes took Ginnie's breath away, forcing her heart to pound in her ears at the same time it drained the air from her lungs.

She felt like she might have drowned right then and there, except Calliope snorted, shook her head, and sent a ripple from her neck to her tail, jerking each of them.

Sliding down the saddle, Ginnie fumbled for the edges.

One hand gripped, one didn't.

Her upper arm muscles burned as she tried to right herself, but her lower body kept going. She landed in a squat on the gravel lane, the soles of her feet protesting the sudden stop, squishing her toes against the leather limits of her cowboy boots.

Saliva swished by her teeth as she sucked in a breath.

Pain vibrated under the pad of her right foot where her boot hadn't dissipated the pressure from landing on a pointy rock.

"Are you all right?"

Ginnie glanced up.

Tillie's concerned voice swept the gloom away.

Relief made Ginnie bob her head. "Are you?"

Tillie shrugged. "I will be."

Will you? Ginnie wanted to ask. *How can you be?*

Ginnie didn't believe her. She had just peeked into Tillie's darkest place and Ginnie couldn't escape the hurt imprisoned there, the fragrance of doom permeated every breath in that ink-black void. If Ginnie couldn't shake off the misery, how could her best friend?

Her quick visit to Tillie's private dungeon stained the incredible joy she had experienced just moments before ... making her happiness at finding Aunt Roni seem like a dream that happened a lifetime ago.

Tillie lifted her leg high enough to arc over the saddle and slide off Calliope's rump. She landed next to Ginnie pretty much on her feet, with more grace than Ginnie had.

"You can't tell him that. I'd die." Tillie's words gripped her throat as surely as her friend's hands now grasped Ginnie's arms.

Tillie shook her. "Promise me you won't tell him. *Please.* You have to promise."

"But it's not true. Daddy *does* love you. Even if he didn't marry your mom for some crazy, unthinkable reason, he could never *not* love you, Tillie. It just wouldn't happen."

"It already did. With *Jasper.* He supposedly *had* to love me ... and he doesn't." Her nails drilled into Ginnie's arms. "Your dad doesn't have to, but he might."

"You're not listening, Tillie. Daddy *already* loves you."

"Just as your friend. And my mom's daughter. Not as *his* daughter. I need him to want me, maybe not as much as he wants you ... but almost as much." Her cheeks reddened more as her tears flowed freer. "My mom loves *you* like that, and ... you don't even want her too."

Ginnie shook her head. "No, she doesn't."

"*Yes. She. Does.*" Tillie swiped at her cheeks. It didn't help, new tears replenished the stream. "But you don't care about that. You only care about *your* mom. And even though your mom died, you get to have a zillion great moms and I can't even have *one good dad.*"

Tillie's tone turned from pleading to poisonous, striking an ugliness in Ginnie that she didn't want to comprehend.

She took a step back. "What are you talking about?"

Tillie rolled her eyes. "I don't want Jasper, but I do want *one* good memory of him. I don't have *any!* Your mom dies and you get Vi. Then Vi gets engaged and you want your mom. And just like that, you find her journals! And you get a zillion great memories of your mom. What do I get? *Nightmares*, that's what."

"Hey!" Ginnie objected. "*Hello-o-o!* My mom is *dead.* You have yours. *And she's great.*"

Tillie waved Ginnie's protest into the cloudless blue sky. "*You* get your mom's journals, you get *MY* mom, *and now ...*" Tillie spat the words. "You even get an aunt, who looks just like your perfect, gorgeous, beauty queen mom ... who loves you, *too.* It's. Just. *Wrong!*"

Ginnie raised her arms as Tillie's hand flew at her face. She grabbed at the hand, but realized too late that timid, mousy Tillie had disappeared.

Instead of immobilizing her friend, Ginnie struggled to keep from being clawed.

After digging her boots in the lane, Ginnie pushed against Tillie's fury while gripping her friend's wrist. "Stop it! I don't want to hurt you!"

"It's not fair!"

"What am I supposed to do about it?"

Glaring, Tillie snatched her wrist from Ginnie's grip. "I dunno, but whatever happens, it'll be good ... for *you.* It always is. You always get what you want and I get *nothing.*"

"That's not true."

"Yes. It. Is." Tillie's hand flew in slow motion this time.

Ginnie lunged under it and bulldozed her friend.

Tillie dropped.

Her scathing glance disappeared as her mouth formed a capital "O."

She hit the gravel lane, bouncing slightly, like a ten-pound bowling ball.

Ginnie's mouth mimicked Tillie's, making it easy for the bowling ball to jump down her throat and knock her on her denimed rear.

63

HOUSE OF CARDS

illie felt like a lead balloon, free-falling until her palms scraped the gravel lane and she hurt her wrist on impact. "Oomph!"

After jerking her head forward, Tillie watched Ginnie push herself into a sitting position. "Thanks, Til."

"Any time," Tillie snapped, sliding her hands down her jeans to brush off the tiny rocks sticking to her sweaty palms. "And by the way, *you* pushed *me!*"

"Because *you* started it. I was just defending myself."

Tillie started to protest, then realized her friend was right.

She *had* tried to hit Ginnie ... again.

Leaning back, the fury that made her charge at her best friend, fizzled.

Horror and disgust swooped in to fill the void.

What have I done? No way will Ginnie be my sister now. What if she tells DT? He'll never forgive me. Never.

Blinking back tears, Tillie thought back to the one and only time DT had ever punished her.

Just before school ended she, Ginnie, and Toran had gotten into a fight with the biggest bully in sixth grade at the movies and kept it from their dad.

When DT found out, he made all three of them sweep and vacuum the floors and dust all of the furniture. But before he did, he had asked Tillie what happened and had really listened when she explained that Pierce had started it.

DT had even said he wouldn't have punished them at all, if they had only been honest and told him about the fight before Pierce's dad ratted them out.

After he talked with Tillie, DT had offered her a cookie almost as an apology for punishing her, while Ginnie and Toran finished their chores. He gave Tillie the choice of being an honorary West kid or an honorary Taylor-West kid before he made the three of them start the chores. Tillie was so happy that she was an honorary West that she wasn't even bothered that he punished her.

For once, she really believed that she could be a West--for real.

But that was different. *Ginnie* had knocked Pierce down.

It was one thing for DT to blame Ginnie for that fight, and bust all three of them, but Ginnie was still his daughter.

I'm just her friend. And I'm not even a good one anymore. He won't send her away ... and he won't stop loving her. An acidic burning clawed her throat, rushing upwards.

She tried to swallow the rising bile, but gagged instead.

Tillie flipped onto her hands and knees and threw up.

As she heaved, she barely noticed Ginnie crawling up next to her to hold her hair out of the way.

Her throat burned.

Her belly hurt.

She couldn't stop her tears any more than she could stop heaving.

So she quit trying and gave in to the tears ... again.

It's not fair. It's all ruined. All of her plans, all of her hopes. DT would never love her now and Ginnie would stop being her friend.

When the dry heaves subsided, Tillie crawled a few feet away from the mess and collapsed onto the grass.

Ginnie followed her. "Tillie, it's okay."

"No, it's not." She shook her head. "It's never gonna be okay again. Go away."

She couldn't pretend that she was normal anymore ... or that she was lovable.

Maybe people could love the Tillie who tried hard to please everybody, but she couldn't be that Tillie any more.

She didn't have the strength.

As soon as everybody found out what she did, they would be done with her.

They certainly wouldn't miss *her*.

Mysti was Uncle Jake's *real* daughter and Aunt Roni was Ginnie's *real* aunt.

Real family.

It didn't matter how much she wanted it to be true, Tillie would never be a *real* West, even if her mom married Ginnie's dad.

Tillie was just a Taylor and she would always be just a Taylor.

A loser ... just like Jasper.

She squeezed her eyes shut until the sunlight vanished, wishing she could make herself disappear just as easily.

64

THE COMPROMISE

*T*illie stop crying." Ginnie shook her friend. "You're scaring me." The only response she got was silent tears that creeped her out.

"Go away! You have your aunt now. Leave me alone." Tillie rolled onto her side and then into a ball. "You don't need me anymore."

"What are you talking about?" Ginnie shook her again. "Quit being a drama queen. Of course I need you. You're my best friend and you're gonna be my sister. *Talk* to me."

Calliope snorted and pawed at the ground.

Ginnie hitched a thumb at her horse. "Even Calliope thinks you should talk to me. Why are you so jealous of Aunt Roni?" Ginnie sat back on the heels of her cowboy boots. "And why do you hate my mom so much?"

Tillie sat up quickly, looking surprised that Ginnie would say that. "I don't hate your mom."

What does she expect me to think?

"Well, you coulda fooled me."

"You don't understand."

"*Duh.*" Ginnie clamped her jaw shut to keep from finishing her

snarky thought. *Yeah, you're huge drama scream about all of my "moth-*
ers" made no sense. YOUR mom is alive.

"Go away." Tillie pushed her hair out of her face. "Or bring me a
drink and *then* go away."

Ginnie glanced at her friend. She was pale and shaking. She
probably did need a drink. "Fine. I'll bring you a drink. Do you want
to talk to Vi or Uncle Ben? They can help you feel better."

"No! You can't say anything to them!" Tillie dropped her head
onto her knees. "Please."

"Tillie, what gives? Why are you so mad at me?"

Tillie clamped her mouth shut and locked her eyes on Ginnie.

The pain in them forced hot tears to well.

Ginnie turned to concentrate on the corn growing on the other
side of the lane. "I thought you *wanted* your mom to be my mom ... so
we could be sisters for real. Or did you just want *my* dad to be *your*
dad?"

A gasp escaped Tillie.

She shook her head.

That's it!

"You don't want to share your mom ... just my dad?"

The thought irritated Ginnie.

Tillie shook her head.

"Then what?"

Moaning, Tillie hid her face on her knees.

"I'm running out of ideas." Ginnie searched the crazy schemes
bouncing around her brain like bingo balls in a cage.

Unable to find a brilliant solution to this craziness, Ginnie offered
a compromise. "I'll get you a drink. Will you promise to tell me everything when I get back?"

Tillie didn't respond.

"Fine, then I'm bringing back Vi."

That did it.

The desperation in Tillie's eyes turned to panic.

She grabbed at Ginnie. "You can't!"

Moving out of her reach, Ginnie stood, feeling much better.

She smirked. "Then you better be ready to spill when I get back, or I'm bringing *both* Vi and Uncle Ben."

"You better not."

"Then get a grip." Panic might not be better than desperation for Tillie, but it was a lot easier for Ginnie to deal with.

She tried not to smile when Tillie glared at her. "Sorry, but you gotta snap out of this."

"Says you. *Your life is perfect*," Tillie snarled.

"Whatever." They exchanged glares until Ginnie mounted Calliope. "I'll be right back." She tried to make her voice light, even though she was getting angry with Tillie's accusations.

You've totally ruined Aunt Roni coming.

So my life really rocks right now.

NOT.

65

TRUSTING TORAN

*G*innie leaned into the breeze as she rode Calliope toward the farmhouse and rubbed at her cheeks. She hoped the wind would finish drying her face so that no one could tell she'd been bawling. *Sugar beets!*

No way could she let anyone know Tillie was nutburgers at the moment.

Even though Ginnie was frustrated with her best friend, she couldn't make good on her threat to involve Uncle Ben or Vi.

Tillie was too upset for Ginnie to ignore her plea ... unless she absolutely couldn't figure out how to help Tillie get a grip.

Why is she so jealous of Mama? She's not even here ... and why did Tillie say I don't need her now that I have Aunt Roni?

Ginnie slid off Calliope. She slipped the leather reins through the large metal circle hanging from the mouth of the black horsehead hitching post, slid her hand down Calliope's neck, and followed the sidewalk to the side porch door.

She swiped at her cheeks and forced a smile to her lips before quietly opening the door and stepping onto the porch.

Ginnie scanned the doorway leading to the kitchen.

Vi was stirring something on the stove. Uncle Ben and Aunt Roni sat with their backs to her at the kitchen bar, chopping cucumbers and carrots for a salad.

Ginnie tiptoed to the porch fridge to sneak a root beer.

She snatched the brown can, turned back to the red painted screen door, and slipped out as quietly as she came in, catching the door before it could slam.

She fled down the sidewalk.

"Hey!"

Chilled blood sludged through her veins.

Ginnie stopped, then turned slowly toward the voice behind her.

Her hand flew to her heart. "Toran! You scared me."

Relief warmed the blood.

He grinned. "That's what you get for sneaking. What are you hiding?"

Smirking, she jiggled the can of root beer. "*Where* were *you* hiding?"

"I wasn't hiding. I came out the kitchen doorway the same time you dodged out the screen door. I said 'hi', but you didn't hear me."

Ginnie rolled her eyes. "I just needed a drink."

She headed back to Calliope.

"Hold up." Toran caught up to her and sucked spit through his teeth. "Ow."

"What's wrong?" Ginnie turned.

"My ribs." He held his side. "What's wrong with *you*?"

"Nothing. *You're* the one who said 'ow.'"

"That's not what I meant *and you know it*." He leveled her with his "magnifying glass" look.

Ginnie swiveled, uncomfortable with the intenseness of his stare. "No, I don't."

"Yes. You. *Do*. You know you're supposed to ask for sodas. And you're wearing your 'guilty' face."

"Nuh-uh."

"*Uh-HUH*." Toran's understanding tone turned harsh. "There's been enough secrets. What's up?"

Ginnie turned away.

He grabbed her upper arm. "I asked you a question."

"*Let. Go.*" She colored each word with warning.

"I'm done with all the secrets. What's going on?"

"What're you talking about?" She jerked her arm. He held on for a second longer before releasing it. "You know—the *secrets.* The journals, Mysti, Aunt Roni, and whatever you're hiding *right now*. I'm tired of you knowing things before me and not telling me. When did you decide not to trust me anymore?"

The hurt in his voice made her pause. "What are you talking about? I trust you."

"Yeah ... right." He shoved his hand into his front jean pocket. "I only found out about Mama's journals because you were mad at Uncle Jake for taking them away from you."

"*He* didn't take them away from me—Dad did. *YOU were there.* So no secret."

Toran ignored her protest. "You knew about Mysti the night before I found out—"

" ... *because* I had a nightmare—in the middle of the night. Then Uncle Jake made me prom—"

"You still could have told me."

"No, I couldn't!" Ginnie shook her head. "I wanted to, but Dad said not to tell."

Anger or hurt ... or maybe both, flashed through his eyes.

Ginnie softened her tone and reached for his elbow. "I found out about Aunt Roni just before you did. I'm sorry you weren't here when she came. But I honestly had no idea. I was just as shocked as you."

Toran moved his elbow out from under her hand and backed up a step. "Fine."

He didn't sound the least bit fine.

"It's the truth. I swear."

"Whatever." He turned away from her.

"Tor, I'm telling you the truth."

He swiveled toward her and hung his thumb on his pocket. "Fine, then tell me your *new* secret."

"I don't have a secret."

"You should stop lying. You're not good at it."

She grimaced. "I'm *not* lying."

"Then *don't* tell me." Toran scowled at her and whirled toward the porch. "See if I care."

Ginnie knew he cared very much.

The sludge-y chilled blood feeling returned.

Apparently it was *his* turn to deny the truth.

She followed him. "Toran."

He ignored her and reached for the door handle.

"Toran!"

He turned long enough to let his scowl deepen to a glare before shaking his head in disgust.

The same awful helpless feeling she'd had in the lane not very long ago swept over her, forcing the confession to her lips and out her mouth before she could stop.

"It's not *my* secret ... it's *Tillie's*."

66

TEAM WEST

Something about the way Ginnie said "It's Tillie's" panicked Toran. He took a good look at his sister. Her gaze didn't quite meet his. Her lip trembled. She blinked like she might cry ... something she rarely did. "Is Tillie okay?"

"I don't think so." Ginnie's quiet whisper made his heart hammer. "She's talking crazy ... and she just threw up. The soda is for her."

As one, they swiveled toward the lane and jogged quickly down the sidewalk.

All of Toran's anger fizzled as he followed his twin to Calliope. "Where is she?"

"In the lane." Ginnie untied Calliope's rein.

Toran mounted.

"Tillie's scaring me. She hates Mama and Aunt Roni and I've no idea why."

That can't be right. Toran shook his head. "Tillie doesn't hate anybody. It's not in her to hate." He reached a hand to Ginnie, pulling her when she put her foot in the stirrup.

He scooted forward as she swung up behind him, then adjusted behind the saddle.

"It is now." Ginnie wrapped her arms around his waist. "And she thinks Daddy doesn't love her."

"That's insane."

"*You* tell her. She's not listening to me."

Toran might have accused his sister of exaggerating, but the misery in her voice couldn't be faked.

He wheeled Calliope toward the lane, and pushed down the rising concern.

Whatever was going on couldn't be good.

Toran knew one thing for sure: Ginnie wasn't a very good liar.

Tillie must be in real trouble.

67

THRUMMING

Tillie's head throbbed. Each thrum made her queasier. She just wanted her stomach to settle so she could think of more important things ... like disappearing forever.

Moaning through her misery, she slid her cheek off her arm onto the cool grass, squeezed her eyes shut, and breathed in the relaxing scent of the growing plants around her. The sweet smell of cornstalks calmed the thrumming and eased her nausea.

The alfalfa wasn't as soothing, but still pleasant.

The grass smelled more like dirt than grass.

Duh. Because my nose is practically in the ground.

She wondered if Ginnie was ever going to come back.

Tillie couldn't blame her if she didn't.

If she were Ginnie, she wouldn't.

Well, she would, but she wouldn't want to.

What if she brings Vi or Uncle Ben even though I told her not to? Tillie sat up way too quick, instantly regretting the motion.

The thrumming pounded her head and her nausea returned full force.

Uncle Ben would take one look at her and know she'd been nothing but a fake all these years.

The Tillie he knew ... was gone.

She moaned again, hating her uncooperative body.

There was nothing left to throw up ... except maybe the lies she'd been telling herself for the last few months.

Lies like DT could actually love her when even Jasper didn't.

Lies like Ginnie really wanted to be her sister.

Lies like Tillie could be a *real* West.

When those lies came up, Ginnie would see the horrific mess she'd been concealing for so long.

Tillie eased to the ground and curled into a ball, trying to shut out the sounds of her own mind.

Every thought burned like a hot needle.

Somehow the rushing, splashing sounds of the brook poked through the symphony of self-loathing and cooled the hot poking enough to offer a reprieve so she could take a breath every now and again.

The panic slowed.

Her tummy settled.

Tillie clung to the sounds of water crashing against the rocks, hoping each wave would whisk away the ugliness that overwhelmed her and whirl away her worries.

Eventually the pounding in her head softened to gentler humming that she almost welcomed.

Her breathing eased.

She drifted into the dream-like state that hovered between reality and blissful sleep.

The sun felt too warm on her face, but Tillie dared not move.

Inside she felt nothing.

I can deal with nothing.

Nothing didn't hurt.

Then nothing disappeared.

The pounding returned ... but not in her head.

Where's it coming from?

The pounding grew louder.

Tillie opened her eyelids only to be blinded by the afternoon sun.

Her eyes watered.

She snapped them shut.

Pounding hammered her ears.

She buried her face in the crook of her arm.

"Whoa, girl." A boy's voice said just before boots hit the ground.

Toran. Ginnie brought Toran? How could she? She promised ... well ... sorta she promised.

Tillie couldn't let Toran see her like this.

He was like Uncle Ben ... a human lie detector.

Maybe he would believe that she was lying here because she was sick, but if he looked into her eyes ... he would know that she was a fraud.

And she couldn't bear it if he found out.

BUNNIES AND BULLDOGS

*T*he whole way down the lane, Toran hoped Ginnie was wrong. But as soon as he saw Tillie lying pale in the grass, he knew she wasn't.

His heart pounded as he rushed to Tillie, only stopping when she buried her face deeper into the crook of her arm instead of looking at him.

He knew why.

Tillie didn't like attention being called to her, even when she deserved it for doing something good.

They were alike that way, happy to go quietly under the radar and let people like Ginnie or Austin live in the spotlight. Ginnie thrived in the center of attention.

Toran managed okay when he needed to, and on occasion, he even enjoyed it.

But Tillie didn't ... she withered.

If Ginnie was right about Tillie hating Mama and Aunt Roni, then there was a lot more going on with her that she didn't want them to know.

Tillie didn't feel things lightly.

She stewed and simmered forever, just like he did.

After putting his hand up in a 'whoa' motion to Ginnie, Toran nodded at their friend.

Ginnie scowled, then seemed a little relieved.

Toran knew Ginnie's love for Tillie was great.

He also knew his twin didn't deal well with situations that called for an extra dose of patience.

He squatted until he sat on his boot heels. "Hey, Tillie."

She stiffened before covering her red-rimmed eyes with her hand to shield them from the sun.

Tillie kept them closed.

"Hey, Toran." Her lips forced a surprised smile.

He decided to play along and returned the smile even though she couldn't see it.

"Ginnie said you threw up. Are you feeling sick?" Toran motioned at his sister for the can of root beer.

Ginnie handed it over.

When Tillie nodded, Toran popped the top, then offered first his arm to help her sit up, and then the soda. "This should make you feel better."

Tillie gave Toran a grateful smile, but narrowed her eyes at Ginnie, before taking a small gulp of soda.

Pink colored her cheeks.

Tillie took another sip and seemed to perk up. Only she still wouldn't look at him.

"Better?" Toran asked.

She lowered her chin and nodded.

"Good." Toran glanced at Ginnie.

Her eyes widened expectantly.

He shook his head and sat next to Tillie. "Wanna talk?"

"Nothin' to talk about." She turned toward the alfalfa field. "Must've ate something I shouldn't have. Thanks for the soda. It's making me feel much better."

Toran might have believed her bright tone ... *if* she had looked at him.

When she didn't, he knew she was going to hide inside herself again ... because that's what she did.

He suspected that's why Uncle Jake called her 'Turtle.' She protected her rawest feelings by shoving them so deep no one could see them, just like the inside of a turtle shell.

Ginnie sat down beside them and drummed her fingers impatiently on her knees.

Toran knew he wouldn't have long to figure out how to get Tillie to open up before Ginnie barged in. "Are you sure? Because we're your friends. Ginnie and I just want to help."

The sideways glance Tillie threw his twin could only be described as scathing. "*I'm fine.*"

Toran didn't miss the warning in their friend's tone.

When Ginnie's jaw tightened, he knew she hadn't either.

Toran made sure his next words sounded welcoming. "Good. Want to go back to the farmhouse? You can ride Calliope or we could walk." He hoped she would choose the latter.

Before Dad and Miss Amanda started dating, Toran had considered dating Tillie when they were older. Now that she was going to be his sister, he tried not to think of her as a regular girl, but still, they understood each other in a way that Ginnie and he didn't, even though they were twins.

She squeezed his knee and brightened her smile. "I'm fine. *Really.* Must've been bad tuna fish or something."

Ginnie rolled her eyes. "Or something."

Toran gave his sister a quick shake of his head. "Must be. But if it's not, we can still talk about it. We're family, you know. It's what we do: Uncle Ben Lecture Number Four. Memorize it, there'll be a test."

Tillie groaned at his joke and then giggled.

He laughed softly with her.

She relaxed for a few seconds and let her guard down.

This was the Tillie he liked to see. She reminded him more of a bunny rabbit than a turtle ... gentle, quiet, and ready to flee at any hint of trouble.

Although when Tillie pleaded with Dad to let Aunt Roni stay,

Tillie reminded Toran of Piglet sacrificing his home for Eeyore. Going wa-a-a-y out of her comfort zone—at a high personal cost—all because she loved her best friend.

Like the timid, but brave, unsung hero she was.

Toran had wanted to applaud Tillie's plea, but knew that would send her running—and his dad probably wouldn't have been very understanding either.

Toran's thoughts tumbled about his mind like convoluted Tetris blocks.

If he thought about it long enough or kept manipulating the blocks of this situation, he could figure this whole thing out and maybe help Tillie in the process.

He smiled at Tillie and stood, offering her his hand.

She looked away and down, before staring straight into the alfalfa.

Her lips trembled. She licked them and sighed, before lowering her head to her knees.

Ginnie stood. "Tillie, I promised not to bring Vi or Uncle Ben if you'd talk to me. This *isn't* talking to me."

If Tillie was timid like a bunny rabbit, then Ginnie was tenacious as a bulldog.

69

SNAP OUT OF IT

Ginnie ignored Toran as he waved away her impatience. She'd had enough of Tillie's misery. It had always been Ginnie's job to look out for Tillie and she wasn't about to quit now that she'd seen that horrific, sad, dark place hiding deep inside her best friend.

"Ginnie," Toran said, using his warning voice.

"What? She *promised*. I can't stand seeing her like this." Ginnie's hands flew to her hips. "She's stuck in a bad place and I want her to feel better. I *also* want to know why she hates Mama and Aunt Roni."

Tillie jerked her head from her knees and looked at Toran. "I don't hate your mom." She swiped at her tears and scrambled to her feet. "Or Aunt Roni."

"That's not what you said a little while ago."

"I said 'you don't need me,' not that I hate either of them." Tillie turned to Toran. "I don't hate your mom. I *promise*."

"I know you don't." Toran glared at Ginnie and took a step in front of Tillie. "Ginnie just misunderstood."

Ginnie crossed her arms. "Fine, you don't hate them, but you *are* jealous. Why? Mama is *dead*. It's not like she's gonna come back and break up Daddy and Miss Amanda."

Tillie gasped and hid her face in her hands.

"Ginnie!" Toran scolded.

"Don't *'Ginnie'* me. Tillie started the plan of us being sisters and getting Daddy and Miss Amanda to date." Ginnie moved around her brother so she could see straight into Tillie's eyes. "I love your mom. But just because she's gonna be my stepmom doesn't mean I don't want to know my *real* mom. Aunt Roni just wants to help me get to know her. Why isn't that okay?"

"It *is* okay." Tillie dropped her hands. "You don't understand."

"*Duh.* Help me figure it out." Ginnie rolled her eyes. "You're talking in riddles."

"Ginnie, stop!" Toran stepped between them.

Tillie burst into tears.

Toran slid his arm around her shoulders and glared. "I mean it, Virginia West! Don't say another word!"

The warning in her twin's voice stopped Ginnie's protest in her throat.

Tillie melted into Toran's arms and sobbed.

Toran rubbed her shoulder. "It's okay, Tillie."

Ginnie glanced between the two of them several times like a hiccupping kangaroo, in turn wanting to protest Toran's decree, as well as apologize for causing Tillie more misery.

She finally went with neither.

"Tillie, I love you. But I can't stand seeing you so sad. I'll listen to what you have to say, but you actually have to *talk* to me." Ginnie offered the brightest smile she could muster and wiped her cheeks. "And quit crying ... you're giving me a headache."

70

TOTALLY DOUBLE DUH!

*T*he silence screamed.

The scream joined the loud hammering of Tillie's heart and the thrumming of pulsating blood through her ears. For how long she stood like that, Tillie didn't know.

Then a warm breeze swept the lane and a soft rustle of growing alfalfa accompanied the melody of quacking ducks flying overhead.

Tillie's panicked thoughts swirled wildly in her head while Ginnie waited expectantly in front of her and Toran to her side.

No matter how hard she tried, Tillie couldn't find the words that would make her friends understand.

Even if she wanted to, she had no voice to speak the things she had shoved into the darkest corners of the closet of her memory ... and she did *not* want to speak them.

Speaking them might bring them out where she couldn't control them.

She'd been safe for a while now, but only because she'd locked the door, pushed a dresser in front of the closet, and leaned against it with all her might.

Her memory flew to first thing that morning when Mom arrived early to help the family welcome Mysti and Miss Clarissa.

Tillie had felt special because she, Ginnie, and Uncle Jake were the only ones to have already met Mysti.

For once, Tillie was a charter member of the inner circle of Club West ... and she liked it.

Then her thoughts bounced to when Uncle Jake scolded DT about taking his time proposing to Mom and she had *really loved that*.

It was all Tillie could do not to add: "So *when* are you gonna ask? *Now* is good for me."

Her thoughts kept bouncing from one random memory to another like a ping pong ball, making no sense until her thoughts landed on Toran getting hurt and everything turning awful.

She glanced at him.

His eyebrow arched when he caught her gaze. He deepened his sympathetic smile.

Her cheeks flamed.

She dropped her gaze to his side, but seeing no sign of his injury, concentrated on his blue T-shirt instead.

"Take your time. *We'll wait*," Toran said quietly.

Tillie surveyed each of their faces.

Toran's emphatic "we'll wait" had been a warning for Ginnie, who stood impatiently like a racer for the starting gun.

Ginnie smirked at Toran and pasted on a more pleasant expression for Tillie.

Tillie might have laughed, but the humor quickly evaporated when she realized that *she* held the starting gun and she had nothing to say.

She didn't even know where to begin.

Her thoughts pinged to Toran, Mysti, and herself happily playing with the kittens, then Toran angry about not telling him about Mysti.

Then Uncle Jake and Tillie making butter with Mysti.

Uncle Jake had made Tillie feel like they were teammates with the same goal: helping Mysti feel at home. He had winked gratefully at her when she made Mysti laugh before he did, making her feel like a real member of Team West.

Then her thoughts ponged to seeing Aunt Roni and Ginnie hugging on the front porch and Tillie realized once again that she was just fooling herself.

Maybe if Aunt Roni didn't look so much like Ginnie's mom it would be different. But how could she compete with Ginnie's mom's ghost, even if Ginnie's mom's ghost turned out to be Ginnie's aunt?

DT was going to see Aunt Roni and realize that his *real* family didn't include a girl with straight mousy-brown hair who looked like the man who used to be his friend.

"Please say *something*," Ginnie pleaded. "Tell me why you hit me or why you don't think Daddy loves you. Or why Aunt Roni bugs you so much."

Toran's jaw dropped. "You hit Ginnie?"

"I didn't mean to! It just happened." Tillie swiveled to the alfalfa field before continuing her protest. "She was dissing your dad. I couldn't help it. I said I was sorry."

"All I said was I wasn't sure why Mama and Miss Amanda loved Daddy *so much*." Ginnie locked her gaze on Toran. "Miss Amanda said he's like Prince Charming." Toran smiled at the news. "I just don't see it."

"You said he was *lame!*" The flames from Tillie's cheeks lit the anger in her heart, threw the dresser across the room, and blew open the closet where she hid her darkest feelings.

Tillie swiveled angrily back to Toran.

Her hands flew to her hips as fury and hurt spewed out her mouth.

"Ginnie has *no* idea how lucky she is. Your dad's the best and I can't stand it when she calls him lame." Tillie swiveled to Ginnie and stabbed an angry finger at her. "'Lame' is a dad who hurts you and runs away instead of doing the right thing. Lame is NOT *your* dad. *Your dad* is the UN-lamest dad I know. And now he'll *hate* me."

As one, Ginnie and Toran widened their eyes and took a step back from her. "No, he won't!" they said together. Then Ginnie added. "You didn't even hurt me. He won't hate you over that. And I wasn't going to tell him anyway."

"Dad could *never* hate you Tillie. *Ever.*" Toran gripped Tillie's hand firmly. "It's just not possible."

Tillie wanted to believe him, but the monster she'd set free wouldn't let her. "What about Aunt Roni?"

"What about her?" Toran asked.

"She looks just like your mom."

"So?" Ginnie moved closer. "She's *not* my mom. And Daddy loves *your* mom now. He didn't even tell us about Aunt Roni. She came on her own. If Daddy had his way, we *still* wouldn't know about her." Ginnie looked at Tillie like her hair was on fire as well as her temper. "And she's married, with *two* kids. Why are you worried about Aunt Roni?"

Tillie swallowed, not knowing what to say. All her fears sounded stupid coming out of Ginnie's mouth. " ... and anyway, she dated Uncle Jake, *not* my dad."

Toran's mouth popped open. "She did?"

Ginnie nodded. "That's what she said."

"Really?" Tillie didn't know why, but that made her feel much better. "What about Mysti?"

"What about her?" Ginnie and Toran asked as one.

"She's *real* family. I'm not."

Ginnie and Toran exchanged looks that suggested they might need to commit her to an insane asylum.

Tillie glared at each of them. "I'm not crazy."

"Tillie, Tillie, Tillie ..." Toran shook his head. His voice had a kind, teasing tone. "Is that what this is about? You don't think you're part of our family?"

Tillie jiggled her leg uncomfortably. "Kinda, 'cause I'm not *real* family."

Ginnie grabbed Tillie's upper arms and shook her once before squeezing her into a bear hug. "You're nuts. Or as Vi would say, certifiable. Daddy even told you last night."

"Told me what?"

"That *you* look more like our family than he, Toran, and I do, AND that *you fit right in ... just fine. Duh.* Pay attention."

That's right, he did.

"Everyone in my family loves you. And my dad *is* gonna marry your mom." Ginnie squeezed her again. "If he wasn't, he wouldn't have been kissing her last night. *Double duh.* He's not gonna act all lovey-dovey if he wasn't planning to be serious. *Triple* duh." She rolled her eyes again and frowned. "You're being dumb. Get with the program. You've been family for *years.*"

Tillie didn't know what to say.

None of her arguments worked anymore, even for her. "But Jasper left ..."

"So? *We* didn't." Ginnie waved her hand, dismissing Tillie's argument without even listening. "And it doesn't matter anyway. Uncle Ben considers Jasper family."

"Don't say that." Tillie shuddered, not wanting Jasper to be any part of her life and most especially not part of her dream family.

"Too late." Ginnie folded her arms across her chest. "*You* argue with Uncle Ben about it. Jasper may be the *lost* sheep of our family, but he's family. So that makes you *double* family."

Arguing with Uncle Ben about *anything*, and most especially, Jasper, didn't appeal to Tillie in the least.

Uncle Ben had asked her many times to let her anger with Jasper go, promising Tillie that she would feel better if she did, but she never could.

Tillie wanted to let her anger go, *sometimes*, but she could never completely forgive Jasper for hurting Mom and her, and then abandoning them.

"*You're* the one who's certifiable. I'm *not* gonna argue with Uncle Ben about anything." Tillie returned Ginnie's hug, feeling lighter than she had all day. "But how do you figure I'm *double* family?"

Ginnie smirked and mimed pulling something out of her back pocket. She wiggled it in the air. "A notebook." She pretended to take a pencil from behind her ear. "I'm gonna write this down. Pay attention. You ready?"

Tillie rolled her eyes. "Sure."

"You're *double family* because you were Jasper and Miss Amanda's *before*, and you're *Daddy's* and Miss Amanda's *now*. Are you with me?"

Tillie smirked and then nodded.

Ginnie scribbled in her imaginary notebook, and then pointed the "pencil" at her. "You and Miss Amanda are a 'two-for-one-special.' Daddy, Toran, and me are a 'three-for-one-special.' Are you following?"

Tillie smirked again.

"Dad told me he couldn't date anybody who couldn't love me and Toran. So that means he wouldn't date your mom if he didn't love *you*. Uncle Ben adopted Jasper a long time ago. He and Miss Amanda had you. Daddy has always been a West and he's *choosing* you. So that makes you *double* family. Daddy wouldn't date your mom if he didn't want you as his kid." She rolled her eyes. "So there, double *duh*. Got it?"

Ginnie pointed her thumb at her brother. "Tell her, Tor."

"I've gotta go with Ginnie on this one, Tillie." Toran chuckled and rolled his eyes as well. "You're the only one besides us that Dad gives an allowance to. So, Ginnie's right. Do the math. You're *double* family."

Tillie's gaze pinged between Ginnie and Toran one more time and then she saw the truth in each of their eyes.

Definitely ... she *was* family ... and had been all along.

She smiled at her friends and lightly smacked her forehead.

Totally double DUH.

71

TILLIE'S TRANSFORMATION

oran watched as Tillie's eyes darted between his face and Ginnie's. A transformation occurred as the reality of their words soaked into Tillie's understanding.

The pale, sad, shaking girl alternating between voiceless and raging that had stood before them disappeared as quickly as an albino cat in high cotton.

A gentle breeze swept the lane.

Toran blinked. Before him now stood a completely different girl in the same jeans and T-shirt the other Tillie wore. A beaming smile radiated a new confidence.

"Yay! You're back!" Ginnie squealed as she grabbed this Tillie's hands and happy-danced with her.

Tillie giggled softly, then found her voice.

A joy-filled, robust laugh erupted from the pale face, coloring her cheeks a bright pink.

Her hollow blue eyes deepened and filled with purposeful life.

She bobbed up and down with Ginnie a few times before they fell into each other's arms twittering the relieved laughter of people who'd been scared half-silly only to realize they were perfectly safe.

Toran's cheeks hurt from grinning so hard. His legs felt wobbly, but he didn't know why.

Tillie hugged Ginnie hard and then caught Toran's gaze.

Time froze.

The timid bunny emerged long enough to assess the situation.

A few sniffs must have determined all was well.

It turned tail and disappeared.

Toran softened his smile and held out his hand. "Let's go home."

Nodding, Tillie released Ginnie from their hug.

Tillie's eyelashes fluttered slowly closed, then opened shyly as he took her hand in his.

Her lips closed, sealing in the hysterical mirth.

A welcoming sort of bliss radiated from her eyes.

Ginnie hooked her arm in Tillie's other one, took hold of Calliope's reins, and started chattering about horses and breeding, and some competition their dad probably wouldn't let her do anyway.

Toran didn't really pay attention, too busy trying to decide if Tillie felt the same electricity buzzing through her that he felt surging through him.

72

SISTERS?

hen they reached the farmhouse, Toran offered to put Calliope up so Ginnie and Tillie could sneak to the upstairs bathroom to wash away all signs of their tears, dirt, and drama before any of the adults spotted them and could ask what happened.

None of them wanted to share the events in the lane.

After dabbing her cheeks with a soft blue towel, and checking her face in the mirror for missed smudges, Tillie hugged Ginnie again, happy to be free of the doubt and ugliness that had been hovering over her ever since Ginnie told her that she'd found her mom's journals. "You're really okay with my mom and your dad getting married?"

"Of course. Duh." Ginnie waved her hand dismissively and then lowered her voice. "But you have to let me be happy about finding Aunt Roni. Daddy doesn't really want her here, and I don't want to fight both of you."

The seriousness of Ginnie's tone stunned Tillie. Alarmed, she searched her friend's face.

"I mean it. Dad hid her from us for a long time and I forgot all about her. That's just wrong. I *need* to get to know my mom ... *and*

Aunt Roni. And I need *you* to be okay with that." Ginnie squeezed Tillie's hand. "Vi's on Dad's side. She's playing nice for now, but if Dad starts not being okay with Aunt Roni coming around, Vi, Buzz, and Uncle Ben will run her out of town."

Tillie shook her head. "No, they won't."

"Oh, yes they will." Ginnie rolled her eyes. "That's how my family is. Uncle Jake might not agree, but he's always loyal to my dad, even if Daddy is wrong. And in this case, Daddy was *really* wrong. Look at what they did to Jasper."

Tillie gasped. "What did they do?"

"*You know.* Uncle Jake beat him up after he found out Jasper hurt you and your mom. And then Uncle Ben told Jasper to leave if he couldn't keep his hands to himself."

"Oh ... yeah." Tillie thought back to Uncle Jake telling her that a while ago and exhaled. She smiled at the memory. "I'm actually okay with that. I'm glad Jasper's gone."

"Me, too." Ginnie grimaced, then shook her head. "But it's all part of the same thing—good when you agree, but bad when you don't. Uncle Jake didn't think Aunt Roni was a problem, but because Daddy thinks Cabot is, Uncle Jake kept Dad's secret." Ginnie hung the towel over her shoulder. "Then Daddy took Mama's journals away from me. I know that's weird for you, but I *Need. Them. Back.* You met Aunt Roni. She's not gonna hurt me. She misses Mama even more than I do."

As much as Tillie wanted to sympathize, part of her was still jealous of Aunt Roni. She stuffed the jealousy down and nodded. "Okay, but promise me you'll give my mom a chance. She loves you. You know that, *right*?"

"You still don't get it." Ginnie rolled her eyes. "I *already* love your mom. Aunt Roni doesn't want to be my mom. She just wants to share Mama with me. She and Mama were best friends, like you and me. That's cool, isn't it?"

"Yeah. I just don't want you to like her more than my mom." Tillie blurted, not believing that she admitted it out loud.

But she couldn't take it back.

And she didn't want to.

She was tired of secrets.

Ginnie hugged her tight. "Tillie, you're *still* certifiable. Knock it off. I love your mom. I want her to be my stepmom. You don't have anything to worry about." She let go of her. "Besides, I asked Daddy how he could be happy with your mom after being married to *my* mom ..."

"Hey!"

"Let me finish." Ginnie frowned and then had the decency to look embarrassed before she continued. "*I meant* because they're so different and all, not anything bad about Miss Amanda. My mom was a little crazy and your mom is so quiet. But Daddy says that's why he can be happy with your mom. They're different in *good* ways."

Tillie wanted to protest, but couldn't figure out how she had been insulted.

Ginnie didn't seem to notice and kept right on talking. "And I think he *likes* that your mom isn't so crazy, like me or Mama. I also think that's why he likes *you* so much. You're like Toran. You don't make Daddy nuts like I do."

Hmmm. She *did* like being compared to Toran.

"Well, except that you kind of make being quiet sound like a *bad* thing, I *like* that you're a little crazy." Tillie dropped her gaze to the floor. "You aren't afraid of dumb things like I am."

"Being afraid of a dad who hurt you, isn't dumb."

"Being afraid that your best friend's dad—who's gonna marry your mom—won't love you, *is* dumb."

"Why is that dumb?" Ginnie asked in all seriousness.

Tillie searched Ginnie's face. "*You* acted like it was dumb."

"Only because *my* dad is the dad you're talking about." Ginnie popped her head out of the bathroom doorway and looked both ways, before she continued.

"What *is* dumb is that you didn't know how much my family cares about you. Ever since Jasper left, you've practically lived here ... even before our folks started dating. Uncle Ben, Vi, Buzz, Uncle Jake, Dad, Toran, me—we all adopted you and your mom—a long time ago."

"Well, you don't know what it's like to have a father like Jasper!"

"You're right. I'm sorry." Ginnie blinked, then lowered her voice. "I'm really sorry he hurt you. He shouldn't have done that. And even though I'm not sure I need another mom, I know *you* need a good dad, so I don't mind sharing." Ginnie offered a smile. "Mine is pretty good, but he's *not* perfect. You gotta get over thinking he is or you're gonna be *really* disappointed."

Tillie shook her head. "He's perfect enough." She giggled. "He gave me a cookie when he busted me for getting in that fight with Pierce. That's pretty cool."

"Yeah." Ginnie scrunched her nose. "He didn't give *me* a cookie— just a lecture."

"Sorry."

"It's okay." Ginnie shrugged. "Your mom hugged me after busting me last night. That felt kinda good. So maybe my dad'll be soft on you and your mom'll be soft on me." She met Tillie's gaze and giggled. "That could be fun."

"Why did Mom bust you?"

"Same reason you got all mad. I dissed my dad." Ginnie mimed putting her fingers down her throat and then laughed. "She told me he was Prince Charming. Ummmm ... gag city."

"Knock it off." Tillie threw her towel at Ginnie. "You deserved to get busted then."

"Thanks a lot."

"You're welcome."

"I see how this is gonna go." Ginnie raspberried her. "I get a wicked stepsister to go with my stepmom. Oh, joy!"

"Only if you're dumb enough to disrespect my stepdad." Tillie tossed the towel over Ginnie's head and left, calling, "So don't," over her shoulder.

73

SASSY GIRLS

*G*innie pulled the towel off her head and glanced in the
mirror. Blonde strands flew around her head. She undid her
braids, brushed them out, and reached for a green
scrunchie. Straightening, she watched her wavy curls bounce around
her shoulders ... like Aunt Roni's ... and Mama's.

For once the curls didn't disgust her.

In fact, they fascinated her.

She shook her head and watched the curls follow along. She
tilted her head every which way and watched how they floated
around her shoulders.

Ginnie brushed a portion of her hair until it pulled taut, then
quickly tugged the brush all the way through. Her curls bounced like
coiled ribbons a couple times before framing her face.

She smiled and fluffed her bangs.

She ducked her head, recalling an argument with Dad about her
hair.

He had forbidden her to cut it and she refused to show her curls.
Their final compromise was braids. Regular braids, French braids,
and on occasion, fishtail braids. Once, Miss Amanda had braided her
hair around her head in a "waterfall" braid that was kinda cool. It

looked like a wreath with dangling curls so Ginnie had insisted on making a double wreath to hide them.

Now she felt bad about it.

Miss Amanda had tried talking her into letting her curls show, but Ginnie wouldn't hear of it.

Remembering how Miss Amanda scolded her last night, Ginnie entertained a new thought.

I wonder if Miss Amanda will be bossier when she's married to my dad?

When Vi made up her mind about something, Dad usually let Vi have her way, unless he *really* wanted his way ... like not having Aunt Roni around.

Ginnie opened a drawer and fished out a pink comb. After parting her hair, she set the comb on the sink. She felt a swish behind her.

Turning quickly, she caught a flutter of curls in the mirror, only they weren't hers.

"Gins, honey, stand still. I can't very well make a straight part with you wiggling like a little worm, now can I?" For a moment Ginnie was three again and pulling away as Mama tried to part her hair.

She heard every word Mama spoke in Mama's soft Southern accent.

"No, Mama. Only *one* ponytail. Two takes too long. I wanna ride Love with you. Just *one* ponytail." She jerked backward and bumped against Mama's pregnant belly.

"Sugar, be careful. You'll hurt the baby." Mama took Ginnie's chin in her hand. "Be soft."

Present-day Ginnie felt a rush of sadness and shame as young Ginnie stomped her foot. "Sorry!"

Little Ginnie pulled her chin from Mama's hand. "Just *one* pony."

Mama frowned. "Be nice. You're a big sister now. You have to be a good example."

"I just wanna ride with you. I don't want you to do my hair."

Young Ginnie grabbed Mama's hand and pulled.

"In a minute. Be patient and let me finish your hair."

"No!"

"Excuse me?" Both Ginnies shuddered when Daddy's stern voice came through the doorway. He knelt in front of young Ginnie at eye level. "I sure hope I didn't just hear you sassing your mama. Sassy girls don't get to ride horses. *Sassy* girls take time-outs."

Both Ginnies blinked.

Goosebumps dotted their arms.

"Todd, I'm handling it. No need to growl," Mama chided softly and pulled young Ginnie close. "You'll stand still and let me finish, won't you, Fidgets?"

"Yes, Mama." Ginnie watched her dad out of the corner of her eye. "Sorry, Mama."

"I didn't growl," Daddy said in a quiet voice and stood. "I wouldn't have to scold her if you wouldn't allow her to fuss so much in the first place." Daddy crossed his arms over his chest. "You want to make a good impression on your dad next week. Make her mind. She knows how."

"Don't start." Mama pointed the comb at Daddy before parting Ginnie's hair and fastening one side in a ponytail holder. "I'm nervous enough as it is."

"Owie, Mama. That's too tight."

"Sorry, sugar." Mama kissed the top of Ginnie's head and loosened the band.

Daddy frowned at Ginnie, then offered a more sympathetic look. He rubbed Ginnie's cheek with his thumb and kissed Mama's, squishing Ginnie a little. "I'm sorry. I know you're nervous."

He scooped Ginnie up, set her on his hip, and wrapped his arms around each of them.

"I know you want to fix things with Cabot, but *he* should be making the bigger effort. *He's* at fault here, not you. It doesn't take four-and-a-half years to realize you've been a stubborn fool. I've got a bad feeling about this, Queenie. I can't explain it, but something's not right."

"You're just hormonal. It comes with the pregnancy," Mama teased.

"Very funny." Dad leaned in for a kiss.

"Hey!" Little Ginnie protested, pushing them apart.

Mama put a finger on his lips. "Let me finish with Gins, then I'll spend some time with you, okay?"

Daddy wiggled his eyebrows at Mama, then pretended to eat Ginnie's arm, making her giggle, and push him away. "Silly Daddy. You don't eat little girls. You eat *pizza!*"

"What about little girls who taste like pizza?" He pretended to eat her hand. "Arummm. Mmmm."

Little Ginnie giggled. "Daddies are silly, huh Mama?"

"Yes, sugar. Daddies are most definitely silly." Mama rolled her eyes, brushed Ginnie's hair, and fastened the last ponytail holder. "Especially *your daddy.*"

Daddy puckered his lips and pressed them against Mama's neck, tickling her.

Mama giggled.

Daddy stopped kissing Mama to look Ginnie in the eye. "Your mama's daddy is the *silliest*. Of course I haven't had to share her with him for a long, long time, so maybe his being silly is a good thing."

"Todd Benjamin. You're as naughty as she is. You blame me, but she gets it from *you*."

"Fine. I'll take a time-out ... as long as it can be with *you*." Daddy set Ginnie on her feet in the hallway. "Go see what Toran's doing. He's out front with Buzz."

Ginnie shook her head. "I wanna ride with Mama."

"In a minute. Go on." He tried to close the door, but Ginnie pushed it. "Mama!"

"Don't tease her." Mama kissed him and opened the door wider. "The sooner we go, the sooner we'll get back. Remember that you and Pete are taking the kids to the play place so Lauren and I can go shopping. Behave and I'll buy you a treat."

"Me too, Mama?"

Mama smiled at her. "Of course."

"I don't want you to go," Daddy said.

Mama pinched his cheek and laughed. "I said I'd bring you a treat, Sugarlips."

He smirked. "I meant I don't want you to go riding."

"I can't disappoint Fidgets. Quit being silly."

Daddy blocked her way. "I mean it, honey. Something doesn't feel right. I don't want you to go riding. Let's all go to the play place ... *together*. You can ride another time."

Mama rolled her eyes. "We'll be back in two shakes."

"Don't take Ginnie then. I mean it, something's *not right*."

The worry in his voice sent a shiver through present day Ginnie.

Young Ginnie stomped her foot. "Mama!"

"Stop it, Todd. I already promised her." Mama gently pushed him aside and took hold of young Ginnie's hand.

Tillie poked her head in. "Hey! What's taking so long?"

Ginnie leaned around her, but it was too late.

Mama had disappeared.

74

ANOTHER SECRET

*G*innie. *Hey.* What gives?" Tillie waved her hand in front of Ginnie's face, pretty sure her friend didn't see her. "Are you mad because I walked off? You know I don't like you dissing your dad, but I didn't think you'd get mad about me teasing you."

"What?" Ginnie's voice sounded hollow.

"Hello? Are you here?" Tillie teased.

"Yeah." Ginnie shook her head, like she was trying to reboot her brain. "Did you see her?'

"See who?"

Ginnie sighed. "Nobody."

"There's just us."

Disappointment crossed Ginnie's face.

"What's wrong?"

"Nothing." Ginnie picked up a comb from the sink, then moved toward the door.

Tillie backed up and followed Ginnie's gaze as she entered the hallway, glancing one way and then the other. "I promise. Everyone's downstairs. No one's up here."

"Okay." Ginnie followed the railing and turned to go downstairs.

Tillie caught her eye as she went down the first step.

Ginnie looked straight through her.

Swallowing hard, Tillie struggled to keep a pleasant expression on her face.

Great. Another secret.

75

SUGAR IS SWEET

There you are. I was hoping you'd be back soon." Aunt Roni crossed the dining room and enveloped Ginnie in a hug as she passed the cherry wood dining table set for eight. "Did you have a nice ride?'

Ginnie hugged her back and breathed in the smell of her perfume.

It wasn't Mama's.

Aunt Roni fluffed Ginnie's hair. "Vi says you never wear your hair down. It's pretty."

Ginnie clenched her fist. The teeth of the comb jabbed into the palm of her hand. She held the comb out to Aunt Roni. "Can you fix it? Please?"

"Sure, sugar. How do you want it done?" Aunt Roni smiled at Ginnie and then looked past her. "Hi, Tillie."

"Hi," Tillie said.

Feeling bad about how she'd treated Mama all those years ago, Ginnie shrugged. Then she remembered Miss Amanda. "Could you do a waterfall braid? You know, braid it around the top and let the curls hang?"

"If you'd like. Tillie, honey, are you alright?" Aunt Roni reached a hand to her friend and hugged her as well. Before her friend could respond, Ginnie blurted, "Did Mama call me 'sugar?'"

"I'd imagine." Aunt Roni revved up her smile. "We're from the south. We call everybody 'sugar' or 'honey.' It's what we do."

Between Aunt Roni's smile and her accent, each of her words dripped with sweetness.

"I like it." Tillie hugged Aunt Roni. "It's friendly."

"Why thank you, sugar." Aunt Roni squeezed Tillie again and then took Ginnie's chin in her hand. "Is something troubling you?"

"Mama talked like you. *With an accent*, didn't she?"

"Well, we didn't sound alike to each other, but to *you*, we probably do. Why do you ask?"

"Why didn't I remember that?" Ginnie blinked, and swept the room with her eyes, her final look to a painting that hung over their cherry wood sideboard.

The picture was a present from Aunt Sadie to Mama on her second Mother's Day. A young mother played with two blond toddlers. One boy. One girl. Each child held a basket of purple flowers.

"My mom talked with a southern accent and I didn't remember. What's wrong with me?"

"*Nothing* is wrong with you!" Aunt Roni gave her chin a gentle squeeze. "You were three when she passed. No one expects you to remember everything about her."

"I didn't even remember *you*. There aren't too many people that look like a person's mom. You'd think I'd remember that, being's how I'm a twin too."

"What is this *really* about?" Aunt Roni leaned closer and held Ginnie's chin firm. "Did something happen or is my being here too upsetting for you?" She sighed. "I didn't realize I would be such a surprise. But if it's causing you a lot of distress, I can leave and come back when you've had time to get used to the idea. I certainly don't want to cause you anymore grief."

"Don't go." Ginnie clasped Aunt Roni's wrist with both hands. "I want you to stay. I just want to remember Mama." She lowered her eyes. "But I don't remember much."

"Not to worry, sugar. I'll help you." Aunt Roni released her chin and smiled her million dollar smile. "I have a whole lifetime of stories to share with you. Your mama wasn't anything if she wasn't colorful. I've remembered enough for both of us."

76

CHATTING WITH AUNT RONI

*G*innie kept one eye on the clock and one on the lane.

Ever since Aunt Roni fixed her hair, she'd been waiting impatiently for Miss Amanda to show. So much had happened that she felt like a jumble of raw nerve endings.

"Why do you keep looking down the hallway?" Tillie asked, sidling up next to her in the dining room door frame.

They looked together out the screen door. "I want your mom to come home."

"Really?" Tillie's tone offered happy suspicion. "Why?"

"Just because." Ginnie tried to force her tumbling thoughts into a cohesive explanation.

Seeing Tillie's dark place and her friend's worries had been bothering Ginnie.

Recalling herself treating Mama and Miss Amanda badly when they had styled her hair also bugged her.

Tillie was right. It was time to grow up and try something new.

Ginnie glanced through the kitchen doorway when Aunt Roni laughed at something Toran said. She was getting used to Aunt Roni *being* Aunt Roni and not a real-life version of the pictures of her mom that she had been poring over the last few weeks waiting impatiently for Dad to share his secret.

Still, Ginnie waffled back and forth between being angry with him for keeping such a great secret and relief that he was willing to let Aunt Roni stay when he really didn't want her here ... and great joy that his secret was working out well, so far, at least.

Aunt Roni didn't seem to be a manipulative monster waiting to steal her away from her dad. She seemed like Ginnie herself, just sad that she couldn't have Mama in her day-to-day life.

But after seeing Tillie's jealousy, Ginnie was worried about Miss Amanda.

What if her future stepmom was concerned that Aunt Roni was going to ruin everything?

Aunt Roni entered the dining room holding a platter of corn-on-the-cob.

Toran followed with a bowl of peas.

"Give me a minute, okay?" Ginnie whispered to Tillie.

When Tillie nodded, Ginnie approached Aunt Roni. "Can I see you for a second? Please?"

Aunt Roni glanced at Toran, who gave a quick nod. "Sure thing, sugar." She followed Ginnie into the living room off the dining room and waited for Ginnie to close the door. "Is something the matter?"

"No, I just have to ask you something."

"Be my guest. *Anything.*"

"Aunt Roni ..." Ginnie stopped.

"Yes?"

Ginnie licked her lips. "Ummm ..."

"Spit it out honey, you're starting to worry me again."

"Are ... are you gonna be okay meeting Miss Amanda?" Ginnie blurted. "I mean ... she's gonna be my stepmom and I love her ... and Daddy loves her and she's not my mom, but still. She says she doesn't want to take Mama's place, and Tillie'll be crushed if you want to break them up and ... and ..."

"Whoa now, sugar. Slow down." Aunt Roni put her finger gently on Ginnie's lips. "I came to get reacquainted with you and Toran. I've considered that Todd may be remarried or contemplate doing so."

"Really?"

"Of course. It has been over eight years. I'll admit I was a little surprised to hear about Amanda, but I am fine with that. It's good for your daddy to be happy."

Relief washed over Ginnie.

"And I think Tillie is darling. I loved having my sister as my best friend. Why would I spoil that for you?" Aunt Roni strengthened her smile. "Uncle Ben assures me that Amanda is a wonderful woman who only has your best interests at heart. I'm a little more concerned how she will perceive *me*, but I truly just want you and Toran to be happy. If that includes Amanda and Tillie ... then so be it. Don't worry your pretty little head another second."

"You're sure?"

Aunt Roni hugged her tight. "You have my word."

"Thank you. 'Cause I want you to stay and I don't want Tillie or Miss Amanda to worry. If they do, Daddy might send you away." Ginnie squeezed her tighter and blinked back hot tears. "I can't lose you again."

"That won't happen." Aunt Roni slid her hands to Ginnie's arms, pushed her gently back, and looked her in the eye before lightly touching their foreheads together. "Even through the ugliness, Todd knows I've never been a threat to him. I'll jump through whatever hoops he deems necessary to prove that to him if it's still a concern. But I won't lose you and your brother again. I promise."

Overwhelmed by too many emotions to define, Ginnie stood speechless, for once, trying to soak in the sincerity of her aunt's words.

Ginnie hoped they were true. She needed to believe them, as much as she had needed to help Tillie earlier.

Recalling Uncle Ben's cautious greeting/warning and Dad's initial animosity toward Aunt Roni had worried her. Each act had been completely out of character for Ginnie's experiences with her great-uncle and dad, and yet she knew she had witnessed the hard truth that Aunt Roni represented a horrific time in her family's life, in too many ways to count.

She blinked again, and breathed out her doubts. "Okay. I *really* want you to like Miss Amanda. She's *totally* awesome sauce!"

Aunt Roni laughed. "I didn't know 'awesome' came in a sauce, but if you like her that much, I know I will."

"Oh, it does—awesome sauce is the best."

"Then I look forward to meeting her."

The front porch screen door squeaked open.

Two pairs of high heels clicked on the wooden entryway.

"Mom!" Tillie greeted.

"Mommy!" Mysti squealed.

"I guess it won't be much longer then. There she is," Ginnie said, taking a quick breath.

Aunt Roni nodded and pointed toward the living room door that opened into the hallway. "Please do the honors."

"Yes'm. And I forgot about Miss Clarissa, so this oughta be really fun." Ginnie smiled at her aunt and reached for the porcelain knob.

"For sure, sugar, for sure." Aunt Roni didn't look so certain when Ginnie turned the knob, but by the time Ginnie opened the door and looked at her again, Aunt Roni wore a welcoming smile.

77

CHAIN REACTION

*T*illie hugged her mom and waited anxiously for Ginnie and Aunt Roni to join them. Mysti chattered non-stop, telling Miss Clarissa about the farm animals and how much fun she'd had with Uncle Jake.

Then the living room door opened.

Ginnie followed Aunt Roni into the entryway.

Mom greeted Aunt Roni. "It's nice to see you again."

"You too. Much better circumstances." Aunt Roni returned Mom's smile and lengthened it for Tillie. "I understand congratulations are in order."

"Congratulations?" Mom echoed.

"On your engagement." Aunt Roni motioned from Tillie to Ginnie. "The girls are so excited that you and Todd are to be married."

She raised an eyebrow at Ginnie.

"Um, it's not official yet. They're *gonna* get married, but Daddy hasn't asked her yet," Ginnie explained, and then caught Tillie's eye. "But he will."

Aunt Roni's cheeks pinked. "I'm sorry, I was under the impression it was a done deal. Everybody here speaks of you like you're already part of the family."

"Because she is," Ginnie insisted.

Relief tingled through Tillie as Ginnie nodded at Mom.

Mom gave a nervous laugh. "We haven't even been dating a month. We didn't realize there was a time table. *Vi's wedding* is the priority at the moment."

"It took Preston three years to get around to asking Vi. So I guess three weeks isn't very long," Ginnie teased.

"Well, now that Mommy is sharing me with Daddy, they're gonna get married too, huh Mommy?" Mysti proclaimed more than asked.

"I'm sure we'll talk about it," Miss Clarissa said quietly, her cheeks flaming a bright crimson.

Tillie felt sorry for her, knowing that in Uncle Jake's present mindset, an engagement wouldn't happen any time soon. Aunt Roni's mouth dropped, and Tillie knew she was trying to figure out how to backpedal out of this bad chain reaction of misinformation.

Mom saved the day. "Why don't we leave the speculation to another time? I, for one, am enjoying the dating phase and am looking forward to getting to know Clarissa, Mysti, and Roni." She smiled at each of them, locked her eyes on Ginnie, and ran her fingers through Ginnie's platinum springs. "And Virginia West! Do I see curls? They're gorgeous! Your auntie has been a good influence on you already."

Miss Clarissa looked relieved to have the attention removed from her.

Aunt Roni's smile rejuvenated.

Ginnie gave a shy nod. "I had her do it like you did, because I realized later that I really liked it." Ginnie whirled slowly, like a pageant princess. "Do you think my dad will like it?"

"Of course." Mom laughed and bent her forehead to Ginnie's. "He'll love it. *And* he'll hate it because you look like a sweet young lady and not his tough little tomboy."

It was Ginnie's turn to pink. "Yeah, he's like that. I just can't make him happy," she teased.

"Not when it comes to you growing up," Mom agreed. She stared straight ahead when they heard footsteps. "Uncle Ben, is that your lasagna I smell?"

"Why yes it is." Uncle Ben's welcoming grin took them all in. "Mysti helped me layer it. Why don't we all enjoy some dinner while we get acquainted? This is a great day for a family reunion."

He didn't need to tell any of them twice.

Everyone, except maybe Mysti, seemed happy to escape the awkwardness permeating the entryway.

78

WEST WOMEN

$\mathscr{A}$fter dinner, Ginnie, Tillie and Toran did the dishes together while the adults gathered in the family room to visit. Toran offered to wash while Tillie dried the dishes. Ginnie found plastic containers for the leftovers and noticed that Toran seemed more chatty than normal with Tillie.

By the time Ginnie put the extra food away, wiped down the table, and the countertops, Toran and Tillie were having a lively discussion about Toran's new computer game and standing closer than necessary. Tillie's face shining with a new confidence.

When there were only a few dishes left to be washed and dried, Ginnie joined Uncle Ben, Aunt Roni, Vi, Miss Clarissa, Miss Amanda, and Mysti in the family room.

Aunt Roni patted the spot next to her on the big couch.

A huge smile lit Vi's lips when she caught sight of Ginnie. She waved a hand to indicate everybody in the room. "Finally, Gin. Check it out. The West women outnumber the West men. This is a historical occasion."

Ginnie sat between Vi and Aunt Roni and glanced around the room.

With only Uncle Ben and Toran representing the men in their

family, there were indeed, for once, far more women and girls present than ever seemed to be in the farmhouse at any given time.

Even at their family reunions where the great-aunts and great-uncles were balanced, every single West child or grandchild was a boy or man, with only Vi, herself, and a few of her dad's cousins' wives representing the opposite sex.

But those wives had all married into the West family.

Vi's smile ignited Ginnie's. "That is *way* cool."

"I'm not sure Jake would consider me a 'West woman' at the moment," Miss Clarissa said, "He's trying to be kind, but he's still aggravated with how things turned out."

"Don't worry about Jake, he'll get over being aggravated soon enough. He's already in love with Mysti--and the two of you are a matched set. Just like Amanda and Tillie. And Todd, Toran, and Ginnie. My cousins are Neanderthals but they are loyal." She nodded at Uncle Ben. "And if Jake doesn't come around soon, Dad'll take care of him."

Uncle Ben gave a slight shake of his head at Vi. "You make me sound like a bully, Violet. And I believe Jake can figure out his love life without any extra persuasion from me." He offered Miss Clarissa a friendly smile. "Clarissa is a wonderful person and although Jake might be a bit thickheaded on occasion--he *isn't stupid*." He nodded at Mysti. "And he wants to do right by his little girl. That's a very powerful motivation."

"Well, I am glad that Daddy is dating Miss Amanda," Ginnie turned to Vi, "and that you two take Tillie and me for Girls Night Out every once in a while. Daddy tries hard to be both a good mom and a good dad--but you guys definitely do the 'mom thing' better."

Vi laughed and hugged her. "Well--we are still going to do that, even after I get married. I love spending time with Preston--but I'm already missing Amanda, Tillie, and you." She glanced at Miss Amanda and then Miss Clarissa. "And it'll be fun to add Clarissa, Mysti, and Faith as well." She smiled at Aunt Roni. "And if you and your girls are in town--we'll have a grand ole party."

"That's really sweet, Vi. If we're in town--we'll definitely be there," Aunt Roni assured her.

Ginnie liked that Vi included Aunt Roni. She could get used to spending more time with her newfound aunt. And even though Mama was the official "West Woman," it was nice that she could be included in spirit with Aunt Roni attending the gathering as well.

"When will we get to meet Genna-Maie and Niqi?" Ginnie asked, hoping it would be soon--because then she wouldn't have to wait as long to see Aunt Roni again.

"My family is still in England. If it's alright with Uncle Ben and Todd--I thought I'd arrange a time after they return next week. Then Vi and I can try bridal hairstyles and such, so I know what I'll need to do at her wedding."

Vi reached across Ginnie to squeeze Aunt Roni's hand. "I know you're not Queenie--but since you are her sister and we are friends again, I feel like I've gained another sister." She turned to Miss Amanda, then included Miss Clarissa in her welcoming smile. "And trust me, Amanda and Clarissa--*more* sisters are better. Since you will both be expected to attend the West family reunion next month--as well as see the family at my wedding, having more West women than less is a great and beautiful thing. Right, Gin?"

"Absolutely. I can't wait for the family to meet Mysti. Then maybe I can get through the family reunion without bruised cheeks." She rolled her eyes and grinned at Miss Amanda. "The family already likes you and Tillie." She motioned to Miss Clarissa. "And I'm sure they'll love Mysti and you. But it gets old being the half-orphaned daughter of one of the completely orphaned nephews. The extended family love Uncle Jake, Daddy, Toran, and I a little *too* much."

"True that," Toran agreed, coming into the living room with Tillie. "Mysti will be fresh meat. And since she's a girl--even better for Ginnie and me."

"What does that mean?" Mysti asked, wide-eyed.

"Just that there's a whole lot of new people who want to meet you. You'll be like a rockstar," Ginnie said, trying not to giggle.

Concern lit Miss Clarissa's eyes.

Mysti smiled. "Rockstars are cool."

Tillie sat next to her mom while Toran sat on Tillie's other side, filling in the last two spots on the love seat.

Uncle Ben cleared his throat. "Please don't scare Clarissa and Mysti off before they even meet the extended family." Uncle Ben winked at Miss Clarissa. "No need to be afraid. My brothers and sisters-in-law are a friendly, loving bunch. You will find them to be great allies."

"As long as you don't cross Jake or Todd," Aunt Roni added, then smiled at Miss Clarissa. "But if you stay on Uncle Ben's good side-- you'll probably do just fine. For my part, I will be staying in South Carolina during this West reunion. The last time I saw Uncle Tom, it didn't go so well."

Miss Clarissa turned a little green.

Uncle Ben chuckled. "Tom is my oldest living brother. He can be a little prickly, but we'll introduce you to my folks, Oma and Opa, before then. My mama is the best ally to have. And since you have a little girl, she will stop my brothers from giving *you* a bad time-- though Jake will probably have to jump a few hoops." He chuckled. "Mama always wanted to have a little girl. So Violet, Sadie, Ginnie, Queenie, and her daughters-in-law always got *lots* of good attention from her and my sisters-in-law."

"That is true. My sister *loved* Aunt Sadie and Oma to pieces. She couldn't say enough good things about them," Aunt Roni assured, meeting Miss Clarissa's gaze. "I managed to attend one family reunion with my sister while still in Todd's good graces. It truly was a lovely experience. The Wests are good people to be on the right side of."

"But they aren't a lot of fun to be on the wrong side of," Vi added, glancing at Aunt Roni. "But Dad and I will vouch for you--so if you happen to be in town, feel free to stop by."

"Thank you, but again, I will need to decline that invitation." Aunt Roni shook her head, offering an apologetic smile. "My sister was the courageous one. It's one thing to have you, Jake, Todd, and Uncle Ben be open minded, but I don't think I could show up at a

West family reunion looking so much like my sister. The Wests adored Queenie. But our father crossed her. It took my last nerve to come here--I don't think I could face Uncle Tom or Aunt Kate and the rest of your family any time soon. At least outside of your wedding, Vi. *You* will be the focus of attention then. The first West woman to be married in what, a hundred years?"

"Ninety-four years to be exact. Viola Josephine West married Bjorn Torgerson. She was my daddy's great-grand aunt. They had 5 sons. Violet was the next West girl born, one hundred and four years and two weeks after Viola's birth."

"Is that where Vi got her name then?" Ginnie asked, scrunching her eyebrows in question. "Because I thought Aunt Sadie named her after her favorite flower, violets."

"Sadie had always wanted to name a daughter, Violet--and I had always thought it would be nice to name a daughter after Oma. When we realized how close Vi was born to Viola's birthdate, Violet Elizabeth won out." He turned to Ginnie and Toran and smiled. "Her Elizabeth came from your grandma West's name, Eliza, and Sadie's sister, Beth. Sadie and Eliza were best friends and sisters, much like our Ginnie and Tillie here."

Tillie smiled big. "I can see naming a daughter after my sister."

Ginnie rolled her eyes. "I can see naming a daughter after you as well--but I don't like it when Daddy uses my full name when he is mad at me. I don't think I want you to use it for my future niece. She might grow up hating me if she doesn't like it either."

"If Tillie has a 'Virginia'--she might actually be a quiet little girl who likes to wear dresses and follow rules. She probably wouldn't hear her formal name very much," Toran suggested, laughing.

"But probably not," Aunt Roni replied, winking at Ginnie. "Your mama and Ginnie are not the only 'Virginias' in our family--and the other two also tended to walk to a beat of their own drums. I think being independent and courageous and determined are traits borne by those named Virginia."

Toran laughed. "Which is a nice way of saying they were also stubborn and defiant."

Ginnie smirked at him. "You're so funny."

"Hey--I was named after two grandfathers, and a good friend and hero," Toran pointed out. He buffed his fingers across his t-shirt. "I'm good with that."

"Ginnie was named after her mama, an extremely lovely woman who knew her own mind, very well," Aunt Roni interjected, shaking her head at Toran.

"*Another* nice way of saying stubborn and defiant," Toran insisted, a teasing gleam in his eye.

"You are a bit precocious, aren't you Victor Alexander Stratton West?" Aunt Roni asked, her eyes narrowing in mock sternness.

"I think you meant to say, he's a bit *obnoxious*," Ginnie corrected, frowning at her twin and rolling her eyes. "Who were the other Virginias?"

"My daddy's mama--who was named after her mama's sister, so my grandmama and great grand-aunt. Both women, who, let's just say, also knew their own minds very well and were quite the force to be reckoned with. Each a highly successful woman, well known for their entrepreneurial prowess and very respected by all who knew them."

"Mmm-hmm. Probably bossy, defiant, and stubborn *as well*," Toran added.

"You better stop, *Victor*. Take it up with Daddy--it was his idea to name me after Mama."

Toran chuckled. "I don't have a problem with your name--I just happen to think that Virginia is synonymous with stubborn and defi-ant--and Aunt Roni is proving that I am right."

"It's also synonymous with: you better stop or you will wish you had," Ginnie threatened.

"Alright you two, behave." Miss Amanda glanced between them and then at her watch. "It's getting late and I need to finish a project tonight before bed. Tillie, please get your things." She shook her head as Tillie opened her mouth to protest. "I miss you and I want you to spend at least one night at home this week. And Virginia Maie--I'm going to let you ditch our sleepover tonight because Aunt Roni is here--but we are going to do it soon, understood?"

"Yes ma'am, understood." Ginnie revved up her grin. "I'm thinking the name 'Amanda' might *also* be synonymous with bossy."

Miss Amanda rolled her eyes. "You keep ditching me, and you'll see how bossy I can be."

"Yikes, Toran. Nobody said anything about getting a *wicked* step-mom. Are you still up for Daddy and Miss Amanda getting married?" Ginnie teased.

"Sure, why not? Miss Amanda is nice--*to me.*" Toran shrugged, laughing.

"And she's nice to Ginnie as well." Aunt Roni wagged a scolding finger. "And I suggest you mind your manners, young lady. Amanda is lovely, and you are lucky to have her."

"Miss Amanda knows I'm just teasing--don't you?" Ginnie turned to her future stepmom. "And besides, she said we can just be friends."

"I do know you are teasing." Miss Amanda offered a friendly smile, then stood, pointing her finger. "And I'm still serious about you not ditching our next sleepover. I never see you girls anymore. You ditch me a third time and I may very well try on the wicked step-mother role."

"Wow, Gin, you probably shouldn't push her," Toran said, eyes wide in mock fear.

But something about Miss Amanda's stance made Ginnie realize that Miss Amanda wasn't quite the pushover that she had thought and that made Ginnie respect her even more.

Ginnie kind of liked the fierceness of her words--at least the part that showed that Miss Amanda cared about her and wanted to spend time with her.

"Yes ma'am, understood." Ginnie rose from the couch and met her gaze. "Not sure I can actually picture you as a wicked anything--but something tells me that I don't really want to find out."

Miss Amanda touched her forehead to Ginnie's. "Good--because I like the relationship we have." She gave her a hug. "But if you keep ditching me--I *will* have to do something about it." She nodded toward Uncle Ben. "And if I can't come up with something creative, I'm sure he can help me out."

"I'd just go on the sleepover, Gin. You don't want her bringing out the big guns." Vi stood, laughing as she shook her head. "Not that she needs Dad's help. Because I was invited as well. And I don't mind being considered bossy. And that isn't a surprise to you."

"No ma'am--it is *not*." Ginnie agreed, laughing along with her cousin.

She hugged Miss Amanda and Tillie goodbye.

After Ginnie promised to wait on gathering the eggs until after Mysti showed in the morning, Mysti walked hand-in-hand with Miss Clarissa to their car.

Aunt Roni stayed a little longer, showing Toran the photograph album she had shown Ginnie as well as shared a few more stories of Mama in her younger days.

After Aunt Roni left for her hotel, Ginnie said goodnight to Uncle Ben and Toran and caught sight of the pink journal. Before she could pluck it up and read it again, Ginie spied the gel pens that Miss Amanda had given her and decided she should take a few minutes and write three things she was grateful for.

Ginnie scanned her previous entries and realized that she was even more grateful for Miss Amanda tonight than she was in the last couple of entries.

I am VERY grateful for my family.

1. Miss Amanda doesn't pressure me or make me feel bad about getting to know Mama. She even postponed our sleepover tonight so I could keep visiting with Aunt Roni.

2. I can't believe that Mama has an identical twin sister! Her name is Aunt Roni and she showed up today. She wants to get to know Toran and me and has been very open about sharing Mama

with us. She even loves Tillie already and wants to be friends with Miss Amanda!

This has been a TOTALLY AWESOME SAUCE day!

3. Uncle Jake--he's been trying to convince Daddy to let us know about Aunt Roni all along--and when she showed up without permission--he let her stay--even though he could have told her to leave. He really has been on my side--trying to get Daddy to tell me about Aunt Roni so that Daddy will give me back the journals. It turns out that Cabot is Mama's daddy--and he tried to take Toran and me away from Daddy after Mama died.

4. Daddy didn't like that Aunt Roni showed up without permission--but let her stay even though he didn't want her here. And he really came through for me today--I realized that he really does love me--that he didn't take the journals to be mean--just that he didn't know how to tell Toran and me about Mama's family. Aunt Roni has been really cool--but her father, Cabot Stratton, was a big problem for Daddy. Even so, Daddy is giving Aunt Roni a chance to make amends.

5. I remembered seeing Mama today when I was 3 1/2--talking with Daddy about reconnecting with Cabot. I think Miss Amanda might be right--she gave me this journal because she thought maybe Mama directed her to it. I swear I smelled Mama's perfume when I met Aunt Roni today. Maybe Mama *is* nearby--helping Toran and I get to know her family. I'm not really sure I ever want to meet Cabot, but I sure am loving getting to know Aunt Roni.

6. Vi scared me a little when she realized Aunt Roni was in town, but once she decided that Aunt Roni wouldn't hurt Toran or me, Vi welcomed her and shared stories of Mama with me --and invited Aunt Roni to her wedding--so I'll get to see her again soon.

7. Uncle Ben helped Daddy decide to let us keep visiting with Aunt Roni--after Daddy told her to leave. Uncle Ben seems to like Aunt Roni--which made everything better.

8. Tillie went a little nutburgers after Aunt Roni came--but it's all good now. I'm really glad we're gonna be sisters--and that Tillie is okay with Aunt Roni now--because at first she was jealous. She

also helped talk Daddy into letting Aunt Roni stay. So I'm really glad about that.

9. Miss Clarissa, Mysti and Faith are adding to the "West Women." Eventually, the West Women will outnumber the West Men--at least here on the farm.

10. Toran got hurt today--but he's going to be okay. He really came through for Tillie today--and me. He stood up to Daddy when Daddy told Aunt Roni to leave--and he wants Mama's journals back too. I think together, we can talk Daddy into giving the journals back quicker.

11. All-in-all, I am very grateful for my family. We stuck together today, and Toran and I are getting to know Mama through Aunt Roni. Uncle Jake and Uncle Ben helped Daddy get a grip. Tillie and Miss Amanda are being supportive and Aunt Roni has been amazing. I can't wait until tomorrow when she comes back. Hopefully Daddy will feel better about her being here--she almost left today when she realized how much Daddy *didn't* want her to be here. I'm glad Daddy said she could stay. :)

Ginnie added some hearts around the entry with her red, pink, and purple gel pens, then decided she was too excited to sleep. Knowing her dad would be home in an hour or so, she crawled into bed and tried to recall the long ago conversation when she was a little girl, while listening for him to get home, so she could thank him again for letting Aunt Roni stay.

79

STUCK IN MAD

Good morning, Gin," Dad called, opening the emerald green curtains to let in the morning sun. "Rise and shine."

Ginnie squeezed her eyes shut harder.

"Hey now, 'Good morning' is code for 'time to wake up, sleepy-head,' not 'pretend you didn't hear me,' Virginia Maie," Dad said in a teasing voice.

"Talk to me when sunrise comes at noon."

He laughed. "Sorry, but we're haying today, so we need an early start. Breakfast is almost ready and I need to help with Toran's chores. He needs a few minutes for his pain medicine to kick in."

Ginnie sat, panic starting her heart. "Is he okay?"

"He'll be fine." Dad's reassuring tone calmed the thudding in her chest.

She slid her feet up and wrapped her arms around her knees. "Good. Is Mysti coming over?"

Dad nodded. "Vi'll be here until after noon. And I'm sure Aunt Roni'll stop by."

His voice changed when he said Aunt Roni's name.

And not in a good way.

"Aunt Roni just wants to get to know us."

"I know." Dad sat on her bed. "I just have to get used to seeing her again. She complicates things."

"How?"

"She just does. If I let her in, Cabot isn't far behind and I'm not ready to go there."

Ginnie scooted next to him and laid her head on his shoulder. "It probably doesn't help that she looks like Mama and you're falling in love with Miss Amanda, huh?"

"That's not really a problem for me. Even though they are identical twins, they never really looked alike to me. I know who is who. Is their looking alike a problem for you?"

"Only at first. For being identical twins, they seem very different from each other--not that I remember much about Mama."

"In some ways they are like night and day, but so are you and Toran." He blew out a breath. "I'm sorry I didn't tell you before. When I read one of your mom's journal entries about her and Roni shopping and planning a birthday party for Cabot, I realized I'd forgotten Queenie had a family that I didn't want in your life." He ducked his head, and lowered his voice. "Since you never talked about your mom, there never seemed to be a reason to bring up the Strattons. But I knew as soon as you found out about Roni--you would want to connect with her. And the truth is--for the most part, I like Roni. But I can do without Cabot Stratton."

He stopped talking, searching Ginnie's face.

"I get it. After seeing how upset you were when Aunt Roni showed up--I realized there was more to the story than keeping us apart."

"Thanks." He let out a slow sigh. "I'm also not comfortable with the Strattons taking over--which I'm *not* going to allow--in case you are interested." He met her gaze. Her mouth dropped open. "I like our life the way it is." He sprung one of her curls. "Roni has only been part of your life for a few hours--and you're already trying new hairstyles. Which looks beautiful by the way--and too grown up for my liking." He grinned. "See? She's complicating things already."

"You just like being an ostrich," Ginnie said, trying to make her tone more teasing than accusing. "And this hairstyle is Miss Amanda's doing, not Aunt Roni's. But then I found Mama's journals."

"Yeah." He tweaked her nose. "*You* complicate my life too. It's hard being an ostrich with you around. You're like your mama that way."

Ginnie smiled. "Is that a good thing?"

"Sometimes. Your mom catapulted me out of my comfort zone on many occasions--and mostly it was a good thing--but sometimes I'd like it if the two of you could just be happier leading a calmer life." He gave a slow shake of his head, looking uncomfortable with this conversation. "Keeping up with you gets a little crazy at times."

"Aunt Roni said she'll do whatever you need her to so she can keep seeing us," Ginnie offered, not wanting him to spend any time trying to figure out how to send Aunt Roni away.

"I know. But Cabot is the real problem. He's not an easy man to be on the wrong side of."

"Why doesn't he like us?"

Dad lifted her chin and locked his eyes on Ginnie's. "It's *not* about him not liking you or Toran. Cabot didn't think I was good enough for his daughter. And as the dad of two daughters myself, I get that-- but I'd like to think I'd at least *meet* your future boyfriends before I decide they aren't good enough to date you and Tillie." He offered a playful wink. "And while I *have* made a few of Vi's boyfriend's squirm, Preston stood the test of time. I'd be pretty surprised if he treats her badly." His tone sobered. "But like Uncle Ben once said, it wasn't about *me* either. Cabot never got to know me before he forced your mom to choose between us. When she chose me, he got stuck in mad and couldn't move on."

"Why was that such a big deal? You loved her, she loved you. It's kind of a no-brainer." Ginnie shook her head, still a little surprised to see lots of messy curls framing her face instead of her braids. "Why didn't he just say he was sorry? You would've forgiven him, wouldn't you?"

"Yes, but that's not how Cabot works. It's his way or *no* way."

"Why did he ignore us while Mama was alive, but wanted Toran and me after she died?"

"*That* I understand. You are a part of *her*. And you especially--are her mini-me. I'm sure he thought he could make up how he treated her the last few years through you and Toran. But by then, I'd had enough of him." Dad clenched his jaw. "I held your mom while she cried way too many nights to count because he wouldn't make amends with her. After she died, he wanted to take her back to South Carolina and bury her in the Stratton family plot." Dad let go of Ginnie's chin. "I wouldn't let him."

"Why not?"

"As far as I was concerned, he made his choice by disowning her. She was a West when she died. And so was Cody. He doesn't have Stratton in his name like you and Toran do. Cabot had his chance to make amends while she was alive and he threw her away. End of story."

Ginnie held her breath while his face tensed with anger and disgust.

Finally he seemed to remember she was there.

His features softened.

"But that wasn't the end?"

He shook his head. "When I wouldn't let him take her, or let you and Toran go off with him unsupervised, he went to court and tried to say I was an unfit parent."

"No way!"

"*Yes* way. But the judge said there was no evidence to back his claim." Dad gave a humorless laugh.

Ginnie swallowed hard.

"Just the opposite." A snarky glint lit his eye. "People who actually *knew* me, testified on my behalf. Since Cabot had never even met you and Toran prior to the funeral, it wasn't a hard sell." Dad's voice turned firm. "There was *no* way I was going to lose you and Toran after losing your mom and Cody."

The dark look on Dad's face made Ginnie shiver.

He didn't anger easily, at least at *other* people.

She wanted to see where his imagination would run. "What would you have done if Cabot had gotten us?"

"Let's not go there." His jaw tightened even more. He stood. "He *didn't* get you ... and ... he ... never will." Dad turned away.

"But I want to know." Ginnie slid to her feet.

"No Ginnie, you really don't." His animosity only stoked her curiosity.

"Why not?"

"Because."

"Because *why?*"

"Because I don't like remembering the rage and hate I had for that man." He spit the words like moldy bread. "It was bad enough he made your mom miserable the last few years of her life, but the thought of losing *our* children to him was the last straw. That *wasn't* going to happen and I didn't like what I'd consider doing to make him go away."

When his face contorted with indescribable fury, Ginnie knew better than to pursue this line of questioning.

His hateful expression blanked her mind.

She had to look away.

But somehow, knowing he would go to great lengths to keep her safe was reassuring.

She better understood Tillie's need to be his child.

Dad offered an apologetic smile and pulled her close. "Let's change the subject. The thought of Cabot Stratton curdles my breakfast and I haven't eaten yet."

Ginnie let him hug her. "Aunt Roni said Mama loved Cabot very much. Is that true?"

"Yes. That's why it hurt her so much for him to reject her." The muscles in his arms became as hard as his voice. "And that's why I get so angry when I think about him."

Ginnie recalled the long ago conversation that she remembered between Daddy and Mama.

Something in Mama's voice made Ginnie think that maybe

Daddy should give Cabot a chance to redeem himself. That it would help him as much as Cabot.

Maybe Cabot isn't the only one "stuck in mad."

She slid her arms around Dad's waist, hoping she could figure out how to make things better for all of them. If Mama wanted to fix things with Cabot so much, maybe they should make the effort.

80

AS IT SHOULD BE

illie glanced around the breakfast table, happy to see all of the people who belonged to her future 'for real' family gathered with her and Mom ... just like they should be.

Normally, Mom didn't stay for breakfast and Buzz would be

leaving for an early morning class, while DT and Uncle Jake would be rushing off to work.

In just a few short weeks, Vi wouldn't be here at all. She'd be in her new home with Preston.

Of course, if DT would ever ask Mom to marry him, Tillie and Mom could be here every day, helping Uncle Ben cook breakfast before Mom had to leave for work, instead of rushing to get ready at their apartment so Mom could drop Tillie off at the farm before going to work.

This morning though, everyone enjoyed breakfast before the men left for the field and Mom left for work. DT had insisted Mom join them for a minute. She kissed him and let him lead her to the dining room, making Tillie very happy that this day was starting out well.

The peaceful feeling only lasted until Mysti rushed through the doorway and threw herself at Uncle Jake, squealing, "Daddy! I missed you so-o-o-o much!"

Miss Clarissa followed behind, looking a little out of place. "I told her to knock, but she was so excited."

Uncle Ben stood and pulled a chair from the wall, motioning for Miss Clarissa to sit with them. "No need. I told you yesterday that you're family now. Have a bite with us before we head out to the field."

DT, Toran, Buzz, and Uncle Jake stood for a quick moment, murmuring greetings around mouthfuls of food. Uncle Jake tickled Mysti, making her squeal louder. "Uncle Ben makes the best biscuits and gravy. Try some."

"We already ate, but it looks fabulous," Miss Clarissa said, as she sat in the chair.

"Have a little, it's delicious," Mom invited.

Uncle Ben placed a small plate of breakfast in front of Miss Clarissa before she could protest. "Eat what you want, leave what you don't. You won't hurt my feelings."

Miss Clarissa gave him a grateful smile. "Thank you."

"You're welcome." He made a small plate for Mysti and set it next to Uncle Jake's. "Jake, you can get the chair from my room for Mysti."

"That's okay." Uncle Jake snuggled Mysti in his arms. "I'll share mine."

Mysti beamed.

Uncle Jake winked at her.

A twinge of jealousy crept over Tillie.

She tried to force it away by concentrating on a bite of sausage gravy, but couldn't.

It was so easy for Mysti to be a West.

Too easy. Why did Mom have to marry Jasper?

Tillie remembered what Ginnie said yesterday.

That Tillie was "double family" because Jasper had been an honorary West for years.

She glanced at DT and Mom.

They were looking into each other's eyes, like they didn't see anybody else.

Why couldn't Jasper look at Mom like that? Wait, then he'd still be here.

Tillie shook her head, not believing that lame thought had crossed her brain.

Ginnie's right. You are dumb, Matilda. This is better. I get a great new dad, a new sister, and a new brother.

She peeked at Toran.

He smiled at her, causing her cheeks to heat.

Just as the heat turned to flames, Tillie's fork tumbled from her hand and clattered onto her plate.

The happy chattering around the table came to a complete stop as all eyes locked on her.

81

ORANGE MARMALADE

*A*fter taking a quick peek at Tillie's crimson cheeks, Ginnie slipped into "protector mode." She glanced around the table to see who or what caused the extreme reddening.

The silence deepened.

Her gaze flew to Dad and then Toran.

Must be Toran, Dad's trying to figure it out too.

Toran shoved a bite of biscuit in his mouth and became very interested in the three decorative plates hanging on the wall leading to the kitchen.

Ding! Ding! Ding! We have a winner!

"Hey, Mysti." Uncle Jake said, jiggling her on his knee. "What did one chick say to the other chick when the mother hen laid an orange instead of an egg?"

"I dunno." She scrunched her face in thought. "Hens don't lay oranges ... or do they?"

Uncle Jake winked at her. "Not usually."

Mysti smiled. "I didn't think so. What did he say?"

"He said, 'look at the orange Mama-laid.'"

Everyone groaned and the chattering started again, this time more stilted as everyone scrambled to give Tillie time to recover gracefully.

Toran rushed a second forkful of biscuit and gravy into his mouth.

Tillie gulped her glass of milk.

Dad and Miss Amanda exchanged knowing looks after Dad sent a slight nod in Toran's direction.

A small smile lit Miss Amanda's lips.

Oh, man! She musta figured out Toran and Tillie's 'not-so-secret' secret.

Ginnie could tell by the look in Dad's eye that Toran and Dad would be going for a walk later. It didn't take a genius to figure out if Dad was gonna marry Miss Amanda, Toran wouldn't be dating Tillie.

"I don't get it, Daddy." Mysti rubbed her chin. "Why did the hen lay an orange?"

Stifled laughter circled the table.

"It's a play on words, honey," Miss Clarissa said. "Orange marmalade is a type of jelly."

Mysti's expression turned even more serious. "Ohhh. Is orange jelly any good?"

Uncle Jake chuckled. "Vi's marmalade is the best. I'll bet she'll let you try some."

Mysti turned to Vi. "Will you?"

Vi nodded. "You can help me make peanut butter and orange marmalade sandwiches for lunch."

"Yay!" Mysti reached toward her mom.

"Sounds like you're gonna have a fun day." Miss Clarissa hugged Mysti and then glanced from Uncle Jake to Vi. "Are you sure I should leave her? I know Jake's gonna be in the field. I don't want her to be a burden."

"She's *family*, Clarissa," Vi replied, her auburn waves swaying as she started to clear the table. She ramped up her smile and made her tone more teasing. "You heard me say I'm planning to put her to work. We'll have lots of fun."

When an accepting smile crossed Miss Clarissa's lips, Ginnie watched Tillie drain the last of her milk.

Check it out! The white from her milk is turning her red cheeks a light pink.

Ginnie considered pointing out the-not-so-scientific observation, but glanced at Toran instead.

His cheeks turned a color similar to Tillie's.

With the adults ignoring the obvious, Ginnie realized any joke she made would not go over well. *Better let this one go.* She caught Dad's eye.

He frowned and gave a quick shake of his head.

She grimaced. *How does he do that?*

The doorbell rang.

After glimpsing Aunt Roni's platinum blonde curls, Ginnie leapt from her chair, hurried down the hallway, and happily squealed her aunt's name, reminding herself of Mysti.

She didn't care if she was acting eight, she had a plan, and she needed Aunt Roni's help.

82

GATHERING EGGS

*A*unt Roni showed up ready to help with their chores. Ginnie wouldn't have guessed that such an elegantly dressed woman could be such an eager worker.

The only chore that didn't get completed before breakfast was gathering the eggs. Uncle Jake had asked them to wait until Mysti could help. For some reason the chickens fascinated her new cousin.

Ginnie let Mysti gather all the eggs she wanted.

Aunt Roni seemed to be having almost as much fun as Mysti. "Maybe we'll get some chickens. Genna-Maie and Niqi would love gathering eggs. Kind of like Easter morning all ye-ah round."

Grinning, Ginnie handed her aunt an egg near her own cowgirl boot.

Aunt Roni pushed her hair back with the crook of her arm. "What's so funny?"

"I just like your accent. Do your girls have accents too?"

"Yes, but theirs vary depending on who they're around." Aunt Roni straightened. "Right now, I imagine they're speaking with hoity-toity British accents. My husband is a transplant from Great Britain. He and our girls are on holiday with my in-laws. I'm sure my mother-in-law is schooling our daughters on the proper way to speak, even as *we speak.*" She rolled her eyes. "Which in her mind would be more in a British accent than a Southern one."

Ginnie giggled. "Did Mama roll her eyes a lot? Daddy hates it when I do it."

"All the time." Aunt Roni nodded and then laughed. "It annoyed *our* daddy as well. They have that in common at least." She sighed. "Maybe it's a place to start."

After recalling Dad's rare display of uncontrolled anger this morning, Ginnie shook her head. "My dad's willing to give *you* a chance, but I don't see him forgiving your dad anytime soon."

"I know." She sighed again. "But I can hope."

"Me too. I didn't like seeing Dad so upset." Ginnie tried to erase the horrible feeling of that moment. It clung to her like cold wet denim. "I wanted to talk to you and Tillie about that."

"Really?" Aunt Roni asked.

Ginnie nodded. "Daddy's really mad at Cabot ..." When Aunt Roni's smile turned from a 'u' to a line, Ginnie hurried to finish her thought. "But I was thinking—"

"Umm, you can't blame him for being upset," Tillie interjected, dusting straw from her jeans. "Cabot *did* try to take you away from your dad. That was wrong."

Ginnie nodded. "True, but I think I remember Mama telling Daddy she *wanted* to see Cabot."

"Oh?" Aunt Roni's eyes widened with surprise.

"Mama wanted to fix things." Ginnie tried to remember her mother's face and words more clearly. "Dad told me this morning that Cabot was 'stuck in mad', but I don't think Cabot's the only one stuck."

"I'll say. He kinda scared me when he yelled at Aunt Roni yesterday." Tillie lowered her gaze and then her voice. "He reminded me of Jasper and that's never happened to me before."

"Yeah, he shocked me too. Maybe we can figure out how to help them both." She turned to Aunt Roni. "Can your dad come here? I don't think Dad'll go to him, even if he wasn't so mad. With morning and afternoon chores to do, we don't travel very far."

"Not right now." Aunt Roni shook her head. "I came back early from England last week because Daddy took a turn for the worse. He's recovering now, but he's far too weak to travel."

It was Ginnie's turn to be surprised. She couldn't imagine a man strong enough to hold a grudge for so long would show any signs of weakness. "If he's so sick, why aren't you with him?"

She wasn't in any hurry to meet Cabot, but Aunt Roni had made it clear that she loved "the old coot."

"Because we need to mend this fence." Aunt Roni pushed her hair out of her face and looked Ginnie in the eye. "Once he recovered, I realized that his main problem is a broken heart ... and not the physical kind."

"Well, he did *cause* the problem," Ginnie reminded her. "I know if he'd given him half-a-chance, Daddy would've worked something out with him. It's not like my dad to hold a grudge. He always tells me and Toran not too."

"And me." Tillie grimaced. "I try not to, but I make an exception for Jasper."

Ginnie chuckled. "I guess you're even then, because Daddy seems to be making an exception for Cabot."

"You know, Ginnie Maie," Aunt Roni scolded. "Your grandfather wasn't the only one at fault. He offered Widget several olive branches that she refused to accept."

Ginnie bristled with indignation. "My dad said Cabot didn't even try to get to know him. *You* said Cabot called my dad 'a farm boy.' So what if we live on a farm? People have to eat and farmers make that happen. We also grow hay for peoples' animals. *You* have horses. Being a farmer is good, honest work. It's *nothing* to be ashamed of."

Aunt Roni's mouth opened wide and stayed silent while Ginnie spewed the lecture she'd heard from her dad and Uncle Ben many times over the years.

Only this time, she heard the words in a new way ... a way that made her proud to be a farmer's daughter.

Not only did they grow food for people and their animals, Dad and Uncle Jake delivered truckloads of necessary items to stores so people could buy whatever they needed. Mama's passions might be flashier and more exciting, but Daddy's jobs made people's lives better.

For the first time ever, Ginnie truly understood why Mama and Miss Amanda could be attracted to her dad. Flashy and exciting may be fun for a while, but loyal and steady made people feel safe and loved.

And if Mama had a dad who could just up and throw her away, she needed a man like Daddy to cherish her and make her feel special.

"Sugar, you just put words in my mouth that I simply did *not* say. Yes, your grandfather did use the words 'farm boy,' but I want you to understand that I don't look down on your dad for that ... or anything else." Aunt Roni took Ginnie's chin in her perfectly manicured hand. "And I understand why my sister gave up our family for yours."

Dad's angry words leaped into Ginnie's mind.

She shook her head. "She didn't leave, Cabot threw her away." Ginnie took a step back, breaking free of Aunt Roni's grasp. She tried not to let the betrayed look on Aunt Roni's face make her feel terrible. "Even Miss Amanda thinks Mama was wonderful. And she's gonna be my stepmom."

"Honey, we adored your mama, *especially* our dad." Aunt Roni protested. "He most certainly didn't throw her away."

Ginnie backed up. Her curls flashed in her face. Ginnie wished she had put her hair back in braids. She didn't want to look like this aunt—who looked like her mom—anymore.

Aunt Roni shook her head. "Honey, Widget left. She made that choice. Our daddy offered her a way out of the ugliness and she refused. It wasn't entirely his fault."

"*My dad* said Cabot threw her away. Daddy doesn't lie."

No way was she betraying her dad like Cabot betrayed Mama.

Tillie was beside her in a split second, angry hands on her hips. "He sure *doesn't* lie. If *he* said your father threw away Ginnie's mom, then that's what happened."

Ginnie closed the distance between her and Tillie.

"Tillie, dads simply don't throw away their children," Aunt Roni said, her tone insisting that the idea was the craziest notion she'd ever heard.

Ginnie wasn't prepared for the hurt and hardness that resonated from Tillie's two-word answer. "Mine did."

Her friend's reply felt like a slap.

Ginnie searched Tillie's face. It was unwavering.

Tillie *absolutely* believed what she said.

Aunt Roni and Ginnie's jaws both dropped wide open. Ginnie scrambled to come up with a response that would fix Tillie's truth ... only to realize that she didn't need to.

Tillie folded her arms across her chest. "And I don't care anymore. Ginnie's dad is gonna fix it."

Aunt Roni glanced between them. "Fix what?"

Tillie's cheeks flamed bright red.

Mental light bulbs exploded in Ginnie's head.

She recalled Tillie's question in Calliope's stall.

Tillie turned even more crimson, then tightened her jaw before giving a firm nod.

The question made more sense now.

Tillie had already "adopted" Dad.

She just needed Ginnie to be okay with it--and be okay with Daddy adopting Tillie.

Ginnie smiled at her friend.

Tillie got the message ... Ginnie would share.

"Tillie—honey." Aunt Roni reached a hand to her. "Daddies are *people*, and people aren't perfect. Heaven knows I'm not. But most people try to do right by the ones they love."

"Jasper doesn't love me." Tillie waved away Aunt Roni's words. "And it doesn't matter anymore, anyway. Ginnie's dad is better than Jasper ever was."

"Tillie, I'm glad you have Todd, but that doesn't mean Jasper doesn't love you. My daddy never stopped loving my sister, even when she turned her back on him."

Silence pummeled the air as Ginnie processed her aunt's words.

She threw her arms up and swept away the thought. "Mama didn't turn her back! *Your dad* threw her away!"

Aunt Roni's jaw dropped again. "Todd may feel like your grandfather threw my sister away, but I felt like my sister threw *me* away. Perhaps somewhere in the middle is where the *real* truth lies. Maybe we are all wrong."

"No way." Ginnie shook her head. "Daddy doesn't lie. He told me today—*this morning*—that Cabot threw her away. Mama used to cry in his arms about it. It hurt him that he couldn't fix it. And Mama *tried* to fix it." Ginnie recalled Mama's plea to Daddy to not make her more nervous than she already was about seeing Cabot. "They were gonna get together. But she died too soon."

"That part is true." Aunt Roni nodded. "She and I made up for a while. You saw the pictures to prove it. But it didn't stay fixed. Other things happened. On *all* sides."

Ginnie shook her head.

Aunt Roni took a step closer and lowered her voice. "You said Todd believes that although each person has a side, there's also the *whole* truth. Maybe we should try to find *that* truth, no matter how ugly it looks. I suspect *that* truth will look like each of us made mistakes, including my sister."

"Mama only left *us* because she died." Ginnie yelled. "She wouldn't have left if she got to choose. So she wouldn't have left *you*, unless you did something to hurt her. What did *you* do?"

"Stop being mean!" Mysti scolded, standing straight up. "Aunt Roni's nice. Don't yell at her."

"She's not even *your* aunt." Ginnie snapped. "Mind your own business."

"Ginnie!" Both Tillie and Aunt Roni scolded.

"What?"

Tillie grimaced. "She's not my aunt either, but she *is* nice ... and she might be right."

"About what?" Ginnie crossed her arms.

"About your mom."

"No way. Mama wouldn't do that." Ginnie shook her head so hard her curls kept bouncing even when she stopped moving. "I thought you believed my dad?"

"I do. And he's right, too." Tillie looked from Aunt Roni, to Mysti, to Ginnie. "There can be many sides to a story. If Aunt Roni's right about your mom, she might be right about Jasper."

Tillie's voice betrayed a hope that Aunt Roni's words were true.

As much as Ginnie knew that Aunt Roni was absolutely right about Jasper, she didn't want to believe that Mama could have been at fault for the break with Aunt Roni and Cabot.

It was easier to believe her mom had been a victim ... like Tillie.

Then something nagged at Ginnie.

Everything she'd ever been told about her mom didn't point to a weak person who let others make decisions for her. Mama's independence and desire to try new things was the ruler everyone seemed to use to measure Ginnie's spunkiness, her courage, her stubbornness, and her tenaciousness ... *with* Mama.

It's what made Dad both frustrated and proud of her.

Mama's independence is what Ginnie embraced about each of them. That strong, fearless person who welcomed new adventures was the person Ginnie wanted to be.

When Daddy had begged Mama to go to the play place with him and ride Eternal Love later, Mama didn't waver. She had made up her own mind and pushed past Dad, the obstacle that would have kept her safe.

The man who always tried to keep Ginnie safe—even when it made her furious.

The man who made Tillie feel safe, when her own father didn't.

The man Mama loved, but didn't let get in her way.

Daddy had *tried* to keep Mama safe, but he couldn't, because *Mama* hadn't let him.

He kept Ginnie home, but he couldn't make Mama stay.

Maybe Cabot wanted to keep Mama safe, but Mama wanted Daddy more than she wanted to be safe.

That doesn't make sense. Daddy IS safe.

Ginnie shook her head, not knowing what to believe.

Daddy's pain and anger that morning had been real.

She studied Aunt Roni's face.

Her expressions churned through hurt and loss, trying to find words to help them both.

Ginnie knew her aunt's pain was real.

She glanced at her friend. Tillie was waiting for Ginnie to make it all better and for once, Ginnie didn't even know how to *pretend* to make it better.

Mama isn't here anymore. That was real. *Too real.*

Being here was real. Here *hurt*.

Ginnie didn't want to be here anymore. "Sorry," she apologized as she pushed past Mysti.

She flung the coop door further open and fled.

Ginnie didn't know where she was going, but she knew where she didn't want to be.

83

MAMA GETS A SAY

Once she was free of the chicken coop, Ginnie bolted toward the gate. She needed to think ... and to make the pain stop. Riding Calliope always made her feel better.   That's what she would do.

That's what Mama would do.

While Ginnie fumbled with the gate latch, she heard footsteps approach.

"Please wait, sugar. We can talk this out."

"I don't want to talk to you." Ginnie opened the gate and rushed through, slamming it shut before Aunt Roni could reach her. "I want my mom."

When she saw the farmhouse, Ginnie changed her mind. Instead of Calliope, she would get her journal.

Maybe Mama *could* help.

She bolted down the sidewalk, threw the side porch door open, and rushed inside. She hurried into the kitchen doorway and heard the side porch door squeak open. Ginnie turned right and ran through the dining room, down the hallway, and flew up the stairs.

When she reached the top, Ginnie grabbed the banister as she made a U-turn toward her room.

Vi's door opened. "What in the world?"

"Make her go away," Ginnie yelled and kept going, past the bathroom door, to Toran's room. She didn't bother to knock, she just flung it open.

She barely noticed Toran sit up. He was reading a book, like usual. "Hey, what's the hurry?"

Ginnie started to shut the door, but Vi was right behind her. She let go of it and caught a glimpse of Aunt Roni's platinum blonde curls bouncing up the stairs. "Ask *her*."

Ginnie pointed over her shoulder and bolted to her room, opened her desk drawer and plucked out the pink journal Mama had kept for her.

Vi, Toran, and Aunt Roni converged on her doorway all at once.

Ginnie held up the journal and glared at Aunt Roni.

Toran glanced from Ginnie to Vi to Aunt Roni. "What's the matter? Why are you crying?"

"I'm not." Ginnie touched her cheek.

It was wet. She rubbed away the evidence, before repeating, "I'm not."

Vi stepped between Ginnie and Aunt Roni. "One of you needs to tell me what's going on and *right now*. What did Roni do that you want me to make her go away?"

"She said ..." Ginnie tried to catch her breath. She swallowed hard and tried again. "She said ..."

"She said ... *what?*" Vi asked impatiently, her 'Mama Bear' face plastered firmly in place.

Tillie and Mysti came through the door as Ginnie finished her thought. "She said it was Mama's fault."

Vi hugged Ginnie and glared at Aunt Roni. "*What* are you blaming Queenie for?"

"She didn't blame Ginnie's mom for anything." All eyes riveted to Tillie. "Aunt Roni said there was probably a mix-up and everybody misunderstood."

"What mix-up?" Toran asked.

Ginnie held up her journal. "Daddy said Cabot threw Mama away. Aunt Roni says Mama left. Mama doesn't mention either of them in my journal. It doesn't make any sense. If Mama and Aunt Roni were best friends, why doesn't Mama mention her? Even once?" Ginnie waved the journal at Toran. "Does she talk about them in yours?"

Toran shook his head. "No, and that's weird to me, too."

"That's a good point, Roni." Vi glared at Aunt Roni. "Why wouldn't she mention you?"

"I have no idea. If you remember, she wasn't on speaking terms with me when Ginnie and Toran were born. She was mad at me for not leaving home when she did. But she conveniently forgot she had some place to go and I didn't. I was all Daddy had left. I kept hoping I could make each of them see reason." Aunt Roni waved her hand and grimaced. "But they're both so pigheaded they wouldn't give an inch, either of them. *You* know she was stubborn."

Ginnie bristled.

"She had her moments." Vi loosened her grip on Ginnie's shoulder. "But why would you badmouth her to Ginnie?"

"I didn't mean to. That certainly wasn't my intention."

"What *was* your intention?" Vi reached a hand to Toran, enveloping him as well. "I told you yesterday that I won't let you hurt Todd and the kids. I mean that."

"Vi, slow down. I came here thinking the kids knew more than they do about their mama. I didn't consider that the truth as I saw it may be vastly different than the truth as *Todd* sees it. We've spent eight years thinking about things from our own perspectives." She pulled her cell phone out of her front pocket. "I've listened to this a thousand times. I know Widget wants us to put away the past and forge new memories. I want to respect her wishes."

"Wow!" Toran reached for her phone. She let him take it. "This is the latest iPhone! Can I check it out?"

"In a minute. For now, I want you to hear something." Toran handed it back. Aunt Roni touched the screen and swiped it with her thumb until she found what she was looking for. "This is the last message Widget left on my phone. I reinstall it when I upgrade my phones."

"You mean it has Mama's voice?" Ginnie broke free of Vi and stood next to Aunt Roni.

She nodded. "And yours and Toran's, when you were three. This was the night before her accident." She held the phone out so that they could all hear it. "Ready?"

Everybody nodded and crowded around Aunt Roni to hear. She pushed the play button.

"Gidget! Where are you? Pick up already, we have a surprise for you." Several seconds of silence. *"I guess your auntie didn't hear the phone. Gins, Grins, let's sing the song anyway. Are you ready?"*

"Yes, Mama," a very serious Toran replied.

"Let's sing it!" an excited Ginnie squealed.

Faint handclapping could be heard on the recording. The whole room giggled.

"You sound so cute," Tillie said.

Heat rushed to Ginnie's cheeks while she waited eagerly for whatever was coming next. She looked at Toran. "Do you remember this?"

"Not yet." He shrugged. "Maybe when we sing?"

Mama started singing with them to the tune of "We Wish You A Merry Christmas":

"We miss you so very much, we miss you so very much, we miss you so very much, dear Auntie and Grandpapa, and can't WAIT. TO. SEE. YOU!

They heard young giggles and more handclapping.

. . .

Then Mama said: *Lovely singing guys. Tell Auntie you love her.* They heard two young voices say: *"Love you!"*

"Gidge. Call me when you get this! Tell Daddy that Gins is about ready to burst at the idea of riding a 'her size' horsie. And Toran can't wait to check out his new telescope. Love you!"

The recording ended with a click and a dial tone.

A reverent quiet permeated the room.

"That's it?" Ginnie whispered happiness and disappointment battling within her.

Toran's mouth beamed the same joy that was starting to overwhelm her.

Aunt Roni nodded and wiped her eyes. Her smile grew in brilliance.

Tears shone in Tillie's eyes, making Ginnie feel torn between savoring this glorious moment and guilty at being so happy.

Then Tillie moved toward her, arms outstretched, and hugged Ginnie tight. It took a second for Ginnie to realize that Tillie didn't feel threatened by Ginnie's joy at 'finding' Mama again.

Tillie was just as happy for Ginnie's new memory as Ginnie was.

She hugged Tillie and blinked back joy-filled tears.

Aunt Roni enveloped them both in her arms.

"Family cuddle!" Vi shouted, motioning Toran and Mysti close. "Everybody in."

Toran shook his head, but let Vi corral him up.

Mysti giggled loudly and set off a chain reaction of jubilance as the whole room echoed with laughter.

Happy tears overwhelmed each of them until Aunt Roni let out a gasp.

Alarmed, Ginnie locked her eyes on her aunt's. "May I see your journal?" Aunt Roni asked.

Ginnie nodded and handed it over.

Aunt Roni opened it from the back. She flipped through a couple pages, then looked at Ginnie and smiled. "That's why." She held the book so everyone could see.

"I don't get it." Ginnie saw the same sticker of a pink birthday cake with one candle to represent her first birthday that she'd seen many times before, as well as Mama's thoughts about how much she loved Ginnie.

"Your first birthday," Aunt Roni said, like somehow that made everything crystal clear.

Ginnie shrugged. "I know. I still don't get it."

"Sugar, we didn't reconnect until *after* your first birthday. I'll bet if I read through this, there would be a whole lot of 'I love you's' and great memories and positive thoughts on you and your daddy and brother, but not much of anything negative. Would I be right?"

"Yes." Ginnie nodded, puzzled. "How do you know?"

"Because I have several diaries just like it, as did Widget." Aunt Roni smiled and handed the book back. "Every year on our birthday, our mama started a new diary for each of us, and wrote how much she loved us, our first smiles, steps, days of school, dates, everything. I don't think I ever heard her say a bad thing about anybody and if she did have something bad to say, she most certainly wouldn't write it where just anyone could read it."

"That sounds so cool!" Tillie gushed.

"It was. I've read them many times since she passed. Those diaries are a great source of comfort to me." Aunt Roni beckoned Tillie to her and slid her arm around her shoulders. "I suspect—*at least I hope*—my sister felt it was better to ignore our squabbling rather than writing it down for anyone to remember before we made up."

Aunt Roni slid her other arm around Ginnie's shoulders. "Your Grandmama Serafina was big on 'not airing our dirty laundry.' My mama would've been downright mortified had she been alive during that time."

Ginnie rolled her eyes heavenward. "Why didn't your dad just give in? It wasn't wrong for my mom to fall in love with my dad. You said so yourself, he's a good man."

"If my mama had been alive that wouldn't have happened. She

didn't abide with cross words and fits." Aunt Roni sighed. "But she wasn't there and that was the main problem. My dad was still grieving her passing. He really wasn't in his right mind. That's not meant to be an excuse, but it is a big part of why he dug in."

"I still don't get it. If he was sad, why wouldn't he want to see Mama happy?" Ginnie wiggled out of the hold to face her aunt. "Wouldn't that make him feel better?"

"Maybe he was hurting too much to see Mama's pain," Toran suggested.

"Yes, that was certainly part of it. When our mama found out she was terminally ill, our parents talked about a lot of things, including who we should marry. Mama worried a lot about Widget especially and had a few suggestions about which young men would make good suitors for us. Daddy wanted Widget to stick with one of those suitors, forgetting of course, that the final decision was really up to her. Marrying Todd messed up his plans in other ways as well. She was on the fast track to being a lawyer for our father's company."

"A lawyer? Really?" Toran's eyes widened like jumbo-sized eggs. "She was a beauty queen. How does that translate into being a lawyer? Or are you kidding?"

Ginnie planted her hands on her hips. "Just because she was beautiful didn't mean she wasn't smart."

"Very true Ginnie. And Toran, I'm serious as a heart attack. My sister could argue that sky was green and she'd win." She raised an eyebrow at Vi. "Right?"

Vi laughed. "Well, she did get her way more often than not. Of course, I remember her saying that your dad encouraged her to speak her mind. If he hadn't, she probably wouldn't have defied him to marry my cousin."

"That's also true. Our dad has spoken his regrets about that many times." Aunt Roni laughed softly. "Even if Widget was flat-out wrong, he'd let some transgressions go, provided she could come up with a good reason why she did something she shouldn't have. He admired her spirit. Not many people have the nerve to stand up to him."

Toran laughed and jabbed his thumb at Ginnie. "He hasn't spent much time with Ginnie. I'll bet that changes."

Ginnie smirked at him. "If he ever tries to justify cutting her off, I'll have something to say about it."

"Well, like you heard, they were looking forward to reuniting. Daddy was absolutely devastated when we found out about the accident. The only thing that kept him sane was knowing they were pointed in that direction when she passed. Had she passed before they made up, I know he would've died of a broken heart right then and there."

"Maybe, but it seems like it shouldn't take years to figure that out." Toran held out his hand. "Can I listen to the recording again? And put it on my computer?"

"Certainly." Aunt Roni handed him the phone. "I have a couple others, but as you heard, she was excited about you guys coming to visit." Aunt Roni turned to Ginnie. "I'm sorry about before. I can see why Todd said what he did. But after listening to this, can you see why I didn't think of her as 'thrown away,' sugar?"

Ginnie nodded. "Maybe you can let Daddy hear it and he'll feel better."

"I'll do that. I would never ask you to choose between him and me." Aunt Roni leaned toward Ginnie until their foreheads touched. "My sister chose him and I can see he's been a good dad to you. I'd just appreciate you having an open mind to letting me introduce you to your grandfather."

"I'm open to it," Toran said as he pocketed the phone. "But good luck getting past Dad."

84

MAKING A DECISION

*T*he trees flew by on either side of the car as Dad drove further out the county road. They'd been driving for half an hour. Ginnie was starting to feel squished.

Tillie sat between her and Toran, with Miss Amanda straight in front of her. Dad's mid-sized car felt smaller than it used to now that the five of them traveled together more and more.

"Are we almost there?" Ginnie asked, her curiosity getting the best of her.

"We'll be there when we get there," Dad replied, his tone betraying his amusement at stumping her.

Ginnie turned to Tillie and rolled her eyes, while mouthing Dad's answer in a mocking way.

Tillie giggled, then shook her head in disapproval.

"And don't roll your eyes," Dad said.

"You didn't see me do it," Ginnie protested.

"And yet, I know you did." He arched his hand over the front seat to squeeze her knee until it tickled. "Don't."

Ginnie laughed while struggling to remove his hand.

He tickled her knee again before letting go and made his tone more serious. "I mean it."

"Yes, sir. Got it."

"You know, Todd, sometimes I'm not sure who the bigger tease is." Miss Amanda turned in her seat to smile at Ginnie. "You or her."

"Her." Dad hitched his thumb toward Ginnie as she pointed her finger at Dad.

"*Definitely* him."

"You're *both* teases," Tillie declared.

"Wrong answer." Dad tickled Tillie's knee until she squealed.

Ginnie laughed at her friend. "See? It's him. Right, Toran?"

"I'm staying out of it." Toran leaned forward. "Hey, look. Hot air balloons."

All five looked up in the sky in time to see a lemon-yellow balloon sporting royal purple eyes, nose, and mouth of a smiling face. Several yards away, but not as high up, sailed a black balloon decorated with squares that made it look like a pixelated rainbow.

"How pretty!" Tillie gushed, leaning past Ginnie. "I love rainbows."

"Me too." Ginnie lowered her gaze when she felt the car turn to the right.

A sign read: Welcome to Stella's Hot Air Balloons: Where every ride is a STELLA-R experience.

"Hey!" Toran and Ginnie chorused.

"Straw is cheaper, grass is free, buy a farm and get all three," Dad answered in a sing-song voice.

Miss Amanda grabbed his arm and hugged it. "Are we really going on a balloon ride?"

"Only if you want to." Dad glanced at the clock. "Our reservation is in twenty minutes."

"Of course I want to." Miss Amanda swiveled toward the back seat. "You guys want to go as well, right?"

"Well, yea—ah!" Ginnie sang.

"Totally!" Tillie high-fived both Toran and Ginnie.

"Definitely!" Toran replied.

Miss Amanda laughed. "I guess it's unanimous."

"Sounds like it." Dad pointed ahead. "There's our ride."

"Oh my goodness! Todd, that's perfect!" Miss Amanda's squeal made Ginnie jerk forward and adjust so she could see out the front window as well.

In front of them loomed a balloon decorated as a huge strawberry, complete with yellow seeds scattered over a rosy red bulb with kelly green leaves crowning the top.

"It's gorgeous." Tillie squished with Ginnie to get a better look. The car followed the curvy road around a bend. They were able to straighten and see out the side window.

Toran grimaced. "That's a little girly, don't you think?"

"Maybe." Dad winked at Miss Amanda. "But I wanted to impress a girl, so I think it works."

"It *totally* works," Miss Amanda assured them both.

"Too bad it isn't real." Toran motioned toward the balloon. "Can you imagine how much strawberry jam that would make?"

"Maybe enough to fill you ... but probably not," Dad teased. He pulled into a parking space. "Go look, but keep your feet on the grass until I talk with the balloon pilot."

"Yes, sir," all three said, before scrambling out of the car.

Ginnie and Tillie rounded the back of the car on the way to the balloon. Ginnie slowed when she didn't see Dad and Miss Amanda leave the car and follow right away.

She ducked her head and watched as Dad kissed and then slowly separated from Miss Amanda. When he finally left the car, he wore the happiest and most satisfied grin she'd seen on him for too long to recall.

The grin ignited many emotions in her: happy, relieved, peaceful ... as well as confusion and panic. Each emotional kernel popped and exploded like a bag of microwave popcorn, filling her chest until she thought it might burst.

Then Dad caught her eye.

His smile faded.

Worry and doubt glanced back at her.

The glow on his face dimmed as they locked eyes.

The kernels began to wither.

Ginnie's struggle between embracing Miss Amanda and her own mom crystalized at that moment ... so she made a decision.

She wanted them both ... just like Dad did.

Ginnie threw her dad the most brilliant smile she could muster, and gave him two thumbs-up.

She didn't even need to see his face to know he understood her message.

His relieved smile radiated warmth through each of them.

85

FLOATING ON AIR

*H*old on," Ian, the hot-air balloon pilot, cautioned.

The balloon basket rose, shifting as one side, then the other, lifted into the air.

A current of adrenaline coursed through Tillie's bloodstream, infusing a mixture of excitement and fear into each of her cells.

DT stood between Mom and Tillie, on one side of the six-man basket, while Toran, Ian, and Ginnie stood on the other. The quarters were fairly close, but Tillie liked that everyone was in an arm's reach or two. She sucked in a breath and peeked over the side of the basket.

Her insides fell and then jelled.

Her knees buckled, jerking her whole body toward the center of the balloon.

"It's okay. Take a breath," DT instructed quietly while reaching for her elbow to steady her. "Nothing to be afraid of. Look."

She followed his pointer finger to the mountains west of them and tried to make out clumps of trees. "Look over there instead of down. Enjoy the beauty of just being here."

Up, up, up, they soared.

A soft breeze swept Tillie's face.

She breathed in and out slowly, trying to steady her nerves.

Glancing at DT she let his kind smile calm her hammering heart and tried to take his advice.

She concentrated on the wonder that started replacing her fear. Before long they were closer to the clouds than the ground. The scene below them held a dream-like quality.

The fields of growing corn, soybeans, wheat, alfalfa, and whatever else wove together like giant quilt squares colored in a variety of green hues, stitched together by winding threads of highways and back roads.

The whooshing sounds of the burner made Tillie look straight up inside the balloon. She saw a faded inside-out version of the strawberry.

The balloon pilot let Toran turn a valve. An orange flame lengthened several feet into the hollow cavern.

"How far up are we going?" Toran asked.

"About twenty more feet. The wind is blowing east. The only way to control the direction is by riding the currents." The pilot jutted his thumb up, pointing inside the balloon. "We'll open those flaps when we're ready to go back down or catch a current going a different way. Enjoy the ride. You don't often get to fly without wings."

Tillie inched to the side and braved another peek over the rim.

Ginnie scooted beside her. "It's beautiful!"

"It's awesome." Tillie could hardly whisper the words, her heart was so full of awe and wonder. "Not 'just saying' awesome, but 'for real' awesome."

Excitement and joy mingled with not-too-scary fear, like the Ferris wheel or bumper cars at the fair.

Red barns, white silos, brick homes, tractors, backhoes, and other miscellaneous farm equipment dotted the quilt blocks like textured buttons.

They flew over housing developments and stores.

People milled around on the streets like ants.

Cars and buses moved along ribbons of highways.

Toran asked the pilot non-stop questions about motion and velocity. He wanted to know how the altimeter and variometer worked and how and when they were going to adjust to the currents' movements and directional changes.

The balloon pilot seemed happy to answer his questions.

Tillie only half-listened. She didn't care about the mechanics of the ride.

She was more interested in memorizing every detail of the landscape so she could recall it later to write in her journal or think about when she drifted off to sleep.

"No, *way*!" Ginnie squealed. "Miss Amanda, *look*! Daddy, that's *too* cool!"

Mom gasped. "Todd!"

Panicked, Tillie swiveled toward Ginnie's frantic pointing, barely noticing the buzzing of a small plane as she turned.

The crop duster continued to unfurl a bright pink banner with white lettering that read: *Amanda, I love you to the moon and back. Will you marry me? Love, Todd*

"It's for *our* Amanda, right?" Ginnie asked.

DT took Mom in his arms and hugged her tight. "She's the only Amanda *I* care about."

Right then and there, time stopped.

It took a second to process that *this* was the moment Tillie had been waiting years for.

This moment.

Right here.

Right now.

No Jasper.

No Mysti.

No Ginnie's mom.

No Aunt Roni.

Just the family she had been dreaming of forever.

Mom's hands flew to her face, not quite covering the 'o' formed by her lips.

DT kissed the top of Mom's head, fished a red velvet jeweler's box out of his pocket, took her hands in his, and then bent on one knee. "I finally feel like I can be truly happy again, all because of *you*.

Amanda, will you *please* do me the incredible honor of becoming my wife?"

When Mom froze, Tillie's heart stopped cold.

She didn't have to think. She *knew* what to do.

Tillie threw her arms around each of them. "*Yes!* She says '*yes*'!"

Laughter rippled through the balloon basket.

"I love your enthusiasm Tillie, but ..." DT slipped his arm around Tillie and gave her a reassuring hug. "I kinda need to hear the answer from *your mom*."

Any other time, Tillie might have melted from embarrassment, but right now, she was too anxious for Mom to give the right answer. "Mom, say *yes!*"

This decision was too big to risk any hesitation.

Ginnie giggled. "And you guys say *I'm* impatient."

"Tils, I got this." Mom took Tillie's chin in her hand. "Thanks for making this so easy for me." Mom kissed her forehead and then let go of her chin, before turning back to DT. "I would be extremely honored to be your wife, as long as my daughter doesn't object."

"She absolutely *doesn't* object." Tillie jumped up and down, pushing them together. "Kiss already."

D.T didn't need to be told twice. He sprang to his feet and swept Mom into his arms, pulling her in good and tight. Once Tillie saw their lips touch, she grabbed Ginnie's hands and happy-danced with her, until the balloon bobbed and swayed.

"Whoa, now!" Ian called.

Ginnie and Tillie dissolved into giggles.

Toran shook his head in mock shame. "Girls. What're you gonna do? Can't live with'em, can't live without'em."

"I guess that's a 'yes,' Mr. West?" Ian asked.

"I believe it is." DT kissed Mom again before nodding at Ian. "Go ahead."

"I'll be happy too." Ian rummaged in a pocket bolted to the side of the basket and pulled out a flare gun. He handed the gun to Toran and motioned toward the plane. "Fire this that-away. You can handle that, right son?"

"Yes, sir." Toran took the gun and shot it.

Ian handed the flare gun to Ginnie. "Your turn, young lady."

Ginnie grinned and pulled the trigger.

Within a minute, a second banner unfurled from the plane.

Tillie glanced at DT who arched an eyebrow and grinned.

"Well?" he asked.

It was Tillie's turn to freeze with disbelief. Her gaze darted to the second banner. It read:

Tillie, I love you. Will you be my daughter?

"Say yes, Tils." Mom laughed and enveloped Tillie in her arms. "Say yes."

Tillie hugged her mom and then glanced at DT.

"*Yes!*" Her legs turned into gelatin.

Her mind blanked.

DT swept her up in his arms.

She clung to him, speechless.

Happy tears burned her eyes and then flowed down her cheeks.

Tillie was barely aware of Mom, Ginnie, and Toran crowding into the hug. For once, everything was completely right in her world.

DT whispered, "thank you" in her ear.

She didn't know why he was thanking her, she just knew she didn't want him to let go of her.

Mountains of doubt and fear withered to nothing and disappeared.

For the first time in her life that she could remember, she felt safe and filled with true joy.

She knew she truly belonged somewhere.

Here.

Right here.

With *her* family.

The one she chose long ago.

86

THE END

"Wow! Maybe Daddy really IS Prince Charming," Ginnie mused as she dismounted from Calliope. She slid her hand down her mare's satiny neck, and unfastened the lead from the bridle.

Remembering the balloon ride and the unfurled banners bubbled joy through her all over again. She giggled as she recalled happy dancing with Tillie and rocking the balloon.

Miss Amanda had said *she* felt downright "giddy" and had kissed Dad over and over while squeezing Toran, Tillie, and Ginnie into numerous hugs.

Ginnie liked how "giddy" felt. It was both fun *and* a funny word ... just like "twitterpated."

Dad couldn't stop grinning and Ginnie didn't want him too.

She couldn't remember when everybody in her family had been so happy, all at once. Ginnie even hoped Dad could become 'twitterpated' with Miss Amanda, even though she suspected he might be already.

This had to be THE. BEST. DAY. *EVER!*

After she got over Aunt Roni leaving that is. But even that wasn't as sad as she imagined it would be. Aunt Roni had said she'd come back for Vi's wedding and promised a big surprise.

Even though Ginnie didn't know her aunt really well yet, she was certain whatever the surprise was, it would be *totally* awesome sauce.

Calliope snorted and shook her head.

Ginnie laughed and uncinched the saddle, recalling all the happy events of the day. She would never forget Tillie's absolute jubilation as Dad 'asked' her to be his daughter. Ginnie blinked tears of joy for her new sister and patted Calliope before freshening the water in her water bucket. "I'll be back soon, girl."

After a final pat, Ginnie turned, grinning as she ran to the gate.

Uncle Ben stood at the end of the sidewalk leading to the farmhouse.

He motioned to the open kitchen window. "I left you a piece of cake on a plate. The last two are for your dad and Toran, when they get back from dropping off Tillie and Amanda. See you in a bit."

Uncle Ben waved before heading up to the main barn.

"Thanks." Ginnie latched the gate and walked to where her great-uncle had just stood. She heard the family room phone ring as she passed the kitchen window. She quickened her pace and glanced up the hill.

Uncle Ben was closer to the barn than the house.

She hurried through the side porch door and reached the kitchen doorway as the answering machine picked up. Ginnie glanced at her slice of red velvet cake on the counter and snatched up the clear glass plate, listening for the speaker to start talking as she moved toward the phone.

When he spoke, her feet grew instant roots in the doorway between the kitchen and family room.

"U-Uncle Ben? Hey, it's Jasper."

Ginnie's chest tightened.

The speaker blew out a breath. **"Uncle Ben? Aw, man. I really wanted to talk to you. Okay, here's the deal ..."**

A few seconds passed like fudge sauce through a strainer. **"Today's the one year anniversary of my sobriety. I want to cele-**

brate by coming home. I know I've been an idiot, but I've gotten help."

Two seconds of silence passed before he spoke again.

"Uncle Ben, w-will you help me get my family back? I miss my little girl. I'm ready to keep all the promises I made to Amanda and Tillie, and be the husband and father they deserve."

His voice lost some of its confidence, before sounding determined again. "I've really changed this time ... *for good*. I'll do right by them, I swear it. This is a borrowed phone, so I can't leave a call back number. Please, Uncle Ben? Will you help me? It would mean ..."

BE-E-E-EP!

The machine cut off the rest of his message.

Ginnie swiveled back to the kitchen.

Her hands turned to cooked spaghetti. The glass plate tumbled to the hardwood floor, shattering into several pieces around the blob of red velvet cake.

All of her joy evaporated instantly as she realized ... if Jasper got *his* family back ... then Ginnie, Dad, and Toran would lose theirs.

I can't let that happen.

Ginnie didn't know how to stop it from happening ... but for Tillie's sake, as well as her own, she would have to figure it out.

THE END: For now 😊

Author's Note
The Story Continues in
Book 4: *BEING WEST IS BEST:*
A Ginnie West Adventure

AFTERWORD

A MESSAGE FROM
THE AUTHOR:

I hope you have enjoyed reading this book as much as I have enjoyed
writing it.
Writing empowering and entertaining books has always been a
dream for me, so I truly appreciate your support.
If you like my books, I would really appreciate it if you would leave a
review at Goodreads.com, Amazon.com, Audible.com,
Barnesandnoble.com, or anywhere else reviews are given,
I'd love to hear from you. It's easy and would help me immensely.
Just type my name in the search bar:
Monique Bucheger, and all of my books will show up.
Please write a sentence or two about why you
liked it. You can copy and paste the same review to all places. This
would really help me reach new readers.
Thank you.
-Monique Bucheger

If you want personalized signed copies of any of my books, please

visit my website:
http://TheHeroInsideMe.com
Or message me on Facebook: I'd love to be Facebook friends! You can
find me at:
https://www.facebook.com/Author-Monique-Bucheger-
193789017310198/
or Author Monique Bucheger on Facebook.com

ABOUT THE AUTHOR

MONIQUE BUCHEGER

When Monique isn't writing, you can find her playing taxi driver to one or more of her 12 children, plotting her next novel, scrapbooking, or being the "Mamarazzi" at any number of child-oriented events.

Even though she realizes there will never be enough hours in any given day, Monique tries very hard to enjoy the journey that is her life. She shares it with a terrific husband, her dozen children, a dozen granddarlings, too many cats and many real and imaginary friends.

She is the author of several books and hopes to write many more.

You can find more about Monique and her works at:

www.moniquebucheger.blogspot.com

A new website is being built at: http://www.TheHeroInsideMe.com

Downloadable free content will be available as soon as the website is live.

OTHER BOOKS BY MONIQUE BUCHEGER

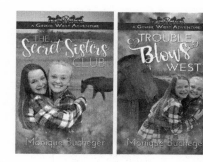

The Secret Sisters Club:

Twelve-year-old BFF's Ginnie West and Tillie Taylor, want to be sisters. Ginnie's widowed dad plus Tillie's divorced mom could equal a lifetime of round-the-clock girl talk and slumber parties. Too bad Dad vowed to never marry again. Ginnie and Tillie come up with the perfect scheme to change his mind: 'Operation Secret Sisters' (aka OSS). After all, if they can't get Dad to move on, Tillie can't move in.

Things get more complicated when Ginnie stumbles across her mom's hidden journals. Ginnie can finally get to know the mother she doesn't remember and her dad doesn't talk about—if Dad doesn't take them away.

Trouble Blows West: A Ginnie West Adventure

Putting her body in motion before her brain is in gear creates a mountain of problems for 12 year-old Ginnie West. She is certain that defending her twin brother, Toran, from the biggest bully in sixth grade was the right thing to do. But Ginnie couldn't be more wrong. She quickly learns that Toran doesn't appreciate being rescued by a girl any better than Pierce likes being

knocked down by one.

When Pierce seeks revenge on Ginnie, Toran sets aside his anger and helps her plot a payback prank at Pierce's house. Sadly, Ginnie learns that Pierce has a reason for being a bully when she sees his dad drop him to the floor like a ragdoll. Realizing he's a boy in big trouble, Ginnie decides to be his ally, because he won't let her be his friend.

Simply West of Heaven: A Ginnie West Adventure

Twelve-year-old BFFs Ginnie and Tillie are matchmaking geniuses. Sweet! Not long after they schemed to get Ginnie's widowed dad to fall in love with Tillie's divorced mom, Ginnie stumbled upon her late mom's journals, making life even more awesome sauce ... until her dad confiscated the journals, determined to protect Ginnie from a danger he won't name.

Ginnie is counting on her future sister's help to make Dad change his mind, but Tillie's not so sure the ghost of Ginnie's mom will make a good addition to their new family tree. The girls' world gets flipped upside-down when a blast from the past shows up and makes Tillie go nutburgers. Ginnie is torn between helping her best friend and what could be the answer to her deepest wish.

Being West is Best: A Ginnie West Adventure

Twelve-year-old BFFs, Ginnie West and Tillie Taylor, are matchmaking geniuses. Together, they maneuvered Ginnie's widower-dad into proposing to Tillie's divorcee-mom. Sweet! Certain they are well on their way to sisterhood, each girl is floored when Tillie's lousy-excuse-for-a-father puts in an appearance after a six year absence. Too bad "lousy dad repellant" doesn't come in a can.

Even though Tillie's dad has sobered up and is determined to make amends, Tillie would rather he just disappear again. If he stays, "Operation: Secret Sisters" may need to be renamed "Operation: Not Gonna Happen."

If that's not bad enough, the biggest bully in seventh grade comes over often and wishes he could call the West's farmhouse "home." When the bully's abusive dad shows up as well, Ginnie thinks it's time to change her family's motto from "When you're here, you're family" to "There's no more room at the West's."

The Ginnie West Adventure Collection

Multi-Book set (Featuring Books 1-3)

Popcorn:

When hunger wakes little Ginnie from her dreams she sets out to makeherself a midnight snack. Hilarity and trouble ensues as she wrecks the kitchen in her attempts to make homemade popcorn balls.

(A Picture book featuring Ginnie and Toran West when they were 3 ½ years old)

For More Great Content

Including Free Downloads Visit:

https://TheHeroInsideMe.com

For more about about the illustrator,

Mikey Brooks, visit:

www.insidemikeysworld.com

Resources for Child Abuse Help
Child Abuse Resources
National Coalition to Prevent Child Sexual Abuse and Exploitation:
www.preventtogether.org
Prevent Child Abuse America
www.preventchildabuse.org
Healthy Families America
www.Healthyfamiliesamerica.org
Stop It Now!
www.stopitnow.org
Darkness to Light
www.d2l.org
Association for the Treatment of Sexual Abusers (ATSA)
www.atsa.com
Prevention Institute
www.preventioninstitute.org
Child Help USA
www.childhelp.org
Child Care Aware
www.childcareaware.org
The National Child Traumatic Stress Network
www.nctsn.org
National Children's Alliance
www.nationalchildrensalliance.org
Kempe Center for Prevention of Child Abuse and Neglect
www.kempe.org

International Society for Traumatic Stress Studies
https://istss.org
National Children's Advocacy Center
www.nationalcac.org
National Alliance of Children's Trust and Prevention Funds
www.ctfalliance.org

33869382R00220